Shelter from the Storm

Perfect Storm
Book 2

Mari Carr

Cover Photography: WANDER AGUIAR PHOTOGRAPHY LLC

Cover Design: Qamber Designs & Media

Editor: Kelli Collins

Final Line Editor: Nan Mabbitt

Shelter from the Storm

A storm never felt so safe.

Desperate for a new life, Gretchen escapes her abusive ex and finds refuge in the small town of Gracemont. Her plan is simple: lay low. But when she meets Theo Storm, her sexy new boss, everything changes. Drawn into the warmth of his world, Gretchen discovers the possibility of happiness, love, and family—things she thought were out of her reach.

For Theo, it's love at first touch. From the moment he takes Gretchen's trembling hand, he knows he's found someone worth fighting for. Though he senses she's hiding something, he's determined to help her overcome her painful past.

When old demons come knocking, Theo calls on his family to help protect the woman who's quickly claimed his heart. The Storms are a force of nature, and they step up, ready to defend their own at any cost.

Will they succeed in keeping Gretchen safe, or will her dangerous past tear her and Theo apart?

Trigger Warning

Shelter from the Storm contains scenes and descriptions of domestic abuse—physical and emotional, as well as grooming.

Chapter One

Theo Storm rubbed his tired eyes, then leaned back in his office chair and closed them. He'd been staring at the computer for too long and it was giving him eye strain. Maybe it was time to finally break down and buy a pair of those blue light glasses his cousin Nora raved about. Glancing at the keyboard, he considered opening a tab to shop for a pair online, but even that felt like too much effort at the moment, so he closed his eyes again.

He'd been burning the candle at both ends the past few months—not that that was unusual for August and September, but today, he'd slammed into a brick wall. His energy level was nil, which *was* unusual. His brothers called him the Energizer Bunny, insisting he didn't possess an *off* button. Usually he agreed with them, but lately, it felt as if he'd not only found the *off* switch, he'd also lost his *on* button, which bothered him more than he cared to admit.

Maybe he should skip the blue light glasses and go to the doctor for a checkup.

He sighed, rejecting that idea the second it came to him. He was healthy as a horse.

Maybe he was getting too old to keep burning the midnight oil, working long hours.

He dismissed that idea too. He was only thirty-four, for God's sake.

Which left him with only one answer. The right one. Sadly, it was also the one he didn't want to confess, not even to himself.

Because the truth was, he was stuck in a rut, one so deep he feared he'd never find his way out. The worst part was, he hadn't even realized he was stuck until his oldest brother, Levi, fell in love with Kasi Mills.

Theo was one of seven Storm sons, all of whom shared a farmhouse on Stormy Weather Farm. Well, he supposed he couldn't say they *all* shared it anymore. Levi had one foot out the door as he made plans to move in with Kasi. Although, considering Levi had spent every night on the Mills' farm for the past week or so, maybe it was more correct to say his brother had *both* feet out the door.

And while Theo was genuinely happy for his brother, Levi's newfound love had shone too bright a light on his own lacking love life.

"Knock knock."

Theo looked up. "Hey, Sam."

"Got a minute?"

Theo gestured to one of the chairs across from his desk. "Of course. What's up?"

Sam released a long, slow sigh, a sure sign his brother was struggling with something, as he dropped heavily into a chair.

He, Sam, and Levi were the oldest of the Storm sons, Theo number three in line. He was close to all his brothers, but he felt a stronger bond with Sam. Probably because in addition to living together, the two of them had both spent almost every single day for the past ten years working tirelessly in this brewhouse, building the Rain or Shine Brewery brand and making it a success.

There were precious few people Theo could spend pretty much every waking hour with, but Sam was at the top of that sparse list.

"What's wrong?"

Sam grimaced. "Just wanted to give you a heads-up about how much time I'm going to be away from the brewhouse this fall. It's more than I thought."

Theo leaned back in his chair. "We talked about this before you even threw your hat in the ring, Sam. We'll be fine here."

This past weekend, Sam had announced his intention to run for mayor of Gracemont, Virginia. Theo had been one of only two family members to know he was even considering it. Sam had called a meeting with him and their kid brother, Jace, to let them know he was thinking about running and to get their opinion, since it would mean a heavier workload for them.

Jace had come on as brewmaster last fall after their cousin, Lucy, gave up the job, opting to hit the open road with her boyfriends. Both of them. Theo was still blown away by the fact their sweet little cousin had found love in the middle of a real-life menage. While it had taken a couple of his brothers a little longer to get accustomed to the fact Lucy was in love with Miles *and* Joey, Theo thought it was one of the coolest relationships he'd ever seen, and Lucy's happiness these days shone so bright it was almost blinding.

"I know you guys said it would be okay, but I don't think I realized how much time I would have to take off from work," Sam said, concerned. "I hate to leave you shorthanded because that means you and Jace will be picking up the slack for the next couple of months. And if I win—"

"You *will* win," Theo interjected.

Sam ignored him because he never put the cart before the horse, considering it serious bad luck. "This campaign is coming on the heels of harvest season. You and Jace have already been busting your asses to help with that. Now I'm asking you to—"

"Bro. Take a breath," Theo said, raising his hand. "We've got this. Seriously, man."

Like Theo, Jace had encouraged Sam to run for mayor, both of them convinced he'd be incredible in that role. It would be hard to find someone who loved their small hometown more than Sam. The only two people Theo could think of were their dad, Rex, who'd been a member of the town council for close to twenty years, and Edith Millholland, the unofficial first lady of Gracemont. At eighty years young, Edith had been born in the house she still lived in, and there was very little that happened in town that she didn't know about. Perhaps that would be an annoying attribute in another person, but Edith had a heart as big as the state of California and a sense of humor that was unmatched.

"Yeah, but you're about to have a new employee to train as well," Sam added.

Most of the year, Theo spent the majority of his working hours in the brewhouse or brewery, either in his office or the tasting room, but whenever harvest time rolled around, he split his time between those two places and the vineyards, helping his family pick the grapes that would be used to create Lightning in a Bottle wine, one of the other major businesses on his family's farm.

While it was backbreaking work, he enjoyed harvest time because sometimes it was good to get back out into nature after spending too many hours riding a desk.

By now, he should be seeing a light at the end of the tunnel, as most of the grapes were picked—but he and his family had decided the time was right to expand by opening an event barn on the property and hiring a coordinator to run it.

It meant more work for him, as he and his cousin Nora had taken lead, working with the contractor as they designed and built the barn the past six months. Not that he minded. The truth was, Theo loved his job, loved working on the same farm where he'd grown up with his brothers and cousins. There wasn't a day that passed that he didn't feel truly blessed.

"And Jace is still pretty new at the brewing." Sam and his anxiety had made quite the list.

"Jace might be new in the big chair, but he's been working in this brewery since high school, helping you and Lucy every chance he got. He knows the job, and, while he probably wouldn't admit it to you, I think he's looking forward to the opportunity to put his own spin on things for a bit. You cast a big damn shadow around here."

Sam was one of the few Storm brothers to leave the mountain for four years to attend college. He'd graduated with a bachelor's degree in microbiology from Virginia Tech, then went on to earn his brewing certification.

"Not that big." Sam rubbed the back of his neck. His brother was shit when it came to accepting compliments, one of the humblest men Theo had ever known.

"Besides," Theo continued, "you can't drop out of the race or we'll have to endure four more years of Scottie Grover as mayor. I swear to God, I can't deal with that douchebag strutting around Gracemont like he's all that and a bag of chips for five more minutes."

Gracemont's current mayor, Scottie Grover, had been running unopposed—for a second time—before Sam entered the race. Theo felt confident his brother was a shoo-in, but Sam, crazy guy, genuinely thought he had a serious race on his hands. Simply because Scottie had experience. It wasn't in Sam's genetic makeup to phone anything in, always going the extra mile on basically everything. So it made sense he would feel strongly about taking the campaign seriously.

Sam frowned. "After all the shit Scottie pulled with Lucy and Kasi, I'd like to see him knocked down a peg or twenty."

A year earlier, Scottie had come on way too strong with Lucy, pissed off when she'd started dating Joey and Miles. Levi had been forced to intervene when the mayor got physical with her.

Once Lucy left town, Scottie turned his attention to Kasi, using threats and intimidation to try to get Kasi to marry him. Again, Levi had stepped in. It was those actions that had encouraged Sam to pursue the office now rather than wait. His brother had always planned to run for office—either mayor or town council—but he'd pushed it off, claiming it would take him away from the brewhouse too much. Scottie's poor behavior and overweening sense of self had forced Sam's hand.

Theo leaned forward. "Exactly. So you're not dropping out of the race. Send me a list of the dates you know you'll be out shaking hands and kissing babies, so I can get some extra help in here for Jace."

Sam nodded. "Will do. I appreciate your support, bro. Gonna owe you big-time after all this."

Theo shook his head. "You don't owe me a damn thing. This is what family is for."

His brother gave him an appreciative grin. "So what are you working on?"

Theo gestured toward the open document on his computer. "Compiling a list of job duties for Gretchen Banks, the new event coordinator."

"She starts Monday, right?"

"She does. I created a general list when we first posted the job online, searching for applicants," Theo said. "But it was nowhere near complete. Now that we've hired her and she's arriving in a few days, I figured it was time to get serious about deciding exactly what we need her to do."

Sam glanced at his computer, his eyes widening. "That's a hell of a list."

Theo smirked. "I might have gotten a little carried away, because the truth is, I'm trying to off-load some of my more tedious tasks."

Sam laughed. "Clever man. If that's how we're playing this game, can you add cleaning and sanitizing the barrels? I fucking hate cleaning."

Theo shook his head and gave him a shit-eating grin. "I'm afraid she's not going to have time to do your crap jobs because she'll be too busy doing mine."

He glanced at his list. Sam was right. It was bordering on too long, but Theo couldn't help himself because, while he was constantly hiring extra help for Sam and Jace, he'd refused to do the same for himself in the past, always determined to do it all.

Sam walked around his desk, skimming the list. "I think it's smart to reassign some tasks. God knows you've got too much on your plate."

He appreciated Sam's support. "When I started my job as brewhouse manager, I didn't anticipate how many tasks would fall to me."

"That's because it was just the brewhouse back then. We hadn't opened the brewery, hadn't invited the public in," Sam added.

"True. It was a hell of a lot easier running just the brew-house, ordering supplies, paying bills, organizing work sched-ules, and hiring extra help for you guys during busy season."

When the family decided to add a brewery, Theo's job

duties expanded to include basically running a restaurant, hiring and training people to work the tasting room and serve food, buying swag with' their Rain or Shine Brewery logo, and coordinating special events with Nora.

"You alleviating some of Nora's duties too?" Sam asked. "Because she's spread as thin as you these days."

"I asked for her input earlier and told her to give some thought to other duties she'd like to move over to Gretchen."

Nora had the same job as Theo, only she managed the winery, so the two of them typically met a couple times a week to compare notes, share ideas, and pool employees as needed. Most of their servers had been trained to work in both the winery and the brewery, in case one business or the other was short-staffed due to illness or vacations, or if they were running special events that required more workers at one location over the other.

When the family unanimously voted to build the event barn, it became instantly apparent the expectation was that he and Nora would run it. That was when the two of them had cried uncle and expressed the need to hire someone else to serve as event coordinator.

Mercifully, the family agreed they needed the new position, so Theo and Nora decided what parts of their jobs to reassign to a new employee. In the past, the two of them had worked together planning special events at the brewery and winery, but because their lists of job duties were already quite · large, they were never pleased with the end results of their party planning, certain every event could have been better if only they'd had time to do more.

So, between handing those duties as well as the running of the event barn over to someone else, the new position was created.

Theo was thrilled to leave the event coordination to

someone else, because while he loved a good party, he preferred to be the one *attending*, not the one planning. He'd volunteered to serve as the direct supervisor for the new coordinator, primarily because the brewery was positioned closer to the event barn on the farm, so now Gretchen's shiny new office was located right next to his.

"Still feeling good about your choice for the job?" Sam asked. "Nora mentioned Gretchen's lack of experience."

"Yeah. Nora had some concerns, and she was definitely gunning for another candidate." Clicking onto a different file, Theo pulled up Gretchen's resume. "I hope I made the right choice. Problem is, most of the interviews Nora and I conducted were through video conference calls. I prefer interviewing people face-to-face. It's too hard to get a good feel for someone over the computer. But, since the list of qualified candidates in Gracemont was pitifully small, we had to widen the search. Hence the online interviews."

"You've got good instincts when it comes to people, so you probably hired the right person."

"Well, I'll know soon enough because Monday is only a few days away. Crazy thing is, Gretchen didn't even make the initial cut when Nora and I went through the resumes."

"So why did you interview her?" Sam leaned against his desk, arms folded over his chest.

Theo grinned. "Because we'd narrowed it down to four candidates."

Sam shook his head, grinning as well. "Gotcha. You added Gretchen to keep Nora from twitching."

He and his brother laughed. Nora's OCD was well-known in the family, and a source of humor—even to Nora—who owned her special brand of crazy with pride. Theo realized as soon as they'd narrowed down their list, he'd either have to add one more name or take one away...because Nora hated even numbers. *All* even numbers. Interviewing four people would have kept her up at night.

So Theo had reached into the pile of remaining resumes and pulled one out at random. It had been Gretchen's.

"It must have been one hell of an interview for you to choose her, considering she wasn't even in the running originally," Sam mused.

Theo wasn't sure why he'd chosen Gretchen over all the other, more experienced applicants, or why he'd defended that decision so strongly to his cousin. Nora had been sitting in on the interviews, and she'd read the same resumes and listened to the responses of the candidates, so she knew—just as Theo did —that Gretchen was by far the least qualified.

"It was," Theo lied. Her interview had been a good one, but she hadn't exactly blown everyone else out of the water.

Sam's eyes twinkled with humor. "Nora also mentioned Gretchen is pretty."

"Nora's got a big mouth," he joked.

Sam barked out a loud laugh. "Got a picture of her?"

"No, I don't," Theo grumbled. "I didn't hire her for her looks." He didn't dare admit he'd found Gretchen *very* attractive.

Sam chuckled. "Suuuure you didn't."

Theo rolled his eyes. "You're as bad as Nora."

It had been difficult for Theo to explain to Nora why he'd moved Gretchen to the top spot on his list. Because it wasn't what Gretchen had said in the interview, so much as her demeanor. He'd tried for weeks after that Zoom conversation to figure out why he was so sure she was the one.

In the end, all he knew was that Gretchen had a determination and a quiet strength that had called to him in a way he'd never experienced before.

Nora ultimately capitulated to his choice because, as she

pointed out numerous times, he was going to be Gretchen's boss. And, because Nora was a minx—like all his girl cousins—she'd winked and wished him luck if it all went to hell.

Then she had added that she looked forward to saying "I told you so" for the rest of their lives.

Theo had flipped Nora the bird, then fired off an email, offering Gretchen the position before his cousin could change her mind about supporting his decision or he could second-guess himself.

It wasn't until he'd received Gretchen's immediate acceptance that he realized it wasn't her determination that had prompted him to hire her.

No.

There was something in her eyes—a vulnerability—that had captured his attention and held on to it.

"So, you got any big plans this weekend?" Sam asked. "Now that the harvest is over, Jace and Maverick are chomping at the bit to go out. Apparently, picking grapes has cut into their," Sam finger-quoted, "prowling for women time."

Theo snorted. "I haven't exactly noticed Mav suffering too much from longer work hours. Didn't he hook up with Susie Watkins that night we all went to Whiskey Abbey for ladies' night?"

"He did," Sam replied. "But as he pointed out, that was all of three weeks ago."

"Guy better pace himself or he's going to run out of women available for one-night stands in Gracemont soon," Theo commented, though a part of him was concerned about Maverick's horndog, never-gonna-settle-down ways. Mav was two years younger than Theo, and at thirty-two, his brother was way too young to be so jaded about love and relationships.

"I hear that," Sam seconded, walking back around Theo's desk and reclaiming the chair he'd vacated.

While Theo and the rest of his brothers didn't date much, that didn't mean they weren't looking to find a girl and settle down one day. Levi going out with Kasi and making serious plans for the future had lit a place inside Theo that he'd locked in the dark for too long.

He didn't live like a monk, but he wasn't out every weekend, hooking up with single women like Maverick, either. Whenever anyone asked, Theo blamed his lack of dates on the fact he worked long hours, saying he preferred hanging out with his brothers, playing video games and chilling after work.

However, that wasn't the whole truth.

While Theo could list a million things that were awesome about living in a small town, there was one big downside—he'd already met every available woman in his age range. Hell, he'd gone to school with almost all of them, because very few people moved into Gracemont.

As such, he knew the woman he was looking for didn't live here. Sure, there were plenty of girls he'd dated for a short time, but ultimately, none of them had set his heart racing or had him thinking about rings and kids and white picket fences.

Which meant he needed to widen the search. Something that wasn't easy because...well, refer to his first excuse. He really did work a lot. Maybe having Gretchen here and taking over some of his tasks would offer him more free time to date.

"Maverick thinks we should bypass Whiskey Abbey and head over to Henley Falls Saturday night. Apparently, some local band he likes is playing in a bar there," Sam continued.

"You going?"

Sam shook his head. "Hell no. I've agreed to attend the fall craft show the ladies auxiliary organized to raise money for the fire station that afternoon. I suspect I'll be all *peopled* out after that."

Theo chuckled. "Too early in your campaign to wear out on people."

"Which is why I intend to pace myself," Sam said. "But you should go. When's the last time you went out on a date?"

"You sure you want to throw that stone?" Theo joked. "Because your entire house is made of glass."

Sam smirked. He and his brother had discussed the lack of "the one" in Gracemont before, Sam feeling the same way he did. They were both certain their Miss Right didn't live in town. They also agreed that fact sucked. Big-time.

"I'm just saying," Sam began, "we need to at least try to put ourselves out there. I mean, I'm sure if we'd asked Levi six months ago if his dream woman was in Gracemont, he would have said no. Yet, Kasi's been here all along. Hell, she practically grew up on this farm."

"She did." Theo had to admit his brother had a point. There was always a chance he'd overlooked someone, though that seemed unlikely.

"And now, here's Levi, uprooting his whole life for a woman he's known since she was a kid," Sam added.

Levi, in addition to moving out, had also given up his current job managing the Stormy Weather Farm's vineyards and gardens. A born farmer, he'd spent every single day with his hands in the dirt. However, his agricultural interests over the years had evolved from working with the grapes, to growing vegetables, to starting a small patch where he could plant hops and barley for the brewery.

Levi was always interested in learning new things—something that had served their businesses well. With his move to the Mills' farm, his brother would now have enough land to grow all the barley and hops they required for the brewhouse, as well as other produce that could be incorporated in their beer or served in the B&B their parents ran. Mom was a huge fan of farm to table, so now they wouldn't have to outsource their produce anymore. It was a win-win for Levi—finding true love as well as an exciting new farming direction.

Theo rolled his eyes. "Which is why our too-serious brother is suddenly smiling all the time. And whistling. And walking around with an actual goddamn spring in his step."

"Because none of that is annoying. At. All," Sam replied sarcastically, the two of them laughing. They were happy for Levi, but damn if it wasn't a bit of culture shock, seeing their stoic big brother fawning over a woman who was thirteen years younger than him.

"Regardless," Sam pressed on. "You should go check out the women in Henley Falls. Who knows. Maybe your girl lives the next town over."

"Wouldn't that be nice?" Theo mused. "But I think I'm going to sit this weekend out. Gretchen starts on Monday, and I'm trying to get my ducks in a row. I need to finish making a list of job duties then run it by Nora. Plus, the contractor is coming that day as well to do one final walk-through of the barn."

Sam gave him a commiserating look. "I'm glad it's finally built. Talk about a major pain in the ass. I swear I kept expecting you to lose your shit at some point and take a match to it."

Theo agreed. "Not going to say there weren't days when burning the damn thing to the ground wasn't tempting."

They had run into one setback after another building the barn, between long delays on the delivery of lumber to their construction foreman, Roy, taking six weeks off after becoming a first-time father. They were happy for Roy, but his next-in-charge, Bryant, had screwed up more than a few things that had required renovations after Roy returned.

"Alright," Sam said, rising. "I've left Jace alone too long.

When the cat's away... Twenty bucks says he's kicked back watching TikTok videos and not doing a damn bit of work."

Theo shook his head. "I'm not taking that bet. I don't like to lose."

Sam gave him a playful salute, then walked out.

Theo sank down on his chair and forced himself to get back to work on his list...then he considered Sam's campaign. It looked like he was going to be burning that two-ended candle a little longer.

Fucking awesome.

Chapter Two

Gretchen jerked awake as the bus hit a nasty pothole, her head banging against the window that had been serving as her pillow.

Reaching up, she rubbed the soreness away, ignoring the pain.

Because really...what was one more bruise? It wasn't like she wasn't currently wearing matching ones on her neck and back, and at least this one would be hidden by her hair.

She blinked several times, trying to clear her vision. Sleeping on a bus was nearly impossible, even given her current level of exhaustion.

She'd spent the past six months secretly saving money and stowing clothing at work, while making arrangements for what she hoped would be a happy future. This was the last leg of the journey, and as the bus crept ever closer to Gracemont, her emotions wavered between relief—that she'd almost made it—and fear. Because life had taught her countless times that the other shoe could drop at any moment.

She pushed those negative thoughts away. There was no room for them here, since she was determined that this time, she would succeed.

Gretchen had made a few weak attempts at leaving Briggs in the past. But they'd failed because she always ran while her emotions were high, and she never had a solid, practical plan in place, turning to unreliable people who never had her best interests at heart.

This time, she had dotted all the i's and crossed all the t's, determined to start a new life on her own. One where she didn't walk on eggshells, didn't spend a fortune on concealer, didn't live in fear of saying or doing something that might set someone off.

She had to hand it to her ex. Briggs had chosen his victim wisely. He'd known exactly how to isolate her, how to keep her reliant on him, from controlling all the money, to discouraging her from getting her driver's license, to driving a rift between her and the only real family she had, her brother Shaw.

She peered out the window, taking in the scenery. It was mid-September in northern Virginia, too early for fall to paint the mountain in an array of bright reds, yellows, and oranges as the leaves changed color.

Right now, everything was still green and lush. If it had been any other day, she might have enjoyed the view, marveled at the beauty of the nature surrounding her, but as she got closer and closer to her final destination, she found herself second-guessing the plan.

What if she'd missed a step somewhere and failed to cover her trail?

What if, when she arrived at the bus station, Briggs was there in uniform, and he forced her into his police car? She'd learned the hard way no one would step forward to save a woman from a cop. That lesson had come the last time she'd run, and he'd caught up with her as she was buying a bus ticket out of town. The other people at the station simply stepped away when Briggs pretended to arrest her, cuffing her and dragging her home in the back of his cruiser. That weak attempt at escape ended with three cracked ribs and marked the end of her running for two long, painful years.

She'd drifted into a dark place during that time, believing the life she was living was the best she could hope for, and she gave up dreaming for happiness or love. Gretchen spent two years as a ghost in her own life, disappearing into romance novels, trying to make herself invisible, and when that failed, taking Briggs's abuse without fighting back.

As the bus pulled into the station, she took a deep breath. This was a critical juncture, and she needed to be alert, focused. Gretchen scanned the parking lot as well as the front of the building and the area where they would disembark, terrified Briggs would be there.

She didn't see anyone who looked like him and there were no police vehicles in the parking lot, but that didn't ease her anxiety as she waited until everyone else got off the bus before making her own trip down the aisle, stepping into the crisp morning air.

Gretchen stood near the bus until all the bags were unloaded. Once she claimed hers, she stepped closer to the building and pulled out her brand-new Tracfone, prepared to call for an Uber, when she noticed an older gentleman standing by the bus station door holding a piece of paper with her name on it.

Her new name.

One of the first steps she'd made toward creating a new life for herself had been dropping her father's last name and changing it to her beloved great-aunt's name instead.

Gretchen Parker was now officially Gretchen Banks.

Her heart stopped beating for a moment when the man glanced in her direction. Shit. She'd been staring. He smiled as he took a few steps toward her.

Had Briggs sent this man? He didn't look like a cop, but maybe that was by design. Briggs had to know Gretchen would avoid anyone in uniform.

"Miss Banks?" the man asked.

Gretchen didn't reply, fear constricting her throat.

"Gretchen?" he added. "Gretchen Banks?"

Gretchen's gaze traveled from the man to their surroundings as she calculated her chances of escaping. She felt certain she could outrun this guy, who was at least fifty pounds overweight and probably thirty years older than her.

But what if he wasn't alone? What if there were others, hidden, waiting to capture her and drag her back?

God, she needed to act *now*.

"Who are you?" she asked, rather than confirming her identity.

Identity...wait. He was using her *new name*.

"I'm Manny Millholland, Edith's nephew. She sent me to pick you up. You *are* Gretchen Banks, yes?"

Gretchen nodded as she took a shaky breath. This new life of hers was beginning in a room she was renting from Edith Millholland, an elderly woman who lived in the tiny town of Gracemont, Virginia. When she let Edith know she'd be arriving this morning by bus, the older woman had offered to send her nephew to "fetch her," but Gretchen had assured her she could make her own way.

"I am," she said. Then hastened to add, "I'm sorry for my behavior. It's impossible to sleep on a bus and I'm kind of groggy."

Manny smiled widely, easily accepting her excuse for

acting like a trapped lion cub. "Nothing worse than trying to sleep while sitting up. I took the red-eye to California once to go visit some college friends a few years back. Didn't sleep a wink." Manny gestured to her suitcase. "That your only bag?"

She nodded. She hadn't dared to sneak out more than just the essentials from her house, taking care to make sure Briggs didn't notice things were missing.

"Someone sending the rest of your stuff along?"

She was renting the room at Edith's because she'd gotten a job in Gracemont. As far as Edith was concerned, Gretchen was moving to town permanently, and obviously someone relocating should probably have more than one small suitcase.

"Um, yes," she lied. "A friend is shipping the rest."

Once again, Manny accepted her words as the truth, attempting to take her suitcase from her. She stopped him. "Um. I hope you don't mind but, uh, could I see your ID?"

Manny froze for a second, clearly surprised by the request, but then he reached into his back pocket, pulling out his driver's license, which did indeed confirm he was Manuel Millholland from Gracemont. "Suppose you can't be too safe as a woman," he said genially. "Good for you. Looking out for yourself."

She was relieved she hadn't offended him or set off any alarms. She needed the room in his aunt's house, so she was walking a thin line between protecting herself and not coming off like a lunatic.

"My car is over here." This time when Manny reached for her suitcase, she let him take it.

"It was nice of Edith to send you, but I told her I was fine getting an Uber to Gracemont."

Manny waved her words away. "Gracemont is a bit of hike from here. No sense wasting thirty, forty dollars when I'm happy to give you a ride."

"I appreciate it. I hope I didn't drag you away from work or anything," Gretchen said, as Manny placed her suitcase in the trunk. She climbed into the passenger seat, doing one last scan of the parking lot, just in case anyone was watching.

"You didn't drag me away from anything I wanted to do," Manny said with a wink. "My aunt owns quite a few properties in Gracemont and the surrounding towns. I work for her as property manager. This trip let me put off fixing a clogged toilet in one of the rental homes over in Henley Falls. So thank you."

Manny proved himself to be an entertaining storyteller, and the ride to Gracemont passed quickly as he regaled her with all the "need to know" information regarding his aunt Edith, who sounded like quite a character. Gretchen had gotten a similar sense from the emails they'd exchanged, but hearing Manny recount some of the older woman's hijinks confirmed it. According to Manny, Edith was an amazing cook and baker with a cutting wit, who, despite her advanced years, managed to keep everyone she knew on their toes.

"So you don't have a car?" Manny asked, curiously.

She shook her head. "No. I'm from Harrisburg, Pennsylvania, which, while not a huge city, is large enough that I could get around by using public transportation and rideshares."

"Ah. Well, I should warn you now, we don't have any of that in Gracemont."

Gretchen frowned. She wasn't surprised to learn there was no public transportation, but she'd been counting on the rideshare option.

"I checked online, and I swore Gracemont offered Uber services."

"Well, now, I suppose that is true," Manny replied, and Gretchen breathed a sigh of relief. "One of the local fellas, Koda James, started offering the service a year or so back. That young man is obsessed with his car and driving, and completely unimpressed with set work hours that begin before noon and involve sitting behind a desk."

"Oh."

Manny continued. "Koda will Uber people around town but usually only in the evenings. Truthfully, that seems to be the only time anyone needs a ride. Koda drives folks home from Whiskey Abbey, our local bar. In addition to his Uber services, he's our only DoorDash deliveryman. And because neither of those jobs earn him enough money, he also delivers pizza for the local pizza place. Between those three things, he's managed to avoid the dreaded day job and make Gracemont sound cool, because we get to say we have Uber and DoorDash now, like the bigger cities around us."

Gretchen bit her lower lip. Now she was faced with a dilemma. She'd looked at a map when she'd first rented the room from Edith, so she knew it was a little less than five miles from Millholland House to Stormy Weather Farm, where she'd taken a job. She'd seen that as good news, thinking it would mean a cheap Uber trip back and forth to work.

Score yet another one for Briggs. He'd convinced her when she was younger—and stupider—that she didn't need to get a driver's license, assuring her that he would take her wherever she needed to go. It was one of many ways he'd managed to keep her trapped.

It looked like she was going to have to get creative. She wondered how long it would take to walk five miles. Luckily, she didn't start her new job until next Monday. It was Wednesday now, so that gave her four days to practice the trek and time it. She tried to tell herself the exercise would be good for her. Then she mentally moved "get a driver's license and car" up on her "New Life" to-do list and added "get a bike and learn how to ride it," as well.

"Here we are," Manny said, pulling her from her thoughts. "Gracemont."

She glanced up in time to see the pretty sign announcing they were indeed entering the town of Gracemont. As they traveled along Main Street, Manny pointed out the businesses, filling her in on what they provided, who owned them, who offered fair deals, and who overcharged.

Her eyes widened when he pulled up in front of a grandiose three-story white house with a wraparound porch, bright green shutters, and huge azalea bushes in the front yard that were probably gorgeous in the spring. There was a small sign hanging from a pillar in the yard that said Millholland House.

"Welcome to your new home, Miss Banks," Manny offered cheerfully.

Home.

She liked the sound of that.

Manny pulled into the driveway as Gretchen tried to calm her nerves before climbing out of the car. She waited while Manny retrieved her suitcase from the trunk, then before they even reached the top of the porch, the front door swung open and the tiniest woman Gretchen had ever seen emerged.

When Manny told her all the stories about his aunt, Gretchen had pictured Edith as a much taller woman, sturdier and more imposing.

Edith Millholland looked like a light breeze could blow her away, with her petite frame. However, the woman's looks were obviously misleading. Gretchen fought not to wince when Edith stepped forward, arms outstretched, and pulled her in for a hug, gripping her tightly.

Of course, it wasn't the hug that hurt but the pressure on the hidden bruises beneath her clothing.

"There you are! I've been looking forward to meeting you,

Gretchen." Edith released her, eyeing her from head to toe. "Well, let me have a look at you. Aren't you a beauty!"

Gretchen smiled, doing her own once-over of the elderly lady. Edith had snow-white hair pulled up in a loose bun, bright blue eyes, and deep creases by her eyes and mouth that seemed to indicate she laughed and smiled a lot. "It's very nice to meet you, Ms. Millholland."

Edith waved her hands. "No, no. None of that. You and I are going to be roomies and future besties, so I insist you call me Edith."

Gretchen was amused by the elderly woman's use of the words *roomies* and *besties*.

Edith looped her arm through Gretchen's, guiding her into the house before looking over her shoulder. "Well, don't stand there with your mouth hanging open, Manny. You'll catch flies. Bring in her bag."

Manny, whose mouth was *not* hanging open, rolled his eyes, then hastened to follow them inside. Like her nephew, Edith was taken aback by Gretchen's lack of belongings.

"That's your only suitcase?" the older woman asked.

Gretchen nodded, but before she had to repeat her lie, Manny told it for her. "A friend is sending the rest of her stuff along later."

Edith accepted that fib as easily as her nephew. "She'll be staying in the blue room," she said to Manny, who climbed the stairs with her bag.

"Let me give you a tour of the house, dear." Edith's eyes drifted down to Gretchen's neck, narrowing.

Gretchen tugged on her turtleneck sweater, pulling it higher. She hadn't had a chance to touch up her concealer, so she feared the bruises must be at least partially visible by now. Explaining away bruised arms and cheeks was a lot easier than a neck. Especially when the bruises were fingerprint-shaped.

Briggs had an unnatural fondness for choking her during his fits of rage.

Mercifully, Edith didn't ask her about her injuries, and for the next twenty minutes, Gretchen followed her around the large house as her host took her through each room, pointing out the interesting artwork, collectables, and various other knickknacks—all of which had fascinating stories—that she'd acquired over the years. Edith was obviously very proud of her home, and she should be. The elegant décor reminded Gretchen of pictures she'd seen in magazines.

According to Edith, there were four rooms available for rent upstairs, but Gretchen was currently the only guest staying there.

When Gretchen had first gotten the job as event coordinator for Stormy Weather Farm, she feared she might have to turn it down due to the lack of available apartments. Gracemont seemed to be one of those towns that time forgot. When she began researching places to rent, she'd come up painfully shy on options because there wasn't a single apartment building within the town limits. The closest place she could find was a condo that was way out of her price range, just outside Leesburg.

Between the astronomical monthly rent and the fact she didn't drive, she'd started to worry she was going to lose what honestly felt like a dream job.

When she'd mentioned to her new boss, Theo Storm, that she was struggling to find housing, he said he'd see what he could find. He'd called her back less than an hour later and given her Edith's number. It was the answer to a prayer. Lodging at Edith's was very affordable, and she wasn't even tied to a lease. Edith basically told her she could stay as long as she wanted.

The tour ended in Gretchen's room, and she failed to hold

in her gasp as she walked into the large, beautiful bedroom. It was a suite, so in addition to the bed, nightstand, and dresser, there was a small sitting area complete with a love seat and chair, arranged together in front of a fireplace.

There was a *fireplace* in her room!

Edith pointed across the hall. "The bathroom is there. Ordinarily it's shared between the guests, but as you're the only person here, you get it all to yourself."

"This is wonderful." Gretchen suddenly felt guilty because Edith was seriously undercharging her to stay here.

Not that she was able to pay more. While she'd managed to squirrel away nearly two thousand dollars, she'd already dipped into that, paying for the bus fare that took her from Harrisburg to Atlanta, where she'd disembarked, taking a rideshare to a different bus company called Southeastern Stages. From there, she'd traveled to Raleigh. In North Carolina, she'd gotten a rideshare to a Greyhound station, where she bought the third and final ticket to Leesburg.

It had taken her two days to travel what should only have taken four hours by bus, but it hadn't felt like overkill because she was determined to make finding her as hard as possible on her ex.

Briggs was a cop with too many resources on hand to help find her, so she'd been very careful to cover her tracks. In addition to the bus swaps, she'd bought the tickets with her new ID, using cash only. She prayed the care she'd taken would be enough to throw him off her scent permanently.

Maybe if she managed to stay hidden, he'd stop looking eventually.

"Now," Edith said. "Why don't you take some time to unpack and rest for a little while? When you're ready, come downstairs and I'll make us some tea and sandwiches to go with the cookies I baked last night."

"I would love that."

Edith gave her a warm smile as she left, closing the door behind her. Gretchen walked to the bed and sat down. The mattress sank in just right, so she fell to her back and groaned in delight. She'd never slept in a bed this comfortable.

That wasn't exactly true. There was nothing wrong with the bed she and Briggs had shared, except for the fact he was in it. It was difficult to relax while lying next to him.

She'd caught only catnaps on the bus before fear woke her up, trembling over the possibility of Briggs catching up to her. Staring at the ceiling, she let out a long sigh, her tired body begging for sleep.

Unfortunately, her mind was the stronger—and it was currently racing a million miles an hour, showing no signs of stopping soon.

Gretchen didn't want to consider what Briggs would do if he found her. After six years with the man, she had a very full understanding of exactly how possessive he was.

She rolled over and willed herself to fall asleep, but after an hour had passed, she gave up and decided to answer the call of her growling stomach. She'd been living off vending machine food at the bus stations, the crackers and chips doing very little to fill her stomach.

Running a comb through her hair, she quickly changed clothes, anxious to get out of the jeans and turtleneck she'd been wearing. She pulled on another high-necked sweater, then touched up the visible places on her neck with more concealer.

Feeling as refreshed as she was going to get without taking a shower, she stepped out of her room and made her way downstairs. She found Edith in the kitchen.

"That wasn't much of a nap," the older woman observed.

Gretchen shrugged. "I think I'm overtired. Couldn't fall asleep."

"Well then, that decided what tea we're drinking. Nothing like a nice cup of chamomile to help you relax. You have a seat right there." Edith pointed to the kitchen table. "And I'll get you something to eat."

Another perk of staying with Edith was the fact her nightly rate was a room-and-board deal.

"I don't mind fending for myself for meals." Gretchen felt like she was taking advantage of the woman, now that she'd seen her amazing room. "Manny pointed out a couple of places to eat on this street that I can walk to."

"And those are fine places, but I hope you'll humor an old woman and dine with me most nights. The only time I get to cook the way I like is when I have guests or when Manny joins me, which is only two or three times a week."

"You and Manny are close," Gretchen observed.

"We certainly are. His father—my brother—and his mother fancy themselves jetsetters. Those two never live in the same city for more than a year or so, and they discovered—after having their son—they preferred a social life over parenting, so Manny spent every summer with me from the time he was old enough to talk."

"You didn't have kids of your own?" Gretchen asked.

Edith shook her head. "Never found a man who could keep up with me. Besides, between you and me, I've found them to be more trouble than they're worth."

Gretchen was tempted to add "tell me about it" to that statement but feared that would open the door to a conversation she didn't want to have.

Edith continued with her story. "His parents dragged poor Manny all over the country for most of his childhood, until he put his foot down in ninth grade and begged to live with me. Manny, like me, is a homebody."

"So he moved in with you?"

Edith nodded, smiling fondly. "Moved here when he was fourteen and never left, except to go to college. He never married either, but that's because he's completely hopeless when it comes to women. He has no game."

Gretchen laughed, the sound cut short by shock. She honestly couldn't recall the last time she'd laughed.

Edith worked as she talked, pulling the kettle off the stove when the whistle began to blow. Before ten minutes had passed, she'd made Gretchen a delicious egg salad sandwich, served with a dollop of macaroni salad on the side as well as a huge pickle, all accompanied with the promised chamomile tea.

Gretchen had to fight to eat slowly, her hunger too great and the food too damn good.

Edith poured herself a cup of tea and joined her at the table.

"You aren't eating?" Gretchen asked.

"I had a nibble earlier." Edith took a sip of her tea. "So you're here because you'll be working for the Storm family?"

"They hired me to be their event coordinator. I'll admit, I was thrilled when Theo Storm emailed to tell me I got the job." Gretchen didn't bother to add that she'd applied for the job out of desperation, with zero expectation of getting it. For the better part of six months, she'd spent her entire lunch break at work filling out no less than a hundred job applications, tossing her hat in the ring for anything—most things she wasn't even qualified for—in hopes that something would come along.

It helped that Brenda had written her one hell of a recommendation letter, which she'd given Gretchen carte blanche to change according to whatever job she was applying for, promising to give her a great reference if anyone called.

"The Storms are a wonderful family," Edith said. "They've

been growing grapes on the side of the mountain for three generations, their winery one of the most popular in the area. Theo's oldest brother, Levi, has been the vineyard manager for years, but if the gossip is to be believed, that'll be changing soon."

"Oh?"

Edith leaned forward, clearly delighted to be doing her part to keep the rumor mill churning. "He's fallen in love with a lovely local girl, Kasi Mills, who lost her mother, Katrina, at the beginning of this year. It was such a terrible loss for our community. Trina was a kind, giving woman, and Kasi is a lot like her. According to Levi's mother, Claire, he's hired someone to take over his role on the vineyard so that he can work with Kasi on her family farm. Claire expects we'll hear wedding bells ringing before too long."

Gretchen had gathered from her research that Gracemont was a small town, but she hadn't anticipated the locals knowing so much about each other. She worried it might be hard to lay low in a place like this. "It sounds like there are a lot of farms around here."

"There are indeed. You're from Pennsylvania, right? That's farm country as well, isn't it?"

Gretchen nodded. "Oh, sure. There are lots of farms, but I lived in Harrisburg, which, while not exactly large, is more city than rural."

"I suspect it will be a bit of a culture shock for you, moving to Gracemont. You'll learn that life moves at a much slower pace around here."

"That sounds very appealing to me," Gretchen admitted.

"So when do you start work at Stormy Weather Farm?" Edith asked.

"My first official day is Monday, but I thought I might visit before then to introduce myself and take a look around." And time the walk, now that she knew ridesharing wasn't an option.

"I think you'll be impressed. The view from that side of the mountain never fails to take my breath away, and I've lived here my whole life. On a clear day, you can see all the way to Washington, D.C."

Gretchen's eyes widened. "Really? I can't wait to see it."

"Now, I was thinking that Saturday night, we'd have a special meal, a Welcome to Gracemont dinner for you. I've already invited Manny to join us. What's your favorite food?"

Gretchen didn't know how to respond—because she couldn't recall anyone ever asking her that. Her life hadn't been overly full of nice people. She'd grown up in a rough house with an abusive stepfather and a milquetoast mother. The house parents at the residential home where she and Shaw lived after entering the foster care system had been nice enough, though they'd been harried and overworked most of the time.

So Gretchen couldn't understand why Edith, a stranger, was rolling out the red carpet.

"I can't let you go to all that trouble. You're already doing so much by letting me stay in that beautiful room. You aren't charging me enough," Gretchen added, guilt forcing her to voice that concern.

Edith waved away her apprehensions. "I'm an eighty-two-year-old woman, rambling around in a big empty house. I have more money than I can ever spend before I die, and I enjoy the company of others. This place gets damn lonely with only Manny stopping in at the end of each day. While the boy is entertaining company, sometimes a person craves variety. After all these years, there's not much Manny and I haven't already talked about a dozen or so times. It'll be nice to have someone else to tell my stories to, and to listen as they share their own."

Gretchen smiled, even as her chest tightened. Unlike Manny and Edith, Gretchen's stories weren't the kind you shared over a nice dinner.

Edith continued. "And please don't worry about not paying enough. You're a young girl starting a new job in a new town. I'm happy to be able to help you while you find your footing. Maybe one day, sixty or so years down the road, you can pay it forward."

Gretchen had vowed not to cry in front of anyone, but Edith's words broke a dam that had already been on shaky foundation. She lowered her head, trying to hide her tears, but Edith didn't let her get away with it.

She reached out and took Gretchen's hand. "There, there, child. There's no need to cry."

"I'm sorry. It's just...it's so nice of you. No one's ever—"

She stopped short, refusing to finish that statement.

Not that it mattered. Edith was an astute, observant woman.

"If that's true, then I'm even happier to have you here with me."

"Thank you," Gretchen whispered, wiping her eyes. "Starting fresh is exactly what I need."

"I can see that," the wise woman said, her eyes dropping down to Gretchen's neck.

She acted on instinct, lifting her hand to pull up the neck of her sweater. Before Edith could question her about the bruises, she hastily stood. "If you don't mind, I think I'll go up to my room now." She feigned a yawn. "I'm tired from the trip, and your tea did the trick."

Edith nodded, then rose as well. "A nice nap will fix you right up." The woman reached her hand out, and Gretchen slipped hers into it without a thought. "I hope you and I will become very good friends, my dear."

"Besties," she murmured, repeating Edith's earlier assertion.

Edith smiled and gave her hand a squeeze. "Exactly."

Gretchen left the room, climbing the stairs, feeling lighter than when she'd descended.

For the first time ever, she felt the tiniest kernel of hope for her own future.

Chapter Three

Theo pushed away from his computer and stifled a yawn.

"Fuck this."

He decided to call it a day. It wasn't even one on Thursday, but after all the extra hours he'd been pulling, he figured he had earned an early out.

Dammit. There had to be *some* perks to basically being his own boss.

As Theo, his brothers, and cousins graduated high school, all of them but Sam elected to remain at home, assuming roles tailored to their interests in the various farm businesses. There was an abundance of jobs available because running an operational farm, as well as three—soon to be four—businesses required many, *many* hands on deck.

They had each carved out their own niche, creating career paths that suited them. Levi farmed; Maverick and Grayson made the best wine in Virginia; Sam and Jace served as brewmasters; Everett, a computer genius, was their IT department; Remi, an avid horsewoman, led trail rides and served at the brewhouse; and Mila did a little bit of everything, serving as cook at the winery and brewery, as well as taking care of the cabin rentals and pitching in at the B&B.

As for him, he—like Nora—had been drawn to one of the managerial roles, putting his organizational and people skills to use, running the brewery and brewhouse.

Every one of the Storms had found a way to make their own mark on this land that had been in their family for four generations, and with the exception of his cousin Lucy, they'd all remained right here in Gracemont.

So if he wanted to play hooky one afternoon, there wasn't a soul on the place who could tell him no. Not that anyone would. While they all did their own thing on Stormy Weather Farm, every single Storm shared the same trait. They were hard workers, so when any of them took some downtime, it was because it was well earned.

"His office is right down there," he overheard Billy say from the end of the hall.

Great, Theo thought grumpily.

So much for making a quick escape.

His curiosity was piqued when he heard a female voice say, "Oh, that's alright. I'll come back—"

"No, really," Billy insisted. "It's fine."

He heard more murmurs that said the conversation was continuing, but he couldn't make out what they were saying. When no one arrived at his doorway, Theo turned off his computer. Maybe he'd gotten lucky and whoever the visitor was had decided to return later.

"Theo Storm?"

Theo glanced up, trying to place the woman standing in his doorway. She looked vaguely familiar, though he knew in an instant she wasn't from Gracemont.

"Yes," he replied. "That's me."

"I'm Gretchen Banks."

Of course. The new event coordinator.

"Oh, hey. I'm sorry I didn't recognize you." He gave her a friendly smile as he stood. "I wasn't expecting to meet you until next week."

"I know. I'm sorry to drop by like this. I told the guy who found me outside that I was taking a quick look around, but he insisted I meet you."

"That was Billy, and I'm glad he did."

Gretchen looked uncomfortable and he could tell she really hadn't meant to stop in. Problem was, Billy, an affable, too-eager-to-please guy, was shit when it came to picking up on social cues, so he'd obviously dragged her in for this impromptu meeting against her will.

"I arrived in town yesterday, and I was excited to see the farm, so I thought I'd get the lay of the land. But I can see you're busy, so..."

She started backing out of his office.

"No, wait." Theo lifted his hand as Gretchen froze in the doorway, looking like a deer in the headlights. That same vulnerability he'd seen during her interview flashed across her face.

"I'm not busy at all." There were at least ten more things on his to-do list, but since he'd already decided to blow them off, he figured he technically wasn't lying. "I'm glad you decided to stop by."

The video feed on his computer hadn't done her justice. Obviously, he'd noticed she was pretty during the interview—so had Nora—but Gretchen had been sitting during their Zoom chat, so he hadn't been able to get a sense of her height or build. She was surprisingly taller than he expected, though she was probably still three or four inches shorter than his six-one frame.

She was also quite slim, thin even. *Too* thin. The lack of weight meant her cheekbones were more pronounced, and he felt the unexpected desire to take her to his mom right now, simply so she could feed her.

She'd worn her long blonde hair down during the interview, but now, it was pinned up in a high ponytail, though several wisps had escaped, framing her face. She had long dark lashes and full pink lips that he'd yet to see tipped in a smile. She hadn't even smiled during their Zoom.

One of Nora's arguments against hiring Gretchen was that she'd come across as too serious. While the Storms were hard workers, they were just as notorious for playing hard as well. Laughter, teasing, and practical jokes were the norm around here, and Nora was concerned Gretchen wouldn't fit in or get their humor.

Theo had rejected that argument because he hadn't gotten the sense that she was uptight or humorless. Instead, those sad eyes of hers made him long to put a smile on her face, or better yet, make her laugh.

While Gretchen's complexion was fair, she was currently red-faced. His initial thought was that she was either nervous or even a bit shy—which could be a problem in her new position— but as he took a closer look, he thought maybe she was flushed due to the heat. The hair along her scalp was damp from perspiration and her shirt seemed to cling to her uncomfortably.

It was no wonder she was overheated. It was too damn hot to be wearing a turtleneck. While it was mid-September, they were having an Indian summer, today's high reaching nearly ninety. He wondered if fall temperatures were lower in Harrisburg. He'd taken a look at a map after she'd accepted the job. It was only a two-hour drive from there to here, so the weather couldn't vary *that* much.

She'd been soft-spoken during her interview, but she hadn't given him timid vibes. In fact, despite her lack of experience, her answers to his questions proved that her vision for the event barn lined up perfectly with his. He'd gone into the interview slightly distracted, aware she wouldn't be their candidate, so at first, he'd only listened with half an ear because in his mind, all he was doing was checking a box.

But that had changed by the third question, because he'd become enthralled by...well...everything about her. Her looks, her voice, her answers, that look in her eyes that drew him in like a siren's song, pulling him closer and closer to the rocks.

By the end of the interview, he'd known she was the one for the job.

Theo was big on making gut decisions; mainly, they'd never steered him wrong, and his gut...it had screamed Gretchen was perfect for the job.

"Come on in," he invited her. He remained where he was because she still looked rather uncomfortable.

"I really should have called first. Given you some warning." She glanced over her shoulder, clearly intent on leaving.

"Nope. This way is better. I like surprises."

Gretchen's brow furrowed in obvious disagreement.

"Not a fan of them?" he asked.

"Never had any surprises that were good," she said softly.

He wasn't sure what to make of that, and it was apparent Gretchen hadn't meant to say something so revealing.

"I mean, um..." she stumbled.

"Sounds like we might have to work on that while you're here." He gave her what he hoped was another friendly smile that might set her at ease.

"I was only kidding," she hastened to add. Given the way her eyes darted away from him as she spoke, he could tell she was lying.

He pointed to the chairs in front on his desk. "Please. Join me. I'm glad you decided to surprise me with a visit."

Gretchen walked in, sinking down into one of the chairs, though he noticed she remained perched on the edge, ready to bolt at a moment's notice.

Theo sat down as well, keeping his large desk between them.

"So you made it to Gracemont alright. What do you think of the town so far?"

"I haven't seen much of it, but it's very quaint."

"That's a nice word for extremely tiny. I assume you took a room with Edith?" Theo had been the one to suggest Millholland House, so he figured it was a safe assumption.

Gretchen nodded. "I did. She's a wonderful woman. I can't thank you enough for the recommendation. Her house is amazing. It's like living in a museum or an antique shop."

"Yeah, it really is. And I swear she's got a story for every single stick of furniture."

"I might have heard a few of those yesterday."

"Edith is a character, but she's really great," Theo added. "She and my grandma were thick as thieves when they were younger, so she spent a lot of time here on the farm when I was growing up. After my grandmother passed away, Edith sort of stepped in as a surrogate grandma, never forgetting to send birthday cards and stopping by from time to time to see how we're getting on. Truth is, there are probably quite a few people in Gracemont who feel the same way about her. She's adopted a lot of locals, treating them like family."

"Manny mentioned she's quite popular, and I can see why. She's a natural at taking people under her wing."

Theo grinned. "She's already claiming you as her own, isn't she?"

Gretchen shrugged. "I don't know about that, but she used the word 'roomies' to describe us."

Theo barked out a laugh, amused by Edith's contemporary slang. He'd been told the only other Storm who possessed a more obnoxiously loud laugh than him was his cousin Remi. However, he cut it short due to Gretchen's reaction.

She jerked—and if he had to guess, he'd say his boisterous laughter startled her.

Shit.

He studied her face, keeping his smile in place, trying not to let her see how her response concerned him.

Theo was good at reading people, something that helped him succeed in his job because—in a lot of ways—he was the face of the brewery. While Jace and Sam worked behind the scenes, brewing the beer, he was the one working with the employees and chatting with their patrons, making them feel comfortable at Rain or Shine Brewery. Mom said he was blessed not only with an abundance of charm but also a deep-seated empathy that allowed him to read people better than they could read themselves and put them at ease.

Right now, that empathy was telling him that there was a storm raging beneath the surface of the beautiful woman sitting in front of him. She was uneasy sitting here, but she was facing that discomfort with a determination he admired.

He adopted a quieter tone when he spoke again. "I give it one week before Edith starts introducing you as her bestie. She loves using current slang, probably for the humor factor."

"She claimed her nephew has no game, and that's why he's still single."

Theo snorted because that was a fair description of Manny. "I can almost imagine her sitting up at night messing around on Urban Dictionary, searching for new words to spring on the unwitting Gracemont citizens. Just for shits and giggles."

Gretchen winced. "I don't even want to think about that."

Theo was tempted to laugh at what was clearly a joke on her part, but instead, he winked. "Edith's a regular at the winery and the brewery, making an appearance at both at least once or twice a month. Sam, my brother, claims she's 'holding court,' and damn if that's not what it feels like because by the time she leaves, every single patron has made their way to her table to chat. I can't tell you how many times I've watched her draw a crowd, everyone jostling to hear one of her tall tales. She's a regular one-woman show, and I've toyed with the idea of putting her on the entertainment schedule." He held his hand up as if reading a marquee. "'Gracemont Gossip with Edith Millholland. One night only.'"

"I'd pay money to see that show," Gretchen said.

Theo laughed, but this time, he made sure it was softer. "I'm sure Edith loves having you with her. She's happiest when she has someone to fuss over."

Gretchen looked around again, as if seeking an excuse to leave, but Theo wasn't ready to say goodbye yet, so he jumped in first.

"Nora's working over at the winery, of course, but she plans to be here Monday morning to meet you. Before you head out today, I can introduce you to the brewmasters, who also happen to be my brothers, Jace and Sam."

"That's okay," she said, intending to refuse. "I can wait—"

"Sam's currently running for mayor of Gracemont," Theo interjected. "So Jace will be taking on the lion's share of the brewing, once Sam takes office, though I'm sure he'll still be here a fair amount of the time."

Gretchen's eyebrows rose. "Mayor? That sounds like a big job."

"Maybe in a bigger city, but in Gracemont, it's less than part-time. Even so, knowing Sam, he'll work overtime to assure it's done right, because that's who he is. He was made to be mayor, and the whole family is proud of him."

"That's great," Gretchen said. "And it's nice of Jace to step in so that Sam can pursue the position."

"Well, that's what family does, isn't it?"

Gretchen hesitated slightly before giving him a short nod, letting him know in an instant that wasn't how things worked in *her* family. The personal information he knew about Gretchen was limited to superficial things he'd discovered from her resume and during the interview. Things like, she was twenty-four years old and she was born in Harrisburg, where she'd lived her entire life. He knew where she'd graduated from high school, and that she'd only had one other job, as the personal assistant to a real estate agent. She said during her interview that her reason for applying for the job was because she was looking for a change—no, the words she used were *fresh start*—though she hadn't elaborated on why.

Now, it was all he could think about.

It was easy to see that Gretchen's walls were so high, he would need to take a slow approach when it came to getting to know her. Lucky for her, as a Gracemont boy, slow and steady came easy to him, as that was the only pace most folks in this town knew.

Theo decided to try the "lead by example" tactic. Perhaps if he willingly shared information about himself, she would follow suit.

"Jace is the youngest of my brothers, but he's got one of the biggest personalities. He's also a shameless flirt, but don't worry about that. He's harmless. And nowhere near as good-looking as me," Theo added as a joke, when Gretchen nervously licked her lips.

"It must be nice to work with your brothers," she mused.

"For the most part, it is. My brothers are my best friends,

but we're also like most siblings. We get into some knockdown, drag-out fights. Probably doesn't help that we don't just work together but live together as well."

"That is a lot of togetherness." Gretchen was still sitting on the edge of her chair, her hands clenched tightly in her lap. He wished there was a way he could encourage her to relax.

"There are three farmhouses on the property," Theo explained. "I share one with my six brothers. Well, five now, since my oldest brother, Levi, is essentially living with his girl-friend Kasi these days."

"Edith mentioned Levi's new relationship. Said they would probably get married soon."

Theo chuckled. "You've been here what? Twenty-four hours?"

Gretchen nodded.

"I'm guessing there's not much left I can tell you about me and my family, then. Edith's probably already covered every-thing," he joked.

Gretchen gave him a look that proved Edith had been filling in lots of blanks for her. "She's a wealth of information. I considered taking notes for a little while."

Theo laughed at her joke, and this time, Gretchen graced him with a small smile.

Progress.

Though now that he'd managed to break a hairline-thin crack in her thick surface, he wanted to go for broke. Because something told him that she hadn't laughed in a very, very long time.

So Theo had a new goal.

Well, *another* new goal, because before he made Gretchen laugh, he was determined to set her at ease.

Once again, she looked ready to escape as her eyes darted

toward the window, then toward the door behind her. "I—" she started.

"What about you?" he asked, taking a chance. "Any siblings?"

Gretchen visibly tensed. It looked like he'd gone a step too far. "Just one," she replied. "An older brother. Shaw. He's a Navy SEAL."

Theo whistled, impressed. "A SEAL, huh? Pretty cool."

That sadness he'd seen in her eyes during the interview returned. "It is. Unfortunately, it keeps him busy, so I'm afraid I haven't seen him much the last few years."

"That can't be easy. I'd go crazy if I went so long without seeing one of my brothers."

Gretchen glanced at him before looking away again, shrugging in a way she clearly meant to look indifferent. However, he could see she wasn't happy about the estrangement from Shaw. "He's typically deployed overseas. Because of time zone differences and the fact he has to go radio silent a lot of time, we don't get to talk much."

Theo hated the sadness that laced her words. "No phone calls? Emails? FaceTimes?"

She unclenched her hands, rubbing them along her jeans, a sign that his questions were making her uncomfortable. "Not for a while."

"He doesn't come to visit?"

Gretchen shook her head. "He went his own way after he graduated from high school, and there really wasn't any reason to come back to Harrisburg all that often."

"Except to see his sister," Theo said with a bit more bite than he'd intended. It was just that she looked so damn sad about her brother. Theo knew if he had a little sister, he'd do a hell of a lot more than call her from time to time. He and his brothers were very close to—and overly protective of—their cousins, Mila, Remi, Nora, and Lucy, and there was no way they wouldn't make time to see them.

Hell, Lucy left home a year ago and he'd seen her six times since: three times when she'd visited here, twice in Philadelphia—which was where Joey, Miles, and Lucy were living most of the time—and once when he and Maverick made an impromptu road trip to Baltimore to meet them for drinks at Pat's Pub.

Unfortunately, Theo could see he'd stepped over the line with his comment, as Gretchen visibly shut down.

She nodded vaguely, though not necessarily in agreement. "I really should let you get back to work." As she rose, he noticed the slightest wince, and realized she was in some pain. The problem was, he couldn't tell where she was hurt.

Gretchen tugged up the turtleneck of her sweater, despite the fact she was obviously still hot. The air-conditioning wasn't cooling her off enough.

Theo's protector instincts rose to the forefront. He had a white knight personality, like most of the men in his family. The desire to rescue those in danger and help those in need ran strong in the Storm male genetics.

He stood as well. When he moved around his desk, intent on approaching her, she shrank back. Not a lot. Not even enough that most people would notice. But the fascination he felt for Gretchen that started during her interview didn't hold a candle to now—so he was watching her more closely than he might anyone else he'd just met.

"I'm really looking forward to working with you, Gretchen." Theo reached out to shake her hand.

She hesitated for a moment, staring at his hand like it was a snake poised to strike. Then he watched as that strength he'd witnessed during her interview reappeared. Theo would swear he saw her *force* her body into the appropriate position. Like doing something as normal as shaking a person's hand required thought.

Her spine straightened and her shoulders lowered as she lifted her hand toward his. It was shaking slightly, and he couldn't pass off that response as nerves or shyness. The wariness on her face gave her away.

His curiosity about this woman skyrocketed.

When Gretchen placed her hand in his, Theo felt as if he'd been struck by lightning. The Earth tilted on its axis, and a large part of him was shocked he managed to remain on his feet.

He tightened his grip, trying to calm her trembling—and now his own—even though the connection of their hands lingered past the normal length of time for a handshake.

If Theo had his way, he'd never let go.

Gretchen held his gaze, a multitude of emotions crossing her face, too many for Theo to take in. All he knew was that he wanted to understand every single one of them. Wanted to know why she looked scared, confused, sad, intrigued, regretful, determined, and even hopeful. It was all there, reflected in those beautiful blue eyes of hers.

"Gretchen," he murmured, needing to feel her name on his lips again, smiling down at the slim, gorgeous woman, who stared back at him looking slightly startled.

Did she feel it too?

Suddenly, he recalled the story his father had often told about the first time he'd met Theo's mother, the way he'd known in an instant that Mom was the woman he was going to marry.

Then he remembered a more recent conversation between him and Levi, who'd sworn he'd known the second he touched Kasi that she was meant to be his.

Theo had been amused by the story, even though he'd discounted it. Because that wasn't how love worked.

Or so he'd thought.

Right now, though.

In this moment.

It was as Levi had said.

Love at first touch.

Well...

This was inconvenient.

Chapter Four

Gretchen stared into Theo's coffee-brown eyes, trying to repress a shiver. And not one of fear, which had been her standard form of trembling lately.

Nope. This shiver was based on...

Shit.

Attraction.

She hastily pulled her hand from his, aware she'd let that handshake linger longer than was normal. She also broke eye contact, glancing anywhere except his handsome face. She feigned interest in his office, wondering how she could save this first impression. There was no way Theo wasn't regretting his decision to hire her, because could she *be* any more socially awkward?

Pull it together, Gretchen.

Taking a long, quiet breath, she slowly turned to face him again. It had been too long since she'd met new people, Briggs keeping her social circle very small and contained to people who were *his* friends, not hers.

At one point, she'd thought she had a girlfriend, Destiny,

whose boyfriend, Darryl, was Briggs's partner. The four of them did a lot of couple things, and while she and Destiny never spoke away from the men, she'd enjoyed her company, delighted to have a real friend.

Unfortunately, she'd found out the hard way that Destiny wasn't as good a friend as she'd believed.

For the past few years, Gretchen had been relegated to the corners of rooms, watching others interact rather than seeking to join in. When out in public, she'd learned the best way to keep from angering Briggs was to simply look down and never establish eye contact.

She'd earned too many beatings from a jealous Briggs whenever he thought she was paying attention to another man. He also didn't like it when she laughed at someone else's jokes or paid someone a compliment. Fear of setting him off was why she'd waited in longer lines at stores, just to get a female clerk, and why she let him do all the talking whenever she found herself drawn into a conversation with his fellow cops and friends.

Briggs explained away her silence as if she was a weirdo, claiming she was socially awkward—the description his way of humiliating her in front of his friends. The truth was, when she was younger, she'd been quite the chatterbox, always getting in trouble at school for talking too much.

But the days of appeasing Briggs were over, so she needed to learn how to interact with people—well, mainly men—again. She hadn't struggled as much with Manny, because five minutes in his presence and she'd known he was as harmless as a puppy. A big, goofy puppy. And it was virtually impossible to be uneasy around Edith, since the elderly woman did all the work, carrying the conversation.

As a single, attractive man, Theo was her first true test— and she was blowing it.

Lifting her eyes to his face, she sucked in another breath. She'd seen Theo during her interview, of course, but she hadn't really *looked* at him, too nervous to speak to a man, thanks to Briggs. So instead, she'd spent most of the video chat looking at the square that contained Nora Storm's face. It was easier to talk to Nora because she was a woman and seemed closer to Gretchen's age.

As such, she'd avoided looking at Theo the entire time. Something she could see now was a mistake, because she was wholly unprepared for how attractive he was.

He was exactly the kind of man she'd learned to give a wide berth while with Briggs.

Now, however, she not only *could* look, she *should* look. Establishing eye contact was the polite thing to do when in normal social situations.

Her heart started to race when she realized how tall Theo was. She'd been a tiny bit taller than Briggs, so she had taken to living in flats and slouching whenever they were standing next to each other. Even now, she resisted the urge to do the same, though Theo had at least four inches on her.

He wore his light brown hair longer, combing it back off his forehead, and while it was fairly straight, it curled slightly at the ends. He also sported a well-trimmed beard that framed his strong jawline perfectly.

However, it wasn't even his handsome appearance that she found most attractive. It was the crinkled laugh lines by his eyes and the smile that hadn't faltered once since she'd introduced herself.

Gretchen distrusted her instincts when it came to people because too many had let her down in the past. But when she looked at Theo, she saw a friendly, happy guy, and despite that little voice in the back of her head warning her to be careful, she couldn't help being drawn to him. She'd been painfully low on happiness in her life, and she was desperate to experience it.

Even if it was vicariously through Theo Storm and Edith Millholland.

After hiding out in her room the rest of yesterday, Gretchen was surprised when Edith managed to draw her downstairs bright and early today. The two of them had spent the better part of the morning in Edith's kitchen, cooking a ridiculously large breakfast before eating together.

The older woman had succeeded in learning more than Gretchen had intended to share. Edith discovered that in addition to lasagna being Gretchen's favorite food, her birthday cake every year—until she went into foster care—was chocolate.

Fortunately, Gretchen had managed to hold back the foster care tidbit, but only barely.

Edith was a master at conversation, sharing entertaining anecdotes about herself, then slipping in an unexpected question at the right moment, so Gretchen responded without even thinking about it. The CIA should hire the woman to interrogate spies.

Edith's eyes kept drifting to her neck, despite Gretchen's attempt to hide the bruises. Her wardrobe wasn't large by any means, because she had traveled with just the essentials. As such, she only had two turtlenecks, and she'd already worn both in front of Edith.

So this morning, she'd gone the heavy concealer route, then put on a blouse. The collar wasn't as effective at hiding her injuries, and Edith's eagle eyes had slid to her throat several times. Mercifully, Edith didn't ask about them. Because while Gretchen had become a skilled liar when it came to her bruises, she didn't want to be dishonest with Edith, who'd been nothing but kind and welcoming. If Gracemont was truly going to be

Gretchen's fresh start, she wanted to live the life she'd imagined the past few years but had never managed to achieve.

This Gretchen was going to be honest, brave, self-confident, and not, as Briggs put it, socially awkward.

Unfortunately, she was none of those things now, and Gretchen wondered what the hell she was doing here in Theo's office. She hadn't had a chance to mentally prepare to meet her new boss. She'd only intended to see how long it took to walk from Edith's to the brewery, so she could make sure to be on time on Monday.

Time to cut and run.

"I'm looking forward to working with you too, Mr. Storm."

"Theo," he interjected. "My dad is Mr. Storm, although twenty bucks says he'll insist you call him Rex."

"Right. Theo," she said softly. "Well, I'll go and get out of your ha—"

"How about a tour of the place?" Theo interjected, before she could get the hell out of Dodge.

"Oh, no. I couldn't pull you away from—"

"I already decided to quit work early today. One of the perks of being the boss," he said, wiggling his eyebrows. "I was thinking about heading to the brewery for a beer. Why don't you join me?"

Crap. Hadn't she told him she was excited to see the place? She'd been forced to come up with a reason for being here when Billy found her outside, leaning against the building in search of shade for a few moments before starting her journey back down the mountain.

"Um...okay," she said, unable to come up with a reason why she couldn't.

Theo's smile returned, brighter than before, like her joining him was the greatest thing on earth.

"Come on. Let me give you a quick peek of your office, and

then we'll detour through the main floor of the brewhouse to meet Jace and Sam."

The event coordinator position was the first job offer she'd gotten after sending out countless applications, so she'd readily accepted it without thinking about the fact she would be working in a building surrounded primarily by men. God help her if they were all as hot as Theo.

Gretchen followed Theo to the office right next to his, gasping when he threw open the door and gestured inside.

"This is mine?"

Theo nodded. "We cleared out an old storage closet to renovate it into a nice working space. My cousin Mila decorated it."

The office was at least double the size of her previous one, and it had a large window with an amazing view from the side of the mountain. She could see for miles, down into the valley, and it was as breathtaking as Edith had described.

"Not a bad view, huh?" Theo joined her at the window.

"It's beautiful."

Theo gave her another one of those smiles that said her answer pleased him. Then he turned back toward the room. "This will be your desk, and the computer is already set up and ready to go. My brother Everett is our IT guy, and he'll be here on Monday to explain our network, scheduling programs, and to answer any questions you have. I've loaded the desk drawers with basic office supplies." He slid one drawer open to reveal boxes of pens, new packs of Post-its, a stapler, and a variety of other things. "If there's anything you need that's not here, let me know and I'll order it for you."

She shook her head. "You don't have to do that. I'm sure I can make do with what's there."

Theo pierced her with a look. "I don't want you to 'make

do.' If you need something that will make your job easier, you let me know and I'll get it. Okay?"

Gretchen swallowed hard. There was a thread of dominance in his tone that should have had her running for the hills...but it didn't. Butterflies took flight in her stomach, but not the bad kind. These were the ones she'd felt all those years ago, when Briggs swept her stupid, eighteen-year-old self off her feet.

"You okay?" Theo asked.

Shit. *Way to keep acting crazy, Gretch.*

She blinked and nodded her head, though it was another five seconds until she found her voice. "I'm fine. Just overwhelmed by how nice this office is."

She couldn't keep slipping into awkward silences, or she'd lose the damn job before she even officially started. Gretchen slid her sweaty palms down the front of her jeans. "I'll let you know if I need anything," she managed to say in a relatively normal tone.

Theo pointed to one of the walls, and Gretchen followed the direction of his finger, taking in the framed photos hanging there. "We hung some pictures of the farm, but you're free to take them down if you want to put up something different. Family pics or whatever."

"Okay." Gretchen was aware the farm photos would remain. She only had one family picture, and it never left her wallet. It was a small snapshot taken by one of the foster parents at the residential home, right after Shaw's graduation. In it, Shaw was wearing the standard cap and gown, his arm slung around her shoulders. She adored the photo because of Shaw's face. He'd been grinning from ear to ear, something that was rare for her brother. She was smiling too—another oddity—but instead of mugging for the camera, like Shaw, she was looking up at her big brother as if he hung the moon.

It was one of her all-time favorite possessions, which was why she always carried it with her in a secret compartment of her wallet. She'd kept it hidden from Briggs, too afraid he'd destroy it.

Her chest ached with regret and sorrow when she thought of how she'd let Briggs drive a wedge between her and her brother, insisting Shaw was like her mother—indifferent, uncaring.

Deep inside, she'd known that wasn't true, but during those bad years, she let all the evil, cold things Briggs whispered in her ear stick, and she'd pulled away from her brother, making excuses for why he couldn't come to visit, claiming she was too busy at work or lying about Briggs whisking her away for a few days. The fact was, he'd wanted to come home many times, but she'd rejected the suggestion. Then she had the nerve to accuse him of deserting her. She even said as much in a phone call— their last one—before she'd blocked his number.

Thinking of the hurtful, hateful things she'd said to him sent a sharp pain through her heart.

So much time had passed now...she wasn't sure how to bridge that gap.

Wasn't sure if she should even try.

Wasn't sure if she deserved to ask for his forgiveness.

Surely, he wouldn't want to hear from her after what she said.

Theo pulled her out of her heavy thoughts as he continued pointing out different things in her office. "Nora suggested we add the whiteboard. The woman lives and dies by hers." Theo pointed to another wall. "She's also the queen of color-coding, which is why you have every color marker ever made."

Gretchen's eyes widened at the unusually large pile of brightly colored markers in a basket hanging next to the whiteboard. "I'll have to check out her system."

Theo chuckled. "Believe me, I wasn't saying you have to do what she does. Code breakers probably couldn't crack her overly detailed system. We tease her about her OCD, but hey, whatever works, right?"

It was obvious Theo was fond of his cousin. Of his entire family, actually.

"Come on. Let's go grab a beer."

She followed Theo down the hallway, walking into a large warehouse space filled with huge vats and machinery and barrels. She didn't have a clue what any of it did, but it was impressive.

Two men she assumed were Sam and Jace were bent over a clipboard, discussing something when they approached.

"Hey, guys," Theo began. "This is Gretchen Banks, our new event coordinator. Gretchen, this is Sam and Jace."

While she tended to agree Theo was the better-looking brother, that by no means meant Sam and Jace weren't also hot. Genetics had been *very* kind to the Storm brothers. They all had brown hair, though Sam's and Jace's was darker than Theo's, as well as shorter. They also shared those dark coffee-colored eyes, and none of them were hurting in the muscles department, though she suspected their sexy builds were the result of farmwork rather than time spent in the gym.

"Nice to meet you." Sam stuck out his hand.

Gretchen was a little better prepared this time, so she managed to shake both his and Jace's hands without trembling or suffering that brief flash of panic over the memory of Briggs hitting her for daring to touch another man.

Progress...she hoped.

"Checking things out before you start?" Jace asked.

"I'm going to give Gretchen a proper tour of the entire farm on Monday," Theo explained to his brothers. "Today, we're going for a beer and to get to know each other." He paused for a moment. "You want to join us?" he asked, though Gretchen got the sense he didn't want his brothers to come along.

Both men—thank God—shook their heads. She was struggling enough to act normal in front of just Theo. Heaven help her if she wound up surrounded by three attractive men.

"No thanks. Levi asked for a list of things we want him to plant at the Mills' farm for future brews. We're discussing the pros and cons of different varieties of hops. Going to try to get that to him before we call it a day, since he's chomping at the bit to get started with the planting. Plus, it's my turn to cook tonight," Jace replied.

"Cool," Theo replied. "I'll see you at the house later."

"His turn to cook?" Gretchen asked as they walked away, attempting to make conversation that didn't involve Theo "getting to know" too much about her. The next hour or two would be a lot easier if she could keep Theo talking about himself.

"With six bachelors in one house, it makes more sense to take turns cooking rather than all of us piling into the kitchen to make something for ourselves. Tonight is Jace's night, which almost definitely means something Italian. He makes a hell of a marinara sauce, so he usually serves spaghetti or chicken parmesan."

"Sounds delicious." Gretchen wondered what Edith was making them for dinner tonight.

Of course, having dinner with Edith was contingent on her making it back to Millholland House on time and in one piece.

It was a ten-minute walk from the brewhouse to the brewery. Gretchen knew that because she'd set her stopwatch. She'd also timed the entire walk from Edith's house to the farm, and what she discovered was that she was in worse physical shape than she'd thought, and while five miles didn't feel like that big a distance, it definitely was when four of those miles were straight uphill on a winding mountain road.

Gretchen had spent the two-hour walk—TWO HOURS—in fear for her life as she wound around one sharp curve after another, praying no one hit her. She could tell by the looks of surprise on the faces of the handful of drivers who passed her, they were shocked to find anyone walking on that road.

Getting a driver's license and a car had skyrocketed to the top of Gretchen's to-do list, though she knew neither of those things could be done quickly. Even if she was able to get a license in a reasonable amount of time, she was nowhere near financially ready to buy car. Mainly because all the bills had been in Briggs's name, and she'd never had a credit card. So she was currently sitting on the lowest credit score a person could manage.

As they walked, Theo talked about the history of Stormy Weather Farm, about how his great-grandfather had purchased the land and maintained an apple orchard there. The vineyard and winery were apparently the brainchild of Theo's grandfather, Lloyd. She was so enthralled by his easy style of storytelling and the pride in his voice as he talked about his family's rich history, she forgot to be nervous about the fact she was walking through the woods alone with a strange man.

By the time they reached the brewery, Gretchen was hot again. She'd changed out of her blouse and back into one of the turtlenecks before leaving Edith's house because, given the heat, she knew she'd sweat off the concealer. The problem was, she was way overdressed for the temperature. She prayed the bruises would fade enough by Monday that she could dress more appropriately for the weather.

"Are falls cooler in Harrisburg?" Theo obviously noticed she was red-faced and sweating. In addition to the sweater, she'd forgotten to pack a bottle of water for her trek. A mistake she would not repeat next week.

"They are," she lied, uncertain how else to explain what

she'd chosen to wear. "I'll have to pull my short sleeves out for next week."

"We have a relaxed dress code, as I said when you accepted the job, so jeans and T-shirts are fine. We're also going to give you some shirts with the brewery and winery logos on them, which you can wear for special events or when talking to people about renting the event barn. I know Nora ordered at least half a dozen for you after she got your size."

Gretchen recalled how grateful she'd been when Nora emailed to ask for her shirt size, aware those work shirts were going to bulk up her pitiful wardrobe considerably until she could afford to buy more clothes.

They stopped outside the entrance to the brewery. Theo started to say something—then lifted his hand and swung it in her direction.

Gretchen flinched, covering her face and whimpering in fear, the need to protect herself so instinctual that she didn't even consider her actions.

Theo stopped short, quickly pulling his hand back. "I'm so sorry!" he apologized. "I was swatting away a bee. I was afraid it might sting you."

She struggled to understand what he was saying because her heart was pounding so hard, and blood rushed through her ears, deafening her. It took her too long to recover, to figure out how to cover for her response.

"I'm afraid of bees." It was a lame attempt at playing off what had happened.

Theo frowned, and she got the sense he didn't believe her. Why would he? She'd *massively* overreacted.

"I really am sorry," he murmured. "I didn't mean to scare you."

Gretchen wondered how long it would take her to find another job, and if she should start looking now, because she was fucking this up royally, acting like a timid mouse afraid of her own shadow. "I'm fine."

Mercifully, Theo moved on, putting them back on track. "Obviously, this is the brewery. It's quiet now, since it's still the middle of the workday, but come quitting time, we'll probably have close to thirty people sitting around, enjoying happy hour. The weekends are our prime time, same for the winery. We schedule local musicians to entertain on those days. That'll be part of your job. I'll give you a list of performers and their contact information next week."

"Okay."

Theo gestured to the parking lot. "It's not uncommon for our lots to be completely filled on Saturdays and Sundays in the fall and the spring, when the weather is milder."

Theo led her inside, then to a table on the wide deck that ran the length of the brewery and provided that same incredible view of the valley. Mercifully, he chose a table in the shade, so it was somewhat cooler even though they were still outside.

"This is beautiful. I can see why it's such a popular place," she mused, looking around. There were quite a few tables around them as well as inside. Below the deck, on the hillside, were several different sitting areas outfitted with Adirondacks, facing the valley. There was a large firepit off to one side, surrounded by hewn logs that served as bench seats. There was a long bar inside and one outside, both with small lines of people waiting to be served. Even for an off hour, the brewery was doing decent business.

Theo handed her a pad consisting of half-sheets of paper. "This is our current beer list. If you want to try a flight, you tick the boxes of the ones you want. If you want a pint, you check here," he said, pointing to the sheet.

"I think I'd like to try a flight," she said. "So that I'm familiar with your offerings."

"I'll do one too." Theo talked to her about each of the beers on the list, giving her an idea of whether they were dark or light, bitter or sour. He spoke about the alcohol content, warning her against the higher percentages, since she admitted she didn't drink much.

Once they made their selections, Theo handed their slips of paper to the waitress, who stood by their table for a few minutes to talk to them.

Well, to talk to Theo.

The woman was flirting, but Theo either didn't notice or was ignoring it. When she left to fill their orders, he leaned back in his chair comfortably. "I'm afraid I've been monopolizing the conversation."

"Oh, I like learning about the farm and businesses," she interjected hastily, aware she needed to cut him off at the pass. "So Nora has the same job as you, except she runs the winery?"

Theo nodded, even though they'd explained that in detail during her interview. How she would work closely with both of them to plan events, sometimes for the winery, sometimes for the brewery, and sometimes for both.

"She does. Is it too hot out here?" Theo asked, when she tried and failed to surreptitiously wipe away a bead of sweat that rolled down the side of her face.

"No. No. It's much better in the shade. The beer will cool me off." Nothing short of stripping down to her undies and jumping into a frigid lake would cool her down at this point, but it wasn't as if that was an option.

The server returned with their flights, so she had a moment to pretend to listen to her explain which beer was which, while figuring what tidbit about her past to share, in case Theo persisted.

Her anxiety was wasted, because Theo went a different route—a worse one—when he asked their waitress to grab a medium T-shirt from the gift shop for Gretchen. "You look like you're about to spontaneously combust," he said, when they were alone again. "The T-shirt will be much cooler."

"Oh, no. I wouldn't want to take something that's for sale."

Theo waved away her concern. "We have a huge stock of shirts. We won't miss one, and I'm worried about you overheating."

"Really, I—" Before she could come up with any plausible excuse for rejecting his kind offer, considering she was sweating her ass off, the waitress returned with a navy-blue Rain or Shine T-shirt. "Thank you," Gretchen said, because she had no choice but to take it.

"Restrooms are right by the front door." Theo pointed in the direction they'd entered.

Gretchen grabbed her purse and the shirt. She was never without concealer, so she would simply have to cover her bruises and hope it would be good enough.

In the restroom, she ran the cold water, wetting a paper towel that she used to scrub over her face and along the back of her neck. Stepping into one of the stalls, she switched from her sweater to the T-shirt, instantly feeling twenty degrees cooler. Returning to the sink, she studied her neck in the mirror, then grabbed her concealer. Years of covering the evidence had made her an expert when it came to makeup.

Once she felt the bruises were hidden well enough, she pulled her hair out of the ponytail and ran her fingers through it, drawing most of it over her shoulders as a second layer of concealment.

Praying she'd done enough, she stepped out of the restroom.

She felt Theo's gaze on her as she crossed the large open space. One look at his face and she realized this attraction she felt wasn't one-sided, something that thrilled and terrified her in equal parts.

Gretchen had fallen out of love with Briggs by degrees over the years, though it was safe to say that during the past couple, her feelings for him had turned to nothing more than hatred and fear. Every drop of affection she'd felt for the man who'd been her first love had been expelled in the tears of pain she'd cried due to his abuse. Loneliness had been her constant companion for too long, so it was no wonder Theo, with his easy smiles and laughter, had captured her attention.

Gretchen had come to Gracemont for a fresh start. In her mind, that meant a job, a safe place to live, and independence. Sure, at some point, she wanted to date again, but sweet Jesus... even if she was ready, which she wasn't, Theo was the wrong man, full stop. He was her boss, for God's sake, and she needed this job.

Once she returned to the table, Theo gave her a friendly smile. "Feel better?"

She nodded. "Much cooler. Thanks so much."

Resuming her seat, she picked up the first beer. Theo followed suit, tapping his small glass against hers.

"To the beginning of a new adventure," he said as a toast.

"Oh," she said, after taking a sip, "that's good." Gretchen hadn't lied about not being much of a drinker. Briggs never let her indulge, probably because he suspected it would dull the pain, and he certainly couldn't let that happen.

"Glad you like it."

"I can't even imagine what it must take to make your own beer from scratch."

Gretchen had landed on the perfect opening, because Theo was clearly a fan of not only his job and his brewery but his brothers' "mad skills," as he called them, when it came to brewing beer. He walked her through the process, and because she was genuinely interested—as well as determined to steer them away from personal topics—he patiently answered all her questions.

Before she knew it, two hours had passed in quiet comfort. She had the tiniest of buzzes from the beer, which felt nice. Her shoulders weren't tight and the pressure on her chest that never seemed to lift completely was actually gone, something she hadn't thought possible before Theo and Edith.

"Well," she said at last. "I should head back to Edith's." If she didn't start the two-hour return trip now, she would miss dinner. She'd been smart, however, drinking water between each glass of beer. She also ordered a bottle of water after they finished their tasting, claiming she was thirsty. She hadn't opened it, intent on hydrating on the way down the mountain.

Theo rose and started to follow her to the exit. Her mind whirled over how to ditch him inside the brewery, because if he walked her to the parking lot, it was going to become obvious she didn't have a car.

"Oh," she said, as they passed the restrooms. "I think I'll say goodbye here." She tilted her head toward the women's room. "Thanks so much for such a nice afternoon. I'll see you Monday."

Theo smiled and said goodbye, and she walked into the restroom, stalling until she felt confident that he was probably long gone.

Gretchen grimaced when she stepped out—because Theo was right where she'd left him, next to the exit, chatting with a server who appeared to be asking for time off.

She hoped the conversation would continue as she feigned an easy, breezy wave and stepped outside.

She was almost to the edge of the parking lot, well beyond all the cars, when she heard Theo calling her name.

"Hey, Gretchen."

She considered pretending she hadn't heard, but when he yelled her name again, closer, she was forced to turn around. One look at his puzzled expression, and she knew she'd been busted on the vehicle situation.

"Where's your car?" he asked, when he caught up to her.

"Oh, um...I walked today. I foolishly thought five miles wasn't that far."

Theo frowned. "Jesus. Why didn't you say so? I'll drive you home."

"No, no," she quickly replied, aware it would be obvious there was no extra car in Edith's driveway. "It was a nice walk," she lied.

Theo's frown let her know he didn't believe that for a second. "It's not a safe road to walk, Gretchen."

"I don't want to be an imposition."

He pulled keys from the front pocket of his jeans. "My truck's parked right over there." His tone and the light touch of his hand on her back as he turned her in the other direction told her arguing was pointless. Besides, she was so taken aback by how nice his hand felt, she didn't have time to react.

Of course, as soon as that thought landed, his hand was gone.

She wasn't sure how to process her feelings, because it had been far too long since a man had touched her in a way that she wanted.

She closed her eyes briefly, giving herself a mental lecture. She could *not* be attracted to her boss.

Gretchen walked across the parking lot, surprised when Theo opened the passenger door for her. While she'd heard the myth about men who did such things, she'd never seen it happen out in the wild.

Her hesitation must have given her away.

"Dad taught us that a gentleman always opens a lady's door," Theo explained with a charming grin.

"Thank you." She climbed into the truck.

As they headed down the mountain, Theo talked about the improvements they'd made to the road leading to the brewery, chuckling at her surprise when she learned the current road was way better than the previous one.

When he pulled into Edith's driveway, Theo looked around, not seeing exactly what she knew he wouldn't. "Where's your car?"

Before she could think through the repercussions, the truth fell from her lips. "I don't have one."

"What?"

"I'm sorry. I should have told you that right from the start."

"So what was the plan? To walk to and from work every day?" He was aghast, something that made perfect sense, now that she knew firsthand how bad the daily commute would be on foot.

"I thought there would be a rideshare option when I took the job," she confessed.

"Koda doesn't get up before eleven," Theo said.

"Yeah. Manny told me."

"You can't walk to work," he insisted.

"It's only five miles," she countered. Five of the most painful, brutal miles in existence.

"All uphill," Theo countered, stating the obvious. He'd put the truck in park, so now he turned to face her. "You know what? This isn't a problem. I'll pick you up and drop you off every day."

Gretchen was shaking her head before he even finished the offer. "No. No way. I couldn't ask you to do that."

"Fine. Then you'll borrow one of the farm trucks. We

pretty much only use them during the hours when you'd be at work anyway, so it's not like we'd miss one overnight."

Gretchen bit her lower lip, her silence apparently enough for Theo to understand.

"You can't drive."

She didn't miss the tone of surprise. Given he'd grown up on a farm, Theo had probably been driving since he was old enough to see over the steering wheel.

She sighed. "I've spent the first twenty-four years of my life in a city with ample public transportation and rideshare options. Never needed to learn."

Briggs had seen a driver's license as something that would afford her too much independence and give her a way to leave him. Not having a license had slowed her escape, like the lack of money, and the fact he had her phone tied to Find My Friends, so he always knew where she was.

That was why her old phone had been left on her desk at work the day she left him. Brenda always drove her to and from work, and that day, they followed the same routine, in case Briggs was checking her location. Once at work, Gretchen grabbed her suitcase and new phone, leaving her old cell, along with her Dear John letter on her desk, escaping without him knowing.

Theo didn't appear overly concerned about his new employee's lack of car *or* license. "I'll teach you how to drive."

Gretchen frowned. "That's not necessary." Actually, it was, but she couldn't ask her new boss to do that. Could she?

"We'll practice in the brewery parking lot after hours," he continued, as if she hadn't rejected his offer. She was starting to realize that Theo had a bad habit of ignoring things he didn't want to hear.

"Seriously," she said, trying to think of a reason to refuse.

"Once you've mastered the parking lot, we'll take a spin

around town, and from there," he made a horrified face, "we'll move on to the mountain road that leads you to work."

She couldn't help but smile, because that damn road to their farm was treacherous as hell, and he was right to look terrified.

"There it is," Theo said.

"There *what* is?"

"That pretty smile. I was wondering when you'd let me see it."

Gretchen's cheeks felt hot, and she hoped she wasn't blushing. It had been too long since she'd heard kind words from Briggs. Or from anybody, really.

She shut those thoughts down.

Enough.

No more thinking about Briggs.

No more comparing everybody she met to him.

No more wallowing in the past.

She'd moved here to move on, so she was fucking doing it. Moving right the hell on.

From this moment, Briggs Howard was evicted from her thoughts.

Before Gretchen could continue to refuse Theo's offer to teach her to drive—even though she really didn't want to—there was a tap on his window.

Theo rolled it down when he found Edith standing next to his truck. "Hey, Edith."

"I see you met our girl," she said by way of greeting.

"Yep. She walked to the farm."

Edith's brows lifted nearly to her hairline, and Gretchen felt instantly guilty. Because there was no way Edith would have let her walk to Stormy Weather Farm if she'd known that was the plan.

"How on earth?" Edith mused, as her gaze slid to Gretchen.

"I wondered what was taking you so long. I thought you were going to walk around town today and save the farm visit until tomorrow."

That was what Gretchen had told her this morning, since Edith knew she didn't have a car. "It was a whim."

Theo pierced her with a look that said he knew that was a lie.

"Well, I'm glad you brought her home. I want to invite you to dinner on Saturday night. I'm making a huge pan of lasagna for Gretchen's Welcome to Gracemont dinner. And while I know Manny will give it the college try, even *he* won't be able to put a dent in it, so you have to come and help us eat it all."

Theo grinned, because Edith clearly wasn't the type of person to *ask* for what she wanted, which meant her invitation was one that couldn't be refused. Not that it looked like he was going to.

"Thanks for the invitation," Theo said. "I'll be here. Of course, now I'm wishing I'd thought of having my own welcome dinner for Gretchen."

"Oh no," she hastened to say. "Neither one of you needs to make a fuss."

Theo brushed her off. "Even so, I'm going to talk to Mom and get her help pulling something together for next Friday. I doubt you'll have the chance to meet everyone by then, so it'll be easier to introduce you to the whole family in one fell swoop. You're invited too, Edith."

Edith clapped her hands. "That's sounds wonderful! Two parties is always better than one. Now, come by at five on Saturday, Theo, and we'll start with drinks and apps."

Theo chuckled as he glanced in Gretchen's direction, winking about Edith's use of the word *apps*. She was reminded of his Urban Dictionary comment and couldn't help grinning herself.

"Wait there," Theo said to Gretchen as he opened his truck door.

Edith stepped away, giving him an approving look as he circled the truck to open her door for her.

"You don't have to—" Gretchen started.

"When you're with me, I open the door for you," he said, interrupting her.

Gretchen didn't know how to reply to that, since she wasn't used to people doing nice things for her.

Theo placed a gentle hand on Gretchen's back, escorting her around the truck. Edith was waiting at the path that led to the front porch, so he offered her his other arm, the three of them climbing the stairs together.

Gretchen had never experienced anything so charming and old school and peaceful. By the time they reached the front door, she was smiling, overwhelmed with...God...happiness.

Gracemont was her new beginning.

The place where Gretchen Banks, the real Gretchen, was going to come to life.

She couldn't wait to meet her.

Chapter Five

Theo grinned when Gretchen opened the front door of Millholland House on Saturday. He'd put on a pair of khaki slacks and a dark green polo, feeling as if he should put in more effort than the faded blue jeans he usually wore around the farm. He'd also stopped by Gladys Jenkins' flower stand on the way here and grabbed two bouquets of yellow roses.

He pulled one out from behind his back, handing it to Gretchen.

"What's this?" She took a small step back, obviously hesitant to take the flowers. Unlike most women he knew, Gretchen didn't seem happy about his gift. In fact, she looked uneasy.

"Flowers," he joked, hoping it would make her relax.

"I know, but did I...I mean...is something wrong?"

Theo didn't have a clue what to make of that question, because why would she view flowers as harbingers of bad news?

The more time he spent with his new event coordinator,

the more fascinated he became. Not that he was getting any of his questions answered. The woman was locked up tighter than a vault when it came to revealing details about herself.

Which left it to him to use other clues to decipher the puzzle that was Gretchen Banks, like now, when her expression was troubled, her posture stiff, her eyes not quite connecting with his. She looked like she was on the verge of running away.

"It's a Welcome to Gracemont party," he explained. "Didn't feel right to come empty-handed." Then he pulled his other hand from behind his back and revealed the second bouquet. "Brought some for our hostess, too."

Gretchen flushed, her cheeks turning the most adorable shade of pink. "You didn't have to do that. That was...sweet." He was delighted when she gave him a real smile rather than one of those weak-hearted attempts he got at the brewery, even though she quickly hid it behind her hand.

What Theo was discovering about Gretchen was equal parts alluring and concerning. She was an intelligent woman with a sense of humor, though she struggled to express it. Her smiles always faded too quickly, or she covered them with her hand, as if letting someone see her happy was taboo. Not that she was miserable, not even close. It was more like she felt the need to guard her emotions. But why?

It had taken him the better part of Thursday afternoon to get to the point where he felt like she was starting to relax around him, but even then, he'd been very careful not to make any sudden movements or speak too loudly—because he didn't like the way she'd flinched when he laughed and when he'd tried to swat the bee away from her face. She had reacted instinctually both times.

And her instinct was fear.

"Are you going to invite the poor fella in?" Edith stepped

behind Gretchen, wearing an apron. Her eyes lit up when she spotted the flowers. "Those are beautiful, Theo." She took her bouquet from him. "You thoughtful boy. Come on inside and I'll grab us a couple of vases. Mine can serve as the centerpiece for our dinner, and you can take yours up to your room, Gretchen, to brighten the place. There's nothing like flowers to bring cheer to a house."

Theo and Gretchen followed Edith, who quickly put the roses in water.

"It'll be another hour before dinner is ready," she said, "so I thought we could sit together here in the kitchen. I've put together a charcuterie for an appetizer."

"Because we won't get enough cheese from your lasagna?" Theo teased.

Edith laughed, slapping him on the shoulder. "Exactly. I bought a bottle of that new red Maverick perfected from Lightning in a Bottle last week. Theo, do me a favor. Grab the corkscrew and open it for us."

Theo rose, using the corkscrew Edith had already placed on the counter next to the wine, as the older woman pulled her charcuterie from the refrigerator, adding assorted crackers and bread to the large wooden cutting board.

"Manny will be over shortly," she said.

Gretchen's eyes widened when she saw the food Edith began laying out on her large oak clawfoot table. "Edith, you shouldn't have gone to all this trouble."

"Hush," Edith said with a wave of her hand. "Newcomers to Gracemont are too few and far between. I want to make sure you love it here so much, you never want to leave."

Theo noticed the sheen in Gretchen's eyes, saw how touched she was by Edith's thoughtfulness.

He finished uncorking the bottle, pouring three glasses of wine after Edith pulled the crystal goblets from her corner hutch and set them on the counter in front of him. The Millholland House really could be an antique store, every piece of furniture passed down from one generation to the next.

Edith led them to the table, but Gretchen didn't sit down. Instead, she picked up her bouquet of flowers, hugging the vase against her chest. "I'll run these to my room," she said, and this time, finally, Theo caught the delight in her eyes over his small gift. "They're pretty flowers, Theo. Thank you."

Gretchen left the kitchen, and Edith waited until her footsteps hit the top of the stairs before turning to him. "So, what do you think of her?"

Theo grinned. Edith had never married or had children of her own, so she had basically adopted the whole town. Which meant she'd guided countless people toward their future careers, matchmade no less than thirty marriages, and helped more folks find their forever homes than Julie Devereaux, Gracemont's only real estate agent.

Edith was obviously viewing Gretchen as her next project, delighted to have a young woman to lead toward whatever came next. He wasn't shocked by that, but he *was* surprised Gretchen had managed to win the older woman over so quickly. She'd only been here a few days.

"She's very nice." Theo was aware that response would never be enough to appease Edith. But he wasn't sure how much more he could say without betraying the fact he was seriously attracted to his new employee. God, if he did that, he'd never get a moment's peace as far as Edith was concerned.

He'd been caught in Edith's matchmaking web more than a few times, though none of those earlier attempts had taken. For most of Theo's life, he'd viewed his father's love-at-first-sight story as a romantic tale and little else.

Then Levi had come home, head over ass in love with Kasi

Mills, claiming he'd known from the moment she passed out in his arms that she was meant for him.

Again, Theo had laughed it off, but now...

Now, the story didn't seem quite so farfetched. Because while it was far too early to call this love...there was something very powerful drawing him toward Gretchen. That gut instinct that had told him to hire her was now telling him she had the potential to be so much more to him.

But saying that aloud to Edith—or anyone else, for that matter—would make him sound crazy.

"She's more than nice," Edith huffed.

"You've only known her a few days," Theo pointed out.

"Are you saying I'm not a good judge of character, Theodore Storm?"

Theo gave Edith a quick kiss on the cheek by way of apology. "You're the best judge of character I know."

Edith preened. "Which is why I can tell there's something hidden behind those sad eyes of hers. I think it's safe to say something has driven her here, and I'm afraid it was bad."

The woman had noticed the same things he had.

"I agree. But it's not like we can force her to tell us about it. We're strangers to her."

Edith took a sip of her wine, considering that. While Theo had resigned himself to simply building a friendship with Gretchen—aware asking her out, given their work relationship, would be a mistake—Edith didn't work that way.

Instead, she approached everything like a bulldozer, plowing in headlong, relentlessly, and without hitting the brakes. He'd called her on that habit once, gently insisting she should ease back every now and again. Edith had, in no uncertain terms, informed him that at her age, she didn't have the luxury of taking her time. If she wanted something done, she needed it done immediately. And when she put it that way, Theo had been hard-pressed to argue with her.

"I think she'll be a great addition to the staff at the farm," Theo said. "And you know the girls will absorb her into their crazy tribe of girlfriends." By girls, he meant Nora, Mila, and Remi. He was looking forward to introducing Gretchen to his cousins, curious to see if she lost some of her reticence when she was around females, if she was simply uncomfortable around men. While at the brewery, Gretchen had been friendlier to the female patrons he'd introduced her to than the men.

"The two of you spent some time together Thursday," Edith said.

"I took her to the brewery to sample a flight of our beer."

"And you talked about the job?"

"We did." Theo was starting to feel like Edith was fishing, and he was the trout she was trying to land.

"Did she say anything about herself at all?"

So Gretchen had been elusive with Edith as well. Theo wished the young woman well with her endeavors, even though he knew which horse he was backing in this particular race. Edith would get her answers. It seemed Gretchen hadn't become fascinating just to him.

"She has a brother who's a Navy SEAL. Other than that, I got nothing," he admitted.

Undeterred, Edith grinned. "I suspect between the two of us, we can divide and conquer."

Theo snorted. "I'm not trying to conquer her."

"Mm-hmm," Edith hummed, in a way that let him know she wasn't buying what he was selling.

Before he could reiterate his point, Gretchen returned. She was wearing a pretty pale pink blouse with a lightweight cardigan over top and a pair of dark blue jeans. And God help him, she'd opted to wear her hair down, the long blonde tresses hanging in loose waves over her shoulders.

She looked fucking gorgeous, and he forced his gaze elsewhere so that Edith wouldn't catch him staring—and drooling.

The back door to the kitchen opened as Manny walked in. "Hello, all! Oooo. Cheeseboard." Within seconds, Manny had piled up a small plate with chunks of cheddar, slices of salami, half a dozen crackers, and three small gherkins.

"Leave some for the rest of us," Edith admonished good-naturedly.

Theo rose, pouring Manny a glass of wine, and the four of them chatted in the kitchen as they sampled the variety of cheeses and meats.

Most of the conversation was carried by him and Edith, Manny too busy stuffing his face, and Gretchen seemingly content to merely listen.

They talked briefly about the harvest, as well as Levi's plans for the farmland his family was leasing from Kasi's. Edith asked about Sam's campaign, promising to do her own bit of canvasing—determined, like Theo, to see Scottie lose. When Gretchen asked what was wrong with the current mayor, Theo told her about Lucy's run-in with Scottie, how he'd come on way too strong.

"He actually grabbed her?" Gretchen asked.

Theo nodded. "Mercifully, Levi showed up before he could take it too far, but *any* kind of manhandling is too damn much. No man ever has the right to lay his hands on a woman like that."

Gretchen bit her lower lip, her face losing some of its color.

He glanced in Edith's direction and noticed the older woman's gaze was locked on Gretchen, but she didn't appear to be looking at her face.

Instead, she was focused on her neck.

Gretchen tugged on her hair, pulling it forward...and Theo got a sense Edith had noticed something he hadn't.

"After Lucy left town," Theo continued, "Scottie set his sights on Kasi."

"Levi's Kasi?" Gretchen clarified.

"Yes," Edith replied. "Apparently, he made her think the town government was going to foreclose on her family's farm due to late tax payments. In truth, he was trying to trick her into marrying him, so that he could get his hands on the land."

Gretchen's eyes widened. "He sounds horrible! How did he win the election the first time?"

Manny snorted. "He ran uncontested. I heard from Remi that Scottie nearly shit his pants when Sam threw his hat in the ring."

"Language," Edith said, though she was grinning at the image.

"I was there, and he definitely wasn't happy," Theo added. "I think he knows his chances of winning again are slim to none. Sam's pretty popular around town. And he's not an asshole."

"I hope your brother wins," Gretchen said.

After that, the conversation drifted to the unseasonably warm weather they'd been having, then Manny, Edith, and Theo started telling Gretchen all about the upcoming Fall Harvest Festival that was held every second weekend in October.

When the timer on the stove buzzed, the four of them worked together to carry the lasagna, big bowl of salad, and basket of garlic bread into the dining room. Edith had set the table before his arrival, his roses now serving as the centerpiece.

Gretchen smiled when Edith cut a large slice of the lasagna for her.

"This looks and smells incredible, Edith," Gretchen said. "I can't remember the last time I had lasagna."

"What?" Edith asked. "I thought you said this was your favorite meal?"

"It is. It's just...I mean..." Gretchen stammered slightly. "What I should have said is, I can't remember the last time I had *homemade* lasagna. My cooking skills are limited, so the best I could ever manage was heating up the Stouffer's kind."

Theo wasn't sure how he knew she was lying, but his gut told him she was. Which left him to wonder why Gretchen would deprive herself of what was clearly her favorite meal, as she took a huge bite.

They continued their conversation from the kitchen, each of them regaling Gretchen with stories of past Fall Harvest Festivals.

"Before I forget," Theo said to Gretchen. "We're on for dinner next Friday. Mom was excited when I mentioned having you over, so we can all get to know you better. Since the weather's been nice, we thought we'd take advantage of it by cooking out."

"Oh," Gretchen said. "You don't have to do that."

"We want to. And I'm looking forward to showing off my mad skills."

"Mad skills?" she asked.

"I am king of the grill, master of the coals." Theo had already invited Edith, so he turned to Manny. "You're welcome to join us as well."

"Aw thanks, Theo, but I've got plans Friday night," Manny replied.

"What plans?" Edith asked.

Manny rolled his eyes. "I told you, I'm doing dinner in D.C. with some friends. She never listens to me," he added, shaking his head.

"I listen fine. The trick these days is remembering." Edith tapped the side of her head. "You wait until you're eighty-two years old, young man," she admonished Manny, who grinned at being called a young man, considering he was pushing sixty.

"The menu is going to be your basic cookout fare," Theo said. "Hamburgers, hot dogs, deviled eggs, corn on the cob."

"I'll bring my macaroni salad," Edith chimed in.

"I was hoping you'd offer." Theo took a sip of his wine. "I'll never say no to your macaroni salad."

"Me either," Gretchen added, looking at Theo. "I had some for lunch my first day here. It was delicious."

He smiled. "Between that and Mom's potato salad, we'll be set."

Manny's shoulders fell. "Your mom is making her potato salad? Damn. Wonder if I can talk my buddies into meeting for dinner another night."

Theo chuckled.

"It's that good?" Gretchen asked. As the dinner progressed, Theo noticed she was talking more and more, genuinely interested in their stories.

"Best on the planet," Manny said.

"Tell you what, Manny." Theo lightly tapped the table. "I'll send some back with Edith for you, so you can have it for lunch Saturday."

"Bless you," Manny breathed, as if Theo had offered him manna sent straight from Heaven.

Gretchen giggled, covering her mouth with her hand, the joyful sound far too short for Theo. "What makes her potato salad so good?"

"She uses the secret ingredient," Edith said.

"What's that?" Gretchen asked.

Edith said "love" at the exact same time Theo and Manny both replied "bacon."

All four of them laughed.

Once dinner was over, Edith rose and pulled the glass lid off a cake stand, revealing a bakery-worthy chocolate cake. "Well, now. I hope you saved room for dessert."

Gretchen's eyes widened at the sight of the beautiful cake. "Edith," she said, her tone laced with amazement.

"What's a party without cake?" The older woman's eyes twinkled, clearly delighted by her surprise. "Made it this morning while you were out exploring the shops on Main Street."

Theo couldn't help but notice the sheen in Gretchen's eyes, and for a moment, he wondered if she was going to cry. Over chocolate cake.

"It's too pretty to cut," she said, after clearing her throat. "You shouldn't have gone to so much trouble."

Edith, pleased by the praise, brushed off Gretchen's concerns. "I was delighted to have a reason to pull out the recipe. It's been too long since I've made this cake."

"Tell me about it," Manny chimed in, rising from the table to pick up one of the dessert plates next to the cake. "You know...this is my favorite too," he reminded his aunt.

Edith, who had a silver cake server in her hand, poked Manny's plump stomach playfully. "I know it is, which is why I only make it for larger groups. Otherwise, you'd devour the entire thing yourself in a single night."

Theo knew Edith worried about Manny's weight as he got older, just as he knew she blamed *herself* for her nephew's burgeoning waistline. Theo had walked in on Edith and Mom chatting in the B&B's kitchen one afternoon a few months ago, Mom sharing lightweight recipes with Edith, who admitted she didn't have a clue how to cook without butter.

Edith sliced each of them a generous piece of cake, then

went the extra mile, adding a dollop of vanilla ice cream to the plates before returning to the table.

Gretchen closed her eyes, moaning after the first bite, and Theo had to look away because fuck if her expression of pure pleasure didn't send his thoughts down some very naughty paths.

"Big fan of chocolate?" Theo asked.

"Sweets were a treat I didn't get very often when I was younger," she said, before shoving in another large bite.

Theo believed her, because she was eating the cake quickly, as if she was afraid someone was going to snatch it away from her grip.

"No sweets?" Manny said, his mouth full of cake. "I can't imagine. Were your parents health nuts or something?"

Gretchen paused mid-bite, her fork halfway between her plate and mouth. Theo suspected she hadn't meant to let that little tidbit slip.

"No." She put her fork back down without taking the bite. "They weren't very nice."

Edith exchanged a quick glance with Theo, obviously excited that Gretchen was opening the door to allow them a peek inside.

Manny, oblivious to the undercurrents and blissed out on gooey chocolate, gave Gretchen a commiserating grunt. "I get that. I hate to speak ill of them, but my folks aren't exactly warm and fuzzy, either."

Edith snorted, as if that was the understatement of the century.

Without meaning to, Manny had set Gretchen at ease. Not that Theo was surprised. If Manny was a dog, he'd be Marmaduke, big, goofy, loveable.

"Do your parents still live in Harrisburg?" Theo hoped the question was innocuous enough that she would answer.

Gretchen nodded, licking the tiniest smear of chocolate icing from her lower lip. "My mom and stepdad do. My dad left when I was five, so I don't know where he is."

Edith frowned. "You never see him?"

"Not since I was five."

That answer might have bothered Theo—the idea of a man splitting on his two kids and never looking back—but it was clear from Gretchen's tone, her father's departure didn't seem to bother her much.

"That couldn't have been easy." Like him, Edith was choosing her words carefully, hoping it would encourage Gretchen to say more.

"I don't remember him much at all. My brother, Shaw, was eight when he left, and he took it hard. He started getting in trouble at school, acting like a little brat. Mom married Ivan when I was seven. Sometimes I think she accepted his proposal because she couldn't handle Shaw on her own."

"Did Ivan help?" Manny was completely unaware how thrilled Theo and Edith were that Gretchen was giving them this look inside.

Gretchen shook her head, a faraway look in her eyes that concerned Theo, made him believe she was recalling unhappier times. "No." She hesitated, seeming to remember where she was. "Ivan was a strict disciplinarian."

Theo pinned her with a look because he could tell, once again, she was leaving too many things unsaid.

She grimaced under his steady gaze. "Okay," she relented. "Ivan was an abusive asshole and a bully."

"Oh, dear." Edith reached over to place her hand on top of Gretchen's. "I'm sorry to hear that. How did your mother handle it?"

Gretchen lifted one shoulder. "Mom wasn't the strongest of women, so she always took his side, supported him."

"Was he mean to her, too?" Manny had put his fork down, fully invested now in hearing Gretchen's story.

"No. Shaw took the brunt of his anger." Gretchen bit her lip. "It got bad. Some stuff happened, and we ended up in foster care."

Theo frowned. She'd clearly breezed over a hell of a lot.

Edith's fingers were pressed to her lips, upset by Gretchen's admission. "How old were you when you went into foster care?"

Gretchen looked away. They were treading on dangerous ground here. It was obvious she regretted saying as much as she had, and he suspected before they could ask another question, she'd find a way to change the subject.

"I was thirteen. Is it okay if I pour myself another cup of tea?" Gretchen asked as she rose, halfway to the kitchen before she finished her question.

"Of course, my dear. This is your home now. You don't even have to ask." Edith sighed heavily the second Gretchen was out of earshot. "Poor girl."

Theo nodded in agreement, though he didn't add more, concerned Gretchen would overhear them. He might not know her well, but he'd seen enough to let him know she wouldn't want their pity.

Mercifully, Manny recovered quickly, guiding them back to a safer topic. "Got any D.C. restaurant suggestions?"

Theo named a couple of places, his gaze drifting toward the kitchen. He sensed Gretchen was dawdling, uncomfortable with returning.

Three steps forward, two steps back.

She'd just stepped back into the dining room when there was a knock on the front door. Because he was looking at her, he caught the brief flash of panic that crossed Gretchen's features before she managed to school them.

"That'll be Jacob." Edith rose from the table. "I invited him to stop by for a slice of cake after his shift."

"You're giving away more of my cake?" Manny asked, aghast.

Edith chuckled. "It's Gretchen's cake."

Gretchen visibly relaxed, and even managed a weak smile.

Until Edith returned with Sheriff Jacob Anderson in tow.

Theo swore Gretchen's pale complexion faded four shades, until she was ghostly white. She took a couple steps backward, clearly intent on going back to the kitchen. She was forced to halt when Edith called out to her.

"Gretchen, I want you to meet Jacob Anderson, Gracemont's sheriff. Jacob, this is the young lady I was telling you about earlier. She's starting work at Stormy Weather Farm on Monday."

Gretchen hovered in the doorway between the kitchen and dining room, and Theo would bet every cent he had to his name that she wasn't walking toward the sheriff because her legs wouldn't carry her.

She wasn't visibly trembling, but Theo had caught the previous glimpses of fear in some of Gretchen's reactions—to his loud laughter, to him swiping at the bee. She'd flinched in fear, even whimpered.

But both of those times were *nothing* compared to this— what he was witnessing now was absolute terror.

"Nice to meet you, Gretchen." Sheriff Anderson walked over to shake her hand.

Gretchen swallowed deeply, then—impressively—managed to put her hand out without it shaking...much. "You too." Her voice was thin, but luckily, the sheriff and Edith didn't notice.

Sheriff Anderson had a well-known sweet tooth, so Theo was under no illusion the man would have stopped by to meet a newcomer to town if the promise of cake hadn't been included.

That was confirmed when he instantly turned away from Gretchen, rubbing his hands together excitedly when he caught sight of the three-layer chocolate cake sitting on the sideboard.

"I've been thinking about this cake ever since you invited me this morning, Edith."

She sliced the sheriff a big hunk of cake, setting it in front of him at one of the open spaces at the table. Sheriff Anderson dug in with gusto, muttering what Theo assumed was "yes, please" when Edith asked if he'd like a cup of tea.

Gretchen stepped aside as Edith went into the kitchen. She remained there, her eyes darting toward the sheriff, then away.

Theo wondered what had her so spooked. He'd heard of people who were afraid of cops, but he'd never seen anyone have such a visceral reaction to someone in uniform.

Of course, Jacob Anderson had been the sheriff of Gracemont's tiny law enforcement department since God was a baby, and the man was as gentle and jolly as they came. He'd played Santa at the town's annual holiday celebration for so long, even Theo had sat on his lap as a young kid and told him what he wanted for Christmas.

No one in Gracemont was afraid of Sheriff Anderson, because there wasn't a single scary thing about the guy, except for the gun on his belt that Theo had never seen out of its holster. Most folks in town liked to joke that it wasn't even a real gun, just a prop for show, because it certainly hadn't ever been used as intended.

"Gretchen." Theo stepping close to her.

She startled at his voice, clearly so distracted by the sheriff she hadn't seen him approach.

"I..." She licked her lips. "I have a bit of a headache coming on." She watched Sheriff Anderson plow through his first slice of cake before he and Manny both went back for seconds. "I might go up to my room now. Will you tell Edith for me?"

She was determined to make a quick escape. Theo was tempted to tell her Sheriff Anderson was harmless, but he didn't think it would matter if he did.

"I'll tell her," he promised.

She didn't even say goodbye to Sheriff Anderson or Manny, who were too busy happily humming their way to chocolate bliss to realize she'd gone.

Edith frowned when she returned from the kitchen with a fresh pot of tea in her hands.

Theo stepped next to her. "Gretchen had a headache. She went upstairs."

She glanced toward the staircase, confused. "She seemed fine a few minutes ago."

Theo didn't want to voice his opinion about her being afraid of the sheriff in case he was wrong, or in case Sheriff Anderson overheard him.

Edith put the teapot on the table. "Manny, pour the sheriff a cup of tea for me, will you?" She returned to the kitchen for a moment. When she came back, she handed Theo a bottle of water and some Tylenol. "Will you run those up to her?"

Theo nodded, climbing the stairs. Gretchen's door was closed, but he could hear the opening and closing of drawers. He knocked, trying to catch her before she started undressing for bed.

She opened the door a crack, her gaze sliding over his shoulder to look behind him before she relaxed.

He held up the pills and water. "Edith wanted me to bring you these."

"Oh." Gretchen opened the door more fully, taking them from him. Theo noticed the suitcase on her bed, then the open dresser drawer.

"Just now unpacking?" He gestured toward the case, surprised, considering she'd already been in town a few days.

"Um...yeah." She fidgeted with the pills in her hand nervously. Gone was the easygoing woman from dinner. This Gretchen was on edge, and he wished he knew what had set her off.

"I'm getting ready to head home," he said.

"Okay."

"I'll pick you up Monday morning around eight-thirty."

She nodded slowly. "Okay."

"Good night." He forced what he hoped passed for a normal smile, afraid he was too worried to pull it off.

"Goodbye." Gretchen closed the door.

Shit. That goodbye sounded too damn final. It wasn't a *see you later* sort of farewell, but more of a *we'll never meet again* sort of goodbye.

Theo stood in the hall for a moment, fighting the instinct to knock on the door again and ask her what was wrong. Leaving her alone when she was upset was harder than he might have imagined.

Despite every internal admonishment he'd given himself about maintaining a professional relationship, he was failing to resist the pull.

If this kept up, he was going to have to call Levi to see how the hell he managed to keep from losing his mind once he realized Kasi was the woman for him, because now that he'd met Gretchen...

Jesus. He ran a hand through his hair.

Time to get a grip.

Chapter Six

"Have you ever heard of beer donkeys?"

Theo and Nora both looked at Gretchen with equal expressions of amusement and what the fuck.

"I know it sounds silly," Gretchen said. "But when I was doing some research on event barns after getting the job, I came across the beer donkey option as one of the things people can book for wedding receptions and other celebrations. Considering Rain or Shine Brewery is right here, it felt like a great way to promote your beer at parties."

Theo and Nora exchanged a glance, and Gretchen felt a slight pressure on her chest, afraid perhaps she'd finally said something *so* stupid, the Storms would know they'd screwed up in hiring her.

She wasn't sure what kind of cousin-link telepathy they shared, but before Nora finished saying, "Call Remi," Theo already had his phone out and was dialing.

"Remi." Theo smiled at Gretchen as he spoke to his other cousin on the line. "Two words for you. Beer donkey."

Gretchen couldn't hear Remi's reply, but given Theo's chuckle, he'd captured her interest.

Once he explained the concept to her, Gretchen got the feeling this suggestion had been as well received as her previous ones, because for several minutes, all Theo managed to say was "okay" and "mm-hmm" and "sounds great." Then he made a funny, wide-eyed, OMG face for her and Nora's benefit.

Dear God, Gretchen thought. This job really was a dream.

Primarily because of her two bosses.

Well, she supposed she worked for the entire family, but she answered primarily to Theo and Nora, who had been extremely helpful and supportive in getting her started. Because it was a new position for the farm, the three of them had held several long meetings this week, discussing everything from how to schedule events and promote the new event barn, to generating a list of fees for the various things they planned to offer.

Theo and Nora had listened to her opinions and valued her input. One week in, and she was already starting to feel a bit more confident about her ability to do the job.

While Brenda had been a nice boss, her work style involved a lot of micromanaging, which meant she told Gretchen what to do and Gretchen did it. Between that and Briggs dictating how things should run at home, she was absolutely thrilled by the chance to express her own ideas and delighted by how many of her recommendations Nora and Theo had taken and made part of their processes.

"Okay. Hang on a second, Remi." Theo looked at her. "Gretchen, can you share some links of the beer donkey sites you saw, with me, Remi, and Nora?"

Gretchen nodded, adding that note to the growing to-do list on her legal pad.

Then Theo turned to Nora. "Remi's going to look into what it would take to stable a donkey with her horses, and research which donkeys are best suited for this type of thing and where we could buy one."

Gretchen was shocked by how quickly Remi was ready to roll with the idea. She'd met Theo's youngest and—according to him—wildest cousin her first day on the job. Remi, who had more energy than an entire stadium full of toddlers, had stopped by every day without fail to see how she was doing and to chat for a few minutes.

"Gretchen's going to send you some links, Remi. Let's make plans for the four of us to sit down middle of next week to pool information and see if this is feasible." Theo said a quick goodbye and hung up.

"Let me guess," Nora said sarcastically. "She loved the idea."

Theo laughed. "I proposed we buy another four-legged creature for the farm. What do *you* think?"

On every single one of her daily drop-in visits, Remi had tried to convince Gretchen to go on a horseback ride with her along the countless mountain trails that were part of the farm. Gretchen had put her off so far, because she'd seen the horses in the stables during her first-day tour, and they were big creatures. She wasn't sure she could control such a large beast.

After Theo hired her, Gretchen had spent countless hours —when Briggs was on night duty—reading every article she could find online regarding what an event coordinator did, praying she'd be able to learn on the job quickly enough that Theo and Nora would keep her on. With each passing day, while her fear of being fired hadn't vanished, it was growing less.

Now that the barn was officially ready for business, they were anxious to begin scheduling events, certain the space would be ideal for weddings, family and class reunions, as well as other local celebrations.

Until those reservations started rolling in, she would take over the task of planning special events at the winery and brewery and hiring local talent to perform. Fall was peak season, and Theo and Nora had begun planning Stormy Weather Farm's annual Octoberfest—an ongoing celebration held on weekends from mid-September to mid-November. Now, however, they were anxious for Gretchen to begin running the special programs—like grape stomping, special tastings and food pairings, as well as face painting for the kids. They'd also encouraged her to come up with her own ideas of things that might entice people to enjoy the fall foliage with a glass of wine or pint of beer.

"I love the idea of a beer donkey," Nora said. "It'll be an awesome way to offer a fun vibe to receptions and parties, if that's what the customer wants. I can think of at least a dozen people in Gracemont who would jump at the chance to hire a beer donkey for their special occasions."

"I'll add donkey to our list with a question mark for now, and then we can wait to see what Remi comes up with." Gretchen turned to her computer and typed "beer donkey" into their itemized list.

"And that gives us seventeen," Nora said with a smile.

Gretchen didn't have a clue why Nora was happy about that. "Were we aiming for seventeen?"

Theo chuckled. "Nope. Just for an odd number. That was going to keep you up at night, wasn't it?" he said to his cousin.

Nora lifted one eyebrow. "Nope. I was always going to sleep like a baby tonight, because you're crazy if you think I was letting *either* of you leave here until we either added an item or took one away."

"I have no idea what we're talking about," Gretchen said softly.

Nora flashed Gretchen a self-deprecating grin. "I hate even numbers. Prefer to live my life surrounded by nice round odd ones. It's a small, funky part of my OCD and what makes me the coolest Storm."

"Cool, huh?" Theo teased. "That's the word you're using to describe the fact you have to eat all your meals in a very specific order? And that your closet is organized by color and season and article of clothing."

Nora laughed, then looked at Gretchen. "Vegetable, carb, then protein, in case you were wondering. As for the closet, I follow the color wheel—beginning with red—summer is my first season, and then it's blouses, sweaters, skirts, and pants...in that order.

"Wow. I don't think I have enough clothes to do more than the color breakdown," Gretchen murmured.

"A lack of clothing is *not* Nora's problem," Theo joked. "Or Remi's. Or Mila's."

"Retail therapy is real and it's successful. Stop by the farmhouse anytime, Gretchen," Nora offered. "I'll give you a closet tour."

Theo had mentioned Nora's compulsions a few times since Gretchen began working here, but it was the first time Nora had talked about it herself. Given her grin, it was clear Nora didn't give a shit about her OCD and got a kick out of talking about it.

Nora smirked. "You probably think, like my family, that I'm crazy, but—"

"Not at all," Gretchen hastened to reassure her. "To be honest, I have my own little quirks."

"Oh yeah?" Nora said, leaning back. "Like what?"

"Whenever I eat colorful candy, like M&Ms or Skittles, I

sort them by color and eat all the same colors together. Because they wouldn't like being separated." Gretchen bit her lower lip, surprised by her willingness to share something so silly. But Nora's question hadn't been laced with a bit of judgment, so she'd jumped right in.

"Are you saying the candy has feelings?" Theo asked, even as Nora nodded, agreeing with Gretchen.

"I do the same thing," Nora said. "After I count the candy."

"Because God forbid she eat an even number of M&Ms," Theo added sarcastically.

Nora snorted. "I never hear you complaining when I give you the extra one."

"Yeah, one M&M. Super generous," he teased.

Gretchen shrugged. "I think everyone has little quirks. It doesn't make us crazy. Just interesting."

"I've always called my issues compulsions, but I like the word quirks better. See, Theo, Gretchen gets me." Nora flourished a hand in her direction. "She thinks I'm interesting."

Theo rolled his eyes as Nora rose. "And since we have a good handle on this list of options, I need to head back to the winery to finish a couple things before the cookout. See y'all later."

Nora walked to the door but paused in the threshold. Tilting her head toward Gretchen, she looked at Theo. "You were right."

And with those parting words, she left.

"You were right?" Gretchen was slightly worried, since it was obvious Nora's comment had been about her.

Theo, meanwhile, was grinning like the Cheshire Cat. "About hiring you."

While Gretchen liked hearing that, she felt a little nervous. "Nora didn't want to hire me?"

Theo leaned back and crossed his legs. This meeting was

being held in Gretchen's office, so she was sitting behind the desk while her bosses had claimed the two chairs in front of her. With any other boss, maybe that would have felt weird, but not with Theo and Nora. That was one of the other parts of this job she loved. Neither Nora nor Theo was on a power trip. From day one, they simply pulled her into the flock, treating her like an equal member of the team.

"We interviewed other candidates with more experience," he confessed.

"Oh." Gretchen grimaced, then admitted something she'd been thinking since being hired. "I figured I got the job because no one else applied."

Theo leaned forward and tapped his finger on her desk twice. "Hey, don't do that."

"Do what?"

"Sell yourself short," he replied.

This wasn't the first time Theo had addressed her bad habit of putting herself down or lacking confidence. Not that he did it in a bad way, just in a way that made her feel like he saw way more in her than she saw in herself. And she liked it.

"If you don't mind me asking," Gretchen forced herself to ask, "why *did* you hire me if there were better candidates?"

"Because it wasn't about experience to me." Theo leaned forward as he spoke. "Your answers to our questions lined up with my vision of how I wanted us to proceed with not only the barn but our other events as well."

She nodded, grateful Theo had gone to bat for her, giving her a chance. She'd never be able to express how much his offer of a job had meant to her, because he hadn't just given her a fresh start; he'd provided her an escape route.

Given the way Briggs's violence had begun to escalate over the past several months, she wasn't entirely certain Theo hadn't saved her life, as well.

"But I think more than the answers," Theo continued, "I admired your drive and determination."

She almost scoffed but managed to hold it in. Because what he viewed as drive and determination had been desperation and anxiousness. "Thank you," she said, aware how painfully short that sentiment fell, but unable to say more without choking up.

Theo stood. "It's four-thirty. Let's close shop early and head over to the farmhouse. I have a few things to do to set up for your welcome cookout tonight."

"You really didn't need to go to so much trouble," Gretchen said, not for the first, second, or tenth time this week.

"I get the feeling you don't like being the center of attention, so what do you say we share this celebration. Because Nora handed me the opportunity to say 'I told you so' for the rest of our lives. This is a big day, worthy of a party. Don't take that away from me."

Gretchen grinned. "I wouldn't dream of it."

Two hours later, Gretchen took another sip of Lightning in a Bottle red, sitting in one of the countless camp chairs scattered around the front yard of Theo's farmhouse, feeling happier and more at ease than she had in...well, in her entire life.

Usually, it took her ages to become relaxed around strangers, but it was impossible to be in the company of Edith, Theo, and the Storms, and not instantly feel welcome and safe. It was a foreign but appreciated feeling.

She couldn't believe she'd almost run from this wonderful place Saturday night, when the sheriff had arrived. She'd escaped to her room and packed her suitcase, waiting for the sheriff to come upstairs and... Well, she didn't know what he might do. What Briggs might have told a fellow cop to get her back.

When Sheriff Anderson left—with a Saran-wrapped plate containing another large chunk of chocolate cake—she finally relaxed. Sort of. Though she hadn't unpacked her bag again until after work on Tuesday...just to be sure.

True to his word, Theo and his mother had organized a cookout so that she could meet everyone, not that it was necessary. She'd met most of the Storms throughout the week, nearly everyone stopping by at some point to welcome her.

Edith had mentioned that the pace of life in Gracemont was slower, and she hadn't lied. Whenever someone new stopped by to introduce themselves, they always took a few minutes to get to know her, seemingly in no hurry to be on their way. Gretchen had gotten pretty good at keeping most of the details about her life secret, able to deflect by using Shaw whenever someone asked about her family, or where she'd lived. It wasn't like her brother was going to find out she was embellishing the handful of stories he'd told her about his experiences with the military and the SEALS before their estrangement had become an insurmountable ravine.

She hadn't spoken to Shaw in years, and she hated that she'd been the one to push him away, simply because Briggs had turned her thoughts against him, convincing her Shaw had abandoned her, like everyone else in her life—except him. She could have reached back out to her brother during her worst days, but it was easier to withdraw from everyone, herself included, rather than risk any further hurt or disappointment.

After five days, the only Storm she hadn't met was Levi, because he was now working on his girlfriend's farm down in the valley. Of course, she felt like she knew Levi and Kasi simply because the rest of the Storms were all abuzz about Gracemont's new "it" couple.

Gretchen smiled to herself when she recalled Remi dubbing them that.

Tonight, the couple had come to meet her, bringing along Kasi's dad and brother. Kasi, who'd apparently grown up with the Storms—she and Remi having been best friends since birth —had instantly linked arms with Gretchen and playfully asked in a fake horrified voice if she was ready for what was coming.

Gretchen hadn't known how to respond to that, but as the night wore on, she was starting to understand why Kasi had warned her. Gretchen had never been around such a big, boisterous family. It hadn't taken her long to figure out that trash talking and teasing were the family's love languages, along with food, beer, and wine.

Currently, Theo, his dad, and Sam were standing around the grill, drinking beer and flipping burgers and turning hot dogs, while Edith sat nearby, deep in conversation with Kasi's father, Tim. Most of the other cookout attendees had divided into teams and were playing flag football.

Gretchen was invited to join the game but had declined, because the Storms were clearly very competitive. She'd reassured them she would be a detriment to whichever team got stuck with her, since she had a bad habit of flinching whenever a ball was thrown her direction. Her high school P.E. teacher was constantly exasperated with her, insisting she couldn't catch the ball with her eyes closed.

"Overwhelmed?"

Gretchen smiled as Theo's mom, Claire, claimed the empty chair next to her. She'd met Claire on Monday when Theo took her on a tour of the entire farm, the two of them stopping by each of the businesses. Apparently, he'd timed their visit to the B&B Claire and Rex ran perfectly—and on purpose—so that they were invited to stay for lunch. Claire had served them the tallest, most chocked-full of meat and cheese club sandwiches Gretchen had ever seen, along with homemade potato chips.

"A little, but in a good way," Gretchen said. "I've never been around such a large family."

Claire lifted the bottle of wine she'd carried over with her, and Gretchen nodded, accepting her silent offer of more. Claire topped up both their glasses, then set the near-empty bottle on the ground next to her. "I swear that rosé of Mav's is dangerous."

Gretchen agreed. "It's very easy to drink."

"Too easy. Which is why I'm always shocked when I get to the bottom of the bottle so quickly. By sharing with you, I can fool myself into thinking I didn't drink the whole thing myself."

Gretchen laughed, which was another new development, in addition to her rising confidence. She wasn't aware how rusty her laugh had become until she heard it slipping out whenever Manny and Edith got into one of their adorable nephew/aunt spats that were completely devoid of anger or meanness. Or whenever Theo made a joke as they slowly—and she did mean *slowly*—circled the parking lot while he attempted to teach her to drive. So far, she hadn't managed to do more than round the lot at approximately five miles an hour.

Oh, and reverse. She'd attempted that with some zigzagging success—though she was certain she wasn't supposed to swerve quite that much while looking at the backup camera. Yesterday had been her third lesson, and she was starting to think that at this rate, she'd be mugging for that first driver's license picture shortly after her fiftieth birthday.

"How do you like your hot dogs, Gretchen?" Theo shouted from the grill.

She frowned, confused by the question, so she fired back the first answer that popped into her mind. "Done."

Everyone in hearing distance laughed—though she hadn't intended to be funny. Claire, who really *had* been enjoying the wine, had to wipe tears from her eyes. "He means, do you like them grilled the normal way or Levi's way, which is burned to a crisp."

Gretchen crinkled her nose, then yelled back, "The normal way."

Theo gave her a pleased smile, waving his spatula at her. "Good girl."

Claire rolled her eyes as Gretchen blushed. Her instant attraction to Theo Storm hadn't wavered, despite countless mental admonishments to herself over the past five days. She'd already proven herself to be a terrible judge of character, spending the last six years with an abusive, manipulative man. Following that with an affair with her new boss—in a job she needed like water and air—would do nothing to redeem her poor life choices. In fact, something like that would land her on the too-stupid-to-live list.

So...she had to stay strong.

Of course, that didn't mean she couldn't look at the pretty man from afar and dream a little.

Or a lot.

Despite the fact she'd only been officially single for two weeks, it felt like a lot longer than that to Gretchen, whose heart had checked out of her relationship with Briggs years ago. It didn't help that she used romance novels as an escape from her shitty existence, so that eighteen-year-old girl—who'd chosen so fucking wrong—was now twenty-four and couldn't help dreaming big. Couldn't help but wonder if there was a man out there like the heroes in her books, who would love her for who she was, who would be kind and protective and...not hit her.

She pushed those thoughts away, because even if Theo was as nice as he seemed, he wasn't the guy for her.

"Theo tells me he's teaching you to drive," Claire said.

"He is. I grew up in a city with good public transportation, so I never bothered to learn." So far, everyone had accepted Gretchen's explanation for not being able to drive at face-value.

Claire took a sip of wine. "My boys have been driving around the farm from the time they were thirteen years old, Theo even earlier. He was the third boy, after Levi and Sam, and I swear he spent his entire childhood trying to keep up with his big brothers. I knew it had gotten out of hand when I caught him behind the wheel of our old farm-use truck, sitting on one of the pillows from my couch to give him the extra inches he needed to see out the windshield."

Gretchen's eyes widened. "How old was he?"

Claire shrugged. "He probably wasn't much more than ten years old."

"Did he wreck the truck?"

His mom laughed. "Good Lord, no. The only reason I caught him was because I was hanging clothes on the line when he returned. That boy pulled up, cool as an evening breeze, put the truck in park, and climbed out like he was king of the universe. I told him flat out he was too young to drive, and that I'd better never catch him behind the wheel again. Even threw in that 'wait until your dad gets home' line, because I was hopping mad."

Gretchen couldn't help but grin as Claire told her story with serious country charm. "What did Theo say?"

"That scamp hadn't just taken a joyride around the farm. He'd driven down into the valley!"

"What?" Gretchen couldn't imagine a ten-year-old driving off the mountain, then around town, even if Gracemont *was* small and traffic was always light.

"He had the nerve to claim I couldn't be mad because he'd done me a favor. Apparently, he'd driven all the way to the Mills' farm to buy some eggs because we were out."

"Mr. Mills didn't take the keys away from him?"

After she asked the question, Gretchen glanced at Tim Mills and Edith, only to discover they'd finished their own conversation and were now listening to Claire's story.

"Oh, I would have," Tim reassured her. "But I'd been out in the field and my wife was in the kitchen baking. At the time, we had an honor system on egg pickup. Folks put their money in an envelope with their name on it and helped themselves to eggs. When Claire called to tell me Theo had gotten eggs from us, I went out to the money box and sure enough, there was Theo's name on an envelope, the cash inside."

Gretchen couldn't help but laugh. "Wow. He sounds like he was a handful."

"That's what you took from that story?" Theo asked, joining their small circle.

"What *should* I have taken?" she asked.

"Obviously, that I was an extremely thoughtful, considerate child, and a brilliant protégé, destined to be a titan of industry or NASCAR driver or both."

Claire reached over, lightly slapping Theo's forearm. "I don't know about all that, but I'll agree you *are* thoughtful, and you can charm honey from the bees with that smile of yours. Gretchen, I swear he was so sweet and sincere as he handed me those eggs, I forgot to be mad."

"*You* might have forgotten, but Dad's a tougher nut to crack. I spent the entire next day washing and detailing that truck, the tractor, and the family car. Every time I thought I was done, he pulled up another vehicle."

"An appropriate punishment," Claire said. "Theo had an aversion to cleaning anything. His room when he was a teenager was despicable. Told him he was living inside a trash can."

"At least he's gotten a little better about it," Sam chimed in. "Of course, Levi and I had to nag the hell out of him after he first moved in with us, to whip him into shape."

Theo snorted. "I thought this was a welcome party for Gretchen. Must have missed my invitation to the Theo roast."

Sam threw his arm around his brother's shoulders. "Seems only fair Gretchen has a clear picture of exactly who she's working for."

"Gretchen." Theo shook off his brother's arm, gesturing toward an old wooden picnic table that was laden with food. She had to hand it to the citizens of Gracemont. They sure knew how to eat. "Dinner is served. As the guest of honor, you get to go first."

Apparently, Gretchen picking up a paper plate was the signal to go, as the football game abruptly ended, everyone jostling for position in line to fill their plates.

She'd finished her second helping when her cell rang. Pulling it from the pocket of her jacket, her heart raced when she saw Brenda's name.

Gretchen excused herself, stepping well out of hearing distance as she answered.

"Brenda. This is a surprise."

"I wanted to see how your first week at the new job went."

Gretchen hadn't realized she'd been holding her breath until Brenda revealed her reason for calling. "Oh. It's been amazing,"

"Thank goodness. I've been so worried. We haven't talked since you left and—"

"I'm sorry I haven't called. It's been such a whirlwind."

"But a good whirlwind?"

Gretchen was touched by the tone of concern in her former

boss's voice. Brenda had really gone the extra mile for her these past six months. "So good. The place I'm staying is incredible. There's a fireplace in my room."

"A fireplace! Damn. I might come stay with you."

Gretchen smiled. "And while the job is challenging, it's also exciting and even fun. Everyone on Stormy Weather Farm has been so kind and inviting."

Brenda released an audible sigh. "I can't tell you what a load you've taken off my mind."

"I can never thank you enough for what you did for me, Brenda," Gretchen said.

"I should have seen what was going on much sooner—"

"No." Gretchen quickly cut off her boss, unwilling to let her wallow in regret. "I wasn't honest with you, feeding you lies about the bruises."

"And I should have seen *through* the lies. My dad's a therapist and my mom is a divorce lawyer, for God's sake."

"Please. I can't stand thinking you feel even an ounce of guilt after what you've done for me. Everything happened the way it was supposed to, and in the right time. I'm sure of it. My head...it wasn't in the right place to plan and do what needed to be done for such a long time." Gretchen hated how many years she'd wallowed in her own self-loathing and misery.

"You deserve this second chance," Brenda said.

Gretchen hesitated, torn over whether to ask the question burning in her mind. When she boarded that bus and got the hell out of Harrisburg, she swore there would be no looking back. But those words were easier said than done.

Despite feeling safe in Gracemont, she'd suffered too many moments of panic whenever she saw someone who looked like Briggs, or heard a voice that sounded like his, or whenever she woke up to one of the countless moans and groans—as Edith called them—of the old Millholland house. The creak of a floorboard or a gentle bump in the night left her huddling under the covers, shivering, certain he'd found her.

In the end, she decided forewarned was forearmed. Since she was looking over her shoulder all the time anyway, it was better to know if her need for vigilance was called for.

"Do I want to know how Briggs took my leaving?" She'd left her old phone along with a letter on her desk at work, which meant Brenda would have had a front-row seat to his reaction.

"I don't know," Brenda hedged. "Do you?"

"How bad was it?" Gretchen felt that familiar weight pressing against her chest when she thought about her ex.

"I've known Briggs practically his whole life. And I had no idea he carried that much rage in him. I'll be honest, he scared me for a few minutes. I can't imagine what it must have been like for you, living with him all those years."

"He didn't hurt you, did he?" Gretchen was suddenly terrified she'd unwittingly put Brenda in the line of fire.

"No, of course not. But after he read your letter, he picked up your phone and threw it across the office. It smashed against the wall. I think he immediately regretted that impulse, because it made it impossible for him to go through your phone for clues about where you might have gone."

"He wouldn't have found anything," Gretchen reassured her. She'd all but hit the factory reset on the thing, only leaving the Find My Friends app active, so he wouldn't suspect her plans. She'd done the same thing with her computer at work, careful not to leave him the slightest trace of where she'd run to.

"He's been all over Harrisburg looking for you, checking at the homes of friends, your parents' place, even the old foster home where you lived. My brother stopped by yesterday, unannounced—I'm sure at Briggs's request—to make sure I wasn't harboring you. I told Douglas, Briggs was an abusive asshole, but apparently Briggs got there first, admitting to my brother that he'd done things wrong, crying on his shoulder, swearing he'd make it right if only he could find and talk to you," Brenda murmured. "Douglas, the fucking idiot, drank the Kool-Aid, then suggested Briggs talk to our dad. Douglas has always been one of those people who believes in second, third, and twenty-eighth chances."

"Maybe Briggs will give up when he keeps hitting brick walls." Even as Gretchen made the comment, she knew how unlikely that scenario was. Briggs wasn't the type to take getting dumped, lightly. He wouldn't forgive and forget, which meant there was going to be a day of reckoning for her at some point. She'd known that when she left, but she hoped it would be way down the road, and that she was stronger and in a safe place when that happened.

As she glanced around the yard at all the people still eating and chatting, she sent up a silent prayer that perhaps she'd found that place.

She laughed to herself. Apparently, Gretchen Banks—unlike Gretchen Parker—was an optimist. Who knew she had it in her?

"I hope he will, but I'm afraid he's nowhere near finished looking right now. He came by the office this morning, wanting to look at your computer. I told him to get a court order," Brenda confessed.

"Brenda! You didn't have to do that. I didn't leave anything on my computer to give away my location."

"Doesn't matter. My brother might be the forgive and forget type, but I'm not. Figured it was time to throw my cards on the table. Tired of him walking around town like the goddamned injured party. I have to admit, he's smooth. Even though his frustration is off the charts, he didn't lose his cool when I called him every name in the book. I think I should let you know..." Brenda paused.

"What?"

"He's working an angle."

Gretchen already knew which angle because it was one he'd used countless times in the past. So she wasn't surprised when Brenda continued.

"He mentioned to me that he was concerned you'd had some sort of mental break because of childhood trauma and a bunch of bullshit like that. I think he's using that to get his buddies on the force to help him look for you. Told me he handled things poorly, but it was because he didn't know how to help you. He keeps saying you're a danger to yourself."

Gretchen blew out a long, slow breath. It wasn't the first time he'd attempted to gaslight her—and others—by saying she was crazy, that she overreacted, that she blew things out of proportion. Briggs was as good at emotional abuse as he was physical. And for a while there, she'd started to genuinely believe she might be losing her mind.

But not now. "I've never been more mentally sound."

Brenda sighed in relief. "I can tell. You sound so much better already, and it's only been a couple of weeks. Listen, I won't keep you. I wanted to touch base to make sure you were okay."

"I'm great. And thanks again, Brenda. For everything."

"If you need anything..."

"I'll call. I promise." The two of them said their goodbyes.

Gretchen hung up but made no move to return to the cookout, her thoughts whirling over Briggs and his comments about her mental instability, as a new fear crept in.

What if he traced her here?

What if he told the Storms and Edith the same lies?

Would they believe him the same way all the others had?

Briggs had convinced Destiny and Darryl that she was prone to outbursts and violence, and that the bruises they saw on her were the result of him trying to restrain her, to keep her from hurting *him*. He always managed to paint himself as some savior, as the only one who could control her and keep her safe from her psycho self.

The idea of him turning the Storms against her weighed heavy on her mind, and her lungs constricted.

"Hey, Gretchen," Remi called out. "You better come grab a slice of this apple pie before the heathens eat it all."

She forced a smile, drawing in a shivery breath. She'd felt so relaxed prior to Brenda's call. Unfortunately, she couldn't shake the tension in her shoulders, all the old fears and anxieties bubbling to the surface.

Somehow, she kept her fake smile in place and managed to hold the coming panic attack at bay all through dessert, and while it was clear the party was going to carry on for a few more hours, she was grateful when Edith offered her a chance to leave.

"I'm going to head home, my dear," Edith said. "Theo said he'd drive you home later."

"Oh no," Gretchen said. "That's not necessary. I'm kind of tired. I think I'll go with you if that's okay."

Edith tilted her head curiously. "Of course it is. Are you sure you wouldn't rather hang out with the young ones? Kick up your heels a bit?"

Gretchen shook her head. "No. I'd rather call it a night. I'm looking forward to diving back into our book."

She and Edith had fallen into a routine ever since Gretchen moved in. After dinner, the two of them would hang out in the living room, chilling on the cozy couches as they watched a movie. So far, they'd taken turns picking the flicks. While Gretchen was a huge fan of rom coms, Edith's taste—hilariously—ran toward disaster films.

A few days ago, they'd decided to start their own book club

of two, each of them buying copies of the same book. They'd read the first three chapters last night, curled under their own fleece blankets, then they stopped to chat about what they'd read.

"If you're sure." It was clear Edith couldn't believe Gretchen would choose reading a book over hanging around the firepit with the Storms.

"I am."

Gretchen and Edith said their goodbyes, though it took a little while, given the way Theo, Nora, and Remi were working overtime to convince Gretchen to stay. They weren't pressuring her, just genuinely sorry to see her leave, which was sweet, but she'd spent the last hour with her hands tucked in her pockets, trying to hide the fact she was trembling.

She couldn't dismiss Briggs from her mind, and she had suffered enough panic attacks in the past to know that one was looming. If—when—it became full blown, she preferred to be back at Edith's, where she could retreat to the privacy of her own room and ride it out alone.

Once they were in the car, Gretchen turned her face to the passenger window, though she wasn't seeing the same beautiful view she'd been admiring on the ride to the farm this morning.

She was so distracted by her thoughts she was surprised when Edith pulled into the driveway. They'd made the entire trip back in silence.

As they walked into the house, Edith stopped just over the threshold. "I know we haven't known each other for long, sweetheart, but I want you to know that if anything is bothering you, you can talk to me. I've got a few years on me, and while I don't pretend to know all the answers, maybe I'll have something in my arsenal of experience that will help."

Gretchen was tempted to lie once more, to insist nothing

was wrong, but she was so tired of being alone. The pressure on her chest was unbearable and her strength was all but gone.

Edith must have sensed her wavering. "Maybe you could start by telling me about those bruises on your neck that you showed up here with last week."

Gretchen blinked rapidly, trying to stem the tears, but that was impossible when Edith reached out and pulled her into an embrace that was remarkably strong, given her tiny size.

"It's okay, sweetheart. You're safe. I won't let anyone hurt you."

Jesus.

Gretchen had waited a lifetime for her mother to offer her that kind of support, those comforting words. She never had. Not once.

The fight left her as Gretchen clung to Edith, crying out a lifetime of fears and sadness. And then she opened up...and told the dear woman everything.

Everything.

Chapter Seven

Theo tossed the beanbag up in the air a few times, pretending to seriously size up his target, a pyramid of red Solo cups. Gretchen stood next to him, chowing down on pink cotton candy, cheering him on.

The annual Fall Harvest Festival was in full swing and, while Theo always enjoyed the event, he was having even more fun this year. Because he'd spent the entire day with Gretchen. He'd invited her to join him for all the festivities earlier in the week, offering to be her guide to ensure she didn't miss anything fun, and he was thrilled when she readily accepted.

He'd anticipated having to convince her, just as he had with the daily driving lessons...and the welcome cookout...and his weekly Thursday happy hour at the brewery with him and Nora...and Grayson's birthday party at the winery...and the bowling excursion with his family.

Theo had come to learn that her initial rejections of his invitations had nothing to do with disinterest and everything to do with not wanting to be an imposition. Because once they got where they were going, Gretchen was all-in, excited to be included.

She had officially finished her third week as the farm's event coordinator, and in that short time, she'd won over every single member of his large family. She'd also proven herself to be a hard worker with a willingness to learn. She soaked in new information like a sponge, and he'd been granted a few tiny peeks of what he decided was a personality that had the potential to be as vivacious as his own.

Sadly, those glimpses of the witty, fun-loving woman were too brief, often followed by a strange, sudden silence he didn't understand. It was almost as if Gretchen feared some sort of repercussion for having fun. Like she'd be punished for making a joke or laughing too loud.

She was definitely an enigma, one with many layers. Not that he minded, because he happened to love onions, and he was more than ready to peel back every single one of hers.

This morning, he and his entire family made the trip to Main Street to watch Gracemont's Fall Harvest Day parade. Edith, Manny, and Gretchen had joined them, plopping their camp chairs down along the curb, everyone laughing and chatting as they waited for the festivities to begin.

While it was no Macy's Thanksgiving Day event complete with giant balloons and celebrities, the parade was still entertaining, as the local middle and high school bands marched down the street, playing somewhat recognizable music. In addition to the bands, there were four floats—the same four floats that traversed the parade route every year. The only difference was which business took their turn to sponsor them, the signage, and who got to ride on them.

It had been Stormy Weather Farm's turn two years earlier. He, Remi, and Maverick had represented the family, waving merrily to the crowds, while Levi drove the truck pulling them, blasting "Beer for My Horses" and "Hole in the Bottle."

All the town dignitaries were also part of the line-up, as members of the town council—his dad included—rolled by on the back of pickup trucks, waving and smiling. Theo had rolled his eyes when Mayor Scottie Grover went past, perched on the back of some expensive convertible his parents had either rented or bought for the damn event, looking like every inch the smarmy politician he was. He'd even tacked *Reelect Grover* signs to the sides, using the parade as an opportunity to campaign.

Theo had shouldered Sam, telling him next year, he'd be the one riding by. Sam had joked, saying if he won, he wanted to ride the route on the farm's tractor.

"You gonna pitch that thing or what?" Jerry Peterson pulled Theo from his thoughts.

Jerry was Gracemont's Mr. Fix-it, running a repair shop on Main Street. However, today, he was manning the beanbag toss game. All the proceeds from the fair games were being donated to the Gracemont Fire Station, which was in bad need of a new tanker, so Jerry, a volunteer firefighter, was sporting red suspenders and his helmet to help promote the cause.

Theo winked at Gretchen, pointing to the stuffed animal prizes. "Start figuring out which one you want."

Gretchen's barely there smile emerged, but she quickly covered it with her hand, something she still did quite a lot.

Tossing the beanbag, Theo knocked over the entire structure, Gretchen jumping up and down and cheering.

Following the parade, the entire gang had made their way to the fairgrounds, where they split up to play games, ride the rides, and eat themselves into sugar and grease comas. Theo had dragged Gretchen away from Mila and Nora, intent on stealing her for himself all afternoon.

So far—in addition to the cotton candy—he and Gretchen had split a funnel cake, a corn dog, a huge cup of French fries smothered in salt and vinegar, a gyro, and a deep-fried Oreo. They'd thought that by splitting everything, they would get to sample more of the food and—hopefully—not suffer stomachaches afterward.

While it seemed like a solid hypothesis at the beginning, Theo was starting to suspect they weren't going to like the end results of the experiment.

"What toy do you want, Theo?" Jerry asked.

Theo tilted his head toward her. "Ask Gretchen. I promised the prize to her."

"Are you sure?" she asked. "I can have it?"

Theo laughed. "You're going to *have* to take it. I can't squeeze another stuffed animal on my bed."

Gretchen covered her mouth, a breathy laugh escaping, then she surveyed the stuffed animal collection. Her eyes widened when they landed on a black-and-white cat. "Can I have that one?"

"'Course you can." Jerry unclipped the floppy stuffed cat and handed it to her.

She graced Theo with one of her unguarded but too-brief smiles, and he felt the urge to kiss her. It wasn't an urge he should have, since he was her boss for God's sake, not to mention they'd only known each other a few weeks. Pair that with Gretchen's skittish nature, and Theo knew kissing her would be the wrong thing to do.

However, knowing and doing were two different things, and he didn't fool himself into believing he'd be able to hold off for much longer. Every day he spent with her was both a gift and a torment. Theo had never felt like this about another woman, and the more he thought about it, the more he realized the first inkling of attraction had hit him during the interview.

And it had nothing to do with her looks—even though she was fucking gorgeous. No, it was those things he'd attributed as his reasons for hiring her. Her determination and her vulnerability.

He wasn't sure how he knew, but Theo was one hundred percent certain she was meant to be his.

Pushing away the instinct to kiss her, he took the bag of cotton candy from her, grinning as she gave the little cat a squeeze.

"What are you going to name it?" He'd meant his question as a joke, so he was blown away when she replied instantly.

"Boots."

The little black cat had white paws and a white nose, so he supposed it fit. But there was something about her quick response that tweaked his curiosity. Another layer, perhaps?

"You had that name at the ready," he pointed out.

Gretchen nodded. "I had a stuffed cat that looked like this when I was younger. My dad gave it to me right before he split."

Theo's heart broke every time she dropped another glimpse into her past. So far, nothing she'd shared had been good. Even this memory of her dad giving her a gift was tainted by the man's departure.

"I loved Boots," Gretchen said, still staring at the cat. "I slept with her every night, told her all my silly secrets that seemed so deep and serious at the time."

Theo smiled.

"When Shaw and I went into foster care, Boots was one of the few personal things I took with me, besides my clothes."

Her expression was heavier now, the happiness replaced by sadness.

"Do you still have Boots?"

She shook her head.

"What happened to her?" Theo asked, even though he wasn't sure he wanted to know.

"I was a thirteen-year-old girl clinging to a stuffed cat. Obviously, the other kids saw that as a way to make fun of me. There were several girls in the residential home, and we all shared a large, dorm-like room with three sets of bunkbeds. One of the girls, Marci, was older and pissed off at the world. For some reason, she decided to make me the target of her bullying. One day, after school, I walked into our room and found Boots in a dozen different pieces. She'd torn the cat apart...shredded her, really. She didn't even deny that she'd done it, just told me I was," Gretchen finger-quoted the next part, "'too fucking old for toys.'"

"She was wrong," Theo replied hotly, half tempted to track down this Marci bitch. "You're never too old." He reached over and stroked the cat's head. "I think Boots is the perfect name."

Gretchen nodded, though her smile was much dimmer now. "I agree."

"Do you want anything else to eat? There are at least a half dozen stands we haven't hit." He was trying to return them to the fun they'd been having before, even though his stomach hoped she said no. He spun around as he asked the question, his arms spread wide, gesturing at the booths surrounding them.

He must have moved too quickly and spooked her, because Gretchen flinched as if she was expecting a hit.

His jaw clenched.

Gretchen tried to cover her reaction, shaking her head quickly and groaning. "God, no. That cotton candy was a mistake."

"Yeah. It was." As if to prove it, Theo tossed what was left in the garbage. "Do you want to do anything else, or should we call it a day on the fair?"

"I think I'd like to relax some before tonight's Harvest Dance. It's already been a full day and if I don't sit down for a little while, I'll never make it," she said.

"We can't have that. The dance is the best part of the festival."

"I can't imagine that. Everything has already been super fun."

Reaching out, Theo clasped hands with her, feeling her slight tremble and catching the flash of surprise on her face. For three weeks, he'd toed the line, keeping things light and friendly and painfully platonic because he wanted her to feel at ease and comfortable around him.

However, the story about her beloved stuffed cat bothered him, made him realize how scared and lonely she must have been. He couldn't imagine being cast out of his home at thirteen and thrust into a cold institutional place surrounded by strangers.

Then he considered her move to Gracemont. Once again, she'd come to a new place, all on her own, starting over in a town where she knew no one. While Marci had been a heartless bitch, Theo was determined to make sure she understood she wasn't alone here.

He half expected Gretchen to pull her hand away, so he was delighted when her hand tightened around his instead. He swung their linked hands between them, enjoying the soft laughter his silliness provoked.

"Come on," he said. "I'll walk you back to Edith's."

"You don't have to do that." She started to drop his hand.

He clung to it, not letting go. "I'm parked a couple blocks beyond her house, so it's on my way."

They walked together in silence, though they stopped to chat as they passed a couple of his brothers on their way out. If Maverick or Grayson had an opinion about him holding their new event coordinator's hand, neither of them let on. Of course, Theo didn't fool himself into thinking they wouldn't have more than a few questions about it when he got home. Thus far, he'd kept his feelings for Gretchen to himself, but he wouldn't be able to do that for much longer. His brothers weren't just family; they were his best friends, and he valued their opinions. Right now, he was in bad need of advice on how to proceed with Gretchen.

Like Levi, he didn't have the patience to take things slow or pretend his feelings weren't there. However, that was problematic, given the fact he was Gretchen's boss, and she'd uprooted her whole life to move here. It was unlikely she would be willing to risk her job and new home, despite the fact he was certain this thing between them was the real deal.

Then he was forced to acknowledge that most people didn't approach love the same way the Storm men did, blowing in like a hurricane, taking out every obstacle between them and their woman. And while he was trying to be cognizant of that, it wasn't helping. Not really.

When they reached Edith's, Theo climbed the stairs to the front porch. "Want to sit out here for a minute or two? It's a nice day."

"Sure."

Gretchen let him lead her to the large swing and they sat together, gently swaying back and forth. Fall had finally arrived, the sweltering Indian summer of September giving way to cooler temperatures. Soon, the fall foliage would emerge, painting their mountain in bright oranges, reds, and purples. It was Theo's favorite time of year, and he couldn't wait for Gretchen to see how incredible the view was.

"It's so peaceful here," Gretchen mused.

"Here at Edith's or Gracemont?" he asked.

"Both. Sometimes I feel like I've stepped back in time. The days move slower here."

"Is that a good thing?" Theo wanted Gretchen to love his hometown as much as he did. The more time he spent with her, the more invested he became in the idea of love at first touch. Gretchen had sparked something inside him. Something strong, powerful, wonderful.

"It's a very good thing," she replied. "Which is weird because there were a lot of times at my last job when the days moved slowly, and it felt like torture."

Theo considered that. "I suspect there are plenty of people who feel that way about work. It makes a difference when you love your job."

"Absolutely. While I loved my boss, Brenda, at my previous job, the work was... Well, I swear it would have been more fun watching paint dry."

"I hope that's not the case on Stormy Weather Farm."

She grinned. "Not at all. I love working there. Every day holds something new, and it's always cool and fun and everyone there is so nice."

The way she said *nice* so wistfully, it occurred to him she didn't seem to consider kind people the norm.

Theo rested his arm along the back of the porch swing, his fingers inches from her shoulder. She'd left her long blonde hair down today, and he itched to touch it to see if it was as soft and thick as it looked.

"I suppose your time in foster care must have felt torturous too." Theo was anxious to learn more about her. God, he wanted to know every single thing, including all those childish secrets she'd whispered to the original Boots.

"It wasn't bad at first," she said. "Because Shaw was there for the first two years too. After graduation, he joined the Navy, and that was when it got harder."

"You never saw your parents again?"

Her shoulders drooped slightly, and he considered changing the subject, but he dismissed that thought. Especially when she looked down at the stuffed toy in her hands, one finger stroking the cat's head as if it were real.

"I've seen them since."

"You don't have to talk about this if you don't want to," he offered, not wanting to ruin what had been a really great day.

"No. It's okay. I've talked to Edith about…" She paused, and he got the sense she was trying to decide if she should finish her thought. "Some of it. And it's helped. Before coming here, I didn't really have anyone to share these things with."

How in the hell did a woman this interesting, this intelligent, this beautiful, make it to twenty-four years of age without any friends? Especially considering his three cousins and Kasi had already absorbed her into their girl gang as if she'd been there all along.

"Well, you can talk to me." Theo tugged on both ears, wiggling them. "I'm a great listener."

He hoped to make her smile but instead, her expression remained somber.

"I told you that my dad split when I was five."

Theo nodded.

"Shaw was eight, and he took our dad leaving hard. He became belligerent, acting out at school, talking back to Mom and his teachers. Mom couldn't handle him, so she basically washed her hands of him."

Theo recalled her mentioning Shaw's behavior before. "So, what? She ignored him?"

"You have to understand, my mom was *always* distant and cold, so she didn't really change after Dad left. As far back as I can remember, she was short-tempered and disinterested in us.

Dealing with Shaw was more than she wanted to bother with, so she let him run wild."

"Poor kid," Theo said, even though he wanted to make the word "kid" plural. Gretchen had suffered as well.

"Unfortunately, Mom is one of those women who can't live without a man. She finds her identity through who she's with, preferring to be a kept woman." Gretchen rolled her eyes at the term, her disgust evident. "She was forced to go to work after Dad left to support us, and she hated it, resented that the job of putting food on the table fell to her. She became a cashier at a supermarket, and that was where she found the store manager, Ivan."

Gretchen said the name *Ivan* with even more disgust than *kept woman*. Given she'd already mentioned her stepfather was an abusive bastard, he understood why. He was beginning to suspect who might've physically hurt her.

"She and Ivan married after only a few months of dating because they fed each other's egos in just the right way. She deferred to him on everything, and he got to strut around like lord of the manor."

"He sounds like an asshole."

Gretchen tapped the end of her nose. "You got it in one. He's a judgmental prick, always preaching about how people should live their lives. He's one of those 'it's my way or the highway' douchebags. He and Shaw butted heads from day one."

"And your mom never stepped in?"

Gretchen shook her head. "No. She handed all the discipline over to Ivan, and he quickly moved from yelling at Shaw, to grounding him, to spankings. I *hated* it when Ivan hit him."

"Did he hit you too?" If her answer was yes, Theo would be hard-pressed not to drive to Harrisburg to give Ivan the Asshole a taste of his own medicine, while explaining why children weren't punching bags.

"No."

Theo frowned, surprised by her answer—and even more shocked to realize he believed her.

"Ivan hated Shaw, who received the brunt of his anger. With me," she lifted one shoulder, "he felt complete and utter indifference. Sometimes, I wasn't even sure he knew I was living in the house."

"Did your mother hit you?"

Gretchen shook her head. "She was too busy showering all her affection and attention on Ivan. I was white noise in the background."

How the fuck had Gretchen come out of that kind of environment with her humor and kindness still intact?

Sadly, her responses only added to the list of questions he had about her. "What led to the two of you being placed in foster care?" Theo worried he was pushing his luck, getting too personal, but this was the most information Gretchen had willingly offered in three weeks. Most of his questions about her past had been met with one-word, dismissive responses.

She bit her lip, her grip on the stuffed cat tightening. "Shaw was a late bloomer, so he was still quite small at sixteen. It made it easy for Ivan to...hurt him." Gretchen looked toward the road, no longer holding his gaze. "One night, I heard Shaw cry out. I went to his room and Ivan was...hurting him."

It was the second time she'd used the phrase "hurting him" without saying how. Theo was certain if he pressed for details, she wouldn't give them. He was getting good at recognizing which walls he could scale and which were impenetrable when it came to Gretchen's past.

"Neither one of them saw me in the doorway, so I slipped away and called 9-1-1."

"You didn't get your mother?"

She shook her head. "No. I knew she wouldn't do anything to help Shaw. She always said Ivan knew best. When the cops arrived, they saw Shaw's injuries and arrested Ivan. They wanted to take Shaw to the hospital, but Mom said no. Said he was fine."

"Was he?"

Gretchen sighed. "No. He wasn't. But he was as resistant to seeking treatment as my mom. I tried to convince him, and that was when Mom lost her shit in a big way, turning everything around on *me.*"

"On you?" Theo barked. "What the hell had *you* done wrong?"

"I called the cops over something that was a family matter. Then she unleashed on both of us, calling me and Shaw ungrateful assholes. The cops looked a bit shell-shocked by how vicious she was, considering Shaw's...injuries."

Yeah. There was definitely something more to this story.

"After a few minutes of screaming at us, she turned to the police officers and told them to get us out of her house, or she was tossing us out on the street."

"Jesus," Theo muttered.

"The cops kept trying to get Mom to calm down, trying to explain that if they took us, we'd be put into the foster care system, but she didn't care. She got more and more furious. Finally, Shaw stepped forward, said he wanted to leave. He said anywhere was better than there. After that, the cops stopped arguing with Mom and agreed to take us with them. We went to our rooms, packed a few things and, despite Shaw's protests, they took him to the hospital. A social worker picked us up from there, and that was the first night we spent in the residential home. Because of our ages, and the abuse Shaw suffered, they didn't bother to look for foster parents."

"Why not?" Theo asked.

"The chances of finding someone who would take us both were slim, and they didn't want to split us up. I was scared and clinging to Shaw, who wouldn't let go of me."

Theo was grateful she'd had that one fucking crumb of comfort—if he could call it that. "Shaw sounds like a good brother. I'm glad the two of you had each other."

"He was the best brother. He really looked out for me those first two years...before he graduated."

Theo heard the past tense, and he couldn't help but wonder if it was only the physical distance that left Gretchen and Shaw estranged or if something else had happened.

"Anyway, Ivan spent some time in jail, and he lost his job. After that, he became even more bitter and angry, blaming me and Shaw for ruining his life. A few times since, he's tried to hit me up for money, because God forbid he get another job."

"Did you give it to him?"

She shook her head. "I didn't have it to give. These days, he's a heavy drinker, and my mom is still his biggest defender."

"I hate that you went through all that." Theo reached over to tap a finger on her clenched hands, which were squeezing the hell out of Boots.

His action drew her from her recollections, and she smoothed out the crushed cat. "I'm okay," she said, her tone lighter than it should be, considering what she'd shared. "I learned how to live without parents a long time ago, so it's not like I'm missing them or anything."

She *was* missing something, but considering she'd never received motherly love, she didn't realize it.

Leaning closer, he bumped his shoulder against hers. "I'm not sure you're going to *keep* living without family. Edith has already claimed you as hers, and I have a feeling my mom is on her way to adopting you as well."

Gretchen smiled, her hand rising to cover her mouth. "I'm claiming Edith, too, because she's amazing. And I wouldn't mind your mom adopting me," she confessed. "Porch time is awesome."

Theo chuckled. Gretchen had been introduced to his mother's porch time earlier this week. As part of the B&B's offerings, Mom held what she called "porch time" every day starting at three-thirty for the guests. It was basically a happy hour with Lightning in a Bottle wine and Rain or Shine beer, along with some light snacks. Guests could join her on the porch for a drink and to enjoy the view and good conversation.

Gretchen had accidentally happened upon it this week when she walked over to the B&B to ask Mom a quick catering question. Ninety minutes later, Theo had been ready to send out a search party when a tipsy Gretchen returned, apologizing profusely, even as Theo laughed.

"Mom does love her porch time. I swear she purposely finds something worthy of celebrating every day of her life, simply so she can open a bottle of wine."

"That doesn't sound like a bad way to live," Gretchen said.

Theo hadn't really thought about it, but he realized she had a point. "You're right. It doesn't. Did I ever tell you the story of how my parents met?"

Gretchen shook her head.

"They met at the town's annual Fourth of July picnic. Mom was staying in Gracemont that summer with her great-aunt."

"She's not originally from here?" Gretchen asked.

"Nope. Like you, she's a transplant. Dad took one look at her and fell madly in love. He asked her out for a date right then and there, and two weeks later, he proposed."

"Two weeks?!" Gretchen was as astounded as everyone else he'd ever told this story to. "And she said yes?"

Theo chuckled. "Well, yeah. Obviously. Dad said he

wanted to propose at the picnic, but figured he should get a ring first."

"Wow." She leaned back, shaking her head. "So it was love at first sight, huh?"

He'd caught Gretchen reading romance novels on her lunch break on more than one occasion, so he suspected—hoped—she was a fan of the concept.

"Yep. Dad swears it's a real thing. Levi, however, believes in something a little different."

"What's that?" she asked.

"Love at first touch. Levi has known Kasi her whole life, but this summer, when the heat got to her one day, she passed out. Levi caught her—and he said it was like he'd been struck by lightning. He held her in his arms, and he just knew." Theo forced a carefree grin, not wanting to give away the fact he'd experienced the same earth-shaking realization the second he shook Gretchen's hand.

"Knew what?" she whispered.

"That she was his."

"It must be nice to be so sure of your feelings like that," she said.

"It took Levi a bit of work to convince Kasi his feelings were sincere."

"Longer than two weeks?" Gretchen asked, clearly joking.

"Yep. Took Levi three whole weeks."

Gretchen's eyes widened when her joke backfired. "Sounds like you Storm men are relentless."

Theo laughed, tempted to start showing her how relentless they were.

Firsthand.

"That we are. But I haven't finished telling you about my parents. Because Mom tells their love story a little differently."

"How so?"

"When Dad introduced himself, he also included the fact that his family owned and operated a winery. According to her, that was all she wrote."

Gretchen laughed loudly, covering her mouth again.

Theo reached out before he could stop himself and pulled her hand down. "Don't do that."

Her brows furrowed in confusion. "Do what?"

"You have a beautiful smile and a beautiful laugh. Why cover them up?"

Gretchen glanced down at their hands. "I didn't realize I was." He could see the earnestness in her response. "I'll try to stop."

"Good. You should never hide your happiness. And don't worry, you'll have plenty of chances to practice," he reassured her.

"I will?"

Theo wrapped his arm around her shoulders, tucking her against him. "Of course. Because you're hanging out with me, and I'm freaking hilarious."

Gretchen giggled, her eyes twinkling with mirth. "I guess you *are* kinda funny...looking."

"Is that right?" Theo tightened his grip, holding her in place as he ruffled her hair playfully, as punishment for her joke.

Gretchen froze for a split second, but the tension was mercifully brief before she started to fight him off, laughing loudly, the two of them tussling like a couple of teenagers.

They stopped when they heard the screen door open.

Edith spotted them, rolling her eyes in amusement at their antics. "When you're finished flirting, Theodore Storm, I need help loading my pies into the car for tonight's dance."

They untangled themselves, rising, both intent on lending her a hand. Edith walked back into the house, but before Gretchen could follow, he reached out, lightly grasping her wrist.

"Save a dance for me tonight." He probably should have worded that as a request rather than an outright demand, but he was desperate to hold her in his arms, and dancing felt like the easiest, quickest way to get there.

Gretchen pulled her wrist away, and he was subjected to the first serious bit of reticence he'd seen from her all day. "I don't dance."

"You do tonight. With me." Theo stepped closer, slowly moving into her personal space. If she tried to put distance between them, he would stop, but Gretchen held her ground.

Actually, she did one better, drawing in a slow, deep breath, then shifting a miniscule bit closer to him, though her actions felt more like her testing herself rather than tempting him.

Even after everything he'd learned about her upbringing, Theo still felt as if he was in the dark. Today, he'd pulled back one layer of the onion, but there were too many left to go.

"Okay. I'll save you a dance," she whispered, her gaze drifting to his lips.

Fuck him. There was no way he was going to be able to hold himself back for much longer if she kept daring him to kiss her.

Unfortunately, she stepped away before he could throw caution to the wind, wrap his hand around her neck, and kiss her with reckless abandon.

She turned, starting to head into the house again. "After all, I suppose I should take pity on you. Since you're so funny," she paused for effect, "looking."

"Shameless hussy," he called out after her as she took off

running, slamming the screen door in his face when he started to give chase.

Gretchen laughed loudly as she turned to face him through the door, her smile completely unobstructed by her hand.

Beautiful.

Chapter Eight

Gretchen walked around the event barn, taking an inventory of the tables and chairs that had been delivered. She wanted to make sure they'd received the full order and nothing had arrived damaged. She was on week five of Operation New Life, and every day kept getting better and better.

She and Edith truly *were* becoming besties. Most evenings, the two of them worked together in the kitchen, cooking dinner, drinking wine, and talking about their days. Edith was an amazing cook, and she'd been teaching Gretchen how to make some of her "world famous" recipes.

Since coming clean to Edith about her parents and Shaw and Briggs, they'd spent a great deal of time talking about what Gretchen had gone through, and Edith had offered insights that left her thinking differently about everything that had happened, and her emotions and reactions toward those events. She'd encouraged Gretchen to stop viewing herself as a victim or helpless, but as a survivor, someone who'd emerged stronger and wiser.

Edith had missed her calling, because she would have made one hell of a therapist.

Manny dined with them at least three times a week. Like Edith, he was a born storyteller, so most nights ended with the three of them falling about, laughing their asses off.

The Storm family had also taken her under their wing, including her in all their fun after-hours plans. They were huge fans of cookouts and firepits, so in a little over a month, Gretchen had found herself chowing down on grilled burgers and hot dogs around a bonfire no less than five times. She was becoming quite the accomplished s'mores connoisseur, as she and Remi experimented with different flavors of graham crackers, marshmallows, and chocolate bars.

Gretchen had even finally succumbed to Remi's demand to go horseback riding a couple of weeks earlier, and while it was completely terrifying at the beginning, she was sorry when the ride ended. The horse Remi had paired her with had been gentle and so sweet that Gretchen had taken to stopping by the stable every day with a treat for the dear old girl.

But while she'd opened up to Edith, Gretchen still wasn't comfortable talking about Briggs with anyone else. She was trying to take Edith's advice, to stop thinking of herself as stupid—something that had been literally pounded into her head for years—but it was a hard habit to break. Waiting for the other shoe to drop had become second nature to her.

So even though Remi, Kasi, Mila, and Nora had begun to include Gretchen in their BFFs text group, and they'd been incredibly generous in sharing their clothes with her, Gretchen still found herself holding back.

It only took a couple of weeks of Gretchen showing up for work in the same two pairs of jeans and a staff shirt before the girls realized how small her wardrobe was. She'd tried to brush it off as simply not being able to afford much, and luckily, they'd bought the lie. In truth, she was too afraid to spend her money on clothing, stashing away as much as she could for...

God. Would she ever truly feel safe anywhere? Ever stop hoarding money just in case she had to run again?

A couple Fridays earlier, Nora had grabbed her at the end of work and dragged her to the house she shared with her sisters, where all three Storm girls went through their closets, pulling things out, demanding she try them on, then giving them to her if they fit and looked good. She'd gone home that night with two enormous trash bags full of the most beautiful pants, blouses, skirts, scarves, and shoes she'd ever owned—and she'd cried as she unpacked it all, hating that even after all their generosity, she couldn't trust their motives for helping her.

She'd once thought Destiny was her friend, too...so when she'd betrayed Gretchen to Briggs, her ability to trust *anyone* took a big hit.

Part of Gretchen worried that Remi, Mila, Nora, and Kasi were simply being nice because she was an employee and new in town. Eventually, they'd either get bored of her or show their true colors, and she'd be dropped from the text thread. As such, she tried to keep herself from growing too close to them, because she knew how much it hurt to lose someone she considered a friend.

However, that same reticence didn't hold true for Theo. He'd remained true to his promise to teach her to drive, and while there had been some heart-thumping near-crashes—she was shit at parallel parking—he'd been nothing but patient and encouraging. She was currently reading the DMV driver's manual and, if all went well, she was hoping to take the test to get her license early next year. Not that it would matter, because she wasn't in a financial position to buy a car, but at least it was a step in the right direction toward becoming more independent.

Theo was the polar opposite of Briggs, who'd always been too serious and stern. In the beginning, she'd chalked up her ex's stoicism to his age. After all, Briggs was twenty years older than her. Now she could see what she considered maturity, had really been another form of control, as he constantly admonished what he considered youthful behavior, telling her he wanted to be with a *woman*, not a girl.

If she'd had a backbone back then, she would have pointed out that at eighteen, she *was* a girl.

She shut down that self-recrimination, recalling Edith's advice. She'd told Gretchen one of the first steps to healing was to reframe her thoughts. While she hadn't had the courage to speak up back then, each painful experience had been building her strength, instilling in her the bravery she possessed now. She may not have had a backbone then...but she was growing one.

Unlike Briggs, Theo didn't seek to change her behavior; rather, he encouraged her to express herself, building her confidence by supporting her ideas, laughing at her jokes, and offering genuine friendship. Given her issues, she wasn't quite sure why Theo was exempt from her characteristic need to keep a distance from new acquaintances. It had taken him less than a week to draw her out of her shell, and less than two weeks for her to consider him a real friend.

Most shockingly, she was beginning to trust Theo—something Briggs had never truly earned. Even when Briggs came to take her from the foster home, proclaiming love, she'd lived in a constant state of fear, expecting him to abandon her like everyone else. And when he started emotionally, then physically abusing her, she realized she'd been right to hold her trust in reserve.

Gretchen leaned against one of the barn walls, her gaze rising to the strings of twinkle lights she and Theo had hung up last week. They'd decided to make them a permanent part of the décor, since it would be too much of a pain in the ass to take them up and down. They figured if people renting the barn didn't want to use them, they didn't have to plug them in.

The lights reminded her of the ones strung up in the Gracemont Community Center the night of the Harvest Dance. Theo had warned her the event, which marked the finale of the weekend-long celebration, was a big deal, and he'd been right. It felt as if every single resident of the small town had managed to pack themselves onto the dance floor.

Theo had claimed the dance she promised him. Actually, he'd claimed nearly *all* the dances—with the exception of the one she shared with Manny, who had playfully spun her around, jitterbug-style, until she was light-headed and dizzy.

She hadn't lied to Theo when she said she didn't dance. Briggs hated dancing, claiming he wasn't about to make a jackass of himself. He was always overly concerned with appearances and how others perceived him. Whenever they attended social events that included dancing, she was forced to sit next to him, watching everyone else have fun on the dance floor.

She had foolishly tried to join in a few times in the early years, but Briggs always lost his shit, screaming at her the entire way home, claiming she'd been acting like a slut, putting on a show for the other men. In the end, she'd simply stopped dancing because it wasn't worth the hassle.

The night of the Fall Harvest Dance, she never left the floor, drawn into the huge circle of Storms who were all shaking their booties and trying to one-up each other with their crazy dance moves. She still wasn't sure if she was impressed or horrified by the fact Jace knew every single step to the "Thriller" dance. He seriously could have given Michael Jackson a run for his money.

When the first slow song played, Theo had been right there, claiming his dance. She hadn't anticipated the effect it would have on her when he pulled her into his arms, softly humming along to Ed Sheeran's "Thinking out Loud."

Gretchen had been playing that song on repeat ever since that night, recalling Theo's strength and confidence as he led her around the floor. She'd shivered when he placed his hand on her back, his thumb lightly caressing her as they swayed. His cheek had rested against hers, the roughness of his beard sexier than she would have imagined. She hadn't expected him to pull her so close, thinking he would maintain a more proper distance, considering his whole family was there and she was his employee.

Then she realized she felt safe in his arms. She hadn't experienced a single tremor of fear or panic or anxiety. Just warmth and security and...arousal.

As they danced, his breath was hot against her cheek, her chest pressed tightly to his. And the best part was, that had only been one of at least half a dozen slow dances they'd shared that night. He hadn't asked a single other woman to dance. Just her. Her heart fluttered even now as she thought of it.

Ugh.

Gretchen shook herself out of her reveries, trying to shut down feelings she really should *not* be feeling in regard to Theo Storm. There were a million reasons why she should ignore this attraction to her boss, and zero reasons why she should succumb to it. The most they could ever be was friends.

The problem was, she was letting herself get swept away by all these new, unexpected, wonderful feelings because, for the first time in her life, she wasn't afraid or lonely. In five short weeks, she'd started to feel happy. After a lifetime of shit, she couldn't make herself push away something that felt so good.

New Gretchen had apparently kicked old Gretchen, with her trust issues and pessimism, to the curb.

Personally, she blamed the romance books she was addicted to, as well as the rom coms she'd been watching with Edith. For so many years, her beloved books had truly felt like fiction because she was certain those beautiful relationships didn't exist in the real world. Now, as she watched Levi and Kasi together, and as she recalled the story Theo had told her about how his parents met, she found herself wanting to believe in love at first sight or touch.

Because there was no denying the second Theo had touched her hand the first day they met, her world had changed.

She tried to tell herself she needed to proceed with caution, because she'd thought Briggs was going to be the hero of her story and that she was in love with him. Looking back now, she wasn't so sure. She'd been eighteen years old, for pity's sake. She'd never been kissed, and she had been terribly, *terribly* lonely and scared.

What she felt for Briggs had been less about love and more about gratitude. Because she was grateful to be seen and wanted. Two things that hadn't happened before he came along.

So, in reality, she knew *nothing* about love. Except that she wanted it. Desperately. But she couldn't be an idiot about it—and she couldn't let herself fall in love with Theo.

Period.

End of sentence.

He was her boss, and she needed this job. On top of that, she needed time to sort her shit out. Given the fact she was standing here, still comparing Briggs and Theo, proved her ex had done one hell of a number on her. And that was *after* her abandonment issues, thanks to Dad and all the horrors inflicted by her mom and Ivan. Talking to Edith was helping, but she was by no means healed, so it was time to put this unwise attraction to Theo in the rearview mirror.

Unfortunately—or fortunately—Theo was determined to spend as much time as possible with her, and while he wasn't overtly coming on to her, there was definitely some flirting.

"There you are."

Speak of the devil.

Gretchen's stupid heart flickered the second she heard Theo's voice. Turning, she smiled as he walked into the barn.

"Inventory all good?"

"Yep. Just finished. We got what we ordered, and I think it looks nice. I was taking a quick look around to make sure everything was okay for tomorrow's meeting."

Theo scanned the interior of the barn. "Tomorrow?"

"Jenny Wilson is coming to check out the space," she said.

"That's right. I forgot about that."

Now that the barn was ready for business, they had posted an inquiry form on the website. They'd already started getting some interest from people about renting. Jenny Wilson was one of the first to bite. She was hoping to use the barn three mornings a week for a yoga class she planned to offer, certain that the incredible view from the mountain would create a peaceful environment. If things worked out, and Jenny rented the space, Gretchen was considering signing up for the early morning class herself. She could use a little mindfulness in her life.

So far, they'd already booked two other events, including a family reunion and a spring wedding. Gretchen, with Everett's marketing help, had begun advertising the barn rental, and each day was bringing them more and more inquiries. It was her personal goal to book an event for every single weekend by the end of next year. She had no idea if it was feasible, but she was determined to give it all she had.

"It looks terrific in here," Theo said, stepping over to plug in the web of twinkle lights. While it was midafternoon, the sky was overcast and dark. It was the perfect day to curl up on a couch under a blanket to read.

"What are you doing?"

"It's dark in here. Besides, I like the look of them. Reminds me of my junior prom." Theo walked to the middle of the floor to stand under them.

"Oh yeah?"

"Did you go to prom?" he asked.

She shook her head. There had been funds to buy her a dress if she wanted to go, but no one asked, and Briggs had told her it was too dangerous for her to be out that night, as too many teens got drunk and then behind the wheel of a car.

Fuck, she mentally chastised herself. *Enough with Briggs already*.

Theo gave her one of his charming grins, and the butterflies he set loose in her stomach took flight. "I went with Renee Cameron."

"Let me guess. Cheerleader?" Gretchen teased.

Theo shook his head. "Nope. Renee was captain of the debate team and valedictorian of our class. Super-smart and sweet. I sat next to her in anatomy class, and she let me copy her homework whenever I forgot to do it."

Gretchen laughed. "And how often was that?"

Theo wiggled his eyebrows. "I was sixteen years old with a strong aversion to being inside. Me and my brand-new driver's license spent a lot of time cruising around town in my dad's pickup truck with a bunch of my buddies, looking for girls or trouble. We weren't picky about which."

"What constituted trouble for you?"

Theo crossed his arms, drawing her attention to those beautiful, thick biceps of his. "Smoking cigarettes behind the school, sneaking beer from our folks, drag racing on the straight stretch of road behind Roscoe Prescott's farm, shit like that."

"Ohhhh. So you were a bad boy."

"What do you mean *were*?" Theo joked. "There's nothing past tense about my bad boy ways."

"Is that right?" she drawled.

He crooked his finger at her. "Come here, wallflower."

She was, in fact, still hanging out next to the wall, foolishly thinking that keeping a distance would help her resist him. But Gretchen was helpless to stop herself, so she walked closer. She stopped a few feet away, and as was becoming his habit, he cut the distance, moving close enough that she had to tilt her head back slightly to look up at him.

His gaze dropped to her lips, and Gretchen resisted the urge to lick them.

She couldn't remember the last time she'd been kissed without fear lacing the touch. Kissing had stopped being about *her* a long time ago and was simply one of the ways she tried to make a miserable, abusive man happy.

If she kissed Theo...

Kissing him would be *all* for her. Her desires. Her pleasure.

She'd bet every penny she had he was a great kisser.

Gretchen took a step away, needing to put space between them before she did something really stupid.

She cleared her throat. "Um. So, were you and Renee one of those high school power couples or something?"

Theo shook his head. "No. Truthfully, I needed a date for prom. It was the only time we ever went out. She was a little too nice for me."

Gretchen narrowed her eyes. "Are you saying she wouldn't put out?"

Theo barked a loud laugh. When she first arrived on the farm, his boisterous laughter had triggered her. Loud noises always reminded her of Briggs yelling or slamming doors. After five weeks of hearing Theo's laughter almost daily, she was no longer shaken by it.

"Jesus," Theo said. "While I liked to pretend I was a stud and lady killer in high school, the truth is, I probably would have shit myself if Renee wanted to have sex with me. What I meant about her being too nice is, she wouldn't even let me hold her hand or kiss her, and despite the fact prom didn't end until midnight, she still had a ten o'clock curfew because she had to be up early for church the next day. I wound up driving her home, then going back to the school gym to finish the dance stag."

"You're starting to sound less like a bad boy," she teased.

He ruffled her hair, something else she was becoming accustomed to, along with his shoulder bumps, and the way he placed his hand on the small of her back, and how he always offered a hand to help her in and out of his truck during their driving lessons.

Theo found countless ways to touch her, and while it had taken a bit of practice at the beginning not to stiffen or flinch, now she adored his sweet touches as much as his laugh.

"I was a late bloomer when it came to sex," Theo confessed. "Didn't lose my virginity until I was seventeen. Fell madly in love with Sandy Jenkins, and the two of us dated most of our senior year."

Theo had proven himself to be one of those open-book types of people, often recounting stories from his past, even embarrassing ones. She'd discovered there was nothing he wouldn't share if she asked. "Why did that relationship end?"

"Sandy went off to college and I stayed in Gracemont. Neither of us was interested in a long-distance romance. Especially considering she had no plans to return to town after getting her degree, and I was never leaving the farm.

She lives outside of D.C. now with her husband and three kids."

"She was your first love?"

"Yep. First, but not last. I was pretty good at falling in and out of love in my early twenties, but looking back now, I think it was safer to say I was falling in and out of lust," he added with a shameless wink.

She laughed. "Wait. Are you saying you haven't had a serious girlfriend since high school?"

Theo shrugged. "I've done a fair bit of dating, and there were a few women I might have considered girlfriends, though none of the relationships were serious. No discussions of moving in together or rings or stuff like that."

"Is that something you want?"

"Marriage?" Theo asked, as if surprised by her question. "Hell yeah. I definitely want to settle down and have a family."

Gretchen wasn't sure why that answer pleased her so much. It wasn't like she could toss her name into that hat.

Boss. Job.

She repeated those reasons again, wishing Theo wasn't so hot. And nice. And such a good dancer.

"What about you? Any hot-and-heavy relationships in your past?"

It felt as if Theo had dumped a bucket of ice water over her head. She'd surprised herself following the Fall Harvest Festival fair by opening up to Theo about her dysfunctional family. And while she hadn't shared all of it, she'd certainly given him a pretty good peek at her upbringing.

However, that was as much as she was comfortable talking about. The idea of speaking Briggs's name aloud to Theo made her stomach hurt. He was a part of her past she wasn't proud of, that she was truly ashamed of, actually. And while she was trying to reframe those emotions, she hadn't succeeded yet.

She liked the way Theo looked at her. He didn't see a weak, spineless victim. Instead, he saw a strong, confident woman.

She preferred that. *Needed* it.

Because she found herself becoming the woman he saw.

She couldn't lose that.

Not yet.

She shook her head, aware she'd let too much silence follow his question. "I haven't dated much."

It wasn't a lie. With the exception of Briggs, she hadn't dated at all.

"Well," she said, turning away from him. "I guess everything is in good shape here. I should head back to the office. I have a few emails I need to respond to, and Everett wants to show me some graphics he's been working on for the event barn."

She heard Theo's soft sigh, and she felt the slightest twinge of guilt for shutting down their conversation.

Gretchen paused when he placed his hand on her shoulder, glancing back at him.

"Maybe one day you'll feel comfortable enough to tell me all your secrets."

"Some secrets are best left unspoken."

She shouldn't have said that—because it was clear from his expression it only sparked his curiosity. His brows furrowed, but before he could reply, a loud crash of thunder pierced the quiet.

"Shit!" Gretchen jerked in surprise, even though she knew the weather forecast had been calling for afternoon thunderstorms.

She shivered, her heart suddenly racing. So when Theo opened his arms wide, Gretchen moved toward him before she could think better of her actions.

The thunder had sounded too much like the slamming of

her front door in Harrisburg, which was always a precursor to pain.

Gretchen looped her arms around his back, resting her cheek on his chest. Hugs hadn't been a common occurrence in her life, so it was impossible to resist whenever Theo offered one. Apparently he—and his family—were big huggers, because she couldn't recall a day in the past few weeks where she hadn't gotten at least a couple.

Theo wrapped his arms around her, tucking her close. "Hey. It's okay. Just a little storm."

She tried to pull herself together, but then there was a bright flash of lightning and another boom of thunder.

She closed her eyes, hating that she was letting the storm trigger her.

Theo ran his hands up and down her back, murmuring comforting words.

"I don't like storms."

Theo tightened his hold, letting her remain there, safe in his arms for a full ten minutes.

When her racing heart finally slowed, she lifted her head from his chest.

At the same moment, Theo looked down at her, their faces only an inch or so apart.

Gretchen wasn't sure who moved first.

One second, they were staring at each other...the next, Theo's lips were on hers.

One of his hands rose, cupping the back of her head. It was a gentle touch, but damn if it didn't pack one hell of a punch. With that one hand and the slow, soft glide of his lips over hers, she felt cherished and safe, two things that had been painfully scarce in her lifetime.

She wrapped her arms around his shoulders, running her fingers through his thick hair as he upped the ante on the kiss, his lips parting, his tongue stroking her lower lip. She opened for him, drinking in his sweet breath.

With one arm still wrapped around her back, Theo pulled her body tighter against his, and she felt his hardness against her stomach. Desire warred with common sense, and she didn't have a clue which was going to come out on top.

She'd just finished telling herself this couldn't happen, but when another roar of thunder pierced the silence, she pushed even closer, her kisses becoming hungrier, harder.

Theo closed his fingers around her hair, using that grip to tilt her head, his lips firmer as he gave Gretchen her first taste of true passion.

She lost all sense of place and time, but she didn't care. She didn't want this to end. Because she knew the second they parted, her brain would engage, and she'd have to walk away from him.

Theo must have realized that as well, because he showed no signs of stopping. She trembled with arousal when he hummed, low and deep, as overwhelmed by this kiss as Gretchen.

Finally, years later, the need to breathe forced them to part.

Gretchen lowered her gaze, overwhelmed by him.

"Look at me," he demanded.

She raised her eyes, her face flushed from the heat of the kiss and now the aftermath. What the hell was she supposed to say?

Every bit of discomfort vanished the moment she saw Theo's handsome face, his kind eyes, his sweet grin.

When he cupped her cheek with one large hand, she melted because...fuck. Everything he did was Romance Hero 101 stuff, and she couldn't resist.

Theo drew his thumb over her lower lip, which felt puffy following those hot-and-heavy kisses.

"I've wanted to do that since the first time I saw you."

Gretchen blinked, trying to decide if he'd really said that or if she was hallucinating due to the lack of air after that twenty-minute kiss.

"I…" she started, clearing her throat. She could either be honest and tell him she'd wanted the same thing—because she had—or she could start to do damage control. "I'm not sure that was a smart thing to do."

She held her breath, afraid Theo would get angry. But instead, his grin morphed into a full-fledged smile, and he even chuckled.

"Gretchen, I can assure you, that's the smartest thing I've *ever* done in my life."

She shook her head. "Theo." Time to dig herself out of this hole.

"No," he said, her tone clueing him in to what was coming next. "You don't need to say any of that."

"That?"

"You know what," he replied.

"I think I *do* need to say it."

Theo pressed his forehead against hers. At some point, his hands had found their way to her waist. "You don't," he reasserted. "I know all the reasons why you think what we did was a mistake."

"You do?"

"I'm your boss. You need this job. You don't want to screw things up."

Her shoulders relaxed, grateful he'd said the words she didn't have the strength to say. "Then you agree what we just did…" Flames licked her cheeks. Her experience with kissing and men was limited to one man, an asshole, so she was floundering. "It can't happen again."

Theo's hands tightened on her waist, pulling her lower

body against his. She could still feel his erection, pressing against the front of his jeans.

"No. I don't agree with that at all," he said. "But that's because I know something you don't."

Gretchen tilted her head. "What's that?"

"You're mine."

She blinked a few times, now *convinced* that none of this was real. Maybe she'd passed out from a lack of air. Or maybe Theo wasn't here at all, and she was actually in her bed at Edith's having one hell of an awesome dream.

Gretchen reached out, pressing her hands against his chest. He was muscular, his body firm from hard physical labor on the farm, and she was overcome by the desire to see him with his shirt off. She had a feeling he was ripped. However, that touch let her know just how real this was.

"Yours?" she whispered, that assertion equal parts amazing and terrifying. She couldn't be his, and not just for the reasons he'd already listed. She wasn't ready to jump into a relationship with anyone right now. Briggs had broken her, and she was only starting to put herself back together.

If she was a stronger person, she'd explain that to Theo, but the words shriveled inside her.

"Mine," Theo repeated, backing his declaration with a soft kiss.

Gretchen told herself it was time to put a stop to this, but her traitorous lips had their own opinion, welcoming his tongue back into her mouth.

He was only the second man she'd ever kissed, and he had set the bar so high, no other man could ever surpass it.

When Theo broke the kiss, she sighed heavily.

"I can't be yours." She hated how thin her voice sounded. Saying those words cost her something, because all the common sense in the world couldn't convince her heart not to wish she *could* belong to him.

Theo lightly wrapped his hand around the back of her neck, prepared to pull her back into their kiss, but the touch…

Her breath seized and her heart raced as she flashed back to Briggs's hands around her throat, choking her, withholding all air until she nearly passed out. Every time he did it, she was certain that would be the day she died, but he never let it go that far, always releasing her to slump to the ground, gasping and coughing.

On the darkest day of her life, she'd wished he would go all the way, let her find peace in death.

The day after that horrible event was the day Brenda saw the bruises and knew the truth. Her questions, and the way she'd held Gretchen as she sobbed, had pulled her from those dangerous, dark thoughts and sparked the tiniest hope that there might be a way out.

Gretchen shoved Theo's arm away, stepping back, trying not to let him see her sudden panic. Given the way his smile faded, his eyes narrowing with concern, it was safe to say she'd failed.

"I can't…" she started, struggling to finish her thought.

Can't kiss you.

Can't be yours.

Can't be anyone's.

The last thought hurt. A lot.

Pain mingled with the growing panic attack.

She hadn't had one since the night she'd come clean to Edith about her past. Foolishly, she believed that talking to Edith had somehow chased them away for good. She should have known better.

She drew in a breath, but it was too short, too shallow, no air penetrating her lungs.

Fuck.

She took another step away from him, then another, fully prepared to race all the way down this mountain to keep him from seeing her fall apart, thunderstorm be damned.

Theo held his hands up in surrender. "Stop, Gretchen."

Her feet listened, even though the rest of her screamed, *Run!*

"Take a breath, kitten."

Kitten?

The term of endearment caught her off guard, distracted her enough that she was able to draw in a deeper breath.

"Good girl," Theo praised her. "Now, take another."

Good girl distracted her even more.

She was a sucker for romance novels with strong men, who whispered sweet, sexy words in the heroine's ear. She'd learned through those books that she had a praise kink, as those sex scenes were the ones that pushed all her hot buttons. She supposed it made sense, considering kindness hadn't played much of a role in her past. She soaked in his proud tone like she was dying of thirst, and he was a tall glass of ice-cold water.

He kept encouraging her to breathe until she felt the weight on her chest ease and the panic pass.

Once she was more in control, she remained in the middle of the room, feeling like the world's biggest fool.

Satisfied she was no longer a flight risk, Theo walked past her, returning with two of the new chairs she'd inventoried.

"Sit down, kitten."

She dropped heavily into the chair. Then he put his in front of her and sat as well. He kept a few feet between them, something she hated as much as she was grateful for.

"Sorry," she murmured.

"For what?"

Gretchen shrugged. How could she explain the leap she'd taken from kissing him to nearly having a panic attack?

She felt Theo studying her face, but she wasn't brave enough to look him in the eye.

"You don't have anything to be sorry for," he said at last. "I'm the one who should be apologizing to *you*."

That comment had her gaze rising.

"The problem is," he said, a soft smile curving his lips. "I'm not sorry for kissing you."

Gretchen wasn't sure why, but that confession pleased her. Despite all the shit floating around inside her, she liked knowing he enjoyed the kiss as much as she did.

Regardless...

"We can't kiss again."

Theo rubbed his jaw, drawing her attention to his beard. Her lips tingled. She probably had a bit of beard burn around her mouth, something she'd have to hide from Eagle Eyes Edith, or she'd be subjected to a major inquisition.

"You're right, and we won't kiss again," Theo said, his words crushing her...until he added, "today."

She huffed out a breathy laugh, trying to sound annoyed but failing miserably.

Theo took her hand in his. "Tell me what triggered that attack."

"Theo."

"Tell me what. I need to know. You don't have to say anything more than that."

She bit her lower lip, then gave him what he asked for. "Your hand wrapped around my neck."

Theo winced. "I'll never touch you that way again. I promise."

"Thank you," she whispered, hating that she was still so broken.

"We're going to stick a pin in the rest of this for now, because I think you need time to consider what I said."

"Okay." Gretchen did need time to wrap her head around him boldly proclaiming she was his. The last time a man said he wanted her...

She shoved that thought aside. She needed to stop comparing Theo to Briggs. If she continued down that path, she'd never be able to trust any relationship. Loneliness had played too big a role in her past. She would not let it take over her future as well.

"Well, look at that." Theo pointed behind her. She turned, looking outside through the open barn doors. "A rainbow."

She hadn't even realized the storm had passed. She smiled at the beauty of the colorful arc, painted across the now-blue sky.

"Feels like a good omen, doesn't it?" Theo asked.

Looking back at him, she nodded.

Because it did.

Chapter Nine

Theo clicked mindlessly, searching for something to watch on TV, even though he wasn't actually interested in viewing anything. He'd mainly turned on the television hoping for a mindless escape, but he could see now that wasn't going to happen. He had too much on his mind to concentrate on anything that wasn't Gretchen Banks.

A week had passed since that kiss in the barn, and he'd spent every moment since then reliving it. Because it had been one hell of a kiss. He hadn't lied when he told Gretchen he'd longed to do that since the day they'd met, but he hadn't intended to lay one on her quite so soon...or quite so passionately.

He'd been telling himself since her arrival in September that he needed to approach Gretchen slowly, build a friendship with her first, let her get to know him better, and make sure she felt more comfortable in her position and her life here in Gracemont before letting his Storm side out.

So fucking much for that.

When she rushed into his arms, he felt her trembling, afraid of the thunder, and his protective, possessive nature took over. The kiss had solidified what he already knew. Gretchen was his. There wasn't a doubt in his mind.

The problem was, she was carrying around some heavy secrets, things she still wasn't ready to share with him.

He'd kicked his own ass for seven days straight, hating himself for scaring her so badly. Theo had known from the beginning that she had triggers, the flinching when he moved too fast or laughed too loud. He should have proceeded with caution, but that kiss...

He'd lost his head and touched her in a way that frightened her.

He couldn't do that again. Wouldn't.

While he'd managed to calm her down before her panic attack became full-blown, the fear in her eyes had absolutely gutted him.

Theo had continued to spend time with her at work and he hadn't canceled the driving lessons, but he'd forced himself to return to "friend mode," keeping an appropriate distance and eschewing all talk about his feelings.

He hated every single second of it.

Theo glanced up when he heard the front screen door open.

"Hey." Levi walked into the house, peering through the double doors that connected the living room to the foyer. He was carrying a bushel of apples. "Did a fair amount of picking in the orchard today. Thought I'd share the bounty."

Theo nodded his thanks, then listened as his brother carried the apples down the hall and into the kitchen before returning a minute later.

"Everyone still planning to go to the costume party at Whiskey Abbey's tonight?" Levi dropped down next to him on the couch, propping his feet up on the coffee table next to Theo's.

"Yeah. Jace and Sam spent the better part of the afternoon discussing their costumes. They're coming as the Blues Brothers."

Levi chuckled. "Kasi put together a couple's costume for us too. She's been working on it for days, determined to win a prize."

"What are you coming as, or is it a surprise?"

"No surprise." Levi ran a hand through his long hair. Ordinarily, he pinned it up, but today, it was hanging loose over his shoulders. "You're looking at the Han Solo half of a *Star Wars* power couple."

"Is Princess Leia sporting *New Hope* buns or *Return of the Jedi* braids?"

"Buns," Levi replied, grinning widely.

"Sounds great." Theo's reply must've lacked the right level of enthusiasm, because Levi's eyes narrowed with concern.

"You okay?"

Theo started to nod but wound up shaking his head instead. He hadn't told anyone about the kiss. Hell, he hadn't come right out and told any of his brothers that Gretchen was the one, though he hadn't exactly been hiding it. He'd caught more than a few curious glances from Sam and Jace at the brewery whenever he and Gretchen were together. Probably because Theo was constantly coming up with excuses to see her at the office, and he invited her to join them in all their after-hours shenanigans, and whenever she was in the vicinity, he was stuck to her side like she'd bathed in super glue.

"What's going on?" Levi asked.

"It's Gretchen," he said miserably, confused when his big brother chuckled.

"You figured it out, huh?"

He narrowed his eyes. "Figured what out?"

"That's she's the one."

Theo snorted. "Shit. I figured that out the day we met."

Levi leaned back against the couch cushions, clearly settling in for a long story.

Before Theo could launch into it, Sam, Jace, and Maverick walked into the living room.

Sam, astute as always, homed in on Theo's stressed-out expression—and Levi's too-pleased one—and connected the dots quickly. "Is he finally ready to tell us about Gretchen?"

Levi nodded. "You got here just in time."

"Am I that transparent?" Theo asked, even though he knew in this case, he was.

"Jesus. You all but hung a sign around her neck that said Property of Theo Storm the first week she was here," Jace joked.

Then Maverick chimed in. "I reached out to shake her hand when you introduced us, and I swear to God you growled under your breath."

Theo didn't think he'd made a noise, though there was certainly a chance he had. Maverick had a reputation as a ladies' man around town, and while he'd never been the jealous sort, Theo's vision had gone a bit red at the idea of Maverick working his charm on Gretchen.

"You're with her every damn day," Jace added. "Even the weekends. She eats dinner here at least once or twice a week, something no other employee has ever done."

Sam joined the fray. "You're a happy-go-lucky guy, Theo. You always have been, but I've never seen you smile as much as you have this past month or so."

Theo threw up his hands. "You're right! About all of it. I'm crazy about her."

Jace sank down on the recliner closest to Theo's end of the

couch, while Sam grabbed the one near Levi. Maverick remained by the door, leaning casually against the jamb. Probably because, unlike his other brothers, Maverick was the only one who put zero stock in Dad's belief in love at first sight. For some reason, talking about love and romance and happily ever after made his brother uncomfortable.

"When did you know she was the one?" Jace leaned forward, resting his elbows on his knees.

"She stopped by the brewhouse a few days before she started work."

Sam and Jace nodded, aware of that fact, since they'd been there.

"Gretchen came into my office, and we chatted for a few minutes. She started to leave, but I convinced her to join me for a drink at the brewery. I walked around my desk and said I was looking forward to working with her. I held out my hand, and she put hers in mine and..."

"Fireworks?" Levi asked.

"The planet tilted on its goddamn axis. I can't believe I managed to remain standing," he admitted.

"Love at first touch," Jace breathed. "It happened to you just like it did Levi."

Theo nodded in affirmation. "I've never felt *anything* that powerful."

"So why the long face?" Sam asked.

"Let me guess," Maverick said. "Gretchen doesn't feel the same way."

Theo sighed heavily—because that was the million-dollar question, wasn't it? "I'm not sure *how* she feels."

"She probably feels like you're her boss and starting a relationship would be stupid." Leave it to Maverick to speak the hard truths.

"She did mention that, yes."

"Wait." Jace raised one hand. "Why would she say that? Did you come out and tell her how you feel?"

Theo grimaced. "I knew I needed to approach Gretchen differently than the way Levi did Kasi. She and Levi had known each other their whole lives, so when he went all caveman and started beating his chest, she didn't feel threatened."

Levi rubbed his beard. "She might not have felt threatened, but that doesn't mean she wasn't also freaking out at my abrupt about-face, suddenly claiming she was mine and always would be. It took some convincing to get her to understand my feelings were sincere."

Theo knew that, knew Kasi had been resistant at first, but Levi still had an advantage because, on top of Kasi knowing him well, she'd also harbored a crush on him since she was in high school. "I get that, but up until five weeks ago, Gretchen didn't know me from Adam, so I started at square one. Because of that, I was attempting to practice patience. Become her friend first."

Sam frowned. "Can't help but notice the past tense. What did you do?"

"We were in the barn a week ago, the day of that nasty thunderstorm. The thunder frightened her, so I hugged her. One thing led to another, and…" He raised one shoulder.

Maverick filled in the blanks. "You kissed her."

"For a good twenty minutes. I swear to God, I'd still be there now if I didn't need to eat and sleep and work."

"Wow," Jace said. "That good?"

"It was perfect. Heaven on Earth."

"And when it ended, she realized her mistake." Maverick was batting a thousand today.

"She did. Pointed out it couldn't happen again, and the boss thing—"

"Remove the boss thing," Levi interjected.

"What?" Theo asked.

Levi raked his fingers through his hair again. "Take that problem off the table. Make Nora her direct supervisor."

Theo liked that idea. And he was sure if he explained the situation to his cousin, she'd be more than happy to assume that role. It wasn't like it required much extra work, because Gretchen had proven herself to be a competent employee, perfectly capable of working autonomously. Not much managing required at all.

Gretchen was looking at this connection between them differently than him, thinking that if things went south, she'd lose her job. Theo, however, knew that wasn't going to happen because she was it for him. Lock, stock, and barrel.

"That's a good idea. I'll call Nora, but..." Theo grimaced.

"What *else* did you do?" Sam asked.

"I counteracted her arguments by telling her she was mine."

All four of his brothers groaned in unison.

Jace shook his head. "Premature chest-beating, bro."

"I know that! What's worse is, Gretchen came to Gracemont with some pretty heavy baggage. Her upbringing sucked, her mom and stepdad were neglectful and cruel."

Levi scowled, his feelings about parents hurting their kids matching Theo's. "I don't like hearing that. Gretchen is a gentle soul."

"It was bad enough that she and her brother ended up in foster care," Theo added.

Sam nodded, glancing at Jace, who said, "She mentioned living in a foster home in passing a couple weeks ago."

"I'm not even sure if it's the boss thing or the caveman thing I'm fighting against," Theo added. "Sometimes, I get the sense there's something bigger holding her back."

Maverick moved away from the doorway, perching on an ottoman in the corner. "Something besides her shitty parents?"

Theo nodded. There were a lot of unaccounted for years in Gretchen's history. She never once mentioned the years between graduation and her arrival here. All he knew was what was on her resume, and that included little more than her work and education history.

"What do you think it is?" Sam asked.

Theo was touched by the concern in his brother's voice. It was clear it wasn't just *his* heart Gretchen had claimed in her short time here. She'd wormed her way into his family's as well.

Theo rubbed his forehead wearily. "I don't know. While she's opened up to me about a few things regarding her past, there's a big-ass brick wall too tall to scale around the rest of it. She claims she came to Gracemont for a fresh start, but I can't help feeling like she's running from something."

Levi frowned. "If that's true, she'll need you to help her through it."

Theo had every intention of doing that. "I hate that I freaked her out by admitting my feelings so early, but it's hard to hold back when I can see the future so clearly. We're perfect for each other, and every fiber of my being knows we're supposed to be together. This thing between us...it's meant to be."

Levi nodded as if what he was saying made perfect sense. "If she's really yours, really the one, you need to grab her with both hands and hold on until she sees what you do."

Maverick rolled his eyes. "You two are as bad as Dad with this soul mates stuff. What's wrong with playing the field? Dating a few years or so? This love-at-first-touch thing is—"

"True," Levi interjected.

Maverick wasn't finished arguing. "It was only true for you

and Dad because the women fell back. If Kasi had rejected you, then you'd be singing a different tune."

Levi smirked. "I'll bet you a hundred bucks when love comes for you, it's going to take you down just as quick and twice as hard."

Maverick grimaced. "I'll take that bet. Because I'm never going to let some woman tie my dick in a knot, never going to fall in love. It's not in the cards for me."

Theo didn't know how to respond to that, and given the way Levi, Sam, and Jace were frowning, it was apparent they didn't, either.

Sam turned back to Theo. "So what are you going to do?"

"I don't know. I mean...what if I've already fucked up my chance?" Theo forced himself to voice the one thing that had cost him more sleep than he cared to count this week.

"This kiss was a week ago?" Sam asked.

Theo nodded.

Sam tilted his head. "How has Gretchen acted toward you since then?"

"The same," he said, that question and its response one he hadn't considered. "She's acting exactly the same."

"She's not avoiding you? Things aren't awkward?" Maverick asked.

"No. She's as friendly as ever." Theo was the one who'd started acting differently.

"Hmpf," Levi grunted. "So despite the premature caveman act, she's staying put. Not running away."

A big-ass grin broke free on Theo's face. "She's not."

Gretchen hadn't turned down his invitation to last week's cookout, hadn't tried to back out on the driving lessons, hadn't ceased stopping by his office whenever she had a question or wanted an opinion on something work related. She wasn't even attempting to keep a physical distance, leaning over his computer to look at graphics and schedules and playfully slapping his arm whenever he made a joke.

Levi placed his hand on Theo's shoulder and squeezed. "Then it sounds like the door is still open. And as long as that's the case..."

"I can start knocking down the roadblocks." Theo pulled his phone out of his pocket. "If you guys will excuse me, I'm going to kick the first one over." He clicked on his contacts, found Nora's number, and hit call. "Hey, Nora," he said, as he walked out of the living room, catching the smiles on his brothers' faces. "I need a favor."

Theo walked into Whiskey Abbey a couple hours later, a lighter spring in his step, thanks to the talk with his brothers and Nora. Although, he feared he might have permanent hearing damage in his left ear, given the way Nora squeed with delight when he told her why he wanted her to take over as Gretchen's supervisor.

His cousin, like his brothers, hadn't been a bit surprised by his confession, claiming she'd been quite amused by the way he constantly made moon eyes at Gretchen every time he thought no one was looking. And more than that, she started playing matchmaker, giving him ideas for things to do around Gracemont that would be perfect for romantic dates.

"Ahoy, matey!" Levi cried out, when he spotted Theo in his pirate costume. Levi was carrying a pitcher of beer and a couple of glasses. "We've got a big table over there," his brother said, pointing him in the right direction.

Despite the fact it was a Wednesday and everyone in here probably had work in the morning, the bar was packed, no one willing to pass up the chance to kick up their heels. Social events like this were the exception rather than the norm in Gracemont, so whenever something fun cropped up, most of the locals made their way there.

Theo grinned at Levi's Han Solo costume, complete with blaster in a gun belt, then snorted when Levi put down the pitcher and glasses, wrapping his arm around Kasi's waist. She made an adorable Princess Leia.

Then, he took in his family's costumes one by one, chuckling at some of the more outrageous ones. Maverick made an amusing Alan from *The Hangover*, complete with a baby doll strapped to his chest. Grayson was currently acting out his "Where's Waldo" outfit, standing directly behind Superman Everett, and peering over his shoulder as everyone pretended to be looking for him. Sam and Jace had nailed their look, bringing the Blues Brothers to life.

Theo laughed out loud when his gaze finally landed on Gretchen, surrounded by his cousins at the opposite end of the table. Walking toward them, he stopped next to her. "Never really pegged you for a mean girl," he joked.

Gretchen dramatically tossed her hair over her shoulder. "On Wednesdays, we wear pink," she announced. Sure enough, she, Nora, Remi, and Mila were rocking it in several different shades of pink.

"When we realized Halloween was on a Wednesday, we couldn't resist," Remi explained. In addition to her pink attire, she'd created a neck brace for herself out of dowel rods and a foam wreath that was decorated with flowers. "I'm Regina George, obviously. Nora is Cady, Mila is Karen, and—"

"I'm playing the role of Gretchen," Gretchen added, giggling.

"Well, shiver me timbers," he said in a pirate tone. "You all look great."

"So do you." Gretchen reached out to tap his eye patch. "How annoying is the patch?"

He shrugged. "Only just put it on in the parking lot. Suspect it will get old long before the night is over."

While his family had managed to snag a large table, there weren't enough stools for everyone, so while half the group was sitting, the rest were standing around it. Theo parked himself behind Gretchen, leaning over her to pour himself a glass of beer from one of the countless pitchers. For the first time in a week, he made no attempt to avoid touching her or keeping his distance as his chest pressed tight to her back, his arm brushing hers.

She glanced over her shoulder at him, looking confused. Undoubtedly, she mistook the space he'd been giving her as him backing off. Tonight, that was over. He was ready to set the wheels in motion, ready to seduce the socks off Miss Gretchen Banks.

Taking a sip of his beer, he rested his free arm on the back of her stool, playing with her hair.

"Theo," she whispered, her eyes traveling around the table, checking to make sure no one was watching them.

Theo didn't care if they were. He'd come clean to four of his brothers, and given the wink Grayson shot him and the knowing grin on Everett's face, it was obvious the other two had been read in.

He was also certain Nora had filled in Mila and Remi, because those girls told each other everything, secrets nonexistent in their house. And the same held true with Levi and Kasi.

So really, the only person at the table who didn't know he'd made his attraction public was Gretchen.

"Hmmm." He teased the side of her neck with one finger. When she shivered, her eyes growing dark with desire, he decided he needed to pull back a little bit, or he was about to become a pirate sporting a very large plank.

"I love this song!" Remi yelled when a Billy Idol classic from the eighties, "Dancing with Myself," started playing. "Let's hit the floor and get this party started."

Mila, Kasi, and Nora were already out of their chairs, but Gretchen hesitated.

"Aren't you going to go with them?" he asked.

Something crossed her face that he couldn't quite read. For a moment, it looked like anxiety or maybe fear, but she shook off whatever was bothering her quickly. "I think I *will* go dance."

He watched as she joined the other women on the floor, all of them jumping around, laughing, singing along. He lifted his glass to Gretchen in a silent toast, when she turned to look back at him. The smile she gave him was bright and so happy it took his breath away. Then she gave him a shy wave, the gesture so adorable he fell even deeper.

"You've got it bad, bro," Sam said, shoulder-bumping him.

Theo chuckled, but before he could respond, he caught sight of someone over Sam's shoulder and growled. "Scottie is here, doing his slimy politician act."

Sam didn't even bother to turn around. "Saw him when we walked in. Nodded my head, acknowledging him. He gave me a dirty look and turned his back. Because he's an asshole like that."

"He's pissed because he knows he can't beat you."

Sam shrugged. "I wouldn't be so sure of that. I entered the mayoral race pretty late, and there are plenty of people in town who think he's done a decent job. Suspect there are people who prefer the devil they know versus the one they don't."

As always, Sam was selling himself short. Theo spent a great deal of time in the brewery, socializing with their patrons, and all he'd heard was overwhelming support for Sam and relief that they wouldn't have to deal with the pretentious Scottie for much longer.

And to prove his point, he and Sam spent the next half hour chatting with countless locals, all coming over to wish his brother luck. The election was only six days away, and Theo knew Sam, who'd been doing quite a lot of campaigning, would be glad when it was finally over.

Theo was planning a celebration on the down-low with Gretchen. The day after the election and Sam's win, they wanted to hold a victory party at the brewery, where people could raise a glass and participate in a happy hour with their new mayor. If—God forbid—Sam didn't win, he would be none the wiser that there'd even been a party planned.

When a slow song came on, Theo excused himself, quickly moving to the edge of the dance floor, ready to intercept Gretchen on her way off. She smiled when she saw him waiting, and there wasn't a drop of hesitance as she accepted his outstretched hand.

Theo pulled her back onto the floor, lifting both her hands to his shoulders before pushing the eye patch up—he didn't want anything obstructing his view of her—then he grasped her waist, drawing her close.

Gretchen sank into his arms, and he released a long sigh. It had been a rough week of second-guessing himself. For the first time since that kiss, the world felt right again.

Because she belonged here.

In his arms.

The two of them swayed as Rihanna sang "Lift Me Up." The lyrics and beautiful melody felt as if they were written just for them.

"This is our song," he murmured.

Gretchen lifted her face to him as he spoke. "We have a

song?" she asked, her eyes shimmering. Had she been on the verge of crying? Was the song affecting her the same way it was him?

"We do. This one." Theo sang the words of the chorus in her ear as Gretchen rested her forehead on his shoulder.

"It's a beautiful song. The words...they're nice. Peaceful. I like the idea of being safe and sound." She lowered her gaze, and he got the sense she was trying to compose herself.

Theo hated that she considered being safe and sound an idea rather than a reality, and he decided there was a special place in Hell for her mom and stepfather, mistreating her the way they had.

He put the thought away because this dance was too perfect to waste by not living in the moment.

"Lift me up," he sang to her, placing a soft kiss on her cheek. Then he went for broke, his lips touching hers. He intended to steal a quick kiss, but his lips had other ideas, especially when Gretchen returned it.

Sadly, she recalled herself too quickly. She stiffened, broke off the kiss, and glanced around again, searching for witnesses. "Theo," she started, the same tone of warning in her voice she'd used at the table.

"I'm not your boss anymore," he said.

Gretchen stopped dancing, gasping.

Shit. She'd misinterpreted his words, because now she looked panicked and upset.

"Nora is," he hastily added. "You'll answer to her from now on. Which means you and I are nothing more than colleagues."

Her shoulders visibly relaxed, though she rolled her eyes. "I'm pretty sure it doesn't work that way."

"It does," he reassured her, forcing her to start dancing again, a strong arm looped around her back. "You said we shouldn't give in to this attraction to each other because I'm your boss. I'm not anymore."

"That's not the only reason. We barely know each other."

"We've spent every single day together for the past five weeks, and every time we say goodbye, I start counting the minutes until we're together again. Gretchen, I know this is fast, but this has never happened to me before. I've never felt a connection like this with anyone. We can take things slowly if you want, but I'm not going to pretend the attraction isn't there. And we're not going to hide our feelings from everyone. It would be pointless anyway, since I already told my brothers and Nora, and they told everyone else. So you can stop looking around to see if anyone is watching us."

Gretchen's eyes widened. "You what?"

Theo leaned closer, her breath hot against his face. "When I kissed you...you kissed me back. Both times."

"I know," she said, "but I shouldn't have."

"You feel this thing too, don't you?"

She stared at him, biting her lower lip.

Theo reached out, using his thumb to tug it loose. "Tell me," he prodded.

"Yes. I feel something, but I can't act on those feelings. I've made bad decisions in the past, Theo. *Really* bad ones, and now, I don't trust my instincts. I *can't* trust them."

Wow. As far as info dumps went, that was one both telling and severely lacking.

Before he could question her about those decisions, she stepped out of his arms and walked away. Theo reached her at the edge of the dance floor, halting her escape, his hand on her upper arm as he spun her back to face him again.

"Don't run from me, Gretchen."

She closed her eyes, suddenly looking weary. "Sometimes running is the smartest thing a person can do."

That answer upset him. Had he gone too far? "Do I scare you?"

She was shaking her head before he finished asking the question. "No. You don't. Not at all."

"All I'm asking for is a chance to date you. Me being your boss was a roadblock, so I took care of it."

"That's not the only roadblock," she whispered. She was still holding on to some heavy baggage.

"What else?"

Theo watched as she closed down, the walls she erected around herself fortified once more.

While she claimed five weeks wasn't long enough to get to know someone, he knew her well enough to know this conversation was over. "I hope one day you'll trust me enough to tell me." He'd said those words to her before.

"I hope so too," she said quietly.

"I'm not giving up," he warned her, cupping her cheek affectionately. "We Storms are notoriously stubborn. A force of nature."

The heaviness of the moment lifted, and she smiled. "Then you're appropriately named."

"I know life hasn't been good to you, so I understand why you might question this, question me. But I swear to you, Gretchen. I'll never hurt you."

This time, there was no denying the glassy tears in her eyes...or the fact she didn't believe him.

And if that was all he saw in her expression, he would have been hurt. Devastated even. But there was also hope in those bright blue eyes of hers, and that was the part he held on to.

She might not believe his promise right now, but she sure as hell wanted to.

Theo bent his head, sealing his vow with a kiss. Now, as

before, Gretchen returned it, letting it linger. When they parted, she didn't bother to look around.

"You're not going to stop kissing me, are you?"

Theo grinned. "Nope."

"We're taking the pin out?"

He nodded. "Pin is out. Time to see where this thing between us is heading."

Gretchen's mouth quirked in amusement. "Okay. I guess we can take a tiny peek, see where it leads us."

It wasn't the exact answer he wanted, but for now, he'd take it.

Chapter Ten

Gretchen flipped another page in the photo album, the edges yellowed with age. Her eyes widened when she spotted a black-and-white photograph of Edith in a bikini.

"Va-va-voom," Gretchen said. "How old were you here?"

"Probably close to your age," Edith responded. The two of them were sitting side by side on the couch. They'd intended to watch a movie together, but that plan changed when Gretchen spotted the photo album on the bookshelf.

They'd spent the last couple of hours turning through the pages as Edith recounted stories of her younger years, which was way better than watching a movie.

It was the night of the mayoral election, so they were staying up, awaiting the results. Because Gracemont was a small town, Edith said the ballot counting didn't run super late, so they hoped to know the results by ten or eleven p.m.

Theo had promised to call as soon as he heard.

"That was the summer I traveled to Myrtle Beach with a few girlfriends for a week. Oh my," Edith exclaimed. "Didn't we think we were all the rage, smoking cigarettes and drinking Old Fashioneds around the pool, while the boys circled us like flies on honey."

Gretchen looked at the picture again. "If your girlfriends were even half as pretty as you, I'm sure you all were the center of attention."

Edith pressed her shoulder against hers. "Oh, go on with you. I made a lot of bad decisions on that trip, but damn if I didn't enjoy every single one."

Gretchen laughed. "Bad decisions, huh?"

"Sometimes those are the best ones."

They turned another page, Gretchen pointing to another photo, this one of Edith standing in front of the Washington Monument, surrounded by hundreds of other women.

"A protest?" Gretchen asked.

"A march for the ERA," Edith replied. "One that worked, as we were successful in getting the House and Senate to approve an extension of the amendment. I've attended quite a few protests and rallies in my time."

"Good for you." Every time Gretchen learned something new about Edith, she loved the woman even more.

Gretchen laughed when they turned the page, and she spotted a picture of Edith draped over the hood of a car.

"God, I loved my Ford Mustang. Used to drive that thing everywhere," Edith confessed.

As they continued turning the pages, she watched as Edith got older.

"This was the first property I ever bought on my own." Edith's parents had owned several rental properties in and around Gracemont that she inherited following their deaths.

"How many have you bought since then?" Gretchen asked.

Edith tapped a finger against her lower lip. "That's a good question. I'd say at least twenty."

"Twenty?" Gretchen wasn't sure why she was surprised. Edith was a shrewd and clever businesswoman.

"Property is a good investment," Edith said. "Though I'll admit, it took some time for the older generation in town to accept a woman investing in real estate. Especially a woman who was still single in her thirties. By the time I turned forty, I'd acquired a tidy fortune, thanks to some very good stock market investments, so I guess some people around here considered me quite the catch."

"You would be quite the catch without money. You're smart and funny and," Gretchen looked back down at the photo, "gorgeous."

Edith smiled. "Maybe so, but at the time, I was considered an enigma and even a little eccentric. Quite a few of the local men started suggesting I was a lesbian."

"*What?*"

"It was the only way they could explain why I kept turning them down for dates. God forbid they have to accept that they weren't smart enough to capture my interest."

"What assholes."

Edith waved her hand. "Oh, I didn't care about that, because it had nothing to do with me and everything to do with their inability to see a world that wasn't based on the patriarchy. They were threatened by an independent woman capable of making her own money and decisions. They didn't like it."

Gretchen laughed. "So no torrid romance with another woman?" She was joking—until she saw the smug expression on Edith's face. "There was?!"

"I wouldn't call it torrid. One of the friends I traveled to the protests with was a lesbian, and one night she confessed her love for me. We kissed, but..."

"No sparks?"

"Sadly, no," Edith said. "Because she was quite perfect for me in every other way."

"You are so badass. I totally want to be you when I grow up."

"Well, I'd say you're well on your way, my dear."

Gretchen didn't agree, but she didn't have a chance to say so before her phone rang.

"It's Theo," she said, picking it up.

"He won! Sam won!" Theo announced, as soon as she answered.

She and Edith cheered. Then she and Theo spent a few minutes discussing how to get word out about their celebration happy hour.

When she hung up, Edith—who was hardcore Team Theo—suggested that she channel her inner Edith at the party, make a few bad decisions, and go wild with her hot boss.

Gretchen scoffed, dismissing the idea—aloud. While inside, she seriously gave it some thought.

Maybe it *was* time for her to channel her inner Edith. Because God knew that woman had lived a life worth living, and suddenly, Gretchen wanted to do the same.

Time was too precious to keep wasting.

Gretchen took a moment to herself, leaning against the counter behind the bar, enjoying the victory party. Sam had been touched by the surprise happy hour, and given the way he'd circulated the brewery, spending a few minutes with everyone who came to congratulate him, Gretchen had no doubt, he would be a wonderful mayor.

The celebration she and Theo had secretly planned behind the scenes "just in case" had been in full swing for way more than one happy hour. Glancing at the time on her phone, she saw they were approaching their fourth hour of happiness.

Every member of the Storm family was in attendance, and while she wasn't sure, it certainly felt as if nearly every citizen in Gracemont had made a point to drop by. Well, everyone except Scottie Grover, who was probably hunkered down at home, licking his wounds.

Lark McCoy, who provided entertainment at least one weekend a month at both the brewery and the winery, had ensured spirits remained high, strumming her guitar and performing one amazing set after another, packing the playlist with sing-along hits like "Sweet Caroline," "Party in the U.S.A," "Don't Stop Believin'," "Living on a Prayer," "Wagon Wheel," and more.

Gretchen's voice would be hoarse come morning, as she, Mila, Nora, and Remi belted out the words while waiting tables. Because of the sheer number of attendees, it had become an all-hands-on-deck situation for a couple of hours, with every Storm either manning the taps, working in the kitchens, or serving. But as afternoon gave way to evening, a lot of people had finally headed home for a late dinner.

Edith, who'd left half an hour ago, would no doubt be tucking Manny in tonight, the man enjoying one flight too many. He was jovial when tipsy, and he had provided at least five of the countless toasts in Sam's honor that had kept people lifting pint glasses.

With a much thinner crowd, consisting only of Storms and a few stragglers unwilling to call it a night, Gretchen could finally take a moment to catch her breath. It had been an amazing evening—one of the best of her life—something she'd been saying a lot of late.

Every day here was better than the one before. It wasn't anything she'd ever experienced, but damn if she wasn't loving every moment of it. That nagging feeling of waiting for the other shoe to drop was fading away, leaving in its wake this constant state of sheer happiness.

It had been a week since Halloween, since Theo had kissed her senseless on the dance floor at Whiskey Abbey…and then even more senseless on the front porch of Edith's house after walking her home. She was lying to herself when she said she tried to do the smart thing and resist his attention, because there was no denying her efforts couldn't be labeled anything stronger than token at best.

God, she thought, stroking her finger over her lips. They were chapped from all the kissing she and Theo had been doing lately. Since agreeing to see where things led them, he'd taken advantage of the offer, dropping by her office nearly every single hour to steal another kiss. She'd joked earlier in the day that if he kept it up, Nora was going to fire both of them.

After her driving lessons on Saturday and Sunday, they'd parked on a rarely used dirt road on the farm and made out like teenagers who'd discovered their fun bits. So far, they'd limited their embraces to kissing and some hot-and-heavy, over-the-clothing touches. It had been intense and far too innocent for Gretchen, who hadn't felt arousal in years.

Any passion she might have felt for Briggs at the beginning of their relationship was lukewarm compared to her desire for Theo, and nowadays, she felt like a walking live wire, sparking brightly whenever he was in the same room as her.

She wanted him.

That thought was as shocking as it was terrifying. She'd genuinely believed Briggs had beat out of her the part that craved sex and touching and kissing and closeness. If he had, Theo had found a way to bring it all back to life. With his sweet compliments, drugging kisses, and peaceful, gentle, nonthreatening nature, she was smitten.

For goodness sake, the man didn't even hurt bugs. She'd watched him catch a bee in his office the other day then take it outside to release it. On the flip side, she'd seen Briggs kick a dog before, simply for making its way into their yard and rolling in the grass.

When Theo had asked if he scared her on Halloween, she'd almost laughed, because he didn't have a clue what it was like to be truly frightened. Him professing his affection for her didn't even make a blip on her horror radar because...why would it?

She meant what she'd said to him about not trusting her instincts, but damn if she didn't want to believe what they were telling her about the man.

Given her past, she was shocked by how easily she'd let herself be swept away by Theo Storm. The cloak of self-preservation she'd worn like armor for most of her life had fallen off in Gracemont, simply because it was no longer necessary. Everyone she'd met here had been nothing but genuine and kind and welcoming, so it made it simple for her to be herself without fear of repercussions or judgment or violence.

Gretchen grinned when a strong arm wrapped around her waist, Theo's breath warm against the side of her face, the scent of hops and citrus reminding her of the beer they'd both drunk.

"Your party is a hit," he said, giving her a kiss on the cheek.

Gretchen spotted his mom glancing their direction with a pleased grin. She didn't bother tugging away from him because the horse had already left the gate on Theo's pursuit of her. She discovered the day after Halloween that gossip was gold in a small town, and apparently the fact Theo had been seen kissing her on the dance floor was big news, the tidbit making the rounds quickly. Too many of the older women in Gracemont, Edith included, wondering if there were *two* Storm weddings on the horizon. Gretchen had quickly shut that idea down when Edith mentioned it, even though it amused her more than frightened her.

"This is *our* party," she corrected him.

"I tossed a couple ideas at you, and you ran with them, putting in the hard work to make it successful. So *your* party," Theo countered. As always, he minimized his contributions, praising her efforts. After too many years of constantly hearing only what she did wrong, his kind words never failed to lighten her spirits, make her soul sing.

"Looks like things are winding down," she observed.

"With the patrons, yes. But something tells me my family is just getting started. My dad is so proud, he could pop. He ordered four more pitchers for the table, and I've come to drag you back to help us drink it. You're too much fun to stand over here like a wallflower."

Gretchen looked over where Mr. Storm—who insisted she call him Rex—was definitely doing his best to keep the party going. Not that it was much of a struggle, as Levi grabbed a pitcher and started topping up everyone's glass. She grimaced when she watched him fill hers back to the brim.

She was a lightweight when it came to drinking, and she was already two pints deeper than she should be. It was a foregone conclusion that she'd be starting her morning with a headache. "I think this might be the night I'll finally need to use Koda's Uber services."

Theo twisted her until she faced him, his hands on her waist. "Or you could stay here."

"Here?" she asked.

"Spend the night with me."

She narrowed her eyes. "How much have you had to drink?"

Theo chuckled. "Enough. Too soon?"

Gretchen nodded. "It's way too soon," she replied, even

though her body rejected that assertion. "You and I sleeping together right now would be a bad idea."

"Maybe so," he conceded, "but it would be a *good* bad idea."

"Theo," she said, playfully smacking his chest, recalling Edith's assertion that she should make a bad decision.

"Besides, all I heard in that rejection was *right now*, which means my future is looking bright."

"You're incorrigible."

Theo shook his head. "Nope. Just stubborn and determined. But I promised we would take this at your speed, and I don't break promises, so I won't ask you to stay with me again... until tomorrow."

Her heart fluttered.

Even though there was another promise he'd offered that had meant more to her. When he swore he would never hurt her, she tried to dismiss the comment as empty, pretty words, but she had played them over in her mind so much this week it drove home how much that vow meant to her.

And how much it would hurt if he broke it.

Theo had the power to hurt her way worse than Briggs. Which meant there was now another reason why she needed this thing between them to go slower. Probably slower than it was, but what could she say? He was an awesome kisser, and there was a part of her that felt as if she'd inadvertently skipped over this young girl/first love thing when she was a teenager.

At eighteen, she'd moved in with a man twice her age, instantly thrust into a committed relationship without taking the time to flirt or date or make some of those bad decisions.

Gretchen crossed her arms. "Well, if we're going to keep things rolling tonight, I need to grab my sweater from my office. It's getting chilly."

Fall was starting its march toward winter, and while it was still warm enough to sit outside, thicker clothing was required.

"I'll walk with you," Theo offered.

Gretchen playfully pushed him away with a hand on his face. "If you go with me, we'll start making out in my office and we'll never return to the party, and that bad idea of yours really will start to sound like a good one."

"Then I'm definitely coming with you."

She laughed and pointed to the large table and his family. "You are most definitely staying here."

Theo gave her an adorable pout but didn't fight her. "Hurry back, kitten." He gave her a quick, hard kiss, one that ensured she would do just that, because she was becoming too accustomed to always being with him. More than that, she *wanted* to be near him.

The short walk from the brewery to the brewhouse was well-lit, and while she was anxious to return to the party, she didn't rush, enjoying the smell of fall in the air as well as the peaceful sounds of evening. This was the first moment she'd had to herself all day, so she took advantage of it.

She'd just reached her office when her cellphone rang. She pulled it out of her pocket, frowning when she saw Brenda's name. Her former boss had called three or four times, shortly after her escape from Harrisburg, to make sure she was okay, but it had been over a month since the last call. While they'd grown closer during the last six months of Gretchen's employment, it was probably a leap to call her and Brenda friends. It was more that Brenda had stepped up when she'd needed her, offering her help to leave town, and after that, their common bond no longer existed.

"Brenda," Gretchen said.

"He knows where you are."

Gretchen staggered across the office to her chair, sinking down heavily. "Are you sure?"

"Yes. Briggs obtained my phone records without a warrant, which is illegal as hell. Don't think my lawyer mom isn't salivating, ready to press charges for that. Briggs asked my brother if I knew anyone in Gracemont, Virginia. Douglas said he didn't think so, then asked why Briggs wanted to know. That's when Briggs said he'd pulled my phone records. He saw from the records that I'd called someone in Gracemont a few times and he knows the number belongs to a Tracfone, which sparked his suspicions."

"Oh," Gretchen breathed.

"Douglas is finally starting to see the light about Briggs. Because in addition to invading my privacy, he's acting obsessed and more than a little crazy. Briggs has gone off the deep end, Gretchen, and I'm worried about you."

"Oh," Gretchen said again, suddenly breathless, her chest too tight.

He knew where she was. She'd known this day was coming, known Briggs wouldn't stop until he found her.

She thought she was ready for it, but given how quickly this panic attack was coming on, that was another lie she'd been telling herself.

"Okay," she said because her brain had stopped functioning.

"I'm sorry, Gretchen," Brenda said, distraught. "If there's a bright side, I don't think he knows your new name."

Maybe not. But she hadn't met a single other Gretchen in Gracemont yet. She should have moved to a hell of a lot bigger city, like New York or L.A.

"It's okay," she repeated, as if that would make it so. "It's okay. It's okay."

Brenda continued apologizing, but Gretchen couldn't focus on the words.

Briggs knew she was in Gracemont. With that information, how long would it take before he found Edith's address? Gretchen pressed her fingers to her lips, feeling nauseous that she'd put the dear woman in harm's way.

She needed to reach out to Edith. Now. Right away.

"I have to go, Brenda," she said, interrupting the woman who was still quite upset. "I need to..." Gretchen was light-headed, her mind whirling as she pictured Edith at home, Manny sleeping off the party in one of the other guest rooms, as his aunt insisted he wouldn't drink enough water or take aspirin if she wasn't there to look after him.

Disconnecting the call, she tried to figure out next steps, and she needed to do it quickly because her hands were already trembling violently, the edges of her vision going gray, her breathing too rapid and shallow.

She pulled up Edith's name in her phone and sent a quick text, lying and saying that she was having a sleepover with Nora. She couldn't go back to Edith's in case Briggs showed up there.

If she hadn't been out of her mind with terror, the quick thumbs-up and okay gestures Edith replied with might have made her laugh, because Gretchen had only recently taught her how to use emoticons as text responses.

Staying away from Edith's only solved one problem. Just as she wanted to ensure her beloved landlady was safe, she also didn't want Briggs around the Storms. Originally, she feared him showing up here in case they believed Briggs's lies about her mental health. That was no longer as big a concern, because she didn't think Theo or his family would fall for Briggs's bullshit.

But after a lifetime of being hurt and disappointed by

people who should have cared for her, she couldn't shut down that teeny tiny insecure part of her that still worried they would.

She hadn't protected her heart. She'd allowed herself to be swept away in this new magical, amazing, happy place, believing there was some sort of dome over Gracemont that would ward off all the bad shit and keep Briggs out. She thought she'd been getting stronger, but now, when faced with the likelihood of Briggs's arrival, she found herself reverting to that same terrified, weak woman.

Gretchen covered her mouth with her hand, bending over to reach for her trash can. She gagged several times, the contents of her stomach threatening to come up. The idea of facing him again made her physically ill, and a lifetime of insecurities broke free from where she'd buried them, too many voices screaming in her head.

Ivan cursing her out as the police put him in handcuffs, shoving him outside to the squad car after he'd hurt Shaw. *"You worthless, stupid cunt!"*

Gretchen closed her eyes.

Her mother shouting at her after Ivan's arrest. *"Having you was the biggest mistake of my life! You've been nothing but a disappointment. Why do you think your father left? It was because he couldn't stand the sight of you!"*

She covered her ears, wishing the hateful words would go away, but now that they'd escaped, they fell over her head like an avalanche.

When Briggs's voice came next, she began to shake in earnest.

"I treat you like a fucking queen, and you're too stupid to do a simple thing like wash my goddamn shirts! Do you know how fucking hard I work, how stressful my job is? Why can't I come

home and fucking relax? Why can't you do what I say? Why do you make me hurt you like this?"

She hadn't replied to that, hadn't been able to, because his hands were wrapped too tightly around her throat, choking her and leaving behind the bruises Edith had seen upon her arrival.

Stupid.

Worthless.

Disappointment.

A mistake.

Her stomach clenched again, and this time, she *did* throw up. Coughing several times, she emptied her stomach as tears streamed down her cheeks.

When there was nothing left, she rubbed her chest, trying to ease the pain before she reached for her phone. Gretchen clicked on Theo's name. It took her a long time to type out the short text message, her fingers shaking too violently to hit the right keys.

Migraine. Edith picked me up.

She hit send, then placed her phone on the desk, face down.

The immediate swish that followed told her Theo had replied, but she didn't bother to read it. Instead, she closed the door to her office, turned off the lights, then sank down behind her desk.

Alone in the darkness, she curled into a ball and gave in to the panic.

Chapter Eleven

Theo frowned when his message to Gretchen went unread. While the party was still going on around him, he was no longer in a jovial mood. Gretchen was fine when she left to get her sweater, he was certain of it.

But then, she stayed away too long. He'd intended to go looking for her, but Sam dragged him to the brewery's makeshift stage to sing "Friends in Low Places" with him. Once the song was over, he returned to the table and saw the text from Gretchen. He hated that she'd asked Edith to pick her up, but then, he had to admit that he'd had too much to drink to drive her himself.

He had texted to see if she needed anything, but half an hour had passed...and she hadn't read the message.

Which was normal, he told himself. She had a headache. No doubt she'd gone straight to bed and to sleep.

Yet, his gut was telling him something was wrong.

So he gave up trying to reason with himself and called Edith.

"Well, this is a surprise," she said, instead of hello. "I would have expected you and those wild brothers of yours to keep the party going 'til dawn."

"I'm sure they're going to give it the college try. I was calling to check on Gretchen. To make sure she's okay."

The pause that followed told Theo he'd been right to worry.

"Gretchen isn't here. She texted to say she was spending the night with Nora."

Theo glanced down the table to where Nora was laughing loudly at something Remi was saying.

"Theo," Edith prodded, when he didn't reply. "Isn't she there?"

"No. She said you picked her up."

"You need to find her," Edith said, the alarm in her voice triggering his own.

"What's going on?"

"I'm not sure why she lied to us, but I'm worried," she said.

"About what?"

Edith sighed, and for a moment, he thought she wasn't going to tell him. He knew Gretchen had been confiding in Edith, but he didn't realize how much more Edith knew than him.

"I'm afraid maybe her ex showed up."

"Her ex?"

"That's not my story to tell," Edith said. "But he's not a good man, Theo. Please find her."

"I will."

"And call me when you do."

Theo assured her that he would, then hung up, trying to remain calm.

"What's wrong?" Levi said. "Where's Gretchen?"

"I don't know, but I need to find her. She has to be somewhere on the farm." At least, Theo hoped she was. Given that

Edith hadn't picked her up and she didn't drive, he thought that was a somewhat safe bet. Until he recalled her plans to employ Koda's Uber service. If she did that...she could be anywhere.

Or perhaps this dangerous ex—

Theo didn't let himself think about that.

"Levi." Theo was unable to mask his panic. "Edith thinks she might be in danger. An ex."

"We'll split up." Levi placed a firm hand on his shoulder. Within minutes, Levi had gathered the rest of the family, divvying up places around the farm where she could have gone, each of them setting off to search the cabins, winery, big houses, barns, and stables.

Theo raced to the brewhouse, since that was where Gretchen was headed when she'd left the party. The entire time, his mind swirled over what Edith had said. Her ex wasn't a good man.

Now he knew the "who," the person who'd hurt her, who'd caused her to flinch when he moved too fast, tremble or whimper when he laughed too loud or thunder boomed. Who was to blame for the panic attacks.

Bile rose to his throat when he considered exactly why him touching her neck scared her and he recalled that damn sweater she'd shown up here in the day they met. The way it covered her neck.

Running down the hallway to her office, he pulled up short when he saw the door closed, the light off.

He'd needed her to be here, because the idea of her running —or worse, being taken by someone who meant her harm—was too terrifying to consider.

Opening her door, he turned on the lights, his hopes dashed when he found the room empty. Closing the door, he spent the next twenty minutes systematically working his way through every room in the brewhouse, even searching around the machinery in case she was hiding.

Hiding.

Shit.

He was an idiot.

He raced back to her office, because he was almost certain he'd seen...

Entering once more, he turned on the lights—and there it was. Her cellphone, lying face down on her desk.

Theo walked over to it, and as he did...

She came into view.

Gretchen was huddled behind her desk, her legs tucked against her chest, her arms wrapped around them, her forehead pressed to her knees. She didn't lift her head when he slowly walked around the desk.

"Don't hurt me!" she whimpered, her voice so scared Theo felt sick. Then he glanced in the trash can and realized she had been.

Who the fuck had done this to her?

"Gretchen," he said softly, not wanting to spook her. "It's me, Theo. I'm not going to hurt you."

Slowly, she tilted her face to his. And Theo, who didn't consider himself a violent man, was ready to hunt down whoever had put that broken expression on her face and pummel him to dust.

She blinked a few times, the remnants of dried tears on her cheeks. She was pale, and while her breathing was somewhat labored, he didn't get the sense she was in the midst of a panic attack. Actually, he suspected he was seeing the aftermath of one.

"Please don't fire me."

He knelt slowly...so, so slowly, he hoped she wouldn't even

register that he was moving. He was careful to keep several feet between them. "I can't fire you. I'm not your boss."

He hoped that small joke might land, but it didn't.

Instead, fresh tears filled her eyes. "I'm sorry."

He shook his head. "Kitten, you don't have a damn thing to be sorry for."

"I lied to you about the migraine."

"Don't care." Then he lifted one finger, her words reminding him. "Give me one second. Don't move. There are a lot of people out there looking for you, worried about you. I want to tell them you're okay."

A strangled sob was her only reply to that.

Theo quickly fired off a text to the family text thread.

> Found her. She's okay.

That second part was a lie, but he was prepared to move heaven and earth to ensure that by the time they left her office, she would be.

Then he sent one more text.

> Please tell Edith.

After that, he turned his phone off because he suspected his family would inundate him with a bunch of questions he didn't have the answers to. Right now, Gretchen was the only thing that mattered.

Theo's knees were starting to scream at him for his crouched position. "Can I sit with you?"

She wiped her eyes and took a second to consider the question. Mercifully not too long. She nodded.

He dropped down onto his ass, sitting crisscross, trying to figure out what the hell to say next.

Gretchen solved that problem for him. "I swear I'm not crazy."

He frowned. "I never thought you were."

One shoulder lifted slightly.

"What happened after you left the brewery, kitten?"

Her eyes welled with tears. "I like when you call me that."

He grinned, though it was forced. "Then I'll keep doing it. Is this because of him? Your ex?"

Gretchen looked startled, but only for a moment, then she just looked resigned...and so fucking weary, he didn't think a year's worth of sleep would put a dent in her exhaustion.

"I called Edith," he explained. "To check on you. She was concerned perhaps he'd found you."

Gretchen's eyes flew to her phone on the desk.

"My family is texting Edith, letting her know you're okay."

"I can't go back there." Her voice was thick, raspy, further evidence that she'd been crying hard and for a long time. Before, everything she'd said had been spoken in soft whispers.

"Go back where?"

"To Edith's. I don't want him anywhere near her."

"Then we'll make sure that doesn't happen." Theo had zero information, but he managed to piece together enough to know this ex, whoever he was, truly terrified her. Theo couldn't let himself linger too long on what the man had done to Gretchen to produce that kind of deep-seated fear.

Still tucked into a ball, she glanced away from him, her eyes locked on the wall beneath the window. "I was young when I met Briggs," she started, in such a way Theo wasn't even sure she was talking to him as much as to herself. "Only fifteen."

Briggs. He finally had a name.

"Did he live in the residential home too?"

Gretchen laughed at that question, though there wasn't an

ounce of mirth in it. "No. Briggs is a cop. He was thirty-five at the time we met."

Anger flashed hot as Theo's temper exploded. "He was a pedophile," he said, his jaw clenched tight.

Gretchen kept staring at the wall, shaking her head. "No. He was a groomer. He never touched me until I was eighteen."

That did not make it fucking better, but Theo didn't say that aloud because there was no way he could temper the fury in his tone, and he didn't want to frighten her more.

"Shaw had graduated and joined the Navy when we met. I hadn't really felt lost or lonely until my brother wasn't there anymore. Not that I blamed him for going. Shaw had his...his own things to deal with. Looking back now, I can see he was the smarter one, making his escape from that damn city the second he could. But after he was gone, I realized *how* alone I was. And then...there was Briggs. He gave a talk about drugs and gangs to all us kids at the home, and afterward, he chatted with me a little bit. I don't even remember what he said, just that I'd been flattered that out of all the kids there, I was the one he wanted to talk to.

"He kept coming back to see me, visits where he'd ask me about school and my friends, innocent stuff like that. When he brought me a gift on my sixteenth birthday, I almost cried because I couldn't believe anyone even remembered. I mean... the foster parents who ran the home remembered, but they were paid to, and I got the same birthday cake and gift card everyone did. Briggs had bought me the softest, prettiest blue sweater I'd ever seen. He said it reminded him of my eyes. After that, I was under his spell, so flattered to have caught the attention of an attractive police officer. I guzzled down his compliments and praise like a drunk falling off the wagon after years of sobriety."

Theo growled. It was a low, guttural sound, and he hadn't even meant to do it. It captured Gretchen's attention, and for the first time since she'd started talking, she looked at him.

"Why were the foster parents letting this grown man in to see you?" He couldn't fucking understand. He really couldn't.

"I told you, Briggs was a police officer. He spent a lot of time at the home, serving as a mentor to the kids, sometimes returning them after they'd been arrested for doing stupid shit like vandalism or shoplifting. He was a regular face there, and the foster parents liked him. *Everyone* liked him. And I think they thought it was nice that someone held in such high regard in the community had taken an interest in me. He took me under his wing like a big brother, bringing me small gifts and offering advice as I maneuvered my way through high school. I was...what's the word you keep using? A wallflower. Quiet, withdrawn. Briggs was one of the few people I talked to after Shaw left, so why wouldn't they allow the visits? All we were doing was talking, and always in the common rooms. We were never alone together."

That wasn't all Briggs was doing, but he didn't say it. Didn't need to. Gretchen had already used the word. She'd figured out he'd been grooming her.

"When did that change?" he asked.

"The day I turned eighteen, he showed up with another gift—a suitcase. I thought it was the perfect present, because I was only a week away from graduation and when I left my mom's, I'd been forced to pack my things in a trash bag. I told him that, and he remembered me saying how much it embarrassed me to show up at the group home like that. It highlighted to me that from that moment on, I was homeless. The suitcase felt like a new beginning."

"Did you use it? Did you move out?"

Gretchen hesitated, and he could tell this was where the

story got harder for her to tell. "He came to my high school graduation. He was the only one in the crowd who was there just for me. He took pictures and looked at me with so much pride. Then he told me he loved me, that he'd always loved me. He said he knew I didn't have any plans for the future...so he invited me to come live with him."

Theo closed his eyes, swallowing hard against the bile rising in his throat.

"I didn't have anywhere to go. And here was this handsome older man, the one who remembered my birthday, who made me feel special, saying he wanted to be with me. It didn't feel like a hard decision at the time."

"You were eighteen." It was the only thing Theo could focus on without completely losing it. If he considered all the other ways the asshole had preyed on her...

"It was okay at the beginning. I was happy with him. It was a little bit like playing house, you know? I cleaned and cooked and he went to work. We watched TV at night, and sometimes we'd go out with some of his cop buddies and their girlfriends. He was always..." She blew out a slow breath, searching for a word. "Strict. He liked things done a certain way, like the laundry and the way I dressed, styled my hair, the things we ate. He didn't like when I danced or talked to other men. I tried really hard to do what he asked, because I wanted to make him happy." She lowered her head to her knees again, her words muffled when she spoke. "I don't think I... I don't want to relive all of this again."

Theo understood that. She'd been systematically taking him from point A to point B, probably in hopes that he would understand why she went with Briggs and why she stayed. He didn't need to hear anything more than he already had.

"He started hitting you." Theo didn't form it as a question because it wasn't one.

She nodded without looking up.

"How long were you with him?"

"A little over six years."

Theo did the easy math. She'd made her break from the man right before arriving in Gracemont. That was when he recalled her showing up that first day in a turtleneck, completely inappropriate for the temperature. What had she been hiding?

"Is this the first time you left him?"

She shook her head, which was still buried against her knees. "No. I tried three times before."

Jesus.

"Look at me, kitten," he said gently.

She lifted her head.

"Why did you go back?"

Theo had never seen tears flow so quickly. One second, her eyes were dry, the next, they were flooding over.

Every particle of his being wanted to reach out for her, to hold her. "Can I come closer?"

She nodded instantly, her lack of hesitation loosening some of the pressure on his chest.

Theo slid across the floor, keeping a few inches between them. He wasn't touching her anywhere, but at least from here, if she reached out to him, he could.

Gretchen sniffled, wiping her eyes. Theo reached up to the desk, feeling around until he found the box of tissues there. He handed it to her, and she accepted it gratefully, wiping her nose and eyes. "I'm an ugly crier," she said, her first attempt at humor.

Theo couldn't laugh. "There's not a single ugly thing about you."

Her eyes had been darting around, from his chest to his

cheeks to his forehead. For the first time, her gaze met his and held. "You really mean that, don't you?"

"I would never lie to you."

More of that pressure on his chest lifted, because for the first time ever, Gretchen wasn't looking at him with doubt, or suspicion, or even hope. This time, he saw belief.

She believed him.

"Why did you go back?" he repeated, aware that if she started crying again, he wouldn't be able to stop himself from reaching out to hold her. Her tears killed him.

"It wasn't my choice. I ran out of fear, and I wasn't smart about it. I trusted the wrong people."

He frowned. "What do you mean?"

"The first time he choked me..." She paused as her hands rose to her throat.

Gretchen had said she didn't want to relive it. He understood that now, because he wasn't sure he could handle hearing it.

"I was afraid he was going to kill me. When he finally let go, I slumped to the floor, and he stormed off to bed. I waited until I was sure he was asleep, and I ran. Ran to the house of a woman I thought was a friend. Destiny dated Briggs's partner, Darryl, on the force, so we hung out with them a lot, did couples things. They lived a few miles away, and I don't drive, and I didn't have any money, so I ran there."

In the middle of the night, Theo thought, the image of it stabbing him like daggers.

"I told Destiny what happened, showed her the marks on my neck. She hugged me, told me to calm down, then said I could sleep on the couch. It was the first time in a long time I fell asleep feeling safe. I shouldn't have."

"What did she do?"

"She called Briggs, told him I was there."

"Why the fuck would she do that?" he snapped.

"You have to understand, the face Briggs shows the world is very different from the one I saw at home. He showed up there first thing in the morning with a huge bouquet of roses and a big apologetic show that was all for Darryl and Destiny's benefit, not mine. He lied and told them I'd had a psychotic episode, that the bruises were the result of him trying to restrain me. And they believed him. They *always* believed him. Then, he drove me home, ripped the flowers out of my hands, swung them at me like a whip until they were nothing but stems. The thorns cut into my skin. I have a few scars on my shoulder from..." She shook her head. "That doesn't really matter. He told me if I ever left him again, he'd fucking kill me."

"Jesus Christ." Theo grasped Gretchen's trembling hands, holding them firmly in his. He recalled the panic in her eyes when he'd given her the yellow roses. He was never giving her roses again. Any other flower. But not roses.

"I didn't try to leave again for a year. I was too afraid. The second time, I was even more stupid and desperate. I ran to my mother. She blamed *me* for the failing relationship, and Ivan forced me into their car. He drove me back to Briggs and offered some suggestions on ways to punish me. Briggs listened."

Theo lifted her hands, kissing her palms softly, every word she spoke more painful than the next.

"My next attempt was a few weeks later. I stole money from Briggs's wallet and managed to get all the way to the bus station before he came roaring up in his squad car, siren blaring and lights flashing. He said I was under arrest. Handcuffed me, read me my rights, and drove me back home, even as I begged the people at the bus station for help. I didn't try again after that. Not for a couple of years. Not until September."

He wanted to ask why she stopped trying, but he was afraid she might close down again.

Then she answered the unspoken question. "He cracked three of my ribs that last time. I was too afraid after that to..." She lifted one shoulder.

They fell silent for a few minutes, her hands still clasped tightly in his. He was never going to be able to let them go. Never.

With the passage of time, Gretchen seemed to pull herself together, her breathing easing, her eyes dry once more.

"I'm sorry," she said again.

He shook his head, because those words were wrong coming from her. She didn't have a damn thing to be sorry about.

Then he considered the way he'd found her earlier, balled up in panic and fear. "What do you think will happen if he shows up here?"

"I don't know. I've never made it this far."

Theo released one of her hands so that he could cup her cheek, force her to look at him, and really hear what he said next. "This isn't like those other times. He can't force you to go back. He—"

"I know that," she interjected. "My sane brain knows that. But with him, I've never managed sane. Just terror. I hate that I fell apart. I'm pissed off at myself that I'm still letting him have so much power over me."

Theo wasn't sure if she was aware of it, but with every word she spoke, her voice grew stronger.

"I will never go back to Harrisburg *or* him. Never. I was a coward to run the way I did, without facing him, but—"

This time, he did the interrupting. "You were no coward, Gretchen. Jesus. He's a dangerous man. He could have killed you."

"You sound like Edith." She gave him a small, sad smile. It was nowhere near the beautiful ones she was capable of, but it was a start.

"You were smart to escape. Leaving the way you did wasn't cowardly, it was self-preservation, plain and simple. And now? Now, you have something here that you didn't have in Harrisburg."

"What's that?"

He wanted to say "me," but he realized she had so much more. "Support. A family. A whole lot of people who will have your back no matter what."

He hated that his words had provoked more tears, until he realized these weren't bad ones.

"I…" She swallowed hard, clearly moved. His heart cracked when she looked at him and asked, "I do?"

Theo kissed her forehead, then placed his against hers. "You do."

They remained like that, both of them soaking in the much-needed closeness after the confessions of the past half hour or so.

"Thank you for telling me," he said, when they finally separated.

"I was too ashamed before."

He frowned. "Ashamed?"

"I was weak and stupid to stay with him as long as I did."

Theo shook his head. "You weren't stupid. Briggs is an abusive asshole. He preyed on a scared, lonely little girl and took advantage of her. Swooped in and made you believe he was the only one who could ever love you."

She nodded. "I didn't realize it for a long time, but yeah, that's exactly what he did. He was the only person—with the exception of Shaw—who ever paid any attention to me. He made me feel special and worthy of affection. I'd been starved for those things, so I stupidly viewed him as my savior."

"Is Briggs the reason why you haven't talked to your brother in so long?"

"Shaw and I were close most of our lives, even after he joined the Navy. We would talk on the phone at least once a week, and he used to send me postcards from all the cool places he'd been. But after a while...I let Briggs convince me that Shaw only did those things out of obligation. He had a way of twisting things around in my head. I *hate* that I let him do that. That I let him come between me and Shaw. I pushed my brother away, lashed out at him cruelly, and now, I don't know how to fix it."

From the things Theo had learned about Gretchen's brother through her comments, he suspected her fix would be as simple as a phone call. "You can fix it. I'll help you figure out how."

She smiled sadly. "I miss him."

"I'm sure you do." Theo gave her a kiss on the cheek. "You're not alone anymore."

He started to pull away, but Gretchen stopped him, gripping the front of his shirt.

Theo narrowed his eyes, studying her face.

"Please kiss me," she whispered.

Theo placed a soft kiss on her lips, but he didn't seek to deepen it. She was emotionally fragile right now, in need of comfort. Nothing else.

"I guess you understand now why you and I aren't a good idea," she murmured. "I'm a mess."

"There's not a single part of you that's a mess."

Her grin this time was bigger as she rolled her eyes. "You said that about me being ugly, too."

"Applies to both."

She snickered. "Even *you* have to admit I'm not normal."

"You're right. You're not. You're extraordinary. Resilient, brave, strong. God, you could never be anything as lame and boring as normal."

Gretchen stared at him, blinking back tears. "Every time I manage to stop crying, you say something wonderful and all, of sudden, I'm a blubbering idiot again."

Theo ran his fingers through her hair, then brushed his thumbs under her eyes, capturing the wetness there. "Should we get off this hard floor?"

She huffed out a breathy laugh. "Not sure I can. I'm too stiff. I might live here now."

Theo chuckled, rising, then reaching down to help her to her feet.

Gretchen picked up her phone, hesitating. "I can't go back to Edith's tonight. Not if there's a chance..."

"That's okay," Theo said. "Because I can't let you go there. I won't sleep tonight if I'm not somewhere nearby to protect you. Please don't ask me to."

She released a sigh of relief. "I won't."

"The B&B is full this week." Fall was their busy season, as city dwellers escaped to the mountain to enjoy the foliage. "You could stay with the girls if you wanted, but..." Theo paused a moment, then said what he wanted to say. "I'd prefer it if you stayed with me and my brothers. You can have Levi's old room. It's down the hall from mine. I need to know you're safe."

"Safe and sound," she murmured to herself, and he recalled the song they danced to on Halloween.

Their song.

Theo clasped hands with her, the two of them walking along the path that led from the brewhouse to the farmhouse he shared with his brothers. They'd installed solar lights along all the main paths on the farm, so it was easy to make their way through the trees.

When they arrived, Theo was unsurprised to find all six of his brothers, Levi included, sitting in the living room. He wasn't sure where Kasi was. Most likely she was with the girls at their place.

"Everything good?" Levi asked.

"All good," Theo wrapped his arm around her shoulders, tucking her close as he replied for them. Gretchen's head remained bowed as she tried to hide the fact she'd been crying.

Mercifully, his brothers were good at reading social cues, so none of them stared at her or asked questions.

"I'm glad to hear it," Levi replied.

"I'm sorry for being a bother," she said, glancing around at them before focusing on Sam. "And for ruining your party."

Sam stepped closer. "You threw me the best party ever. Nothing was ruined, Gretchen. We're glad you're okay."

She smiled at his brother. "Thank you."

"Gretchen's going to stay here tonight. I offered her your old bedroom," Theo said to Levi.

"Sounds good. I was just heading out. Need to grab Kasi from the brewery on the way back to Lucky Penny Farm. The girls wanted to put a dent in the party cleanup."

"That was nice of them," Theo said.

"We stayed here. Just in case..." Levi paused.

Just in case Theo needed them. He smiled, nodded in understanding. "Thanks."

Levi gave Gretchen one last friendly smile, then said goodbye.

Theo added his own goodbyes, waving to his brothers before guiding Gretchen upstairs. "Let's stop by my room first. I'll grab one of my T-shirts for you to sleep in."

She followed him without hesitation. He wanted to tell

himself that was because she wasn't afraid of him, but part of him suspected she was running on fumes, sapped of all energy.

Theo quickly grabbed a soft cotton shirt for her, then led her to Levi's room. Opening the door, he handed her the shirt. "The bathroom is right across the hall and the sheets on the bed are clean."

Gretchen stood next to him in the doorway, without entering.

"I can walk you over to the girls' house if you'd prefer." If she chose that, he was sleeping on their couch, because there was no way he was leaving Gretchen *and* his cousins unprotected if this asshole was on his way, as she feared.

"No. I'd rather stay here. It's just..."

"What?"

She bit her lower lip, looking uneasy.

"You can ask me for anything, kitten."

He noticed a slight flush rose to her cheeks whenever he used the term of endearment. Considering she'd been pale since he found her own the floor, he was glad to see some color on her face.

"Would you stay in here with me? Not to— I mean, just to—"

Theo placed his hand on her back, pushing her into the room. He followed, then closed the door behind him. He turned off the overhead light, the moon bright enough through the open curtains to illuminate the room.

Taking her hand once more, he led her to the bed. Turning her to face him, he slowly unbuttoned her blouse, his eyes locked on her face. Tugging it off her shoulders, he drew his T-shirt over her head.

She remained perfectly still, allowing him to dress her for bed.

"Toe off your shoes," he murmured.

She did as he asked, never once breaking the connection of their eyes. Not even when he reached beneath the hem of the shirt and unfastened her jeans. Together, they pulled them off.

Theo drew back the covers, gesturing for her to crawl in. Once she was snug beneath the duvet, Theo shed his own shoes and jeans, leaving on his boxers and shirt.

Joining her, he closed his eyes, thanking every god who ever existed when she shifted to her side, wrapped her arm around his stomach, and rested her head on his shoulder, curling into him like the spot was tailor-made for her shape.

That was when she came undone, her body trembling with the tears she tried to shed quietly. He didn't want her trying to hide her pain from him.

"Let it out," he murmured. "Let it all out, Gretchen. I have you."

So, she did. She cried out years' worth of pain and fear, her tears soaking his shirt as he held her tighter, whispering soft words of promise.

"You're safe."

"No one will ever hurt you again."

"I'll never let you go."

"It's going to be okay now."

After several minutes, the crying slowed, and her body softened against his. It felt as if all the bad shit had been expunged through those tears. Theo wrapped his arm around her upper back, holding her close, then placed a kiss to the top of her head.

Gretchen's face lifted to look at him.

"Don't say 'I'm sorry.' You've done nothing wrong," he said quickly, brushing the last traces of wetness from her cheeks with his thumbs.

He noticed the way she changed course instantly. "Okay.

Then thank you," she whispered, shifting up enough that she could give him a proper kiss.

"No thanks necessary. Good night, kitten."

She resumed her original snuggle, sighing softly, asleep within minutes.

Sleep took longer for him. A lot longer.

But by the time it found him, he'd made up his mind that he was going to spend the rest of his life making sure this woman knew she was loved, that she was safe and sound.

He was going to be her shelter in every single storm.

Chapter Twelve

Gretchen blinked a few times, her eyes gritty and puffy from crying. The moment she recalled breaking down in Theo's arms, she remembered where she was and managed to force her eyes open.

Her hand was resting on Theo's chest. Mercifully, he'd slept in his T-shirt because heaven help her if she'd had to sleep on his bare chest.

Trying not to move, she slowly glanced upward, quickly realizing her stealth was for nothing.

Theo was wide awake and grinning at her. "Good morning, kitten," he said cheerfully.

Gretchen attempted to put some distance between them, but Theo tightened his grip around her shoulders.

"Just give me one more minute to savor this," he said, his voice husky from sleep and sexy as hell.

"Savor?"

"This is hands down the greatest way to wake up."

"With a woman in your bed?"

He shook his head. "With *you* in my bed."

Gretchen never knew how to respond when he said sweet stuff like that. Probably because she hadn't been on the receiving end of many kind comments.

Although, while her brain didn't have a response, her body knew exactly how it felt about his compliments and praise. Because it was now wide awake, sitting with paws up like a dog begging for a treat.

For a moment, she considered slipping her hand under his shirt to see if those abs of his were as rock-hard as she suspected. Before she could make that mistake, however, her gaze drifted to the clock on his nightstand, and she quickly sat up.

"Oh my God! It's after eight, and I still need to go home to shower and get clean clothes."

Theo chuckled as she leapt from the bed, belatedly aware of her state of undress.

Her face was suddenly hot, no doubt flushing beet red, as she tried to bend over to retrieve her jeans without flashing him a peek of her panties.

Twisting around, she narrowed her eyes when she saw that he'd pushed to a seated position, pillow propped against the headboard as he watched her awkwardly tug down the hem of his T-shirt while she half bent/half knelt to get her jeans.

"A gentleman would close his eyes," she said.

"And a smart man would enjoy the show. I know which kind of man I want to be."

She couldn't help herself. She laughed. Because he was incorrigible and funny and so fucking sweet. With every word he spoke, it was as if her long-dead self-confidence was slowly being reincarnated.

Gretchen bit her lip after she managed to pull her jeans and shoes on, because Theo still hadn't moved, and he was her ride.

"Um..."

Theo slowly climbed out of bed and, despite her better judgment, she let her eyes slip down to check out his ass in his boxer briefs when he bent over to grab his jeans off the floor. Unlike her, the smug man made no attempt to cover himself—and even went so far as to clench his butt cheeks when he caught her looking.

Gretchen tried to avert her eyes, but it was too late. The damage was done.

Because *damn* that man had one fine ass.

Once Theo was dressed, he reached for her hand. She started for the door, but he tugged her backward, encouraging her to sit with him on the edge of Levi's unmade bed.

"Theo—"

"We're going to be late for work, kitten, and it's no big deal."

"But—"

"I'm the boss, remember."

She tilted her head. "Nora's my boss."

"No one will care if we show up late. Hell, given the way my family was tossing back pints last night, it'll be a miracle if *any* of them start working before ten."

She wasn't sure she believed that—because she'd witnessed their work ethic—but then, there had been a lot of tipsy Storms at the party, so maybe he was right.

"I feel bad enough about ruining the party last night," she said, her hands clenched in her lap. "I'm sorry for reacting like that."

Theo reached over and covered her hands. "You had a panic attack, Gretchen. That's nothing something you ever need to apologize for."

"I feel like an idiot. It's just... Brenda called, said Briggs knew where I was, and my flight-or-flight instinct when it comes to him kicked into high gear."

Theo's lips quirked up at her intentional rewording of the common phrase.

"Lately, I've woken up every day feeling stronger, ready to take on the world *and* Briggs. Then, Brenda said his name, and I felt the overwhelming need to run and never look back."

Theo frowned at that. "You want to run?"

She shook her head. "No. When I lived in Harrisburg, all I could think about was getting out. I was fully prepared to live my life as a nomad if that was how I managed to stay one step ahead of Briggs. But then I came to Gracemont, and met you and Edith and your family, and I can't imagine ever finding another town that feels like..." She sighed. "Like home. Not the shitty kind I grew up in but the good kind."

He smiled, leaning his shoulder against hers. "I'm glad you're happy here." Then he reached over and took her chin between his finger and thumb. "But if you ever feel that need to run again, promise you'll come find me first."

"I promise," she whispered.

Theo sealed that vow with a quick, firm kiss.

"Now, I think we should discuss next steps."

"Next steps?" Gretchen asked, confused.

"Last night, you were worried about going back to Edith's."

Gretchen really had lost her shit in spectacular fashion. Her reaction probably hadn't been helped by the amount of beer she drank.

"I was, but now that I'm thinking with a clearer head, I know how to handle that."

"What do you mean?" he asked.

"Briggs never hurt anyone but me. Whenever he came to drag me back, he never threatened anyone else. To others, he's always cool, calm, collected. I need to make sure Edith isn't around when I talk to him."

"I agree, Edith shouldn't be around, but I also don't want you talking to him alone. I want to be there."

Gretchen had expected the request, but she hadn't managed to come up with a single reason to refuse that offer except the real one—which she hated saying aloud.

Regardless, she felt she owed him the truth after all the kindness and support he'd shown her.

"Briggs is a master when it comes to manipulating people. He's very good at making me look bad, always finding a way to convince others I'm either overreacting, embellishing the truth, or straight-up crazy."

Her reaction last night might have helped prove that case for him, considering how Theo had found her hunkered down behind her desk.

"Briggs is a world champion when it comes to gaslighting. I think it would be better if—"

"If I was there with you," Theo interjected. "He's not going to gaslight me, Gretchen, because I know you, the real you."

She liked the way Theo looked at her. Like she was smart and brave. The idea that Briggs might change Theo's opinion, even a little bit, scared her. But, since she had no idea when or even if Briggs would show up, she would have to cross that bridge when she came to it.

"And to that end," Theo continued. "I think you should stay with me until we sort all the Briggs shit out."

Gretchen shook her head. "No. I could never impose on your brothers that way. They were sweet to let me stay last night, but I can't let my fear of Briggs possibly showing up disrupt everyone's life that way."

"I wasn't suggesting we stay here."

"Where would we stay?"

"We recently finished fixing up one of the cabins for the new vineyard manager we hired to take Levi's place. Boone isn't set to move in until the first of next year, so the cabin is sitting empty for the next two months."

"I..." She was at a complete loss for words, because the idea of living alone with Theo was tempting. Too tempting.

"It's a two-bedroom cabin. Boone's bringing his young daughter with him," Theo quickly added. "We would each have our own room, but this way, Edith is completely out of the line of fire, and I'm always going to be around to keep you safe. I promised we would take this thing between us at your speed, and that still stands. If you hate the idea, then we'll go with plan B."

"You've already come up with a plan A and a plan B?" Gretchen had fallen asleep and slept the sleep of the dead. And she hadn't had time this morning to do more than admire Theo's sexy ass, yet here he was with a million answers to questions she hadn't even thought to ask.

"I won't be able to rest if I'm here on the mountain and you're down in town on your own. If you want to stay there, then I'll move into one of Edith's other rooms and live there with the two of you."

Gretchen blew out a long, slow breath. She had to admit, both options appealed to her. While she was much stronger now than she was when she'd escaped Harrisburg, her bravery hadn't truly been tested. She wanted to believe Briggs would show up and she'd manage to say all the things she'd practiced in her head a million times.

But...what if she couldn't?

She obviously wasn't going back with him regardless, but the idea of having backup sounded pretty damn nice. Given the anger she'd seen on Theo's face last night when she talked about Briggs, she didn't doubt for a second he would have no trouble standing up to her abusive ex.

"What do you think?" he pressed, and she saw something that looked like desperation on his face. He really *was* worried about her. Warmth permeated every dark, cold corner of her heart at the idea that someone as wonderful as Theo Storm would be concerned about her. It felt like the greatest gift she'd ever received.

"I think I prefer the cabin."

Staying at Edith's would be the smarter decision, from Gretchen's perspective, because her resolve to take things slowly with Theo was weakening.

However, staying with Edith and managing to keep her out of the line of fire was a pipe dream. Edith, like Theo, would never leave her alone with Briggs. Knowing the beloved old woman, she'd most likely throw herself between Gretchen and her ex, and that could not happen.

After two months of looking for her, God only knew how angry Briggs was by now. Given the fact he hadn't given up the hunt and had possibly broken a law to find her, she suspected his rage was probably burning out of control.

Theo grinned widely at her response. "I was hoping you'd agree to that one. Edith isn't the type to step aside if someone she loves is in danger."

Gretchen blinked a few times, hating that she was on the verge of crying again. Not because she was sad but because Theo's happiness at her agreement, paired with his assertion that Edith loved her, was too amazing.

Theo rose. "Let's go to Edith's, tell her the plan, and pack you a bag. Then, with your permission, I'd like to invite my entire family over for dinner to let them know what's going on. I like the idea of having an army at your back."

Gretchen laughed, even as a tear slid down her cheek. "I like the idea of that too."

An hour later, Gretchen made her way downstairs in the Millholland House, after packing a bag and saying goodbye to her beautiful room at Edith's. She knew it wasn't forever, but she was still sad to leave the first home where she'd felt welcomed, warm, and safe.

She'd reached the bottom of the stairs when there was a knock on the door. Edith and Theo emerged from the living room, both looking as alarmed as she felt. She drew in a deep breath, steadying herself in case this was it, as Edith went to open the door. Theo, meanwhile, had crossed the foyer to stand partly next to but mostly in front of her.

When she saw Sheriff Anderson standing at the door, her heart started to race. She'd tried to warm up to the man, since making an ass of herself by running to hide in her bedroom the night of her welcome dinner. She and Theo—well, Theo—had chatted with him at the Fall Harvest Festival fair, and then again that same night, at the dance. Gretchen hadn't contributed much to the conversations, but at least she'd been able to stand her ground.

She had even served him last night at Sam's victory party, though she'd done little more than take his order, then deliver his beer and pizza.

When the sheriff's gaze traveled to her, her stomach clenched.

"Edith," the sheriff said, turning his attention back to the older woman. "Can I come in?"

Edith stepped aside—but uncharacteristically, she didn't invite him to sit in the living room. She had noticed the sheriff's interest in Gretchen as well. "What's this unexpected visit about, Jacob?"

Sheriff Anderson took off his hat and raked fingers through his thinning hair. "Got a call this morning from a police officer in Harrisburg, Pennsylvania. He was asking me about a Gretchen Parker," the sheriff said, looking straight at Gretchen. "Your last name is Banks, right?"

Gretchen nodded, her throat closing.

"As I recall, you're from Harrisburg."

"I am," she replied, her voice too weak to hide her unease.

"What did he want?" Theo asked.

While Sheriff Anderson was answering Theo, his gaze was locked on her. "Said he was looking for a mentally unstable woman who'd gone missing a couple months ago. Mentioned she'd gone off her meds and her family was worried about her."

"Bullshit!" Theo cursed. "What was the cop's name?"

Sheriff Anderson pulled a small notebook from his back pocket, flipping through the pages before responding. "Briggs Howard."

"He's her ex," Theo said. "And an abusive prick."

Sheriff Anderson's eyes narrowed slightly. "He's not a cop?"

"He is." Gretchen forced herself to enter the conversation. This was her fight, not Theo's. Jesus. If she couldn't stand up to a sixty-year-old sheriff, what chance did she have against Briggs? "We were together for six years. He... He wasn't a nice guy."

"Is he dangerous?"

"Only to me," Gretchen replied, hoping that remained to be true. She'd die if anything bad happened to Edith, Manny, or the Storms because of her.

The sheriff shoved his notebook back in his pocket. "So your family isn't looking for you?"

Gretchen shook her head. "I'm estranged from my mother and stepfather. My brother is stationed overseas with the Navy SEALs. I'm pretty sure he doesn't know I'm not still living in Harrisburg."

Sheriff Anderson nodded. "And the medication? The mental instability."

Gretchen stepped out from behind Theo, tired of hovering in the background of her own life. "I tried to leave him several times," she said to the sheriff. "Once, after a particularly bad beating, I stole money from his wallet after he fell asleep—because he never let me carry cash—and got a cab to the bus station. I didn't bother with luggage or even a coat, too afraid he'd wake up and catch me.

"I was standing in line to buy a ticket when a siren sounded right outside the station. I turned around to see Briggs dressed in his police uniform, striding over to me. I tried to run, but two guys stepped in front of me, stopped me from escaping. Briggs loudly assured the handful of people in the station that they weren't in danger, that I was only a danger to myself. I realized that I probably looked that way, standing there in disheveled clothing, bruised face and arms, my hair a mess, no coat, crying. Briggs handcuffed me and read me my rights, while I kept begging someone to call 9-1-1, shouting that I wasn't crazy."

Edith stepped closer to her, reaching out to take her hand, as Theo claimed her opposite side, his arm wrapped around her waist.

"Do you know the most surefire way to sound crazy, Sheriff Anderson?" Gretchen asked.

The sheriff shook his head.

"Tell people you *aren't* crazy. Briggs put me in the back of the squad car, drove me home, and beat me so badly, I couldn't get out of bed for two days. I had to crawl to the bathroom, unable to walk."

Sheriff Anderson frowned, his bushy brows furrowed in anger over her story.

"You didn't tell that man she was here, did you, Jacob?" Edith asked.

"No," the sheriff said. "I told him I'd look into it. Now that I have, I'm going to call him back and tell him there's no Gretchen Parker in Gracemont. Because there isn't."

Gretchen stepped forward, reaching out to take the sheriff's hand. "Thank you, Sheriff."

Sheriff Anderson shook it, then offered her one short nod. "If Briggs Howard shows up here, I want you to call me immediately. He's not laying a goddamn finger on you in my town."

"I will," she whispered, overwhelmed by his support.

The sheriff said goodbye, while she, Edith, and Theo talked a little bit longer.

Gretchen, who was becoming a regular crybaby, teared up when Edith gave her one of those nice, tight hugs and made her promise to come back home soon.

Theo took her bag in one hand, wrapping his other arm around her shoulders as they walked to his truck.

"You okay?" he asked when they pulled out of the driveway.

"Yes," she said, realizing that despite all the crap going on, she really was.

Because she was no longer alone.

Gretchen had finished lighting the candle in the center of the table when Theo entered their cabin. A week had passed since the two of them had essentially moved in together. True to his word, Theo gave her the bigger bedroom, moving into the one on the opposite side of the great room.

With each passing night, the separate bedrooms felt more like a punishment than a good idea. Probably because after dinner, they plopped down together on the couch, watched TV, and made out like the plane was going down.

"What's this?" Theo closed the front door behind him. The main area of the cabin consisted of one large living space that contained the kitchen with a small dining table, both separated from the living room by an island. Off each side of the living room were the doors to their private bedrooms and bathrooms.

"You've been feeding me all week," Gretchen said. "Tonight, I wanted to make a special dinner for you."

Theo came over, taking his seat at the table, his eyes growing wide at the meal she'd prepared each of them. Gretchen had been delighted to finally be able to put some of Edith's cooking lessons to good use. Tonight, she'd prepared chicken cordon bleu, twice-baked potatoes, and fresh green beans sauteed in garlic and butter.

"Holy shit, this smells fantastic."

She smiled at his compliment, joining him at the table.

"But I'm not sure I can claim the credit for feeding you all week, kitten, considering we ate at least three of those meals with my brothers and they did the cooking."

"Semantics," she said, waving her hand. "I wanted to find a way to tell you how much I appreciate everything you've done for me. And not just this week, when you uprooted your life to keep me safe here. But for everything that came before, too. The job. The driving lessons. All the fun nights out."

She stood briefly, pouring them both a glass of Chardonnay before resuming her seat. Theo lifted his glass to tap against hers.

"You look beautiful tonight."

Gretchen laughed. "You say that every night."

Theo shrugged. "Because it's always true."

They ate together, the conversation flowing easily as they spent a few minutes discussing work and the weather and a bunch of other subjects, like Remi's obsessive love for the donkey they'd purchased for the event barn, and what Gretchen could expect from a Thanksgiving dinner with Theo's family.

He'd invited her, Edith, and Manny to join them this year, insisting there was plenty of room for everyone. Apparently, Kasi's dad and brother were also new participants. For the first time in her life, Gretchen was looking forward to the holiday season. In the past, it'd been the worst part of her year, as she was painfully aware her holidays were never as festive and bright as those of the other kids in her class.

And sadly, that hadn't changed with Briggs, who bitched that he wasn't about to spend his hard-earned money on a bunch of fancy food and presents, insisting the entire season was a way for big businesses to bleed the little man dry.

The thought of her ex no longer scared her as much as annoyed her. Briggs hadn't shown up in Gracemont, and Gretchen wasn't sure what to make of that. Perhaps Sheriff Anderson had thrown him off the track. Or perhaps he was biding his time, doing his research, trying to find out exactly where she was and what she was doing.

If that was true, more fool him. Because the longer he stayed away, the stronger and angrier she got. The initial fear and panic she'd felt had long since faded, in no small part due to the people around her. Once she came clean to Theo's family about her past, she didn't just find herself with an army at her back but a family at her side.

"No phone calls today?" Theo asked, the question a daily one.

"No. I'm not sure what to make of Briggs's silence."

Gretchen had been convinced now that he had her phone number, he'd begin calling and texting.

"No news is good news," Theo said easily, though Gretchen wasn't sure that applied in this case.

"Maybe."

"You know," Theo said, changing the subject. "If you wanted to invite your brother to Thanksgiving, he'd be more than welcome."

Gretchen took a sip of wine, stalling as she searched for a response. "I'm not sure he'd accept."

Lately, Theo mentioned Shaw more and more, probably because—given his closeness to his brothers—he couldn't conceive of siblings who didn't stay in touch.

"Why not?"

Gretchen leaned back in her chair. Shaw had been on her mind a lot lately as well. Maybe even more than Briggs. "I'm not even sure he knows I don't live in Harrisburg anymore."

Theo tilted his head, one eyebrow raised to let her know he wasn't going to let her get away with her evasive answers.

She grimaced. "I haven't talked to him in a long time. I stopped calling after the last time. I..." She toyed with her fork, struggling with how to explain her mindset. "I went to a very dark place after Briggs dragged me back from the bus station. I started believing his lies, his insults. I even wondered if he was right, that maybe I *was* losing my mind. I let him convince me that I was unlovable and stupid. I let him drive a wedge between me and Shaw, believing him when he said my brother had abandoned me like my parents. The last time Shaw and I spoke on the phone, I was angry, and I parroted back Briggs's words. We haven't spoken since."

"He doesn't know about the abuse, does he?"

"No. During the early years, I defended Briggs to Shaw, claiming it was true love and the difference in our ages didn't matter. Going so far that when Briggs started hitting me, I was embarrassed to admit I'd been wrong. Besides...Shaw would have killed Briggs if he'd known."

Theo smiled sadly. "Sounds like a good brother, one who loves you enough to want to protect you."

Gretchen toyed with the stem of her wine glass. "His phone number is written on a Post-it on my desk. I look at it fifty times a day, but I can't make myself call. What if I ruined things between us? What if I've driven him away forever?"

"If you don't call, you *will* have driven him away forever."

It was a valid point, one she'd considered countless times. It was just... "If I call, and he rejects me... If he hates me and can't forgive me, it'll hurt more than anything Briggs ever did to me."

Theo reached across the table. "This is another one of those moments when you need to be brave."

She shook her head and rolled her eyes. "Those are really stacking up, aren't they?"

Theo laughed. "Yep."

"I think I'll tackle the Briggs one first."

Theo let her get away with that response, though she knew him well enough to know he wouldn't give up on reconnecting her with her brother.

She loved him for it.

Gretchen sucked in a sharp breath, one that Theo, mercifully, didn't hear as he rose and began clearing the table.

She loved Theo.

She was in love with him.

Gretchen sat there and let that fact set in, waiting for... Well, she didn't know what she was waiting for. Maybe panic or fear or self-doubt.

None of it appeared.

Instead, all she felt was how right it was.

For the first time in her life, all the pieces had fallen into place, none of them feeling askew, or jammed in, or wrong.

Gretchen stood as well, quietly helping Theo clean the kitchen. Once they were finished, he flipped the towel he'd been using to dry the dishes, over his shoulder. "Should we change into our comfortable clothes and meet on the couch in five?"

Another part of their nighttime routine included pajamas—both of them trading their jeans for lounge pants and soft cotton T-shirts.

Gretchen shook her head, her response obviously surprising him.

"No?"

"No. I don't want to meet you on the couch." She took a deep breath and decided confronting Briggs wasn't going to be her first act of bravery.

This was.

"I want to meet you in the bedroom."

Theo's eyes darkened with desire. "Gretchen." He wanted her, she could see it, but he needed to hear more from her.

"I want to sleep with you," she added.

"Sleep?"

She laughed. "Fuck," she clarified.

"*Fuck*," Theo breathed, using the word as a prayer and a curse rather than a verb. Then his eyes narrowed. "You and I are never going to fuck. We're only ever going to make love."

Gretchen liked the sound of that. Liked it enough that she rose on tiptoe, kissing his cheek. "You coming?" she asked, as she turned toward her bedroom.

Theo was hot on her heels.

"Hell yeah, I'm coming."

Chapter Thirteen

Theo followed Gretchen into her bedroom, feeling like the luckiest son of a bitch on the planet. And while he could see she truly wanted him and her invitation was sincere, there was something that had been weighing heavy on his mind ever since she'd told him about Briggs.

He didn't want to bring her abusive ex into the bedroom with them, but he needed one more answer before he proceeded. Because Gretchen had confessed a couple days earlier that her panic attack in the barn hadn't been driven by the storm or his kisses or even his proclamation that she was his.

He'd inadvertently triggered it by grasping the back of her neck to pull her in for another kiss. It reminded her of Briggs choking her. Theo felt physically ill, knowing he'd put that memory back in her head, even though she reassured him that she knew he would never hurt her that way.

Gretchen led him straight to her bed before turning and wrapping her arms around his shoulders.

Theo gripped her waist, holding her back.

His hesitance confused her. "Theo?"

"I have to ask, kitten." He paused for a second, searching for the right words. "I need to know if Briggs ever... If when you were together..."

Understanding dawned on her face and she quickly shook her head. "No. No. He never hurt me that way. I guess if there's a small mercy...it's that. His preferred violence was by using his fists. Not sex."

Knowing her asshole ex had never raped her was a relief, but that didn't mean he agreed with what she said. "Nothing he did was merciful."

She nodded in agreement. "You're right. I suppose we should have talked about this before..." Gretchen glanced at the bed.

Theo sank down onto the mattress, patting the spot next to him. "I'm assuming he's the only man you've had sex with." He refused to refer to Briggs as a lover, considering all he'd ever shown her was control and hate.

"He is. And at the beginning, the sex was fine. In the middle, it felt more like a chore, not something I enjoyed but could tolerate. Toward the end, it stopped altogether." She blushed a little. "I think he might have had a little trouble..." She crooked her pointer finger, then straightened it. Theo chuckled at the way she used a gesture rather than saying her ex couldn't get it up.

"Wow. He didn't set a very high bar, did he?"

Gretchen shot him a look that was pure minx. "He didn't. But I should warn you, I read a lot of steamy romance novels, so you're still going to need to bring your A game."

Theo barked out a laugh, enjoying this new side of her. Since coming clean about her past, Gretchen was slowly starting to reveal more of what he suspected was her true personality. She was funny as shit, a bit of a smart-ass, and outspoken on subjects she felt passionate about. She'd shed her reservations, no longer afraid to draw attention to herself or be seen.

Theo had a big personality himself, but damn if he didn't think Gretchen was going to give him a run for his money.

"Challenge accepted," he retorted before rising again. Gretchen accepted his proffered hand, lifting her face as he bent to kiss her.

They'd spent hours the past couple of weeks necking like teenagers. He'd never put a ton of stock in kissing, viewing it only as a prologue while waiting for the story to start. With Gretchen, however, kissing could be the entire first act, leading all the way to the intermission, and he'd still want more.

She ran her fingers through his hair as he slowly untucked her shirt, his fingers dipping beneath to stroke the soft skin of her waist and stomach.

She sucked in a wobbly breath, breaking the kiss. "That tickles," she confessed with a giggle.

Unable to resist, Theo tickled her again.

Gretchen tried to push him away, her hands pressing on his chest, laughing, which only encouraged him to up the ante.

Wrestling her to the bed, he straddled her thighs, tickling her even more as she struggled and laughed in equal measure.

Given what he knew of her past, he would bet the entire farm Gretchen had never laughed in bed, never realized that sex could be hot *and* fun.

"Uncle!" she finally cried.

Theo relented, shifting until his body was completely over hers, resuming their kiss as lips parted, tongues touched, breath grew heavy, and their desire rose.

He ran his fingers over her long blonde hair, then cupped her gorgeous face, taking in her pink cheeks and sparkling blue eyes.

Gretchen looked her fill as well, the two of them speaking volumes with the connection of their gazes.

"I have a condom in my room. I better go grab that before things really heat up."

Gretchen fisted his shirt, holding him to her. "I'm on the pill. If you." She bit her lip. "I mean, we don't need to..."

Theo kissed her again, pressing his forehead to hers. "I genuinely believed the day we met was the best day of my life, but I think tonight might rearrange that order."

"Every single day since that first has been the best of my life." She smiled, pulling him back down to kiss her again.

In between kisses, they undressed each other, stripping one piece of clothing at a time. She lost her shirt first, and Theo took his time, teasing her tight nipples through the lace of her bra.

Once Gretchen tugged his shirt off, she pushed him back a few inches, her eyes traveling over his bare chest. "It's like you're chiseled from stone."

He drew one finger through the valley of her breasts. "Farmwork is better than any gym."

Gretchen arched her back to give Theo access to the hooks on her bra. He snapped them free with a practiced hand, and she smirked.

"You're awfully good at that."

He started to laugh, but it quickly morphed to a growl when he bared her breasts, his mouth watering for a taste. His dick had been rock-hard since he'd walked into the cabin and discovered she'd made him dinner. Every single thing about Gretchen turned him on, and most of it wasn't even sexual.

Her tits, though...

Fuck him.

Perfection.

Lowering his head, he sucked one of her nipples into his mouth, pinching the other between his finger and thumb.

Gretchen jerked slightly. "Oh! Oh my God. That feels so good."

There was a tone of surprise in her voice that gave him pause. Not that he was going to question it, because her ex had no place here. He wasn't interested in comparisons or any more horror stories. His sole purpose tonight was to erase every fucking bad memory from her mind, replacing them with nothing but good ones.

Switching breasts, he treated that nipple to the same ministrations, licking, sucking, even nipping it lightly until she writhed beneath him.

"I need more."

Theo shared her hunger, but there was no way in hell he was going to rush this.

"Mm-hmm." Theo continued to play with her breasts.

Gretchen huffed out a laugh. "You're ignoring me."

Theo lifted his head, sliding up her body so that he could give her another heated kiss. "Be a good girl, and I promise you'll get everything you want and more."

He watched as her already pink cheeks brightened to a darker red, her eyes slid closed, and she drew in a gasping breath.

Awareness dawned.

"You like being my good girl, don't you?"

"Yes," she breathed.

Just when Theo thought this woman couldn't get any hotter, she turned the heat up from bonfire to inferno.

Theo kissed her again, squeezing her breasts as he did so, pinching her nipples until she whimpered. Not in pain. He'd never hurt her. She'd had enough of that to last her a lifetime.

But he knew where the line between pleasurable pain and true hurt lie, and he would never cross it.

Gretchen's fingers closed into fists in his hair, tugging it roughly as she returned his kiss tenfold. He growled when she lifted her legs, wrapping them around his waist, gyrating against his crotch.

Too much more of that, and his vow to go slow would be nullified.

Theo shifted lower again, forcing her legs to drop. He took a second to kiss each turgid nipple before continuing his descent. Kneeling between her outstretched thighs, he unfastened her jeans, then encouraged her to lift her ass as he pulled off her jeans and panties.

After a week in the cabin together, he knew her first order of business upon returning home from work was to kick off her shoes, preferring to be barefoot around the house. With no shoes or socks to add to the pile, he finally—FINALLY—had Gretchen completely naked.

He remained where he was, on his knees between her legs, her body on full display before him. Kneeling was the appropriate position, because he was fully prepared to worship before this altar for the rest of his life.

She was beautiful, inside and out. Upon her first arrival, she'd been right on the border of too thin, but a couple months of dining on Edith's amazing cooking had corrected that, adding gorgeous curves in all the right places. She had a healthy appetite and a huge appreciation for good food, something he suspected she'd never been allowed to indulge in before.

Gretchen's hands drifted to her stomach, covering it. "I've gained some weight."

Theo drew her hands away from her body. "You're perfect."

He slid down, putting himself right over the bullseye, giving her a playful wink before he lowered his head.

Gretchen jolted upward, her hands flying to his hair. "What are you doing?"

Theo gave her a curious glance. "I think it's pretty obvious I'm going down on you."

"Oh." She shook her head. "You don't have to do that. That's okay."

"Don't have to?" he grumbled. "Gretchen, this isn't a *have to* situation. I *want* to. I want to taste you, want to drive you crazy with my tongue and my teeth, want you to come in my mouth."

Her eyes widened, her head still shaking back and forth like crazy, though he didn't think she was telling him no. It didn't take a genius to realize this wasn't something she'd ever experienced. The way she responded to him playing with her tits told him the asshole ex hadn't done much there, either.

Then, something else occurred to him.

Climbing over her once more, he asked, "Gretchen...have you ever had an orgasm?"

She stilled, her silence and beet-red face answering his question.

"I..." she started. "I tried, but I couldn't ever...get there. I guess there's a lot of stuff broken inside of me."

He scowled. "There's not a single fucking thing broken in you. *Nothing.* However, I could list at least a million things broken in your fucking two-pump chump of an ex." He'd spoken the words with more force, more heat than he'd intended, and he worried that he might've scared her.

That fear was for naught when Gretchen grabbed the sides of his face and kissed him hard. When she pulled away, she was smiling. "Thank you."

"I haven't even begun to earn your gratitude yet," he teased. "Now lay down, kitten. Be a good girl and behave yourself."

"Why is that so hot?" she whispered, more to herself than him, as she dropped back to the bed.

He chuckled, deciding that didn't need a response.

It was time for action.

Theo pushed against her knees, which were clenched tightly to his hips. She complied, letting her thighs part more fully.

He lowered himself again, and while Gretchen offered no complaint this time, her shallow breathing let him know she was nervous.

Theo opened her labia with his thumbs, slowly blowing on her clit, his gaze taking in her reaction.

"God," she muttered.

Theo took that as permission, dragging his tongue along her slit. Despite her obvious jitters, she was soaking wet and ready for him.

Gretchen clenched her hands in the duvet, her hips beginning to rise and fall as he teased her clit the same way he had her nipples.

"So good," she breathed.

Theo nipped her clit, then dragged his mouth lower, dipping his tongue into her opening. Using one thumb, he rubbed her clit as he fucked her with his tongue.

Gretchen's hands flew upward, gripping the headboard as she gyrated wildly beneath him. "Too good!" she cried.

That wasn't a thing, but Theo understood why she might think so. She'd never experienced an orgasm. She didn't know what was coming, didn't understand what it meant to splinter into a million pieces, the pleasure so intense it felt as if you might die.

One of her hands returned to his head, half-heartedly

trying to shove him away. "Seriously. I can't take any more. It's...it's..."

He lifted his head and pierced her with a look. "You're going to come in my mouth, then on my fingers, and then on my cock. You're going to do that because you're my good girl, and because you're strong and brave, and you most definitely can take it. Now put your hands above your head like they were before and keep them there."

Gretchen visibly swallowed, but she offered no argument or complaint. Instead, she obeyed, doing exactly as he asked.

Theo resumed his ministrations, driving his tongue inside her as he applied more pressure to her clit. Stroking faster, he gripped her hip to hold her firmly to the bed, lest she break his nose.

Most days, Gretchen held herself in check. After so many years of trying to make herself small or invisible, it made sense that habit would die hard.

None of those reservations were in play right now.

Gretchen writhed, out of control, crying out, the soles of her feet digging into the mattress as she sought more, practically demanding it with her movements.

"Oh my God!" she yelled, as he felt the first clench of her pussy. "Oh my God," she repeated, her tone the perfect blend of shock, panic, and bliss. "Theo. Theo!"

She fell over the cliff, but he wasn't finished with her. This woman had spent her entire adult life deprived of sexual pleasure. He was more than ready to help her make up for lost time.

Theo kept stroking her clit, faster and faster, her main orgasm dying slowly, accompanied by several mini explosions. He only stopped touching her once her body slumped, bonelessly sinking into the mattress.

Her chest rose and fell rapidly as she tried to catch her breath.

Theo lifted his head, grinning.

Gretchen's eyes were closed, but she must have felt his attention on her because she lifted her eyelids slowly, seeking him out.

He didn't bother to hide his too-pleased smirk, nor had he wiped her shiny arousal from his mouth and cheeks.

"Can I say thank-you now?" she asked.

Theo shook his head. "Still too soon."

This time, panic was the prevailing emotion. "I don't think I'll survive another one of those."

Theo pushed up, kissing her, letting her taste herself on his lips and tongue. "Of course, you will. Now, be still. I have more work to do."

She shuddered as he resumed his place between her legs. This time, he used his tongue on her clit, reawakening her arousal before sliding one finger inside. She was fucking tight as shit, and Theo got light-headed thinking about how incredible it would be once he finally buried himself in all her wet heat.

One finger became two as Theo took his time, rebuilding the fire. Gretchen roused quickly, and he grinned to himself when he realized he was creating a monster, a beautiful one, when she asked for—no, *demanded*—more.

"Please, Theo. More. Harder!" Her hips tilted in an attempt to force his fingers deeper. He took his time, because given what she'd told him about her sexual history, he knew it had been a while since she'd had a man inside her.

Theo added a third finger to the first two and heard her slight hiss. Just those three fingers were a stretch, so he needed to make sure she was prepared before he fucked her with his cock.

Her head tossed from side to side as he felt the first telltale quivers of her orgasm. Her pussy muscles clenched, and she cried out, her body jolting as if she'd been struck by lightning when her second orgasm hit.

Theo stroked her through this orgasm, just as he had the first, draining every drop of pleasure from her that he could.

Gretchen collapsed against the bed again, her body shimmering with perspiration, her hair damp along the edges of her forehead. She watched him as he rose from the bed and slowly unfastened his jeans. Theo dropped them and his boxer briefs to the floor, his cock hard, sticking straight up and brushing against his stomach.

Her eyes widened as she looked at it. She was good for the ego.

She licked her lips, then shifted to her side, reaching for him.

He knew her intent, but that wasn't on the itinerary for tonight. It couldn't be. One brush of her lips against his dick... hell, one hot pant of breath and he'd be a goner.

And that was not the way he wanted to go this first time with her. He'd never taken a woman without a condom, but Gretchen was different. She was his, and there would never be anything between them.

For the briefest of seconds, he let himself imagine her stomach swollen with their baby, and his balls tightened.

Holy fuck. He needed to get inside her, or he was going to come simply at the thought of her pregnant.

Theo brushed away her hand. "Not tonight. You put that sweet mouth anywhere near my dick and this doesn't end the way we want."

Gretchen smiled, clearly pleased by his words, by the idea that she could drive him to his knees that way.

He pressed on her shoulder, pushing her to her back before climbing over her.

This time, there was no shyness or hesitance as Gretchen

let her knees fall to the side, making room for him between her legs.

"I want you," she whispered.

"Greatest words ever," he replied, kissing her softly as he reached down and guided his dick to her opening. He'd done his best to assure she was wet enough and stretched enough, but even so...this was going to be a tight fit.

He pushed just the head of his cock inside, his gaze locked on her face, ready to ease up at the first sign he was hurting her.

"You're big," she murmured.

"We'll go slow."

She shook her head. "I don't want that."

"I don't want to hurt you, kitten."

The smile she gave him sent his heart soaring. "Nothing you do hurts. It feels...amazing."

Theo took her at her word, because now that he was tucked inside her, his self-control was gone. He pressed forward, not stopping until he completely filled her.

Gretchen cupped his cheeks in her hands. "So good," she said, though he wasn't sure if she was reassuring him or simply marveling over that fact.

Theo kissed the tip of her nose, and she giggled. For a split second. Then the sound shifted to a groan of pleasure as he started fucking her.

He took his time, assuming a slow and steady pace that gradually grew. Gretchen wrapped her legs around his hips, tilting her pussy in such a way that he slipped in a little bit more. He used that shift in position to his advantage, stroking her inner walls until she screamed.

"Found it," he grunted, taking care to stroke that spot over and over.

Gretchen's back arched off the bed. "I...God...I'm coming again!"

While this hadn't lasted nearly as long as he'd hoped, Theo wasn't strong enough to hold back. She felt too fucking amazing. Reaching between them, he added more fuel to the fire, stroking her clit with his finger and her G-spot with his cock until she exploded beneath him.

Her climax triggered his own, and his balls emptied inside her. Theo wondered how long it would take him to convince her to go off the pill, or move in with him, or marry him, or...

Oh yeah.

King of Patience, he thought, chuckling to himself.

Gretchen's nails raked his shoulders, his badges of honor, scratches he would wear with pride.

For several moments, they simply remained there, locked together, struggling to find their way back, even though Theo didn't want to return. Not to reality or real life or anywhere that required him to exist outside of this room and her body.

Finally, his strength gave out and he shifted to her side, drawing her to him, tucking her close.

Gretchen glanced up at him. "That was... Jesus, Theo. Your A game nearly killed me."

Theo chuckled. "What can I say? You inspire me."

"Time to say thank-you now?" she joked.

He nodded. "Yep. Thank you," he said, beating her to the punch.

She smiled. "You stole my line."

He chuckled, sighing deeply. They lay there for several minutes, both reveling in the aftermath.

Gretchen's breathing slowed, and he thought perhaps she'd drifted to sleep until she said, "I didn't realize I was capable of this much happiness."

Theo kissed the top of her head. "I intend to make sure you feel this way every day for the rest of your life."

Gretchen lifted her amused face his direction. "Do I need

to remind you how many weeks we've known each other? It's a very small number."

Theo tried to be patient, but Gretchen was lying to herself by pretending this wasn't the real deal. "Tell me you don't feel it too."

One side of her lips quirked up, an adorable dimple appearing. "I might be feeling something," she admitted. "But it's too soon to start talking about forever. There are still a million things we don't know about each other."

"We know the important things. The rest is future dinner conversations," he insisted.

She huffed out a breathy laugh, then her expression sobered. "Seriously, Theo. Thank you."

"You don't need to thank me for orgasms, kitten. It was my pleasure."

She lightly slapped his bare chest. "I don't mean for tonight. Though tonight was definitely worthy of some gratitude. I mean for the rest of it. For so many years, I couldn't find a way out of the darkness, trapped in a life that was slowly killing me with no clue how to turn the tide. Then you took a chance on me, gave me a job that led me to Gracemont, and..."

The rest of her words faded, but he knew what she meant.

Then, his thoughts drifted in a different direction, and he realized she had a point about those million things they didn't know. Time to start filling in some of the blanks.

"You know, there's something I've been curious about," Theo said. "Given how controlling the asshole was," Theo didn't think her ex deserved to be referred to by name, "I'm surprised he let you out of his sight long enough to go to work."

"Oh, yeah, that." Gretchen's head rested his shoulder, her fingers toying with the light smattering of hair around his nipples. "That was probably his biggest mistake, because he let his overweening sense of confidence convince him he'd snowed everyone in his life into thinking he was some pillar of the community and a great guy. He found a job for me shortly after I ran to the bus station. It was his way of insuring I had a warden to keep an eye on me during the day, when he was on duty. The sad thing was, he didn't need to bother at that point. That last failed grab for freedom had beaten all the hope out of me, pushed me into a well of depression where I'd spent nearly a year and a half drowning."

Her disgusted tone always gave away how much she hated being what she considered weak, even though the odds were not in her favor back then.

"Who was your new warden?"

"Brenda," Gretchen replied.

"Isn't she the woman who helped you escape?"

Gretchen nodded. "Briggs had known her his whole life. Her younger brother, Douglas, is Briggs's best friend. Brenda was like a big sister to him, so I'm sure he believed he'd found the perfect solution."

"Brenda didn't know what he was doing to you?" Theo found that hard to believe. Edith confided in Theo that she'd noticed bruises on Gretchen's neck the first day she arrived in Gracemont, and that it hadn't taken a genius to figure out they were the same shape and size as fingerprints.

"She didn't. Not at first. I worked for her for two years, and the first year and a half, I got very good at making excuses for the bruises. Though to be fair, she didn't see many of them. I owned a lot of turtlenecks, and I was very good at covering my injuries up with makeup. Then about eight months ago, Brenda walked into my office, closed the door, and asked me how long Briggs had been hitting me. It was the first time anyone had asked that...and I fell apart. Cried my freaking eyes out. Then I told her everything."

Theo tightened his arm around her shoulders, his free hand stroking her bare arm.

"Brenda was incredible. Initially, she tried to talk me into checking into a domestic abuse center in the city, but after the three failed attempts at leaving him, staying in Harrisburg wasn't an option I would consider anymore. I wanted away, you know? So she and I started making a plan. My paychecks went into Briggs's account, so she gave me a small raise and a bonus, both paid in cash, that I locked in a safe she had at work. Then she helped me through the legal process of changing my name."

Theo nodded. "I figured Banks must have been a new name when Briggs called the sheriff asking for Gretchen Parker. Forgot to ask you about it."

"Banks was the last name of my great-aunt. She sent me a birthday card every year until I was ten. It always had five dollars in it and a nice note. Some years, that five dollars was the only gift I got."

"Why did she stop when you were ten?" Theo asked.

"She died. Funny thing is, I'd only met her once, shortly before my dad left, and I didn't remember her very well. Even so, I lived for those cards. I was devastated when I didn't get one on my eleventh birthday. No one had told me she'd died. When I asked my mom about her, she rolled her eyes, and said, 'The nasty old bitch finally croaked. Good riddance.'"

Theo couldn't begin to imagine how someone as sweet as Gretchen had come from such a horrible woman.

"Ordinarily, in Pennsylvania, you have to publish your intent to change your name change in the newspaper, but Brenda's mom is a lawyer, and she got a judge to waive that requirement for safety reasons. I started smuggling clothing out of the house, one piece at a time, so Briggs wouldn't realize I was packing a bag. And Brenda wrote me the greatest reference letter in the history of letters, one that she allowed me to tailor to each job I applied for. I swear I must have applied for at least a hundred jobs, and I rewrote that reference letter every single time."

Gretchen realized what she'd let slip, because she gave him a sheepish look. "Oops."

"You didn't plan the open houses for Brenda's real estate business, did you?" he asked, trying not to laugh.

Gretchen shook her head. "I'd never planned a party in my life, so I was shocked as hell when you emailed to set up an interview. I've never studied so hard for anything, researching everything I could find on event coordination and party barns and breweries and wineries. Are you mad?"

"Not even a little." Though now it was Theo's turn to look sheepish.

Gretchen frowned. "What is it?"

"Your resume was in our rejection pile."

"Then why did you interview me?"

Theo couldn't help grinning. "Because we'd narrowed it down to four good candidates." He paused, waiting to see if Gretchen would figure it out on her own.

"And?" she prodded.

"Four," he repeated. "An even number."

Gretchen's eyes widened. "You added me to the interview list so it would be an odd number for Nora?!"

Theo nodded.

Gretchen laughed so hard she had to wipe her eyes. "Oh my God. That's insane!"

"I basically reached into the 'no' pile and picked one at random. It was yours."

"Holy shit. How lucky is that?"

Theo shook his head. "Luck didn't have a damn thing to do with it."

Gretchen tilted her head. "Hate to disagree, but that was *all* luck."

"Nope." Theo kissed her forehead. "It was fate, plain and simple. You were meant to be here, meant to be mine, and fate made sure it happened. You and me...we were inevitable, kitten."

Her expression was pure awe and delight when she whispered "inevitable" back to him. "I like that word."

"I love you."

Gretchen blinked rapidly, and he saw her lashes were now wet with tears. Sadly, he also saw a shadow of fear.

"You don't have to say it back. I know you're not ready, and that's okay," he reassured her. "I don't want you to say it until..." He ran his thumb under her eye. "Until you can say it without being afraid or worried. Until you know beyond a shadow of a doubt in your heart that you're safe with me, with my love."

She nodded slowly. "I want that."

He kissed her gently. "I know you do, kitten. Don't worry. I'm a very patient man."

She giggled. "No, you're not."

Theo laughed. "No, I'm not. But I'm trying. Let's go to sleep." He gripped her knee, tugging it over his thighs, loving the way she snuggled against him.

This time, sleep did claim her, and Theo wasn't too far behind her.

Just one last thought floating through his brain as he drifted off.

Thank God for fate.

Chapter Fourteen

Gretchen and Remi bumped hips as they passed each other, Remi returning to the bar with a tray of empty glasses, Gretchen delivering a couple of flights to Kasi and Levi, who were on a date.

It was a beautiful November Saturday, sweater weather for sure, but still warm enough to sit outside. The fall leaves were in full color, and the brewery was hopping. Gretchen had volunteered to help wait tables when her driving lesson with Theo was cut short by a call from Nora, who informed him they were down three servers between the brewery and winery, due to a stomach virus.

Theo was currently parked behind the bar, pouring flights and pints, and talking about the different brews. Lark was singing on the makeshift stage again. She was their most popular entertainer, so it wasn't unusual for the place to be even busier, thanks to her.

Gretchen delivered the flights before making the rounds of her other tables. Fortunately, everyone was good for the moment, so she could grab a few minutes of downtime.

And she knew exactly who she wanted to spend it with. The line at the bar consisted of one guy, and since Jace was also manning the taps, Theo sauntered toward her, leaning over the bar to steal a kiss.

"Looks like we've finally hit a lull," he observed.

"Yeah. I was thinking that too."

"Another hour, and I think you and I can clock out. I can't tell you how much I appreciate you helping."

"I like being here," she admitted. "Like being busy and needed."

"You're always needed," he said, stealing another kiss.

A few patrons began to line up at the bar, and Gretchen suspected an order she'd placed for one of her tables was probably ready in the kitchen.

"We better get back to work." She picked up her tray. Spinning around, she stopped dead in her tracks, gasping before dropping it.

The sound it made when it crashed to the hardwood floor drew attention, but Gretchen was focused on one man.

She wasn't sure how Theo managed it, but one second, he was behind the bar, the next, he was standing beside her.

"Is that him?"

She nodded, her gaze locked on Briggs, in his police uniform, who was standing no more than ten feet away scowling at Theo, who had placed his arm around her back.

Gretchen waited for that soul-crushing fear she experienced around him to crash down on her, but she felt none of it. Not even when Briggs walked toward her.

"Gretchen." Briggs gave her a smile he meant to be charming. She was certain there were a lot of women who would probably find him attractive, but when she looked at him now, all she saw was an ugliness that went bone deep.

"What are you doing here?" She crossed her arms, not for protection but because she was annoyed.

Briggs frowned, clearly taken aback by her hostile tone. She'd never dared to speak to him this way in the past, but her days of cowering like a whipped dog were behind her. "I've been looking for you."

"Why?"

"Because I missed you." Briggs glanced around, discovering they'd drawn an audience.

Gretchen looked around too, relieved when she realized how many Storms were now focused on them, ready to step in at a moment's notice. The wagons were circling, shifting closer. Her initial fear that Briggs would show up in cop-mode and attempt to gaslight the Storms into believing she was mentally unstable still hovered slightly, but she pushed it away.

"Is there somewhere we can go to talk in private?" Briggs asked.

"No, there isn't," Theo said firmly, his hand resting on the small of her back. Knowing him the way she did, she didn't doubt he was struggling to remain next to her rather than throwing himself between her and Briggs. Her heart swelled at his restraint, at his faith that she could handle this on her own. Now, as always, he found a way to give her self-confidence the shot in the arm it needed.

Briggs ignored him. "Gretchen. Please."

"I don't have anything to say to you now that I didn't put in that letter. So no, Briggs, I'm not interested in talking to you. In public *or* private."

"We were together for six years," Briggs pressed, speaking in hushed tones. "Surely that's worth a conversation. Trying to end things in a letter...that's the coward's way out."

If he was trying to tweak her pride, he was failing.

Gretchen tilted her head, shooting him an "are you serious" look. "I don't think it was cowardly to protect myself."

Briggs ran a hand through his hair. "Jesus, Gretchen. You never need to protect yourself from me."

She snorted derisively, and for the briefest of seconds, he let his true nature slip, his nostrils flaring with anger before he managed to rein it in.

"I know we had some rough times," he started, in that annoyingly placating tone meant to make her feel like she was somehow being unreasonable.

"We didn't have *rough times*," she interrupted. "Rough times are falling behind on the bills or the car breaking down. You beating the shit out of me does not fall into that category."

She hadn't bothered to lower her voice, so her comment had captured the attention of several patrons who happened to be nearby. Peripherally, she saw at least six people look in their direction. And so did Briggs, who—true to form—had come prepared to throw his weight around by wearing his police uniform. The "mental illness" card was probably his backup plan if she didn't come quietly.

Too bad for him, she wasn't doing any of this quietly.

Now that they had an audience, she'd ripped that card out of his hands. She could almost read his thoughts, could see his regret that he hadn't led with that angle.

His mistake was thinking she wouldn't make a scene or fight back. All she'd shown him the past two years was a timid mouse, afraid of her own shadow. She hadn't raised her voice at him since the bus station, hadn't made a single attempt to fight back or leave. The cocky asshole must have believed his presence alone was still capable of silencing her.

"Gretchen," Briggs murmured quietly. "Please. It's not appropriate to air dirty laundry in public. You need to calm down so we can discuss this reasonably. Let's talk somewhere else."

She shook her head, hating the way he always talked to her like she was a recalcitrant child. "No."

His lips were pursed, his jaw clenched. He didn't take the word *no* well. Ever. "I can see you're going to be difficult about this, but you have to give me a chance to—"

"I don't have to give you a damn thing."

Briggs's brows furrowed as she cut him off once again. She had to hand it to him, he was holding on to his temper better than she thought he could. He leaned toward her, his voice little more than a whisper. "I understand that you're angry, and I know Brenda convinced you that I'm the villain in all of this."

She laughed. "No one had to tell me what your role was. I figured it out after the first black eye."

Briggs glanced around the brewery, then rubbed the back of his neck. None of this was going the way he'd expected. He bowed his head, murmuring the next words so low, she wasn't sure she'd heard him right. "I've been seeing a therapist."

"You?" she said loudly. "In therapy?"

Briggs's eyes went black with anger, but once again, he managed to beat the demon down. "For you. I want to get better for you."

It took everything she had not to roll her eyes. "I'm glad you're getting help, but if you're going for me, then you're wasting your time and money. Therapy only works if you're doing it for yourself."

"Fine," he conceded. "Then it's for me. I wanted you to know that I'm working on myself, trying to be better for you."

Gretchen sighed. "Briggs. There is no amount of therapy in the world that would make me come back to you."

He frowned, and for a second, she got the sense he was struggling to understand her words. "I can make this right."

"No," she said. "You can't."

The utter confusion on his face told her how confident he'd been that he could sweep in here, tell her what he thought she wanted to hear, and she'd fall right back into his arms.

"I mean it, Gretchen. I'm getting better. I swear." He'd lowered his voice again, almost to a whisper, too aware of their audience. He was arrogant enough that he'd never let anyone hear him beg. "I'll never hurt you again."

This was getting tedious. "It's over, Briggs. I don't know how to say that any more clearly to you."

He blinked several times, shaking his head slowly, her words finally starting to sink in. "You can't be serious. You're the only thing that's ever belonged to me."

"You're wrong. Because you can't own a person, and you *definitely* don't own me."

He swallowed heavily. "But I love you. And you love me."

"Briggs. If I ever loved you, I can assure you, you beat every drop of it out of me long ago."

"*If?*" he asked, shocked.

"I was eighteen when you swooped in to claim me. I was lonely and facing an uncertain future. When I look back on that time, I don't think my decision to go with you was based on love at all. I simply saw you as the best of my very limited options. Boy, was I wrong about that."

"Limited options," Briggs repeated. "Why are you saying this stuff?" His gaze finally traveled to Theo, and this time, he let some of his rage escape. "Are you fucking this guy? Letting him feed you all these poisonous thoughts? He's using you for sex, Gretchen, and because you're so desperate for love, you spread those whore legs of yours, didn't you?"

Theo growled, stepping forward.

Briggs straightened, all but flexing his muscles, which was

ridiculous considering Theo had a good five inches on him and was fucking built.

"You've always been too gullible and easily swayed," Briggs continued. "You're too young and stupid to know what's best for you. That's why you need *me*."

"Say one more fucking word to her," Theo said through gritted teeth. "I dare you."

Briggs shot Theo a dirty look, one that he returned with interest. If Gretchen didn't get Briggs out of here soon, this wasn't going to end with just exchanged words. Theo looked ready to pummel Briggs into dust.

"For the first time in my life, I'm thinking clearly," she said to Briggs, shifting to take Theo's hand in hers. "I left you because that's what was best for me, and you have to respect that."

"Haven't I always been there for you? When your mom and stepdad abandoned you. When your brother left you to go live his own life. I gave you a home, found you a job, took care of you." Briggs swallowed hard, something akin to desperation on his face. She'd never seen him backed into a corner, that cramped space always reserved for *her*. "You need to come back with me, Gretchen! I...I can't live without you."

"Of course you can."

"But—"

"I have nothing else to say to you, Briggs. It's over. Your acceptance of that doesn't impact my life one way or the other. I sincerely hope you *are* getting help, because you need it. God forbid you ever treat another woman the way you treated me."

It would appear she'd finally pushed him too far because, eyes narrowed with fury, he pointed his finger at her threateningly. "You can't talk to me like that, you fucking bitch!"

"It's time for you to leave." Theo released her hand as he placed himself completely in front of her.

Briggs stared Theo down as his mask slipped off completely. "Fuck you. I'm not going anywhere."

"Get out," Theo said.

Briggs's fists clenched, but he thought better of throwing a punch when Jace, Sam, and Levi appeared, standing next to Theo, building a wall of muscle in front of her.

Briggs took several steps away, aware he was outnumbered.

"You're making a mistake, Gretchen. This guy's gonna see what a mental case you are, and he'll kick you to the curb. You'll come crawling back to me soon enough, and if you're *lucky*, I'll take you back, you stupid, worthless cunt!"

Theo lunged forward, ready to charge, but Sam held him back. "Easy, bro," Sam said.

His brother's actions gave her time to step around him to place her hands on Theo's chest. "Sam's right. He's not worth it."

Briggs snarled. "*I'm* not worth it?! Me?"

Gretchen twisted around in time to see Briggs move toward her, hand raised. The action one Gretchen had endured too many times in the past.

Mentally, she prepared herself for the blow, her eyes clenched tightly shut. But this time, it didn't land—and when her eyelids lifted, she was shocked to see Briggs being physically dragged from the brewery by Theo, Jace, Levi, and Sam.

"I'm a fucking cop!" Briggs shouted, struggling against their relentless hold. "I'll have you arrested for assault! Get your fucking hands off me!"

"Show up here again and I'll get a *real* cop to arrest you for trespassing," Theo threatened, as the four of them dragged him out of the brewery and to the parking lot.

Remi stepped next to Gretchen, gaping at her. "You are so fucking badass."

"Holy shit," Gretchen breathed. She'd been fired up in the midst of the confrontation, adrenaline taking over, but now...

Now, her hands were shaking, her heart racing, her insides quivering like they were made of Jell-O. Her knees went weak, and for a moment, she was afraid she might fall...but then she felt firm hands on her shoulders, lending her strength.

Theo had returned. He must have let his brothers finish taking out the trash so he could come back to her.

"You were incredible," Theo said. "Jesus Christ, Gretchen. I've never been prouder of anyone in my life."

Gretchen threw her arms around his neck and her legs around his waist, clinging to him, his words the bolster she needed.

Or maybe bolster was the wrong word.

Because she felt something hard in his jeans, and suddenly, her body was aflame.

She pulled back at the same time Theo did, and saw the same thing reflected on his face.

"We're heading out, Remi." Theo didn't bother to look at his cousin, who laughed knowingly as Gretchen lowered her legs. He wrapped a firm arm around her waist, guiding her out of the brewery.

She didn't ask where they were going. Instead, she matched him step for rapid step, all the way along the path to the brewhouse. Theo led her to his office, pushing her inside before closing the door behind them.

Before she knew what was happening, he pressed her against the door as she gripped his shirt tightly, pulling him closer. Their lips clashed in a kiss that was almost brutal in its passion.

"I want you," he panted.

"Then take me," she demanded, a woman reborn. She'd never felt this powerful, this free.

Theo didn't intend to take the scenic route, and she was perfectly fine with that. He unfastened her jeans with steady, quick fingers, shoving the denim and her panties down. Gretchen tried to kick them off, but they got stuck on her shoes.

"Dammit," she muttered, fighting to free herself.

Theo brought his foot down on her jeans, holding them to the floor as he tugged her right knee up, managing to free that one leg.

Apparently, that was all he needed, because he didn't bother to help her tug the left leg loose. Instead, he unbuttoned and unzipped his jeans, dropped them to his knees, and gripped the back of her thighs.

"Wrap your legs around me and hold on," he commanded.

The door at her back and Theo's incredible strength held her up. He didn't bother to touch her pussy to see if she was wet. He didn't need to. She was so hot and ready there was probably steam rising.

"Put me inside you." Theo's fingers gripping her ass tightly.

Reaching between them, she guided his oh-so-hard and oh-so-fucking-huge dick to her pussy. The first time she'd seen him naked, she genuinely worried he wouldn't fit. It had been a tiny stretch too much, but she loved feeling so full, and while she wasn't a fan of pain, she found she didn't mind Theo's satisfying tastes of it.

Once the head of his dick slipped in, she released him, wrapped her arms around his neck, and prepared to hold on for dear life, because she'd never seen Theo look at her with so much hunger.

It was heady...and addictive.

"Do it," she demanded.

Theo might have an alpha side, but for some reason, it turned him on when she was the one asking for what she wanted.

"As you wish," he murmured in her ear.

And then, it was on. Theo slammed inside as Gretchen's head reared back, banging against the door.

"God, yes," she cried out, as he took her with a force and a need that matched her own. Gretchen's ability to move was limited, but she still tried, using her grip around his neck to pull herself up during his withdrawals before slamming back down to meet him on the return.

Theo adjusted his grip on her ass, slanting her hips until he found that previously undiscovered spot inside her.

"Ahh!" she gasped when he stroked what she'd always considered romance novel fiction until their first time together.

Her G-spot.

Theo slammed in and out, their bodies slick with sweat. She was no fan of working out, but she could see herself becoming an exercise junkie if this counted. They came together in a flurry of fast, hard, rough, powerful thrusts.

"Touch your clit," Theo demanded, his voice husky.

Gretchen did as he asked because she was so close, right there. She gasped as she stroked herself, and Theo pounded even harder.

"Theo!" she shouted.

"I'm there, kitten. With me."

Gretchen's entire body tensed, the orgasm so powerful it almost hurt. Her hands flew to Theo's shoulders, riding out the storm as he came inside her.

She loved the way he called out her names as he climaxed. "Gretchen. Kitten!"

Once they landed, her legs dropped from his waist heavily, though she wasn't sure they were strong enough to hold her up. Mercifully, somehow, Theo seemed to have an endless supply of strength, his hands gripping her waist, steadying her until she found her sea legs.

They remained there, leaning against the door for several minutes, simply clinging to each other.

Then Theo pressed his forehead to hers. "I love you."

This was the second time Theo had said those words to her. And now, like the last time, she froze.

She'd said them once before to the wrong man, to a man who only wanted to possess her. She'd mistaken gratitude for love. Facing Briggs had been incredible, but it had also driven home how wrong she'd been.

"Theo—" she started.

He shook his head and pressed his thumb against her lips. "Don't say it back."

It was the second time she'd left him hanging. How long would it take until he decided she wasn't worth it? Her shoulders tensed.

"I don't know exactly what you're thinking." Theo cupped her cheeks. "But I know I don't like it."

She gave him a sad grin.

"This is a marathon, Gretchen, not a sprint."

She raised one eyebrow, and he burst into that beautiful, boisterous, joyful Theo laugh of his.

"Fair enough," he retorted, since she hadn't needed to speak a word. "I'm obviously a sprinter. But you? You're a long-distance runner, and there's not a damn thing wrong with that."

"I've said those words before and…" She gestured in the general direction of the brewery. He'd seen firsthand how that had turned out.

"I don't want you to tell me you love me until you're one hundred percent certain, and until you can do it without fear or without doubting yourself. Can you do that right now?"

She wished she could, but she didn't want to lie to him. She shook her head.

"Then don't say it. And don't worry about *not* saying it. I'm a very patient man, remember?"

This time, she was the one who laughed. "So you keep saying."

"Kitten, you are smart, brave, and beautiful. You're worth the wait."

Unbidden tears sprung to her eyes. "No one's ever said that to me before."

"Then I'll have to say it every day until it finally sinks in."

Gretchen wasn't sure it ever would, but damn if she didn't want him to try. She lifted her face, kissing him, wrapping her arms around his shoulders, and sinking into not only his strength but his belief and his optimism.

When they parted, she glanced down and giggled. "Look at us." Her jeans were dangling off one foot, while his had dropped around his ankles.

Theo smirked. "We look like two people so desperate to be together, they couldn't even take the time to undress."

Gretchen didn't look at him as he spoke because her gaze was locked on what was going on below his waist. "That's some world-record recovery time," she joked.

"What do you say to us doing a little more private celebrating here, badass, before we rejoin my family at the brewery?"

Gretchen tapped her chin, pretending to consider his offer, but it didn't last long when he wiggled his fingers, threatening to tickle her.

"Yes," she said.

"Good girl," he praised. "Now go bend over my desk."

Oh yes.

Chapter Fifteen

Theo sat in the living room in his parents' house with Gretchen right beside him. Sunday dinners were the norm for his family, as it was the one night of the week the B&B was closed to visitors. Mom insisted that—despite the fact they worked on the farm and saw each other all the time—sitting down to dinner once a week was good for them.

No one argued because his family truly enjoyed each other's company. Their Sunday dinners had shrunk by one member late last year when his cousin, Lucy, moved to Philadelphia to live with her fellas. However, they'd more than made up for that loss this fall with the addition of Kasi's dad, Tim, and her brother, Keith.

And now, Gretchen.

They'd invited Edith and Manny to eat with them today, but Edith was at a holiday craft fair in Leesburg with some friends, and Manny had joined her, offering to serve as driver and bag carrier for the elderly women. Manny was as protective of his aunt as she was of him. It was one of the sweetest relationships Theo had ever seen.

Jace and Mila were hanging out with him and Gretchen in the living room. A football game played on TV, even though none of them had a vested interest in either team.

"Where were you guys last night?" Mila asked. "You missed a fun night bowling."

"We had dinner with Edith, then stuck around to watch a movie," Theo replied.

Edith had been missing Gretchen. Over a week had passed since the Briggs showdown, yet he and Gretchen continued to share the cabin, neither of them quite ready to separate. The sex was incredible and addictive. The pull he felt toward Gretchen wasn't a mere tug anymore. He was locked in a vise grip so tight he'd never break free. Never *want* to break free.

Gretchen had admitted a few days ago that she'd never experienced so much lust in her life. He had to agree. In some ways, they were almost feral, coming together in a rush of passion and heat every single night. Hell, he'd had so much sex over the past week, his dick was sore, but that didn't stop the damn thing from getting hard enough to drive nails into concrete every time Gretchen took her clothes off.

Ten weeks.

Gretchen had arrived in Gracemont ten weeks ago, and it had truly been the best seventy days of his damn life.

Theo wanted nothing more than for the two of them to remain in that cabin for the rest of their lives, raising a brood of kids and living happily ever after.

But Gretchen wasn't there yet.

She had feelings for him, that much he knew, and he was certain she was starting to understand how serious he was about the two of them going the distance.

However, as she'd explained last night as they were driving back from Edith's, she'd never really been on her own. She had been dragged from her childhood home to the residential home to Briggs's house. And while her single-girl pad wasn't an apartment, but a room in Edith's home, it felt like her first taste of true independence. She was supporting herself financially and making her own decisions.

Theo got it. He hated it, but he got it. She'd never felt any sense of control over her own life, and considering her only experience in a committed relationship was with a grooming, abusive asshole, he could understand why she didn't realize she would still be free to do those things in a relationship with *him*. In her mind, committed relationships didn't include freedom.

Theo would never break those wings she was just now beginning to spread, but this was another one of those damn "have patience" things, because telling her he wouldn't hold her back wasn't as effective as showing her.

So, they agreed that after tonight, they would return to their normal lives. He'd move back into his room at the farmhouse, and she'd return to Edith's.

"Oh my God," Gretchen exclaimed, digging her phone out of her back pocket. "I have to show you Edith's invitation to dinner last night," she said to Mila and Jace, who muted the game. "It's hilarious."

Theo chuckled, because Gretchen had shown him the text yesterday, the two of them puzzling for ages over why Edith had sent it.

"I made the mistake of teaching Edith how to use emoticons in texts. Originally, she wanted to know how to make the heart or thumbs-up over people's comments." Gretchen and Theo shared an amused look. "I should have stopped there, but I didn't."

Theo jerked his thumb toward Gretchen. "She created a monster."

"Yesterday, she sent me this." Gretchen clicked on the text, then turned the screen toward Jace and Mila.

Mila's eyes widened, while Jace frowned in confusion.

"Why the hell would she send you that?" he asked.

Gretchen laughed. "Right? Theo and I asked when we got to her house what she'd been trying to tell me with the peach and eggplant text."

"What did she say?" Mila asked, grinning widely.

Theo imitated Edith. "She put on her reading glasses, squinted at the screen, and said she thought the peach was a tomato. It was her way of telling us we were having eggplant parmesan for dinner."

"Jesus!" Jace howled with laugher. "Did you explain what those symbols stand for?"

"Oh sure, Jace," Gretchen replied sardonically. "I'm totally going to tell my eighty-two-year-old roomie she basically texted me that she wanted sex."

They laughed loud enough and long enough that several other Storm family members came into the living room to see what was so funny. After retelling the story three more times, Theo had laughed so much his stomach hurt.

"Before I forget," Mila said to Gretchen. "We're doing a girls' night out on Wednesday at Whiskey Abbey. You're coming."

Theo rolled his eyes. "You're getting as demanding as Remi. Maybe I have plans with my girl."

"Do you?" Mila asked.

"No," Theo grumbled, as Gretchen shoulder-bumped him. "I need to get better at planning ahead."

"You're bad at sharing," Gretchen teased him.

"It's not that I'm bad. It's just that I was one of seven boys.

Growing up, you had to get in there and grab what you wanted or you'd never get anything," he explained, giving her a quick kiss.

Gretchen's cheeks flushed pink every time he kissed her or hugged her in front of his family, which was why he did it as often as he could. He loved to see the color on her face, as well as the exasperated eye roll that always followed. Gretchen thought they should keep their blooming relationship more low-key, while Theo would hire a plane to write in the sky that she was his if she'd let him.

"You guys are so sweet, I swear I'm getting a cavity," Jace said, grinning widely.

Theo picked up one of the throw pillows from the couch and tossed it at his kid brother's head. "You're jealous."

"Maybe," Jace admitted. "I mean, I'm looking forward to meeting my girl and falling in love at first touch. But until then, I still have a lot of wild oats to sow."

Gretchen shook her head. "You guys and that love-at-first-touch story. You do realize there are a ton of nice girls here in Gracemont who'd be perfect for you, Jace. Why not ask one or two of them out and try the dating thing? Why do you think there needs to be this instalove connection?"

Jace considered that. "I'm not saying I don't already know my perfect match. After all, Levi and Kasi knew each other forever. It's just that the time isn't right yet for me and *my* Miss Right. When it is, fate will let me know."

"With a touch?" Gretchen asked.

Jace nodded, confidence radiating from him. "With a single touch."

She didn't continue the argument, and Theo knew why. She'd confessed a couple of days ago that she'd felt the same spark he had when they shook hands that first day. She'd also heard Kasi and Levi's story a few times, from both his brother's and his girlfriend's perspectives, as well as Mom and Dad's, and he suspected she was slowly becoming a believer.

"I have been sent from the kitchen to fetch Gretchen to the queen," Sam said regally, acting like some sort of squire.

On Sundays, they referred to their mother as the queen, because she presided over the kitchen and the dining room, treating both as her domain. As such, they were used to following her orders on how to set the table and what the menu would be. Just as they knew a summons to the kitchen meant Mom wanted a heart-to-heart...over wine, of course. No doubt she was worried about how Gretchen was doing following the Briggs ordeal.

The fact Gretchen hopped up without reservation warmed him all the way through, because he loved the way his mom and his true love had bonded.

"I'll be right back," Gretchen said, with a sunny smile.

Theo chuckled. "No rush. I think it'll probably take the two of you a little while to polish off the bottle of wine she's got stashed in there for you."

"Oooh, wine." Gretchen clapped her hands. "I stand corrected. I won't be right back."

Sam waited a few beats, until Gretchen was gone, before he said, "Only two and a half months on this farm and she's already acting like a Storm." His brother's grin told him how much Sam liked that idea. "You're a lucky son of a bitch, Theo."

"Buy the ring yet?" Jace asked.

Mila giggled. "I bet he's had it for weeks."

Theo leaned back and sighed. "Not going to lie. The last three times I've driven by Becker's Jewelry store, I've been tempted to stop. But I keep on driving because Gretchen's nowhere near ready for that. She's just gotten out of a nightmare relationship that lasted six years."

Jace moved to the couch and placed a firm hand on his shoulder. "You're doing the right thing, bro, giving her time. But considering the way Gretchen looks at you, I'd say she's not as far away from where you want to be as you think."

Theo hoped his brother was right, because every day he spent with her solidified his belief that the only life he wanted was one with her.

"Thanks, Jace. Excuse me a second," Theo said, when his phone started ringing. He pulled it from his pocket...blowing out a slow breath when he saw the name on the screen. "I need to take this."

He stepped out of the living room as he answered, quickly walking for the front door. He wanted to have this conversation in private.

"Hello."

"Hi. This is Shaw Parker. Is this Theo Storm?"

"Yes," Theo replied, hoping he hadn't made the mother of all mistakes. After all, he'd spent last night reassuring Gretchen he didn't want to control her life, that he only wanted to be a part of it.

So reaching out to her brother behind her back probably wasn't the best way of proving that. Shaw seemed to be the one mountain Gretchen truly couldn't scale on her own, and Theo could see how much their estrangement hurt her. Fear over losing her brother for good had left her paralyzed in a way she couldn't seem to shake free.

He'd watched her run her fingers over that Post-it with Shaw's number daily, but every time he suggested she dial it, she said she'd do it later.

The pain in her tone whenever the subject of Shaw came up killed Theo...so a few days ago, he'd placed the call. If she was right, and her brother didn't want to see her, he'd never broach the subject again because he didn't want to see her hurt. But if there was a chance to mend that fence...

He told her she needed to be brave and make the call, but in truth, he hated that this was one more difficult thing Gretchen had to face alone. He couldn't stand by and watch her suffer if—in this one instance—he could help her.

Theo's family was everything to him. If Gretchen could reclaim the one good part of her dysfunctional family, then he was willing to do whatever it took. Even if he risked her anger.

Because the fact was, she wasn't alone anymore. And if she'd let him, he'd fight every single one of her battles—not *for* her but by her side.

"I realize I called out of the blue," Theo began.

"You said this was about my sister. I apologize for the delay in replying, but I was on a mission when you called. Is Gretchen okay? Who are you? What's going on?"

The panic in Shaw's tone told Theo everything he needed to know, and he released a sigh of relief. "Gretchen is absolutely fine, I promise." Theo had said so in the message he'd left, but if *he'd* received a message about one of his cousins from a strange man, he would be freaking out too. "She's currently living in Gracemont, Virginia, and working on my family's farm as an event coordinator."

"Gretchen moved?" Shaw asked. "Without telling me?" The panic was now laced with hurt.

"Shaw, I know your last conversation with your sister didn't end well, but she was going through some things. I don't feel like it's my place to discuss them with you. It's just...Gretchen doesn't feel like she has the right to reach out to you after—"

"The *right*?! She's my sister! I've been worried fucking sick about her, but she never answers my calls."

Theo didn't mention that Gretchen had blocked his number during the dark days, when she'd given up.

"Is Briggs there with her?" Shaw asked.

"No," Theo replied darkly. "He's not."

Theo was starting to feel a kinship with Shaw, because he was able to read his unspoken cue, the deep, relieved sigh her brother released.

"Thank God," Shaw muttered. "Where did you say she is?"

"Gracemont, Virginia. My family owns Stormy Weather Farm, and she works here for us," Theo repeated.

Shaw asked for the spelling of their town, and Theo could tell he was writing down all the information. "I have leave this week for Thanksgiving."

"You should join my family for dinner." Theo quickly extended the invitation. "Gretchen is celebrating the holiday with us as well."

Shaw hesitated, and Theo prayed he hadn't made a mistake. Everything in Shaw's responses told Theo that he still loved his sister. It gave him hope.

"I appreciate the offer. I'll book a flight."

He quickly informed Shaw that the farm was a fairly short drive from Dulles Airport. Shaw thanked him for the information and said he'd make plans to arrive Thanksgiving morning.

Theo started to say goodbye, but Shaw had one more question.

"What's your relationship with my sister?"

The easy answer was to say he was her boss or her friend, but Theo wasn't going to lie or minimize his feelings for Gretchen. "She's mine," Theo replied. "I'm in love with her, and I plan to spend the rest of my life with her if she'll have me."

A long silence followed his assertion.

Then, finally, Shaw said, "I'll be there on Thursday to see my sister *and* you." The threatening, overprotective tone was right out of the Storm playbook, and Theo couldn't help but smile. "Don't tell her I'm coming," Shaw added. "I want to surprise her."

Jesus. That would be one hell of a surprise, but Theo agreed. Because he knew beyond a shadow of a doubt, this was going to be a happy reunion, one of those tearjerker Facebook video reunions.

He and Shaw said goodbye...and Theo took a deep breath, hoping he'd done the right thing.

Chapter Sixteen

"Another round," Remi announced as one of the waitresses at Whiskey Abbey appeared at their table with a tray of lemon drop shots.

Kasi groaned. "When the hell did you order those?"

Remi grinned, unremorsefully. "On my way to the restroom. Y'all would have said no if I'd tried to order them here at the table."

Mila rubbed her temple.

"You have a headache?" Gretchen asked her.

"No," Mila replied. "I'm practicing. Because I will tomorrow. Tell me again why I thought ladies' night with Remi the night before Thanksgiving was a good idea? Because I'm on dessert duty tomorrow, and I can already tell tonight is not going to end well."

Remi waved her concerns away with a roll of her eyes. "You'll be fine, lightweight. And please try to remember you're twenty-eight, not eighty-eight, Grandma. You gotta live a little and make all the bad decisions when you're young."

"You sound like Edith," Gretchen chimed in.

"That's the nicest thing you've ever said to me," Remi replied.

"You know, it's funny," Nora said. "Not ha-ha funny, but a-ha funny, that all my bad decisions have been made while with Remi. Coincidence, or is there a common denominator there?"

"Common denominator," Gretchen, Mila, and Kasi replied in unison, laughing afterward.

"All I'm hearing is that I bring joy and fun and wild adventure to your lives. Now...less bitching and more drinking." Remi shoved a shot in front of each of them and, as they'd done all night, they clinked their glasses together in a silent toast, then tapped them once on the table before drinking.

Gretchen had winced at the first shot, the vodka burning her throat. But now, after round three—four?—she was feeling no pain.

"So are we going to dance or what?" Remi asked when "I Don't Wanna Wait" started playing. As the only bar that offered dancing in Gracemont, Whiskey Abbey offered a wide variety of music genres. Tonight, the playlist was one intended to make the small-town locals feel like they'd been transported to some big city nightclub. The beat was thumping and addictive, and the disco ball the owner, Abbey, had hung from the ceiling in the center of the dance floor really did make Gretchen feel like she was in the middle of New York City.

She stood up, intent on following her friends to the floor, but stopped when she felt a hand on her arm. Turning, she was shocked to discover an unwanted memory from her past.

"Destiny?"

"Hi, Gretchen," her one-time friend said.

"What are you doing here?"

Remi must have gotten to the dance floor and discovered her missing, because she returned to the table. "Hey." She pointedly looked at Destiny, leaving Gretchen no choice but to make introductions.

"Remi, this is Destiny. She and I—" Gretchen started to say they were friends but changed her mind midstream. "We knew each other in Harrisburg. Destiny, this is Remi."

The two women nodded, and Gretchen got the sense they were sizing each other up. She and Remi had grown closer lately, hanging out in the stables together some afternoons, feeding the horses and talking about everything under the sun.

Gretchen had shared some stuff about her relationship with Briggs, and Remi told her about her parents' deaths in a car accident, and how she and her sisters had been raised by their grandparents until *their* deaths, when Remi was eighteen.

Gretchen felt a kinship with Remi, realizing they both suffered from abandonment issues. While Gretchen's were based on people *choosing* to leave her, Remi's stemmed from the people she loved dying while she was still too young to fully understand.

"I was wondering if I could talk to you," Destiny said.

Gretchen wanted to chat with Destiny about as much as she wanted to get a pap smear, but she didn't see a way to refuse. Destiny was being nice, and she had driven all the way from Harrisburg. She turned to Remi. "You go on and dance. I'll be out there with you guys in a little while."

For a second, it looked like Remi was going to refuse. Theo's cousin had started to prove she was as overprotective of those she cared about as Theo. Gretchen was touched to be included on Remi's list.

"See you out there," Remi finally said, returning to Kasi, Mila, and Nora. The way all four women put their heads together then glanced back at the table, it was clear they were worried about what Destiny's presence meant.

Gretchen resumed her seat, encouraging Destiny to join her. "Did you want to order a drink or..."

Destiny shook her head. "No, I'm planning to drive back to Harrisburg tonight. Thanksgiving and everything tomorrow."

"Right. How did you find me?"

"Briggs told me where you were."

"He knew I was at Whiskey Abbey?" Gretchen glanced around, suddenly afraid her ex had now resorted to stalking.

"No. He told me you were living in Gracemont at some Millholland House."

Gretchen hadn't been aware that he knew she was living with Edith.

"Apparently, when he came looking for you, he went there first but no one was home. That's when he drove to where you work and found you." Destiny's tone was calm, easygoing, but there was an unmistakable hardness in her eyes that told Gretchen she was angry. "I stopped by the Millholland House, but the old biddy at the door said you were out with friends and wouldn't be back until late."

Gretchen fought to hide her smile when she realized Edith had her back—then she got pissed. "She's not an *old biddy*. She's a lovely woman."

Destiny shrugged. "I did a quick internet search. This town only has a couple bars, a movie theater, and a bowling alley, so I thought I'd take a chance and look for you. This was my first stop."

"What are you doing here, Destiny?" Gretchen decided to cut to the chase. The sooner Destiny spoke her piece, the sooner she could get back on the road and away from here.

"Briggs is falling apart, Gretchen. Losing you has really taken a toll on him. He's stopped working out, rarely shaves, and he's long overdue for a haircut. He looks rough, and Darryl is concerned he's drinking too much." As Destiny rattled off her list, she studied Gretchen's face closely, as if expecting some sort of reaction.

Gretchen felt nothing. "Okay. I'm not sure what you expect me to do. Briggs and I aren't a couple anymore."

Destiny scowled. "You guys were together for six years. You were a great couple."

Gretchen couldn't hold back her scoff. "You've gotta be kidding me. Destiny, I came to you when Briggs hurt me. You saw the bruises."

Destiny rolled her eyes. "Are you still going on about that? It was one time, Gretchen, and Briggs apologized, even though it was *your* fault. He brought you roses, and I could see how sorry he was."

"He *whipped* me with those roses when we got home." Gretchen turned slightly, pointing to a spot on the back of her left shoulder, covered by her sweater. "I have a three-inch scar right here from where the thorns tore my skin."

"Briggs told me you'd say a bunch of shit about him, told me you were suffering from one of your mental breaks. Look, I get that you had a rough childhood, but that's no reason to tell lies about a good man who's only ever loved you."

Gretchen's temper flared. "I'm not lying, and my mental health is fine."

Destiny flipped her bleach-blonde hair over her shoulder. "I stopped by to see your mom when we were all still looking for you. *Worried* about you," Destiny stressed. "She said you've always been prone to drama, always telling lies to hurt people. She told me what you told the police about Shaw. The lies that sent your stepfather to jail. Don't you feel even an ounce of remorse?"

Gretchen leaned back and crossed her arms. The last thing she wanted to do was continually defend herself to this bitch, when it was clear her mind was already made up. She heard a saying once and it had stuck with her. *You can't fight crazy.* And right now, Destiny was saying crazy things because she hadn't just drunk the Briggs Kool-Aid. She'd guzzled it.

"I didn't lie to the police that night, and I'm not lying about Briggs. I'm also not in the mood to argue about it. If you have a reason for being here, please get to it. Otherwise, I'm going to go rejoin my *real* friends." As Gretchen said the words, she realized how true they were. While she'd been trying to play things cool with Remi, Mila, Nora, and Kasi—too afraid of being hurt again—they'd been nothing but open, honest, and good to her.

"You need help, Gretchen. Psychological help. While I don't agree with his choice, I swear if you started therapy, started finding a way to heal yourself, Briggs would take you back. He told me so."

Gretchen barked out a loud laugh. "No thanks."

"You need to listen to me!" Destiny insisted, somewhat desperately. "Briggs is in trouble at work. He's under investigation for searching phone records without a warrant. And then there was this situation where he got too rough during a routine traffic stop. He shoved a guy against the hood of his car when he said he left his driver's license at home. Darryl pulled him away, but the guy called the station and complained to the chief, said Briggs had left him with a sprained wrist and bruises."

"He lost his punching bag," Gretchen mused aloud, unsurprised. Briggs's temper wasn't something he could ever control for long. Without her, he was floundering.

Destiny slammed her hand on the table. "Stop it! Stop saying shit like that! You're destroying his reputation. This is all *your* fault. You broke that man's heart!"

Gretchen shook her head. "He never loved me. At least not in a healthy way."

"Come home," Destiny demanded.

Gretchen gestured around her. "I *am* home. Gracemont is my home."

Destiny looked ready to go another ten rounds, but Gretchen was done. She stood up.

"Briggs and I are finished for good, and I'm not going back to Harrisburg. Now if you'll excuse me, I'm going to go dance."

Gretchen headed to the dance floor, then changed her mind, detouring to the ladies' room first. The conversation with Destiny hadn't bothered her as much as it pissed her off. Walking to the sink, she pulled a paper towel from the dispenser, wet it with cold water, and patted her face in an effort to calm down.

The fact that Destiny had driven two hours the night before a holiday was enough to convince Gretchen that the woman was telling the truth about Briggs's breakdown. And it even made sense that it would freak out Darryl and Destiny. Briggs had been very—VERY—talented when it came to maintaining his "good guy" persona at work or out in public. He'd received countless accolades within the police department and in the community. He'd been Darryl's mentor as well as partner, taking the younger cop under his wing when he'd first started at the station.

Whenever the four of them went out on dates, Briggs put on one hell of an act as the world's most attentive and adoring boyfriend. So much so, Gretchen herself had even bought it for a while, always thinking that perhaps he'd turned over a new leaf, and he meant it when he said he wouldn't hit her again.

She hadn't just been the *fool me twice, shame on me* idiot. Her record was probably closer to fool me thirty times.

After five minutes had passed, more than enough time for Destiny to leave, Gretchen took a deep breath, ready to return to her true friends. A couple more lemon drop shots and a couple hours of shaking her ass on the dance floor and it would be like Destiny was never here.

She surveyed the dance floor but couldn't see the girls, so she turned her attention to their table, praying Destiny hadn't stuck around.

She hadn't. Thank God.

Gretchen rejoined them, pleased to see the waitress was setting them up with another round. "Where's Remi?"

She wasn't sure what to make of the glances Mila, Nora, and Kasi exchanged.

Kasi held out her hand, palm up. "She told me to hold her earrings."

Gretchen giggled, even though she was confused. "Why?"

"Your friend was still sitting here when we came back to the table," Nora explained.

"She's not my friend," Gretchen corrected. "She never was."

"I'm glad. Because she's a terrible person," Mila said.

Gretchen couldn't help but grin, because those were strong words coming from Mila, who was truly one of the sweetest people she'd ever met. "What did she say?"

Nora scowled but didn't reply.

"I can handle it," Gretchen added, when it was clear none of the women intended to share.

"She said you were mentally unstable and a pathological liar," Mila said.

Gretchen felt her cheeks flush, and her chest grew tight. She was embarrassed by the accusation and terrified the women would believe Destiny.

"Remi told Destiny she was an asshole for defending an abusive prick," Kasi added.

"Destiny wouldn't back down," Nora said. "Kept saying we

were being snowed by you and that if we cared about you at all, we'd have you committed."

"Jesus," Gretchen muttered under her breath.

Nora grasped Gretchen's hand and squeezed it. "We just laughed, and I said the only one at that table who needed a straitjacket was her."

Gretchen blinked back tears. "Thank you."

"That was when she went a step *way* too far and called you a worthless cunt," Nora said, clearly furious on her behalf.

Gretchen was touched that they cared enough to be so mad. "I've been called that so many times in my life, it doesn't even impact me anymore."

Mila frowned. "That's terrible."

Gretchen started to reply...then she recalled the earrings in Kasi's hand. "Wait. Where's Remi?"

Nora smirked. "Let's just say Remi didn't let that insult slide as easily as you did."

Gretchen's eyes widened as she glanced toward the door of the bar. "Did she follow Destiny to the parking lot?" Gretchen hopped up from her seat. "To do what?"

"Probably to kick her ass," Kasi replied, as if Remi picking a fight was no big deal. "Destiny said if we wouldn't listen to reason, maybe your 'old biddy of a landlady' would. Sounded like she was going to try to get Edith to evict you."

Edith would be even less receptive to Destiny's lies than the girls. But still...

Gretchen rushed for the exit with the other three women in tow. As soon as she reached the darkest end of parking lot, she spotted Destiny and Remi in an argument, Remi demanding the woman stay away from Edith and leave town immediately.

The bar only had a couple of streetlights in the parking lot, and both were closer to the entrance. The lot had been almost full when they'd arrived, so Destiny had claimed one of the last spots, farther away. She and Remi were cast in shadow and yelling at each other.

Charlie, the bouncer at Whiskey Abbey, quickly passed Gretchen, rushing over to the two arguing women. He took one look at Remi's furious face, then shifted closer to Destiny, attempting to shoo her away.

Destiny was a mouthy redneck—Gretchen had seen her get into a screaming match with a woman in the bowling alley for mistakenly using her ball—and she wasn't the type to back down from a fight, so she shrugged off Charlie's grip and took a swing at Remi, whose back was to Gretchen.

Remi dodged the punch with ease, but before she could retaliate, another man rushed over from elsewhere in the parking lot, wrapping his arms around Remi from behind, as Charlie did the same to Destiny.

Both women continued to scream at each other, while Remi took exception to being restrained, fighting like a wildcat to shake off the stranger's grip.

"Stand down, Hellraiser," the man said firmly.

"Fuck that! This bitch messed with one of my friends!" Remi responded hotly.

"Your friend is a stupid fucking cunt!" Destiny spat. "And so are you!"

Both women struggled to get loose. Charlie almost lost his grip on Destiny, but Remi's guy impressively held tight, considering Remi was putting up one hell of a fight.

"You need to get out of here or I'm calling the sheriff to arrest your ass," Charlie shouted at Destiny, dragging her away from the fight and toward the cars. "And, Remi, you need to settle down, goddammit."

Once Charlie managed to put at least twenty feet between them, he turned Destiny toward the cars. "Which one is yours?"

Destiny shook off Charlie's hand and straightened her shirt as she pointed to her vehicle. Clearly the threat of Charlie bringing in the law was enough to get Destiny to back down. Probably because she was dating a cop, and it wouldn't look good if she got arrested in a parking lot brawl.

"Get in it and leave," Charlie barked. "Now. And don't bother to come back. Consider yourself banned from Whiskey Abbey."

"Like I'd come back to this fucking dive." Then, never able to resist getting the final word, Destiny flipped them all the middle finger as she got into her car and spun tires out of the parking lot.

"Jesus," Charlie muttered, running a hand over his bald head. "What the hell was that, Remi?"

Even though Remi had stopped fighting for freedom, the man was still holding on, as if he didn't trust her not to chase down Destiny's car.

"You can let go, Hotshot," Remi grumbled, glancing over her shoulder.

The stranger hesitated for a second longer, then released her. Together, they turned toward the bar—and for the first time, Gretchen got a good look at the man's face.

She froze when his gaze connected with hers.

"Sorry, Gretchen. I'm sure you don't like violence after everything you've been through, but that bitch had it coming," Remi seethed.

Gretchen's throat constricted, making it impossible to reply. She couldn't make herself look away from...*him.*

"*Gretchen's* the friend you were defending?" the man asked Remi, who nodded...even as she frowned in confusion. "I should have let you kick the bitch's ass, Hellraiser."

"Shaw?" Gretchen whispered, her vision blurry with tears.

Shaw gave her a rueful grin. "Hey, sweet pea. Looks like I ruined the surprise."

She sniffled, his tone and the playful nickname so much the same. Even the way he looked at her.

"You two know each other?" Remi asked.

Gretchen swallowed hard, then cleared her throat. "This is my brother. Shaw."

"The Navy SEAL?" Remi asked.

Gretchen had talked quite a lot about her brother when she'd first arrived in Gracemont, because it was the easiest way to talk about her past *without* talking about herself.

Shaw glanced back at Remi. "Yes. The Navy SEAL."

Remi grinned. "Awesome! Well, we'll give you two a chance to catch up. See you inside." Her use of the word *we'll* reminded Gretchen that the other girls were still standing there, a few feet behind her. Remi walked past Gretchen, linking arms with Mila and Nora...who were seriously checking out her brother.

Gretchen might have laughed at their awed expressions—and the way Nora mouthed the words *holy fuck*. She knew her brother was hot. Was well aware of how many women's heads he turned. And not just women his age but even mothers and grandmothers. He cut an impressive figure, and God had graced him with a drop-dead gorgeous face. The years hadn't diminished those looks either. If anything, he'd gotten even more handsome as he lost every trace of boyishness, now all man.

Turning back to Shaw, she wiped her cheeks, a fruitless endeavor as the tears continued to flow.

The two of them stared at each other for a moment before he held out his arms.

Gretchen sprang forward, racing into his arms as he

wrapped her in his embrace. It was as warm and safe and comforting as Theo's, something that only made her cry harder.

"Hey, hey," Shaw soothed. "It's okay, Gretchen. It's okay. I'm here, sweet pea."

His kindness led to more sobbing, and soon she was a panting, hiccupping mess.

"I'm sorry," she gasped. "I'm so, so sorry, Shaw!"

"What? Sorry? Why?"

She turned her face toward his chest, the soft cotton of his henley wet from her tears. "For the last time we talked," she said, trying to catch her breath. "For what I said. I was so mean."

Shaw's hold on her relaxed, and she braced herself for his anger. She was surprised when he cupped her cheeks, forcing her to look him in the eye.

"Those weren't *your* words. They were Briggs's. I knew that."

"I still said them."

"It's okay, Gretchen. I know you didn't mean it. None of it. I've been worried about you. *Really* worried. I've tried to call you countless times," Shaw said.

"I blocked your number after our last conversation," she was forced to confess. "I don't know how to explain..."

"I called Briggs once, after my calls went unanswered again. He said it was better for you if I stayed away, if I basically showed myself to the door. He said I was a bad reminder of a painful past."

Gretchen's tears turned hot with anger. "He said that?!"

"It didn't stop me from trying to call or email," Shaw said.

"I didn't get any emails." She was pretty sure she knew why. Briggs had most likely gone into her account and deleted them. She rarely checked email because no one ever wrote her, and she didn't bother using it to talk to anyone because she knew Briggs monitored it.

Gretchen swiped her nose with the back of her hand, wishing she had a tissue. She was a blubbering mess.

"It doesn't matter, Gretchen. I never listened to anything that man said." Shaw also had never bothered to hide his disdain for Briggs.

"I'm still sorry. I've wanted to call you for months, but I was so ashamed of myself. I was in a really dark place when I said those things. I don't blame you if you're angry or if," she swallowed hard, "if you hate me."

"I could never hate you, sweet pea. It's you and me. It's *always* been you and me. Us against the world, remember?"

He used to say that to her whenever Mom said something cruel to her, and then in the residential home, whenever she had a nightmare or Marci picked on her.

She'd been devastated when Shaw left for the Navy, even though she understood why he had to go.

"Us against the world," she repeated. "Wait. How did you know where I was?"

"Theo Storm called me."

Just when Gretchen thought she'd gotten her tears under control, something else happened to open the floodgates. "He did?" she whispered.

Shaw nodded. "He said Briggs isn't here with you."

"I finally got away."

His eyes darkened with an anger so intense, it took her aback. "There are two parts of that sentence you're going to have to explain to me. *Got away?* That's a hell of a way to say you left him."

She bit her lip. "I know."

"Gretchen...did he hit you?"

She nodded.

Shaw's expression was pure fury. "Once?"

She hesitated, and Shaw deflated like a balloon.

"He was abusing you? For how long? The whole time?"

Gretchen bit her lip. "No. He didn't touch me the first couple of years."

"You were with him for *six years*, Gretchen. And whenever I talked to you, you acted so happy and in love."

She didn't have it in her to confess the truth. In the end, she didn't have to.

"He was always listening to our conversations, wasn't he?"

"Yes," she whispered.

"I should have known."

"How? I told you nothing."

"I knew the guy was way too fucking old for you. It wasn't okay for a man in his mid-thirties to take an interest in a teenage girl."

"He never touched me until I was legal," she said, because she felt like it was something Shaw needed to hear.

"I don't care. He was a controlling asshole. I should have seen." Shaw raked a hand over his close-shaven hair, regret cutting deep grooves into his face.

"No, you shouldn't have. At the beginning, I genuinely thought I was in love with him, and I was happy—or at least, what I thought happy felt like. Since moving to Gracemont, I've learned what true happiness is."

Shaw considered that. "You said you *finally* got away. You tried before?"

Gretchen quickly recounted the times she'd tried to escape Briggs.

"That woman," Shaw said, jerking his thumb toward where Destiny's car had been parked. "She was the friend you ran to the first time?"

Gretchen nodded.

"I really should have let Hellraiser tear into her," he muttered.

"Remi's a good friend. She had my back tonight."

"She did. And I'm glad. So—who's Theo Storm and why is he saying you're his?"

Gretchen's eyes widened. "Oh my God. He said that?" She threw her eyes heavenward, grinning from ear to ear, uncertain why she should be surprised. "Theo's a big part of the reason why I'm so happy these days."

Shaw crossed his arms, and he seemed to grow at least six more inches. "He and I are going to have a long talk tomorrow, and believe me, if one single thing about that man feels off, I'm not going to ignore my gut this time, Gretchen—and I don't give a shit *what* you say."

She should probably be annoyed by his highhandedness, but it felt too good to have her big brother back, watching out for her. And, to be honest, she didn't blame him for not trusting her words. She'd lied to him about Briggs for years.

"I understand." She gripped his forearm. "Shaw, I promise I'll never lie to you again. About anything."

He tapped his knuckles under her chin. "I'll take that promise. And I'm going to hold you to it."

"Where are you staying?"

"Nowhere yet. My flight landed a couple hours ago. I rented a car and drove straight here from Dulles. Figured I'd grab some dinner, then find a hotel. Didn't realize this town was as big as a postage stamp. Is there even a hotel around here?"

Gretchen grabbed his hand. "You can stay with me at Edith's."

"Who's Edith?"

"Technically she's my landlady, but in reality, she's my

roomie and bestie. She has plenty of rooms, and I know she'd love to meet you."

"If you're sure," he hesitated.

"I'm a million percent sure."

"Good." Shaw wrapped his arm around her shoulders as they walked toward the bar. "Now that I've got you back, I'm not in a hurry to let you out of my sight. I was hoping this place served food," he said, gesturing at Whiskey Abbey.

"Best wings ever."

Shaw laughed, then placed a kiss on the top of her head.

Just when Gretchen thought life couldn't get any better.

In one night, she not only had her big brother with her but realized she really did have four true, amazing friends, who would always have her back.

It was all wonderful and perfect...and it was all she could do not to reach for her phone to call Theo.

Because the only thing that would make this night better was if he was here too.

Chapter Seventeen

Theo walked out onto the front porch when he saw Edith's car coming down the lane to his parents' house. The B&B was closed for the holiday, so the entire family would be dining together at his childhood home, just like they had every year since he was born.

Even when Uncle Ronnie and Aunt Diana had been alive, they'd gathered in this house, where Mom and Grandma Sheila —and Mila, when she was old enough—started cooking the feast at dawn. He could remember waking up those mornings not to an alarm but to the sound of their laughter coming from the kitchen and the smell of apple pie and coffee and bacon drifting through the house.

The holidays were Theo's favorite time of year, but this time around, they felt even more special. Because he would be spending them with Gretchen.

Manny, who was driving Edith's car, parked it, and all four doors of the Cadillac she'd owned for well over a decade opened.

Theo held his breath, waiting to see Gretchen's face. Mila

told him that Shaw had shown up at Whiskey Abbey last night, and as far as his cousin could tell, the reunion had gone well. He prayed that was true, prayed her brother hadn't upset her or made her feel guilty about their estrangement. He'd really wanted to be with her when her brother arrived…just in case.

Gretchen waved at him the moment she emerged from the car, her smile brighter than he'd ever seen it. She waited until the tall man who'd climbed out from the other side joined her.

There was no question Gretchen and Shaw were related, their faces the same shape, with matching cuts of their jaws and brows. Even from the porch, he could see they shared the same bright blue eyes. However, while Gretchen's hair was blonde, her brother's was much darker, cut in a short military style.

Edith reached Theo first, and he held out his hand, helping as she climbed the few stairs to the front porch. She squeezed it, piercing him with an approving look that confirmed conclusively that last night's reunion was a success, and Edith was pleased with him for placing the call.

"Well done, Theodore," she murmured, so only he could hear. "Well done."

He gave her a kiss on the cheek. "Happy Thanksgiving, Edith. I'm glad you're joining us for dinner. I'm sort of hoping…" He glanced over her shoulder at Manny, whose arms were laden with a large casserole dish.

"Yes, yes," Edith replied, gesturing to the dish. "I made my sweet potato casserole."

"With extra marshmallows?" Theo asked.

Edith chuckled. "Just for you."

Theo placed a hand over his heart. "You are an angel sent straight from heaven."

"And you're as big a charmer as your father." Edith patted his arm. "Well, come on then, Manny. Shake a leg, boy. Don't stand there gawking. I promised Claire I'd help with the cooking."

Manny released a sigh, trying—and failing—to sound annoyed. If anything, the man looked more than ready to pitch in with kitchen duty as well. Of course, in Manny's case, that meant he would serve as the official taste tester.

Once they entered the house, Theo turned his attention to Gretchen and Shaw.

"Theo, this is my brother, Shaw Parker. Shaw, this is Theo Storm. I believe the two of you have spoken before," she said to Theo, her eyes sparkling with mirth.

Theo shook Shaw's hand, amused by the slightly too-hard grip the man used. Clearly, Shaw intended to test him.

"Nice to meet you, Shaw. I'm glad you could join us for dinner."

"I appreciate the offer." Shaw wrapped his arm around his sister's shoulders, tucking her close. "Gretchen said she's been working for you and your family since September."

Theo nodded, then gestured in the general direction of the brewhouse. "We have some time before dinner is served. Why don't I introduce you to the rest of the family and then, if you'd like, Gretchen and I can give you a tour of the farm, show you the brewery, winery, and brewhouse."

"I can show you my office," Gretchen chimed in excitedly. "It's huge and the view is unbelievable."

"I'd like that," Shaw said.

Before they could enter the house, they heard a litany of curses coming from the path between his parents' house and the one his cousins shared.

"Fucking goddamn, son of a cock-sucking—" Remi stopped midstream as she lifted her gaze and saw them standing on the porch.

"Hellraiser," Shaw said, the man's nickname for his cousin catching Theo off guard.

Remi offered a weak grin. "Hotshot."

"Did I miss something?" Theo asked Gretchen quietly.

"Tell you later," she murmured.

Theo turned his attention back to Remi. "You're in a chipper mood this morning," he joked.

"Just tripped on the way over here and tore my favorite pair of overalls." Remi reached down, revealing a tear in the denim near the left pocket. Then she rubbed her hands on her thighs, leaving streaks of dirt and—

"Are you bleeding?" Shaw noticed the same thing Theo had.

Remi held up a dirty hand. "Scraped my palm on a stone. It's fine."

Shaw frowned. "You should wash that. Clean out the dirt or it'll get infected."

"Thanks for the suggestion, Dr. Hotshot. That never would have occurred to me," she retorted sarcastically. She must have heard the rudeness in her tone, because she immediately apologized. "Sorry. I woke up late—and slightly hungover."

Gretchen giggled. "Only slightly?"

Remi narrowed her eyes, but the grumpiness was gone. "Why did you let me order that margarita?"

"As I recall," Shaw argued, "everyone at the table said it would be a bad idea."

Gretchen glanced at Theo. "Shaw hung out with us at girls' night for a little bit, while we waited for his take-out order. Then we went to Edith's. He spent the night there in one of the other guest rooms. We talked until three a.m." She smiled fondly at her brother. It appeared all the bridges between them hadn't just been mended but reinforced.

"Sounds like it was a big night. Sorry I missed it." Theo *was* sorry. He would have loved to have seen Gretchen's face when Shaw arrived.

"You don't know the half of it." Gretchen took his hand. "And I wish you'd been there too. More than I can say. I missed you."

Sweetest words ever.

Remi trudged up the stairs. "I need to wash this." She rubbed her injured palm. "Can't decide which hurts worse. My head or my fucking palm."

"That's quite the mouth you have on you," Shaw commented.

Remi shot Gretchen's brother a look Theo couldn't quite interpret. "You," she said, pointing to Shaw. "You owe me one for holding me back last night. I'm on table-setting duty. It's the only thing Aunt Claire trusts me to do. You can set the table, and I'll oversee your work, since I'm injured and all."

Theo was surprised when Shaw snorted—maybe a laugh? A scoff?—then followed her inside.

He started to follow them, but Gretchen grasped his arm. The moment he turned to face her, she pushed up on tiptoe and kissed the hell out of him.

Never one to look a gift horse in the mouth, Theo gripped her waist, pulling her closer and expanding on her tongue work.

When they parted, Gretchen smiled at him. "Thank you. Thank you, thank you, thank you!"

"You're not mad?"

She shook her head, looking at him like he was crazy. "Oh my God, no. Calling my brother, inviting him here, giving him back to me... That's the nicest thing anyone's ever done for me. I'd like to think I would have called him eventually, but I couldn't get out of my own way. Too afraid and ashamed and drowning in guilt. I would have lost even more time with him if it hadn't been for you, so thank you for having my back, for helping me do what I couldn't do on my own."

"Always," Theo said. "I will always be here to help you."

They shared another kiss.

"Come on," Theo said as they parted. "We should probably go inside and rescue your brother from Remi. By the way, what's up with the hellraiser and hotshot nicknames?"

Gretchen's eyes widened as they entered the house. "Oh my God. You missed so much last night."

Nora overheard her comment as they walked inside. "From lemon drop shots to brawls to long-lost brothers. It was a big night by Gracemont standards."

Theo and Gretchen followed Nora into the living room, where most of his family had gathered, football playing on the big-screen. Levi was sitting on the couch, Kasi nestled on his lap, probably because nearly every other seat in the room was filled. Theo reached for Gretchen's hand, tugging her to the last remaining chair and taking a page from Levi's book, drawing her onto his lap. She flushed slightly, though Theo didn't think the color was based on embarrassment as much as delight.

"The shots and brother comment are self-explanatory, but who got in a brawl?" Theo asked Nora.

"Somebody got into a fight?" Everett sat up straighter. His younger brother was a huge fan of gossip.

"It was ladies' night at Whiskey Abbey," Kasi chimed in. "Me, Gretchen, Mila, Nora, and Remi went together. Wanna take a stab at who almost got into a fight?"

Ten people all replied in unison. "Remi."

They cracked up when Remi appeared at the living room entrance with Shaw, whose eyes narrowed when he spotted Gretchen sitting on Theo's lap.

"Were you calling for me?" Remi asked.

Nora giggled, shaking her head. "Nope. We were filling the guys in on last night, and the fight you got into."

Remi scowled, jerking her thumb in Shaw's direction. "*Almost*-fight. Hotshot here got in my way."

"Who were you trying to fight?" Grayson asked.

Gretchen sighed, then looked at Theo. "Destiny. A girl I knew in Harrisburg."

Theo frowned. "What the hell was she doing here?"

Gretchen grimaced. "Pleading Briggs's case."

"I regret holding you back, Hellraiser," Shaw muttered to Remi.

"Destiny has always been Team Briggs," Gretchen replied with a shrug. "She got pissed when I told her that I was never going back to him, and apparently after I went to the bathroom, she said some unkind things about me to Remi."

Theo didn't need the rest of the blanks filled in, because he was well aware of Remi's penchant for throwing punches whenever someone she loved was hurt or threatened. While she was the most fun-loving, easygoing of his cousins, none of that was present when it came to defending her family and friends.

The girls continued recapping the night, how Charlie and Shaw had been forced to drag the women away from each other. Theo kept a close eye on Gretchen, trying to make sure she wasn't putting on a good front over the confrontation. In the end, he could see that she really wasn't upset by the unwanted visit or the woman's cruel words.

"I'm sorry I wasn't there with you," he murmured in her ear.

"I had the girls and Shaw. Remi..." Gretchen glanced at his cousin, who was exchanging barbs with Shaw. "She really had my back. She's a good friend."

After too many years of isolation and being let down, Theo

knew how much it meant to Gretchen to have a friend she could trust.

With the recap of the previous night finished, Theo and Gretchen took a few minutes to officially introduce Shaw to his family.

"How about that tour?" Theo said.

Shaw nodded. "Sounds good."

He and Gretchen led Shaw to the kitchen first, introducing him to Mom and Dad, before leaving by the back door and taking the path to the brewhouse.

Shaw seemed as impressed by Gretchen's office as she had been, marveling over the view. "Nice to see fall colors again. It's been a while."

Shaw was closemouthed about where exactly he was deployed, maybe a requirement of the job or maybe because he had as many trust issues as his sister. As Gretchen told her brother about her role on the farm, Theo took a moment to study the man's face. Shaw had dark circles under his eyes, which made sense, considering the late night spent reconnecting with his sister...but there were deep creases around them that said his weariness wasn't the product of one night's lost sleep.

Shaw looked like a man who'd been tired forever.

Like Gretchen when she'd first arrived at the farm, Shaw's smiles were few and far between and very brief. Theo got the impression he wasn't used to smiling or laughing. God only knew what things he'd seen during his time in the military.

When they left her office, they walked to the large brewing room. Jace and Sam were there, checking on their latest IPA, drawing Shaw into a conversation about the brewing process.

Shaw, clearly interested, asked a lot of questions. So many, Sam invited him to join them at the brewery tomorrow for a tasting, promising to explain what was in each beer and the process used to create it. Shaw readily accepted, then belatedly looked at Gretchen. "Unless you'd rather do something else," he said to her. "My flight out isn't until Sunday morning."

"My plan was for you to do tastings at the brewery and the winery," Gretchen replied, with a laugh.

"Perfect. I look forward to it," Shaw said to Sam.

Theo glanced at his watch. "I think we'd better head back to the house or risk being late to dinner. We can save the rest of the tour for tomorrow," he said to Shaw. "And then maybe Gretchen and I can show you around Gracemont."

Shaw nodded, the warmth he'd shown to his brothers fading a bit. The man was determined to make him prove his worth. Not that Theo minded or even disagreed. Shaw had learned last night that his sister was trapped in an abusive relationship for years. It made sense that her brother circled the wagons tighter around her, wanting to make sure she was safe with him.

Trust was a hard-earned thing for the Parker siblings, and for good reason.

Once they returned, everyone sat down for dinner. While the farmhouse dining room had a big-ass table capable of seating fifteen people, his mother had set up an extra folding table they all jokingly referred to as the kids' table, when four of the youngest Storms—Remi, Jace, Nora, and Grayson—sat down.

As was tradition, once everyone's plates were filled, Dad lifted his glass and said the same things he did every year. "I'm thankful for this family, these friends, and our home. No man was ever more blessed than me."

Those words were the cue to go, so Mom went next, saying what she was thankful for.

Levi, who sat next to Mom, kept the game going, wrapping his arm around Kasi's shoulders. "I'm thankful for Kasi. It took me too damn long to open my eyes and see what was standing right in front of me."

Kasi smiled, then went next. They continued, each person taking their turn.

When it got around to Shaw, he said, "I'm thankful to Theo for placing the call that brought my sister back to me."

Gretchen wiped her eyes, smiling widely, as her brother fondly shoulder-bumped her.

When it was her turn, it took a moment before Gretchen could find her words. But when she did, they didn't stop flowing, as she thanked nearly every single person sitting at the table. And her heartfelt gratitude had Mom and Edith surreptitiously wiping away their own tears. She gripped Shaw's hand, and said she was thankful to have him back in her life.

Then she turned her attention to him.

"Theo, there isn't a word strong enough to thank you for everything you've done for me. Honestly, you saved my life." It looked like she wanted to say more but couldn't, too overwhelmed with emotion.

Theo smiled at her, lifting her hand up to kiss. "I'm thankful for Nora's OCD."

While most of his family gave him curious, confused looks, he, Gretchen, and Nora laughed.

"Because without her compulsions—"

"Quirks," Nora interjected with a grin. "We're calling them quirks now."

"Without her quirks, I never would have scheduled a fifth interview, never would have met you," he said to Gretchen. Leaning closer, he whispered, "I love you."

From there, Maverick went next, but Theo heard very little of the rest of the thank-yous, soaking in the way Gretchen leaned toward him, her hand resting on his knee.

After nearly two hours at the table, they finally rose, everyone pitching in with cleanup.

"I've never been this full in my life," Grayson groaned. "Why is Mom's gravy so damn good, and why do I feel the need to cover my entire plate in it?"

Theo tried to laugh, but he was feeling the same pain.

Once the dishes were done, the leftovers packed up and distributed, Edith reached for her purse and jacket.

"Manny and I are going to head home," she said to Theo, Gretchen, and Shaw.

"Aw," Remi complained, walking up behind them. "We were going to play Charades."

"I can drive you two home after the game," Theo offered Gretchen and Shaw, not wanting to say good night to her yet. The hopeful look Gretchen gave her brother proved she felt the same.

Shaw bent toward her, giving her a kiss on the forehead. "My jet lag is kicking in hard. I'll ride back with Edith."

"Oh," Gretchen said. "I can go too, then."

Shaw shook his head. "Don't cut your night short because of me. My only plan is to fall face down on the bed and sleep until morning, so stay here and have fun."

"Are you sure?" Gretchen asked.

"We have the rest of the weekend to hang out and catch up," her brother reassured her. "Theo can bring you home later."

Theo didn't state that his idea of "later" was actually tomorrow morning. He missed sharing a bed with Gretchen, and he was hoping to convince her to sleep over. Their cabin was still empty until the New Year.

"Okay." Shaw and Gretchen hugged goodbye.

Shaw gave Theo a look he easily interpreted.

"Let me walk them out, and I'll meet you in the living room," Theo said to Gretchen.

She shot her brother a warning glance that Shaw completely ignored, then went to the living room with Remi.

"Catch you on the flipside, Hotshot," Remi said to Shaw as she walked away.

Shaw shook his head, the combination grimace/grin most people wore when dealing with Remi appearing.

Edith and Manny were loading the car with leftovers and her now-empty casserole dish, chatting with his parents, when Theo and Shaw stepped out on the front porch.

"Thank you again for the invitation to dinner," Shaw said, turning to face him.

"I'm glad you could make it. Not sure Gretchen's feet are touching the ground yet. Having you here meant the world to her."

Shaw acknowledged that with a brief nod, then he looked back at the house when loud laughter erupted from the living room. "I think this is a good place for her. I'm not sure I've ever seen her so..."

Theo expected Shaw to say happy.

So he was surprised when Shaw said, "Herself. When we were kids, she was always chatty and laughing and loud. That dimmed a little after our dad left, and it vanished completely when Mom remarried." Shaw didn't say Ivan's name, or even refer to him as their stepfather. "When we moved into the foster home, she was a shell. She looked like my sister, but that was it. And with Briggs...let's just say the light went off and it stayed off. Tonight..." Shaw rubbed the back of his neck, and Theo got a glimpse of the emotions the serious man was trying to hide. "I got my real sister back."

Theo smiled. "She's an amazing woman."

Shaw tilted his head toward Edith, who was standing next

to her car, saying goodbye to Mom and Dad. "Edith cornered me this morning while Gretchen was showering, to plead your case."

Theo grinned, unsurprised. "What did she say?"

"That you were a good man, and you'd treat my sister right."

"I will," he vowed.

"I think... I think I believe that," Shaw admitted. "But if you don't..."

"If I don't, then I deserve to have my ass kicked," Theo finished for him. "But be aware, you'll have to get in line for your turn, because I'm sure Edith and my brothers will beat you there."

Shaw smiled, glancing at Edith. "Yeah. No question in my mind that Edith would finish the job for all of us. She sure does love Gretchen." He held out his hand, shaking Theo's. "I'll see you tomorrow."

"See you tomorrow." Theo returned to the house, grinning when he spotted Gretchen in the foyer.

"Did that go okay?" she asked.

"I like your brother," Theo said.

"Did he give you one of those big brother warnings?"

"Yep." Theo wrapped his arm around her waist and tugged her close. "Promised to kick my ass if I don't treat you right. So...I guess I'm gonna have to be very, very good to you. Wouldn't want to piss off a Navy SEAL."

Gretchen giggled, but he cut it short, stealing the kiss he'd been waiting to give her all damn day.

"Get a room," Everett said as he passed, his arms filled with at least half a dozen beers he was delivering prior to the game.

"I think we will," Theo replied, leaning closer to Gretchen. "Spend the night at our cabin with me?"

Gretchen didn't need a bit of convincing. Instead, she

grasped his hand and pulled him to the door, the two of them racing each other to the cabin.

Theo was panting and laughing when they entered, but all of that ended the second Gretchen dropped to her knees in front of him.

"Gretchen," he murmured, his hand brushing her hair over her shoulders.

She hadn't given him a blowjob yet, but that was because Theo wouldn't let her, aware he'd be helpless to hold back if she wrapped those full pink lips of hers around him. Being with her was still too new, too exciting, so he hadn't wanted to come anywhere except inside her.

Tonight, though, he didn't have it in him to refuse. Especially when she began unfastening his belt, then his jeans, glancing up at him through those thick, dark lashes of hers.

"You're beautiful."

She tugged his jeans and boxers down, gripping his cock in her hands before responding. "So are you."

Theo chuckled. "Are you talking to me or my cock?"

Teasing the tip of his dick with her tongue, she took a moment before replying. "Both."

Theo ran his fingers through her hair, closing his fists around it gently as she opened her mouth, taking just the head in. He had to close his eyes for a moment because the mere image of her on her knees, his cock in her mouth, was enough to push him over the edge.

Despite her relative inexperience, Gretchen knew exactly how to turn him on. Her grip tightened on the base of his dick, sliding along his shaft in time with her mouth. She couldn't fit him all inside, but it still felt as if she was fucking his whole dick. Between her tongue and lips, her hot breath and firm grip, her hungry moans and her eyes locked on his face, this wasn't going to last long.

"So fucking good," he murmured. "Fuck, kitten. You are such a good fucking girl."

Her cheeks grew pink, from exertion and pleasure. She loved being praised as much as he loved doing it.

For several minutes, Theo locked his knees and held on for dear life as she fucked him with her mouth. He was on the cusp of coming when he used his grip in her hair to push her away.

Gretchen frowned, then resisted his tug, trying to take him back into her mouth.

"Not this way. As much as I want to paint those pretty lips of yours with my come, I want to fuck you more." Releasing his grip on her hair, he bent over to help her rise, then kicked off his jeans and shoes. With his hand on her back, he intended to guide her into the bedroom.

He didn't make it any farther than halfway across the living room before he spun her away from him and pushed her over the arm of the couch.

Gretchen gasped in surprise, then delight as he pushed up the skirt she'd worn to dinner, around her waist. Tugging her panties to one side, it took him less than five seconds to slam inside her.

They groaned together.

While they hadn't explored many sexual positions, they'd both professed a preference for doggie style. He thrust again, then tilted his hips, stroking her G-spot as she dug her fingers into the couch cushions, urging him to take her harder.

Gretchen wasn't a passive lover, always finding ways to drive their passion higher. With her grip on the cushions, she pushed herself back, meeting him on every return, driving him deeper. Her body was made for him...everything about her was.

"Mine," he said through gritted teeth. Her blowjob had pushed him too close to the edge for this to last long. Not that Gretchen was far behind.

He reached around her, stroking her clit. He saw stars when her pussy clenched down on him so tight it fucking hurt. In the best. Possible. Way.

"Jesus, kitten. You're killing me."

His fingers tightened on her hips as he plowed in and out.

Gretchen—thank God—got there a split second before him. He always tried to make sure she came first, but tonight, he'd been certain he was going to fail.

Her inner muscles milked every drop of come from him, electricity sparking up and down his spine.

He hovered over her for several minutes, both of them quiet as they fought to find their way back.

Theo winced when he saw the bright red marks on her hips from his grip. "Did I hurt you?" he asked, as he ran his fingers over them gently.

Gretchen giggled as she glanced down at her body. "You and I have very different definitions of the word hurt. I'm fine, Theo. Better than fine." She pushed herself upright, until she was standing in front of him. She wrapped her arms around his shoulders, drawing him down so that she could kiss him.

They remained there, him bare from the waist down, her surprisingly still dressed as her skirt had slipped down over her legs.

Taking her hand, Theo led her to the bedroom and this time, they made it. They undressed each other slowly, kissing and touching as they did so.

Climbing beneath the covers, they assumed what Theo called their sleeping positions, him on his back, her nestled against him, using his chest as her pillow, her arm draped around his waist.

"Thank you," she whispered.

"I already told you, kitten, you don't have to thank me for

orgasms," he joked, perfectly aware that wasn't what she was referring to.

She gave him a breathy laugh, then looked up at him. "Most of my life, I've done everything on my own. It felt wonderful to have someone help me for once."

"Forever," he corrected.

For the first time, she didn't give him an amused, exasperated look when he talked about their future.

Instead, she gave him the greatest gift he'd ever received.

"I love you," she whispered.

Theo cupped her cheek. "Say it again. Louder."

Gretchen blinked a couple of times, her lashes wet. "I love you, Theo Storm. No doubts, no fears."

Theo kissed her softly. Everything about this moment was perfect, and he wished they could live here forever.

"I love you too, kitten."

Chapter Eighteen

Gretchen stepped off the ladder and spun around, surveying her work. The barn had been transformed into a winter wonderland of twinkle lights, white tulle, and red ribbon. She finished sprinkling fake snow on the large pine tree Theo and Sam had bought at a local nursery. The tree would be planted on the farm following the big event.

The town's annual Christmas party was going to be held at the event barn tomorrow night. Ordinarily, the festivities happened in Gracemont's community center—same as the Harvest Dance—but a leaky roof required the place be closed for repairs.

When Edith told her the ladies auxiliary was afraid it would have to cancel, Gretchen suggested they hold the social at the barn. Edith and her fellow party planners had jumped at the chance, and Nora and Theo had been thrilled by the opportunity to show off the barn to so many community members. With any luck, this event would go off without a hitch and increase the number of future rentals. It was a win-win for both the ladies auxiliary and the farm's new business venture.

Gretchen had spent the better part of the day working with the ladies to decorate for the party, all of the other women leaving over an hour ago. Gretchen had hung around wanting to put a few more finishing touches on everything, determined to show the space off in the best possible light. That was when she'd decided the pine tree needed more snow. She was probably being overly critical, but she really wanted the party to be a success. This felt like her first true test as event coordinator. Sure, she'd helped host Sam's election celebration, and she'd made some tweaks and changes to Octoberfest. But this was the first major event to be held at the barn, and she wanted to prove to Nora, Theo, and the entire Storm family that their faith in her abilities wasn't misplaced.

Christmas was five days away and for the first time in too many years, Gretchen was looking forward to it because she had places to go and good, kind, wonderful people to celebrate with.

The Storms had invited her to join them for Christmas Eve as they went caroling along Main Street. Apparently, as tradition dictated, they always ended their holiday singing at Edith's house, where she invited them in for hot chocolate and fresh-baked cookies, warm from the oven.

Then Theo planned to spend the night with her at Edith's, so that they could open gifts together—along with Manny—early on Christmas morning. Edith had changed the menu for her Christmas breakfast at least half a dozen times already, excited that Theo and Gretchen had chosen to spend the morning with her and Manny, whose idea of gift giving—according to Edith—was gift cards. Just gift cards.

Gretchen was determined that the dear woman would have real presents to open this year. She'd bought, wrapped, and hidden half a dozen gifts for Edith in her room, including a pretty cardigan, a couple of new books for their "book club," some perfume, a box of her favorite chocolates, and a new muffin pan, as hers had definitely seen better days.

After the gift exchange and breakfast, the four of them were spending Christmas Day with the Storms, joining them for a midday feast and then games.

Shaw had also been invited, but he couldn't take leave again so soon after Thanksgiving. The two of them had made plans to FaceTime at some point during the day, and she'd already mailed his gift so that he would have it to open while they chatted. His gift to her had arrived the day before yesterday, and she felt a bit like a kid, so tempted to peek to see what he got her.

To be honest, this was already the best Christmas she'd ever had, and it hadn't even happened yet!

She plugged in the lights on the tree, humming "Here Comes Santa Claus." She turned when she heard a side door open, expecting to find Theo, who'd already reassured her countless times today that the place looked great.

She frowned when she found Briggs there, instead.

Destiny said he'd let himself go, but she thought the other woman might have underplayed the situation.

Gone was the uniform Briggs liked to strut around in, walking around Harrisburg like he was freaking Superman, his cape flying. In its place was a ripped pair of jeans, a dirty T-shirt, and a faded zip-up hoodie. His hair was longer than she'd ever seen it—greasy and shaggy—and it looked as if he hadn't shaved since the last time she saw him.

"What are you doing here?" She slowly reached behind her, praying her phone was in her back pocket. She sighed, her eyes sliding to one of the tables they'd set up by the wall for the refreshments. Sure enough, her cell was there, much closer to Briggs than her.

"No. That's *my* question," Briggs barked. "What the fuck are you doing here, Gretchen?"

She looked around the barn. "Decorating."

He scowled. "No, you stupid bitch. What are you doing *here*? In this fucking town? With that fucking guy?"

"Briggs, I—"

"You promised you'd never leave me!" he shouted, cutting her off, and it occurred to her that he wasn't too steady on his feet.

Taking a closer look at his face, she realized his eyes were bloodshot and framed by dark circles.

"You *promised*," he repeated.

She *had* made that vow…right after he dragged her away from the bus station. She'd been lying on the floor at the time, crying, ready to say anything if he would stop kicking her with those boots of his.

Gretchen forced herself to take several deep breaths, because giving in to the panic skirting around the edges of her consciousness wouldn't help her get out of this barn unscathed. She had to keep her wits about her, find a way to talk Briggs down.

Internally, she scoffed. She'd never once talked her way out of a beating, not when he was angry. And right now, he was miles beyond any fury she'd ever seen from him.

"I did make that promise," she admitted. "But, Briggs—"

"No!" He slammed his fist down on one of the tables closest to the door, knocking over the centerpiece. He was moving closer. "No buts. You made a fucking promise to me, Gretchen, and you broke it."

Gretchen shifted, slowly, positioning herself behind a different table. There was twenty-five feet and three round tables between them. If she could cat and mouse her way across the room, she might be able to make it to her phone or even the door.

The fact Briggs was out of his mind with anger—and possibly drunk—worked in her favor because he was too distracted to realize she was moving.

"I lost my job," he said, his voice gruff but quieter. "They fired me for illegally obtaining phone records. They fired me because I was looking for you."

"I'm sorry," she lied, simply to try to calm him down. Because she wasn't a bit sorry he lost his job. He'd abused his position with the force, used it to get close to a young, lonely girl. One of the things she'd worried about since leaving was that he would use that uniform to prey on some other unsuspecting woman.

Briggs stumbled slightly, even though he was standing still. How drunk *was* he? "You have to come home. Nothing's right without you there."

Hell would freeze over first.

"Do you hear me?!" he yelled, when she didn't respond.

"I hear you."

"So you're coming," he said confidently, like he'd actually convinced her.

"No. I'm not."

Briggs picked up one of the new folding chairs and flung it across the room. It crashed into another table, knocking the tablecloth and festive centerpiece off, the potted poinsettia crashing, broken petals and dirt littering the floor.

He looked at the damage he'd wrought with a malevolent grin, as if destroying her work pleased him. Pleased him enough that he kept going, overturning tables and chairs like he was some sort of rampaging Incredible Hulk.

While he was focused on destruction, she moved, rushing toward the exit. She managed to grab her phone on the way by.

Juggling it, her hands trembled as she tried to open it and hold it up to her face, while still running for the door. She managed to hit the emergency button just as Briggs's hand gripped her upper arm, flinging her around.

He grabbed the phone and slammed it down on the floor. She heard it crack. "Who are you calling?" he screamed in her face. "Him?!"

Gretchen tried to pry his fingers off her arm, thinking she would have been smarter to ask Theo for self-defense classes rather than driving lessons.

Had the call connected? Was her phone destroyed, or was someone on the other end, listening?

"Let go, Briggs," she said, as calmly as she could muster. "Let go and I'll leave here with you."

She couldn't remain in this barn with him, not when he was holding on to her so tightly. Staying here, trying to resist him, would only end with him beating her. Right now, her best shot was to get outside, where she could hopefully outrun him.

Oh, and scream her fucking lungs out while praying someone was close enough to hear.

He didn't release her arm. Instead, he tightened his grip painfully. "I was the only one who ever loved you, Gretchen. The *only* one. I took care of you, gave you a home, bought you food and clothes, found you a job. I was the only one! Everyone else left."

Shaw didn't leave, but she wasn't about to say that aloud. She needed to get out of here. He was standing too close, holding her too tightly.

"I know, Briggs," she said softly, desperate to get outside. Every part of her body was tense, remembering this all too well. She tried to brace herself, to mentally prepare for the punches, the slaps, the kicks.

As if those were things a person could prepare for.

"You always blew things out of proportion, always acted like I was some kind of bad guy. All I've ever wanted to do was take care of you, but you wouldn't let me, wouldn't listen and do what I said!"

She nodded, wincing when he reached up with his free hand, grabbing a handful of her hair, pulling her face close enough that she could smell the liquor on his breath.

Her scalp burned as he yanked hard, tilting her face up, fury lining his mouth and eyes. She would be lucky if she didn't leave here with a bald patch.

"You belong to *me*," he said through gritted teeth, his eyes blown, pupils dilated so that she could barely see any of the pale brown irises. His face was blood red, and he ripped out more hair as he shook her roughly, her brain rattling against her skull. She fought not to whimper, not to show any sign of weakness, but her courage was fading fast.

"You let another man touch you—fuck you. *My* property. You're ruined now!"

Fear struck as Gretchen realized there would be no talking her way out of this. Suddenly, it didn't feel like Briggs was here to drag her home.

He was here for revenge, for pain.

In the past, she would have apologized, said she was sorry a thousand times so he would stop hurting her. She could see now all that did was prove to him that he was right, and she was wrong. He took those apologies as justification for punishing her.

He released her hair and arm, and she felt a split second of relief—until both hands wrapped around her throat.

"You're a worthless *whore*," he spat in her face, as he started to squeeze.

No.

No.

No more.

"Fuck you!" she gasped, before he completely closed her airways.

She was done cowering, finished being this man's victim.

So she did what she should have done all those years. She fought back—hard.

She slapped at his head, dragged her nails down her cheeks, then hit him with the big gun.

Briggs's hands fell away the moment her knee slammed into his balls. It was a direct—perfect—hit.

He staggered back in pain, and probably shock, bending at the waist and covering his crotch while coughing. He turned a sickly shade of green and for a moment, she thought he was going to get sick.

"Fuck! *Fuck*," he groaned.

Gretchen didn't wait around to watch him suffer. Instead, she flew to the side door of the barn, bursting free, intent on running as fast as her feet could carry her.

She was instantly stopped when she ran into someone. Still in flight mode, she screamed as strong arms wrapped around her, terrified Briggs had brought someone with him.

"Shh. Gretchen! It's me!" Theo said. "It's me." Theo was panting, red-faced and out of breath, a sure sign he'd sprinted all the way here from the brewhouse.

"Theo!" Tears sprung to her eyes as she sagged in his arms.

"You're okay," he soothed her, as the barn door slammed open and Briggs limped out, furious.

He pulled up short when he saw Theo standing there, scowling when he gently pushed Gretchen behind him, placing himself between her and her tormentor.

"She's leaving with *me*," Briggs said, his tone gruff, pained. "She said so."

Theo shook his head. "Gretchen's not going anywhere. I

told you before if you came back here, I'd have you arrested for trespassing."

"She's coming with me!" Briggs shouted, fists clenched. "This has gone on long enough. Get in the car, Gretchen, and no one gets hurt."

Theo took a step forward, clearly not agreeing that no one was getting hurt, but Gretchen grasped his arm, shifting to his side.

"I'm not coming with you, Briggs. This is over. Leave. *Now*. If you ever come near me again—"

Briggs roared with anger. "Get. In. The. Fucking. Car!" He stepped toward them, fists clenched.

He didn't get within five feet of her before Theo reacted, lunging forward and throwing a hard punch that knocked Briggs's head back, sending him sprawling to the ground.

Briggs grunted in pain, then tried to rise. He was so drunk and dazed—from her kick and Theo's punch—that all it took was one shove of Theo's foot against his shoulder to send him back to his ass.

"If you know what's best for you, you'll stay down," Theo threatened.

For a moment, she thought Briggs wouldn't listen...but then his shoulders sagged, and he bowed his head, beaten.

"How did you know I was in danger?" she asked Theo, certain there was no way her emergency call could have connected before Briggs smashed her phone.

"Billy was moving cases of beer in the brewhouse," Theo told her, though he was staring down at Briggs, daring him to move. "Mentioned someone must have come to help you finish decorating because he saw a car drive by. Wondered who in town had Pennsylvania plates."

While Gretchen had shared her past with the Storms, they hadn't thought to tell the other employees on the farm. Lucky for her, Billy was not only nosy but chatty. There was very little on the farm he didn't see...and then report back to whomever was in hearing distance, simply for the pleasure of hearing his own voice.

Sam and Jace burst through the woods, as breathless as Theo.

"We called Sheriff Anderson," Sam said as they reached them. He looked down at Briggs, sitting on the ground, and frowned.

As if on cue, Gretchen glanced down the gravel lane at the sound of a siren growing closer, echoing off the mountain.

Briggs heard it too. He rolled to his hands and knees, intent on standing up.

Sam, Jace, and Theo all shifted closer, and Briggs seemed to think better of it. Glancing around at the wall of men, he looked at her. "Gretchen. Please..."

She shook her head. "This is over, Briggs. I never want to see you again. Ever."

For the first time, she got the sense that her words had finally sunk in. Every trace of anger in his face evaporated, morphing into deep-seated sadness and regret. "I didn't mean to hurt you."

"But you did," she said quietly.

No one else spoke as the siren grew too loud, flashing lights illuminating the trees and side of the barn as Sheriff Anderson roared to a stop next to them. He hopped out of his car, moving more quickly than she'd have thought possible for the older, chubby lawman.

He pulled up short when he spotted Briggs on the ground, surrounded by three Storm men.

"This him?" the sheriff asked her.

Gretchen nodded. "Briggs Howard, former police officer."

Theo's face lifted to her, when he heard the word *former*.

"He got fired," she explained.

"Good." Sam crossed his arms. "A man like him shouldn't be wearing a uniform. He deserves to be behind bars."

Briggs tried to rise again, stumbling as he did so.

"You drive up here?" Sheriff Anderson asked him.

Briggs was too intoxicated to understand he was walking into a trap. "Yeah. I was just leaving."

He took two steps toward his car, but Sheriff Anderson stopped him with a hand on his chest, shaking his head. "You're not driving anywhere. You and I are taking a trip to the station after I give you a breathalyzer."

Whatever fight Briggs had left was completely gone now, as he lifted one shoulder, shrugging.

Sheriff Anderson looked at her. "He hurt you?"

Theo looked at her closely, his gaze taking in her face, her arms, with genuine concern. Any damage Briggs did—and she knew there would be bruises—was hidden by her clothing.

"Yes," Gretchen answered, as she looked at Theo. "He grabbed my arm, pulled my hair, shook me, choked me."

As she listed her injuries, Theo's eyes traveled to those areas as if he could see the bruises beneath her sweater and hair. He looked crestfallen, guilty.

"Don't," she whispered, stepping closer to him. "None of this is your fault."

"I promised to protect you," he murmured.

"You can't guard me twenty-four-seven," she said, even though it sure looked like Theo intended to give that a try. "You showed up when I needed you. What happened here is no one's fault except his." She pointed to Briggs, who withered under everyone's scrutiny.

"You want to press charges?" the sheriff asked.

"I do. And I want a restraining order."

Briggs looked up, his expression equal parts surprise and

devastation, even though she'd already told him she never wanted to see him again.

"That can be arranged," Sheriff Anderson said. "I'm going to take him to the station, book him with a DUI for now, and let him cool his heels in the drunk tank tonight. You go on with Theo, let him look after you, and come see me tomorrow morning to give your statement, okay?"

Gretchen was grateful for the short reprieve. The burst of adrenaline she'd experienced while in the moment was gone, giving way to exhaustion.

Theo gently wrapped his arm around her waist as Sheriff Anderson cuffed Briggs, read him his rights, and loaded him into the back of the police cruiser. Briggs didn't look at any of them as they drove away, his head lowered, his body stooped.

She looked around, her mind spinning a million miles an hour, landing on nothing. "He broke my phone. And trashed the decorations. I was going to finish setting out some things for the food tables—"

"We can take care of those things," Theo said.

"But the party is tomorrow night and—"

"Gretchen." Theo stepped in front of her. "Don't worry about the party. What do you need? *You?*"

Honestly, she didn't have a clue. She was too tired to think. She blinked a few times, then shrugged.

"Do you trust me to take care of you?" he asked.

She nodded instantly.

"Good." He pulled her against his chest as he spoke to his brothers. "Call Edith and let her know what happened. Tell her Gretchen is okay, but she's going to spend the night at the cabin with me."

Sam nodded, his phone already in his hand.

"Jace, can you let the rest of the family know? And see if Mila and Nora can come here to clean up the mess? They helped earlier so they know what goes where, decoration-wise."

"Will do. Sam and I will stick around and help too. We'll fix it all, Gretchen," Jace said to her. "Don't you worry."

"I should help—" she started.

All three men shook their heads.

"No." Theo grasped her hand. "I'm taking care of you, remember?" He led her to one of the countless paths on the farm. The cabin she and Theo had been sharing was fairly close to the event barn.

"You okay to walk?" he asked.

The only car parked at the barn was Briggs's. She'd walked there earlier when she met the women to decorate, and Theo had obviously run.

"I'm fine. He didn't hurt me."

Theo narrowed his eyes. "Yes. He did. Maybe this time wasn't as bad as in the past, but he still put his hands on you, kitten. I should have..." He ran a hand through his hair.

Gretchen hated the idea that he felt even an iota of guilt for what happened. "I'll only let you take care of me if you promise to stop blaming yourself."

The side of Theo's mouth quirked up. "That might be easier said than done."

"Try," she demanded.

Theo wiggled his eyebrows suggestively. "God, I love it when you get all bossy. Huge turn-on."

"You're a freak," she joked, and the heaviness that had settled between them lifted. Theo always found a way to make her feel better.

Entering the cabin, Theo placed his hand on the small of her back, directing her to the larger of the two bathrooms. The smaller bathroom only had a shower, but this one included a large, old-fashioned clawfoot bathtub.

Theo started running the water, checking the temperature, then he urged her closer.

She stood still as he reached for the hem of her sweater, pulling it over her head before dropping it to the floor. His eyes slid to her neck, gaze growing dark. She didn't need a mirror to know what he was seeing.

Theo ran a finger over the column of her neck, gently brushing the forming bruises.

"I've had worse," she whispered.

"That doesn't make me feel better," he grumbled.

"Sorry," she said with a sheepish grin.

Theo huffed out a laugh, but it faded when he spotted the large bruise on her arm. It hurt worse than the ones around her throat.

Bending forward, he placed a kiss on her arm.

"All better." She was aiming for levity but failed when his lips traveled to the side of her neck, kissing those bruises as well.

Pulling away, he sighed, then helped her take off the rest of her clothing. He stripped his own off, as well.

Turning off the water, he stepped into the tub, sinking down before crooking his finger at her. She climbed in, lowering herself until she was nestled between his outstretched legs. Gretchen leaned back, the hot water and the strength of his arms around her washing away all the fear and pain of the past hour.

Neither of them spoke for a long time.

Then, without words, Theo reached for a cup that sat on the edge of the tub. He filled it with water, pouring it over her hair as she leaned her head back. Once her hair was thoroughly wet, he grabbed the shampoo and gently massaged it in. She groaned when he hit the sore spot where Briggs had pulled, not in pain but relief.

"Okay?"

"That feels so good," she said.

He continued massaging her scalp, then rinsed the shampoo out. From there, he scrubbed her with body wash until her skin tingled and her pussy clenched.

She twisted to face him as the last of the suds were washed away, lifting onto her knees.

"Kitten," Theo started, clearly intent on stopping her, still worried about her.

She shook her head. "I want you. I need you." Gripping his cock, which had been hard since they got into the tub, she guided the head to her entry, slowly sinking down until he was fully encapsulated.

They both released a long sigh of relief and passion.

"I love you," she said, her hands resting on his shoulders, her fingers toying with his damp hair.

"I love you too, kitten. So damn much. Now," he said, with a sexy smirk that was pure Theo. "Be a good girl and fuck me."

Gretchen grinned because...

He didn't have to ask her twice.

Chapter Nineteen

Theo placed a kiss on Gretchen's shoulder, grinning as he watched her toying with the necklace he gave her for Christmas. The holidays had been a whirlwind of activity, starting with the town's annual holiday social and ending a couple of hours ago at his parents' farmhouse.

He and Gretchen had decided to spend the night together here, in what they'd begun to think of as their cabin. Sadly, that would no longer be true in a week, once Boone, the new vineyard manager, arrived to begin work.

Rather than rush to bed, as was their usual routine whenever they were alone together, they opted to relax by the fireplace first. So, as he built the fire, Gretchen made them a cozy nest of blankets and pillows. Then they stripped down to their underwear and crawled beneath the fleece.

She lay in front of him, on her side, her ass occasionally brushing against his crotch. He was hard—a permanent condition whenever she was close by and nearly naked. He was a hundred percent certain those brushes of her ass were teases, but he didn't call her on them, curious to see how far she would go.

He'd stayed with her every night since Briggs's assault in the barn, worried about her suffering from panic attacks or nightmares, but there'd been none of that. Strangely, despite the terror of the moment, once Sheriff Anderson took Briggs into custody, something shifted inside her. They went to the police station so she could press charges for assault and file for a restraining order the morning after the attack. Gretchen was calm and collected throughout the process. After they left the station, she said she was certain Briggs knew it was over this time, and she felt confident he wouldn't come back again.

Theo wished he shared that confidence, aware years would have to pass before he felt secure that the man was truly history. But he didn't say that to Gretchen because she'd found peace in regards to her abuser at last. And he would never take that away from her.

"I love my necklace," she said softly, for the twentieth time since she'd unwrapped it this morning. When he'd explained that the necklace with its heartbeat charm represented the day he met her, the day his heart beat for the first time, she clasped it around her neck, vowing to never take it off.

"More than the photo?" he asked.

"It's a tie."

Theo chuckled.

He'd given her over a dozen gifts, some big, some small, but the two she'd reacted to the most had been the necklace and the framed photograph of everyone taken at Thanksgiving. She teared up when she saw it, remarking that the photo included every single person in the world she loved. She planned to hang it up in her office, next to the older one she'd had framed of her and Shaw at her brother's graduation.

Gretchen had kissed him when she opened it, quietly whispering, "Thank you for giving me a family."

Even now, the thought of those words and her soft kiss warmed him, made him happier than he ever thought possible.

He'd gone on to explain to Gretchen that the Thanksgiving photo was a tradition Mom had kept going since the first year she and Dad were married. Everyone who sat down together for the meal would gather on the front porch to pose. When he mentioned Mom had a photo album dedicated to just those pictures, Gretchen asked if she could see it.

So once they arrived at the farmhouse for dinner, Theo pulled it out, flipping through the pages as Gretchen asked who everyone was in the earliest photos, and then remarked on how much the family had grown and changed. She'd been right. Theo couldn't remember the last time he'd flipped through that album, but it was fun to reminisce.

By the time they hit the final photo—this year's—he and Gretchen were surrounded by no less than ten other people, all jostling for position around the couch so they could look too. This year's Thanksgiving group had been the largest, because they'd added Shaw, Edith, Manny, and Kasi's family.

Gretchen sighed, as she sank even deeper into his embrace. He tightened his arm around her waist, then decided to tease her back, pressing his cock against her ass.

She giggled. "I'm going to miss our cabin."

"I'm not," he said.

Gretchen glanced over her shoulder, eyes narrowed. "What?"

"Because I've got my sights set on a better one. It's farther up the mountain, closer to Remi's stables."

Gretchen's eyes widened. "I know which cabin you're talking about. I helped Mila prepare it for renters one weekend because there was a rush turnaround between the departure of one party and the arrival of the next. The view from the front porch is incredible."

"It is. It's also one of the first cabins we updated when we decided to give them all facelifts. It has a more modern, less rustic feel inside."

"What do you mean, you have your sights set on it?"

"That's the one I'm going to ask for. For us."

Gretchen twisted in his arms, facing him. Theo kept his arm around her waist, refusing to let her shift away, so their faces were close, her ginger-scented breath reminding him of the cookies they'd eaten for dessert. "For us?"

"I plan to live out my life on this farm," he explained.

"I know. If this was my home, I'd never want to leave it either."

Theo loved that she adored his family's farm and Gracemont as much as he did. "That's what I'm saying. It *will* be your home. Obviously, when you agree to move in with me, we can't live with my brothers. So we'll need a place of our own. And that cabin—"

Gretchen drew in a soft breath.

"We're still doing this on your timeline, okay?" he reiterated, not wanting to scare her or put pressure on her.

"I know. It's just... You've really thought this out, haven't you?"

Theo playfully bopped the tip of her nose with his finger. "I've got our whole future planned."

"You do, huh?" she asked, grinning widely.

"Absolutely. Test me."

"Fine," she said. "Where do you see us in a year?"

"Living in that cabin I mentioned. Sleeping together every night, waking up in each other's arms, sharing breakfast, then walking to work, where I intend to slip into your office every hour or so to steal a kiss."

"You do that now," she reminded him, though it was clear she liked sneaking those kisses as much as he did.

"And I'll still do it then," he replied confidently.

Gretchen pressed her hands flat against his bare chest, her fingers toying with his nipples. "I have to admit, I like the sound of that."

"Say the word and it's ours."

She bit her lower lip. "Maybe not yet. But..." She seemed to seriously consider what he was offering. "Yeah. I could see us there in a year."

Theo kissed her slowly, deeply. "You make me so happy."

Gretchen, not finished with their game, stroked his jaw, playing with his beard. "Where do you see us in five years?"

"We'll still live in our cabin, but it'll be bigger. My brothers and I will have put on an addition, doubled the size of it."

Her eyes widened. "Why?"

"Because in five years, we'll already have our first child, a precocious little three-year-old with your good looks and my outrageous personality, and the second baby will be on the way."

"Two children?"

"Within the next five years."

Gretchen tilted her head. "Does that mean you want more than two?"

Theo reached up, slipping her hair over her shoulder, baring it so he could place a kiss there. "Kitten, I want as many babies as you'll give me."

"Two," she replied. "To start. Then..." She lifted her shoulder.

"Two sounds damn fine."

Gretchen ran her hand over his cheek, cupping it. "I have to admit, I never saw myself as a mother until this moment."

Theo was surprised. "Why not? You'll be an amazing mother."

"My biggest fear the past few years was that Briggs might one day decide he wanted children."

Theo understood that fear. Understood that Gretchen would never want to bring a child into a violent home. However, for too many years, she'd been trapped, unable to get herself free, so her fear made sense.

"But you want kids?" he asked.

"With you? More than I can say."

Theo swore his heart pulled a Grinch and grew three sizes.

"I don't have a doubt you'll be the world's greatest dad," Gretchen added.

"I hope that's true. I was blessed with one hell of a role model."

"Rex is awesome," Gretchen agreed.

When Theo told him about Gretchen's dad leaving when she was young, Dad appointed himself Gretchen's "adopted" father, taking her under his wing this past month, teaching her things her own dad should have—like how to change a tire and check the oil in the car.

"So it's settled. In five years, we'll have two adorable children and a beautiful home with an incredible view of the farm."

Gretchen's eyes were glassy with happy tears. "That sounds wonderful. I've spent so much of my life simply going through the motions, taking everything day by day without a thought to the future, because I couldn't see anything good on the horizon."

"Our life together is going to be a long one, and very, very good, kitten. I promise."

"A long one. Does that mean you know where we'll be in fifty years?"

He winked. "Of course I do. We're going to be lying in front of the fireplace in our cabin, just like this, talking about how lucky we were to spend the holiday with our children and grandchildren."

"You do realize we'll be eighty-four and seventy-four in fifty years. Who's going to get us up off the floor?"

Theo laughed. "Good point. We'll have that conversation in bed. And then, we'll make love."

As he spoke, Theo slipped his fingers into the waistband of her panties, tugging them down until she was able to kick them off completely. Then, he removed her bra, bending to worship her perfect nipples, which were hard and tight and begging to be sucked.

Gretchen's hands grasped his hair as he sucked and squeezed her gorgeous breasts.

"Yes," she breathed, her head thrown back, her back arched to allow him better access. She was a huge fan of breast play, which suited him perfectly, because he was a tit man and more than willing to spend hours with hers.

Gretchen broke away first, using her grip on his hair to pull him off with a pop. "Want you."

Theo would never get sick of hearing those words. Lifting his ass, he drew down his boxer briefs, the head of his cock weeping with precome.

One of these days, he swore to himself, he'd manage to work up some level of stamina with Gretchen. God only knew when that would be, though, because every stroke of her fingers, every kiss from her lips, every moan from her throat turned him right the fuck on.

The moment his cock was free, Gretchen was there, her fingers wrapped around his shaft, gripping it firmly as she drew her hand up and down, dragging him into the danger zone within minutes.

Tugging her hand away with a firm grasp of her wrist, he pushed her to her back, coming over her.

Gretchen spread her legs wide so that he could settle between.

"Come inside me," she whispered.

He leaned down to kiss her. However, this time, it was no gentle or quick peck. His lips took what they wanted, demanded her acquiescence.

The head of his cock nudged against her opening, and she pulled away, gasping.

"How do you want it?" he whispered in her ear.

"What?"

"Fast and hard or slow and easy. Your choice, kitten."

She closed her eyes, and she shivered as she responded, "Fast, hard."

He groaned at her request. "God, yes."

Clearly, she'd expected him to thrust in as she'd requested, so she was surprised by his steady, slow entrance.

Her eyes opened, questioning.

"I'm going to give you what you want, but first, I'm going to savor this. You're so hot, so tight, so perfect."

"And you're my dream come true."

Theo's heart flooded with warmth at her words. Her admission spoke directly to his heart and his soul, and he fell even deeper in love with her.

Once he was fully seated, he paused and looked at her. "Love you," he murmured.

"Love you too."

He pulled his cock out until only the head remained lodged in her tight grip. Then he set them free. Theo pushed into her, but this time, he didn't stop. Over and over, he moved inside her, the pace gloriously strong and fast and hard.

Grasping her breasts, he tugged at the sensitive flesh, his fingers squeezing her nipples hard.

Gretchen—his greedy, gorgeous lover—pleaded for more.

Their lips met, even as they panted for breath. He felt her fingernails score his shoulders and back as she tilted her hips, his cock hitting that magic spot inside.

"God!" she screamed, and he felt her release, felt her body explode around him.

Theo clenched his teeth so hard he feared he'd break them, but he was determined that this wouldn't be the end. Not yet.

He rode out the storm, slowing his pace until her orgasm began to wane. Gretchen's hands now rested by her head, palms up as if she was surrendering. It took a full minute before she recovered enough to realize he was still rock-hard and buried deep inside her.

"You're going to kill me," she said, her voice husky from her cries. "Kill me with orgasms."

"Nah," he said, kissing the tip of her nose. "You can take it. Because you're not just my good girl, kitten, you're one hell of a badass."

Gretchen's pussy clenched around him, letting him know without words just how much she liked that.

"So roll over, badass. Because I'm just getting started."

Gretchen did as he said, or at least she tried, flopping to her stomach with all the strength of a rag doll. Once she was face down, he gripped her hips, pulling them up until she was supporting her weight with her knees.

Goddamn, she had one hell of an ass. Unable to resist, Theo lifted his hand and placed a light slap on the right cheek.

Gretchen jolted with surprise; he'd been careful to keep the tease light and painless.

When she looked over her shoulder at him, her eyes dark with desire, he nearly came right then and there.

"Do that again," she said, in that demanding tone that he fucking loved. He loved seeing his little kitty's claws come out, grabbing what she wanted.

He slapped the other ass cheek but kept the smack soft.

She shot him a look. "Do it like you mean it."

Theo narrowed his eyes. "Gretchen," he started.

"I love it, Theo. And I know you won't hurt me. At least, not in a way that won't ensure I come so hard I see stars. So do it like you mean it. Now."

The second she imperiously added the word *now*, he gave her exactly what she—and he—wanted. He spanked her harder —though not as hard as he could, waiting for her response. When she moaned with desire and lifted her ass higher, he set himself free.

He spanked her a dozen more times, varying the placement and force, as Gretchen writhed beneath him, begging for more.

He could have kept going for hours, her pink ass something he would see in his dreams every night going forward, but he was only human, and his resistance was in tatters.

Gripping her hips, he guided his dick back to her opening, and this time, there was no slow entry. Instead, he pounded in, determined she would feel this tomorrow.

Up until now, he'd been a gentle lover, but he could see that wasn't what she wanted or needed tonight.

His kitten was a wildcat, and it occurred to him, she'd learned a hell of a lot from those romance novels she loved to read so much.

Her hand appeared between their legs, and she palmed his balls, toying with them.

"Fuck," Theo muttered, rubbing his hands over her pink ass, squeezing the flesh to keep the burn going.

"Yes!" she screamed. "God, yes. Theo!"

He bent over her back, even as his cock kept thrusting, relentlessly. "You feel that, kitten? Feel how deep I am? How wet you are? You were made for me."

"Fate," she reminded him breathlessly. "Inevitable."

"Fate," he repeated, pounding into her, his balls growing tight. Something else was inevitable too.

Gretchen's body trembled roughly as her climax crashed in on her, and this time, she took him down with her. Theo grunted as pulse after pulse erupted inside her, and he was sorry it wouldn't take root. Talking about the future and children made him long to start right now.

"Love you," he murmured once he came down. He was still curled over her body. Somehow, she was holding the supplicant pose, her lower body resting on her bent knees, her cheek pressed against the blankets beneath them.

"I want to live with you," she whispered.

She pushed herself up, and as Theo shifted back, resting his ass on his ankles, she turned to face him, cupping his cheeks in her hands.

"I want that cabin, those kids and grandkids. I love you, Theo, but maybe even more than that, I trust you. You took a chance on me when no one else would and you gave me a home and a family. You've become my shelter in the storm. You make me feel safe and sound. I don't have a single doubt about us because you made me believe."

"Believe in what?" he asked.

"Love at first touch."

He grinned. Even so...

"Gretchen." He didn't want her to make this decision while still drunk on lust and orgasms.

"I've never been surer of anything in my life."

"I'm glad, but I promise, kitten, we don't have to rush," he forced himself to say, even though he sure as shit didn't want to change her mind. "We have all the time in the world. Forever."

"Exactly," Gretchen said. "We have forever. And I want it to start—truly start—tonight. Please."

Theo grasped her waist, bending toward her to steal a quick kiss.

Then, resting his forehead against hers, he nodded.

"It starts tonight."

Epilogue

Mila reached forward, attempting to grab the final strand of lights still hooked to the porch without having to move her ladder. She'd already gone up and down the darn thing a dozen times, working her way along the edge of the porch roof. Ordinarily, she left the holiday lights up longer, but a strong wind had come through last night, blowing a large section in the center down completely.

Since Mother Nature had already taken care of a portion of the work, she decided to roll with it, taking the lights down now rather than rehanging them, only to have to ascend the ladder again in a couple weeks.

Unfortunately, her laziness wasn't working in her favor, because that last stupid hook was an inch or so out of—

The ladder began to wobble, so she reared back too quickly —and overcorrected. The top of the ladder shifted away from the roof, hovering with no support, her along with it.

Mila was too off-balance to push it forward again, her actions reminding her of a novice on stilts, the ladder shifting from one leg to the other.

She was going to fall. There was no combating gravity. But she fought it for as long as she could.

One last-ditch attempt at recovery failed when her foot slipped. While the ladder fell forward, she went back.

She closed her eyes as she cried out, bracing herself for the painful impact.

It didn't come.

Instead, she heard a grunt that *didn't* come from her.

Opening her eyes, she realized she'd hit the ground. Or at least, the guy *under* her had, leaving her sprawled in his lap. She blinked a few times, fighting to focus, and when she did...

Holy shit.

The rugged mountain man seriously looked like he'd stepped straight out of her fantasies. He was large and muscular, with a thick beard and piercing brown eyes, so dark they looked black. There was a crook in his nose that indicated it had been broken before, but rather than detract, it simply reinforced his attractiveness.

The words *bad boy* flashed through her mind, but she dismissed them instantly because there wasn't one boyish thing about the stranger. He was all man.

"Miss," he said, and she realized it wasn't the first time he'd said it.

Mila shook herself for staring so hard at the sexy man. "I..."

"Are you okay?" he asked, his voice deep and slightly breathless.

No wonder. She'd knocked them both to the ground with her fall.

"I am." She tried to push upright, but the man held her still.

"No," he practically barked. "Take it slow. Make sure you didn't break anything."

Mila wanted to point out that he'd taken the brunt of the

impact, but there was something in his tone, something strong and commanding that had her doing exactly as he said.

Oh yeah. This guy was dangerous...to her libido.

She wiggled her fingers and toes, then her hands and feet.

"I'm fine," she said, and when she tried to sit up this time, he let her. "What about you? Did I hurt you?"

The man chuckled. "A little thing like you? Not likely. All I have is a bruised ass and wounded pride."

"Pride? Why?"

"Because I'm pissed I didn't manage to catch you midair without falling. I'm suddenly looking a lot less like a stud."

Mila giggled...until another voice entered the conversation.

"Gross, Dad."

Mila peered over the man's shoulder, spotting a pretty young girl who looked like she was still in middle school.

Great, Mila. Nothing like ogling a man while his daughter's watching.

She scrambled to her feet, the man rising as well.

When she wobbled slightly, he reached out, gripping her upper arms to steady her.

And that was when she felt it.

It.

The thing Uncle Rex and Levi and Theo all talked about.

Lightning strike.

Earthquake.

Tsunami.

This man was the one.

Mila looked into his eyes, and she felt as if her world had suddenly clicked into place. And as amazing as that should have felt, there was something she couldn't ignore.

The man had a daughter.

So did he also have a wife?

· · ·

Be sure to read the entire Perfect Storm series
Taken by Storm
Shelter from the Storm
Caught in a Storm

Calling all fans of Mari Carr AND Facebook! There's a group for you. Come join Mari Carr's Facebook group for sneak peaks, cover reveals, contests and more! Join now.

And be sure to join Mari's mailing list to receive a **FREE** sexy novella, Midnight Wild.

About the Author

Virginia native Mari Carr is a New York Times and USA TODAY bestseller of contemporary romance novels. With over three million copies of her books sold, Mari was the winner of the Romance Writers of America's Passionate Plume award for her novella, Erotic Research. She has over a hundred published works, including her popular Wild Irish and Italian Stallions series, along with the Trinity Masters series she writes with Lila Dubois.

Follow Mari:
www.maricarr.com
mari@maricarr.com

Join her newsletter so you don't miss new releases and for exclusive subscriber-only content.